PRESSURE POINT

THE BULARI SAGA

JESSIE KWAK

First edition September 2019

Cover art by Dusty Crosley

Cover design by Robert Kittilson

Edited by Kyra Freestar

Map by Jessie Kwak

www.jessiekwak.com

To my grandmas,
for being the kind of rad ladies who wouldn't mind having
space gangster books dedicated to them.

Grandma Anna, I wish you could have read these.

Grandma Betty, thank you for teaching me how to read, and
I'm sorry for all the swearing.

N
W
E
S
To the Maraka Valley
Geordi Jimenez
Space Terminal
Jet Park
Casinos
Downtown
To Julieta Yang's

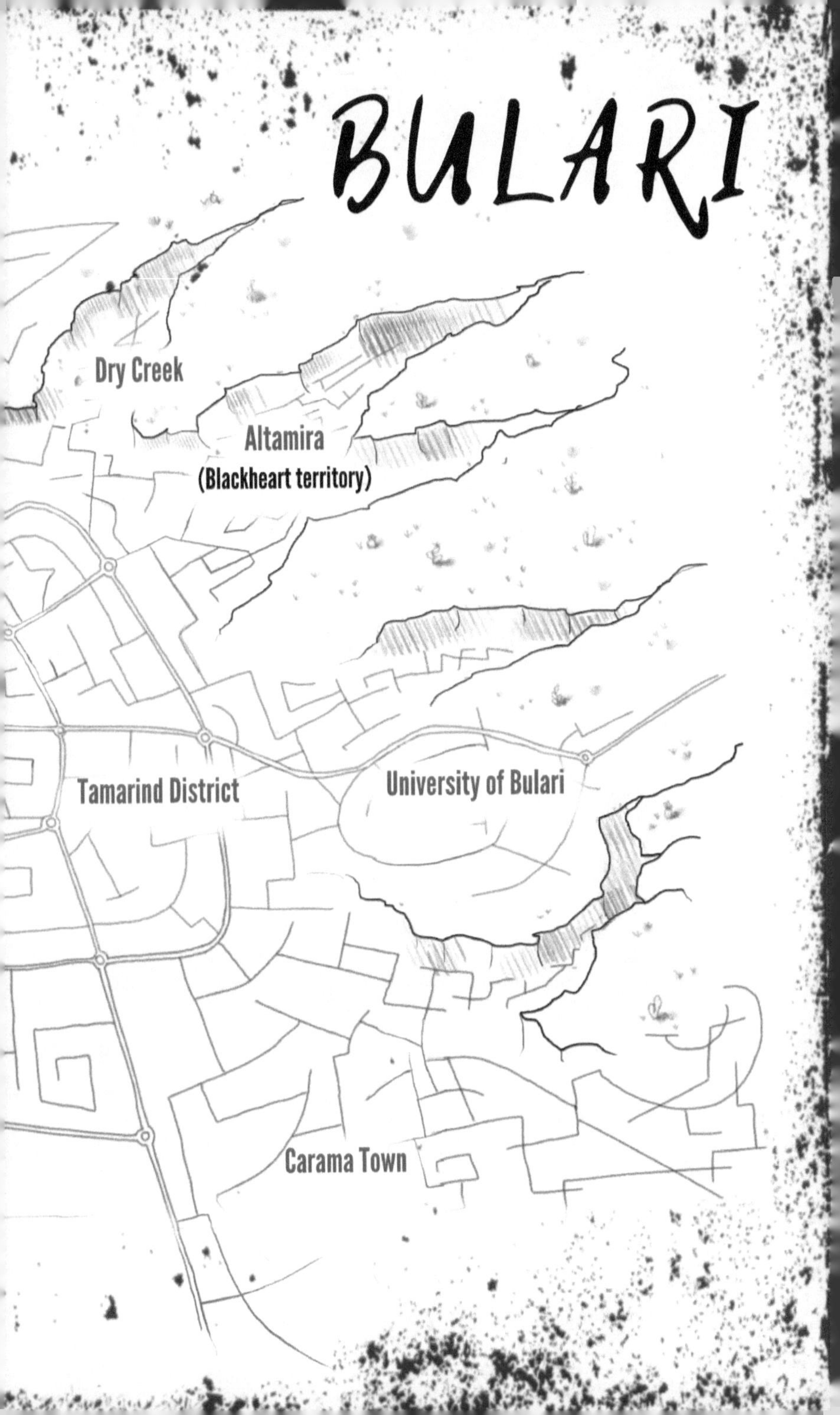

BULARI

Dry Creek
Altamira
(Blackheart territory)
Tamarind District
University of Bulari
Carama Town

PROLOGUE

"I'm not here to make trouble. I just have a few questions."

The figure freezes, silhouetted against the dim light of the hall. The office is dark, though if you've been sitting and waiting in that same dark, eyes adjusting as the evening light faded, it's easy to see the fear etched into the face of the old man standing in the doorway.

The old man's breath quickens, shallow at the top of his lungs. He's thinking about whether to call security. Whether the voice is lying. Why the voice sounds so familiar.

It's a few seconds before his breath deepens, control found again. He clears his throat. "May I turn the lights on, Mr. Juric?" he asks.

"Please," Manu says. "Make yourself at home."

A mildly amused laugh. "I think I shall."

The door closes, the lights bloom, and Alliance Deputy Chief of Mission Marquez ó Lauris is illuminated in the doorway to his own office in the Alliance embassy, a combination of annoyance and intrigue on his features. He crosses to his desk and hitches a hip onto the corner rather than settling in the imposing leather chair behind it. Steam twists gently from the mug of tea in his hands.

Manu has taken up residence on one of the stately armchairs by the bookshelf — one ankle over the opposite knee, his suit jacket unbuttoned, although his shoulder holster is covered. He doesn't miss ó Lauris's glance at where the weapon would be, though. He's been imagining that this chair is where ó Lauris settles with a cigar for a late night of reading, or to puzzle out thorny issues of interplanetary policy. As the deputy chief of mission to the Alliance ambassador on New Sarjun, ó Lauris must have plenty to puzzle.

Hopefully some of the chair's problem-solving charm will rub off on Manu Juric, deputy chief of Jaantzen.

"I didn't realize we knew each other well enough for casual drop-ins, Mr. Juric."

"I didn't think you'd want me on the visitors' log."

Ó Lauris takes a sip of his tea, steam kissing his glasses opaque a moment as he watches Manu over the rim of the mug. "Quite," he says finally.

The last time they met, it was in the back room of a seedy bar, Manu relying on ó Lauris's curiosity to draw him out to a meeting with Willem Jaantzen's right-hand man. Tonight, Manu doesn't have time for games.

Ó Lauris isn't the kind of man to waste time complaining that there were other options for meeting, or asking how Manu got in. Since he hasn't yet called security, ó Lauris has probably decided Manu won't kill him, and Manu's banking on not being thrown out until the man's curiosity has been satisfied. In fact, the way he's watching Manu, seems like he's more amused by a hiccough in his evening's schedule than angry at the intrusion.

Which means he probably has no idea that his government just declared war on the notorious Willem Jaantzen.

"I wanted to pick your brain," says Manu. "Run by you a hypothetical problem we might have."

Ó Lauris inclines his head. "A problem your employer has? Or?"

Manu touches a finger to his chest, tilts it to include ó Lauris. And, with a *What the hell!* smile, circles it to include the whole damn city. "We."

At this, the mild interest in ó Lauris's expression slips to serious. Good. Because what Manu's dealing with is about to get disconcertingly international.

"Indulge me a minute," Manu says. "What's the protocol when an undercover Alliance action against a private citizen in a non-Alliance country goes wrong?"

Ó Lauris considers him carefully, then sets his tea aside. "I saw the news about your employer's place of business. Another 'unfortunate incident of violence by a local crew.'" He's parroting the phrasing; it's clear he doesn't believe that version of the story. "Is everything all right?"

"Nah, man," says Manu. "I'm burying friends tomorrow." He sets both feet firmly on the floor, hiding his wince, watching ó Lauris. The old man has no idea what Manu's about to say; the way his torso leans forward, he's almost off-balance in his desire for inside information. If ó Lauris knew the Alliance was behind the events of last night, he would be on guard. There'd be no way his fight-or-flight response would let him stand so vulnerably.

"An unfortunate and unprovoked attack by a local crew," Manu says. "But what if they'd had help? What if that 'attack' was actually a covert Alliance mission, and the agent got caught?" His smile is sharp. "Hypothetically."

Ó Lauris's expression becomes professionally glass, but

it takes him a few beats to properly react; this was not what he was expecting to hear. "And you have proof?" He straightens, hand clawed on his knee for support. "You have a prisoner?"

Manu lifts an eyebrow.

"Are they being treated well?"

"Course, man." Manu holds out his hands — *We're still friends*. "For the purposes of our hypothetical, let's assume we're not dealing with monsters. Just businesspeople trying to make a living without getting shot up by foreign spies."

Ó Lauris is still. "Mr. Juric, I can assure you that the Alliance doesn't perform operations on foreign soil. That would be in breach of the Eyes of Durga Treaty."

"Oh, I know that. Which is why we're having a friendly conversation." Manu shakes his head in mock disapproval. "Imagine the international scandal this would be if something like that had actually happened. I'm sure your side would be coming up with a plan to react in that case."

Ó Lauris clears his throat. "If they had proof of life."

"And how do they get that."

No answer from the old man; he doesn't know or he's not saying. Manu and Starla went over the Alliance operative's armor and Gia went over her body last night — if she has a transmitter, it's been shut down. Not to mention the room she's being held in is signal-blocked. That should keep her handlers in limbo, enough not to come in guns blazing. With all the effort they went through to embed her with Acheta's crew, they're not going to tip their hands on a rescue mission for an agent they don't know is alive or dead.

Manu knows enough from Oriol about the Alliance's attitude towards its operatives. Unless it becomes a scandal, they probably won't risk much on her.

Only thing is, she was supposed to come back to roost

with the case in tow. The Alliance may not come for her, but they'll definitely come for it. The question is how soon, and what Manu can do to stall them.

"Well," says Manu, "in this hypothetical, let's assume the operative is still alive and being treated very fairly given the body count they left behind. And that their captors have pretty damning evidence."

He reaches into his suit pocket and ó Lauris flinches. But Manu's not reaching for a weapon. He produces a small holoprojector, small enough to nestle in his palm. He tosses it to ó Lauris, who presses the button with a dark expression.

He's probably expecting a threat: an Alliance operative blindfolded and bound with a gun to her head. The clip he views instead isn't long, just long enough to show vid from the stairwell where the Alliance woman's face is clearly visible as she shoots two guards point-blank — they have their hands up, weapons on the ground. The footage cuts to the hallway of floor twelve. The woman's dragging Toshiyo with her when she spins and shoots Elian in the stomach.

"The kid she shot in that last clip was an unarmed medical student," says Manu. "Not a great look for the Alliance. Especially considering the man she's with."

Ó Lauris sighs deeply. "That was Levi Acheta?"

"Only one of the most notorious criminals in Bulari's underground."

"Who has seen this?"

"No one, yet." Manu leans elbows on knees. "I don't know what the standard Alliance special ops response would be in this case, but maybe it would be better to think about a diplomatic option. Particularly since the civilian target is pretty well-connected with people in New Sarjun's government. Oh — and since our governments are on the brink of negotiating a new trade deal." Manu shakes his head. "Terrible timing, yeah? Something like this could get out of hand so fast."

Ó Lauris nods slowly. He's gotten the message: Tell whoever's in charge of black ops on this planet that there will be dire consequences to pulling additional shit. Now it's time to figure out what Manu and ó Lauris can actually do about it.

"I hope you appreciate the respect I did you by coming to you directly," Manu says. He'd already suspected that ó Lauris isn't much involved in whatever illegal tactical operations the Alliance has underway on New Sarjun — but he is in charge of administering the embassy under a parade of rotating ambassadors, and has been for two decades. The ambassadors and the black ops handlers may come and go, but ó Lauris is invested in this country. He's a man whose sole purpose is fixing things. Just like Manu.

"I do appreciate the gesture, Mr. Juric. And I will maintain absolute discretion. What's your next step?" Ó Lauris smiles. "Hypothetically."

"You'll know." Manu stands, straightens his cuffs, doesn't button his suit jacket. "Right now I just need a message sent. And to know there's someone in your government willing to work with us instead of just sending in the dogs."

"Consider it done," ó Lauris says. "In the interest of interplanetary peace."

"Thank you." Manu holds out his right hand to shake, ignoring the screaming pain in his bicep where Toshiyo's hell-beast tore into him last night. The arm should be in a sling, but that's not the way you make a proper impression on a fellow.

Ó Lauris stands to meet him, his grip firm. Polite. His hand is warm and dry.

"Do you have just a moment more, Mr. Juric?" he asks as he releases the handshake. He's feeling more in control of the situation now, Manu can tell, the edge smoothed from his amused Arquellian drawl. "I have a question for you."

"Ask away." Manu doesn't like ó Lauris feeling more in control. He keeps his shoulders relaxed, his gun hand loose.

"I've been hearing rumors over the last few days." The hint of a smile. "That a certain former mayor is alive? And — and this is what has me lingering at work when I should be heading home — that she may have rejoined her old crew?"

He knows about Thala Coeur, he's just waiting to hear Manu confirm it. And, what the hell. It'll be common knowledge soon enough.

"I've heard that, too," Manu says.

"When last we spoke, you came to ask me what we did to contain Thala Coeur when she sought asylum at the embassy. Did you know she was alive at that time?"

Voices pass in the hall, the click of heels rising and fading, a woman's laughter. Ó Lauris doesn't break Manu's gaze.

Manu lets a smile tug at his lips. "I'll answer that question honestly if you do."

An intrigued arch of ó Lauris's eyebrow. "Agreed."

"Yes, I did." Manu lifts his chin. "Your turn."

A breath, ó Lauris considering his answer. "No," he finally says. And the follow-up question he wants to ask is plain in his face, but he'll never say the words: Should I have?

Manu watches him wonder if the Alliance was involved in Coeur's "death" and then revival. If the problem of Thala

Coeur and the attack on Willem Jaantzen are, in fact, linked.

Watches seeds of doubt grow as ó Lauris wonders just how his own government is undermining his peace efforts, right under his nose.

Good.

"Life is cyclical, isn't it?" Ó Lauris picks up his tea once more, sipping contemplatively. "You think you've dealt with a problem, only to find it back on your doorstep."

"Do you think she has a grudge against you?"

Ó Lauris smiles faintly. "One can assume."

"Take a few days and ask some questions," Manu says. "Find out why your government might attack a private New Sarjunian citizen, and who else knew that Thala Coeur was alive. And let the appropriate people know what kind of shitshow they'll have on their hands if they go after the man again. I'll be in touch to set up a meeting, and we can sort this out like adults. Have a good night, Deputy Chief."

"Good night, Mr. Juric. Please convey my sincere condolences to your employer on the tragic loss of life, and let him know I have the best interests of international relations at heart."

Manu nods solemnly at that and lets himself out the door. Ó Lauris may honestly regret what happened last night, but Manu doubts that sentiment applies to the rest of his colleagues. He's still walking through a den of snakes.

This late, the hallways of the Alliance embassy are nearly empty. Manu leaves through the front doors — no one bothers to challenge you once you've gotten in, and the few people still milling about aren't likely to recognize him. Somebody'll check the security vids eventually, though. They'll wonder how he got in, marvel at how casually he strolled back out.

Manu's found that nothing helps a negotiation along quite so well as your enemy knowing just how close you can get to them.

Outside, the baking desert evening is finally starting to cool off as a slight breeze picks up, the air velvety against Manu's skin. It's the sort of night he usually loves, a night meant for sitting lazy in cafes, like the one across the street, where lanterns are strung above cafe tables, waiters pour wine, the kitchen fills the air with the scents of fresh-baked bread and garlic and bitter orange. The government district comes alive in the evenings, a safe place for tourists and the sort of Arquellians who style themselves expats rather than immigrants to sample the evening cafes without worrying they'll get mugged or have to rub elbows with a dirty local.

In the still night, Manu catches snatches of different accents and languages, mostly from Indiran countries, though there are plenty of tourists from throughout New Sarjun come to visit the big city of Bulari, too.

He pauses a moment on the embassy's steps; the first of New Sarjun's moons is rising full just down the street, perfectly framed in the gap between buildings, a deep burnished gold in the faint dust haze of the horizon.

Others have stopped to stare at it, too, others who are leaving the embassy at the end of the day, or stopping on the wide marble steps to enjoy their takeout meals or tie their children's shoes or rest their bones with a cigarette. It's such a captivating sight that, for a moment, it feels like the entirety of Bulari must be appreciating the beauty of the rising moon. It's stunning, both the vision and the sudden vertiginous feeling that everyone else in this city is enraptured by the same glorious celestial object.

Manu isn't looking back at the embassy, but even if he had been, he wouldn't've had warning.

The bomb had been ticking away for the better part of the day. Timed for the hour, not the transcendent distraction of the rising moon, the blast rips through the embassy's facade, thundering through glass and cracking marble, sending bodies tumbling down the steps like windblown leaves. Across the road, the cafe's windows shatter, patrons scrambling for cover.

In the wake of the explosion, an eerie stillness descends. Full minutes tick agonizingly by before bystanders begin to trust that they are safe, shocked onlookers slowly emerge, a few unbelieving moments more before emergency calls are made, before anyone who thinks they might be able to help approaches to see which — if any — of the unmoving bodies on the stairs can possibly be saved.

Through gently raining ash and shifting dust, the shattered facade of the Alliance embassy gapes like a maw.

1

JAANTZEN

Calanthe Yang's husband, Alex, is a phenomenal cook, but tonight everything Willem Jaantzen eats tastes like dust.

When he accepted the invitation, he'd assumed it would only be Calanthe's immediate family and her mother, Julieta. But Calanthe invited her brother and his wife, and her two young sons add the distractive equivalent of another five adults.

Then Jaantzen invited Phaera D, which seemed like a good idea this morning, but now has him on edge. It's been almost two decades since he's brought a woman to dinner with Julieta's family, and having Phaera beside him is digging up old memories.

Tae'd had a quiet grace, where Phaera has a sharp, self-possessed confidence, and the steel at Tae's core was buried far deeper than Phaera's. And, of course, Tae's exasperation with him had manifested itself in muttered prayers instead of profanities.

But for all she's dancing around the edges of his memory tonight, Tae's not here.

She would've adored Calanthe's boys.

Enough.

Phaera's currently entertaining the boys with a magic trick. The older has caught on to the ruse and is trying to copy her with his own napkin while the younger stares at them both with equal parts astonishment and frustration. Phaera's laughter is cool, fresh rain.

He catches himself watching her — not the napkin vanishing through her fingers, but the secret smile in her eyes — and looks up with a start to meet Julieta Yang's amused gaze.

Alex is already making motions towards clearing dinner. Calanthe's brother, Liatris, stands to help him. When Calanthe starts to lever herself to her feet, Phaera waves her back down.

"I've got this, Callie," she says — Do people call this formidable Yang daughter Callie? She doesn't seem to mind it from Phaera. — and begins gathering plates, stacking them gracefully up her arm with an expert hand. She catches Jaantzen watching and winks. A flush creeps up his neck, hidden beneath his dark skin.

Julieta lays her warm, dry hand over his. "Willem, will you indulge an old lady with a walk before dessert?"

"Of course."

Jaantzen helps Julieta from her chair, patient as her hand claws on his arm, though he's never seen her fumble like this. He shares a look with Calanthe over her mother's head and gets a grim smile in response. It's as though she's aged a decade in the past week, since her youngest daughter betrayed them all to the Dawn.

Calanthe and Alex live in an elegant, hilly neighborhood near the University of Bulari, and although there's a lovely view out over the city from the front room of their home, their backyard feels like another world. Acacia and figs arch overhead, all hemmed in by high stone walls in a garden landscaped lushly with native plants and a few of Julieta's strange hybrids. The only illumination is witch lights suspended in the foliage and the glow of the rising moon.

The night is warm and still, troubled only by the faint rustling of birds settling in for the night and the sound of their steps on the paved path. Julieta keeps hold of Jaantzen's arm, fingers tight.

"What is it, Willem?" she says after a moment of silence; something coos softly in the branches above them. "You've been looking like you want to take me aside all night."

He breathes deep. "I have a complicated favor to ask you," he says. "But it's difficult to know where to start."

She knows about the attack on Cobalt Tower, of course — the entire planet does by now. She also knows he's propped Thala Coeur back up into power. What she doesn't know is that the attack was prompted by the Alliance, or about the impossible creature everyone else seems willing to kill to get their hands on.

Jaantzen knows how to rebuild and how to revenge. He thinks he understands, finally, how to deal with Coeur. But the Alliance? The creature? These aren't problems he can take care of the old-fashioned way. He needs advice from an old friend.

"The shipment you asked us to destroy last week," Jaantzen says. "We didn't."

Julieta sighs, but doesn't seem surprised. "I wondered."

"We destroyed the warehouse and everything inside, except for two things: Ximena Nayar, and the case Coeur was sending to her."

Julieta stills, frowning at him. "Ximena."

"Aster called Ximena. She meant her to be in that warehouse when Starla destroyed it."

Julieta takes a sharp breath. "I can't imagine my Aster with blood on her hands," she says after a moment, but it's not denial. It's grief.

"The blood's there," Jaantzen says quietly. Aster Yang may not have succeeded in killing Ximena to cover her tracks that day, and she may not have let fly the bullet that killed Ximena in the end. But she brought the wolf Bennion Zacharia into her mother's house, and Ximena is dead because of it.

"What was in that case you were supposed to destroy, Willem?" Julieta asks.

He glances at her sidelong. Her dark eyes catch the witch lights.

"Zacharia believed the case held the same serum he was using to create his supersoldiers," Jaantzen says. "Levi Acheta believed that, too."

Her fingers smooth absently over his arm. Somewhere in the distance beyond the still serenity of the garden comes the whine of emergency sirens.

"Zacharia and Levi believed," she says. "Surely you've opened it to see for yourself."

"Ximena found out that the Alliance was terraforming the desert around Redrock," he says, and she tilts her head, waiting patiently for him to tie this back in. "She and Coeur believed the cases held a serum that would allow anyone to do the same. Coeur was going to use it herself."

Julieta laughs, amused. "Thala wanted to get into farming? I would've thought she'd be much more interested in the part where it turns humans into killing machines."

"I think she likes that, too. But she's wise enough now to

understand which is the more lucrative business opportunity."

"And is it? A good business opportunity?"

A few weeks ago, Jaantzen wouldn't have known. But now he's paying attention to notices of food shortages and reading the editorials arguing for and against the trade agreement New Sarjun is currently negotiating with the Alliance. Lowering the tariffs against imported Alliance food could potentially lower prices and make food more available. Or it could ruin New Sarjun's already struggling agricultural industry.

Whether the agreement goes through or not, it's the perfect time to get into the business with a competitive technological advantage.

"Thala and I are speaking with the Demosgas."

That earns him a long, cool look.

"Willem. Is that wise."

"We've come to an understanding." It doesn't even seem strange to say anymore. "And I'd rather have her kept busy where I can see her than left to her own devices."

"Tae would have wanted you to move on," Julieta says finally, with a significant glance back at the house; she's not just talking about moving on from his vendetta with Coeur. "So you'll go into farming alongside refrigerators and security systems. Your businesses are mind-numbingly boring."

"And profitable. We can't all make our fortunes smuggling furs and antiques, Julieta."

She smiles. In the semidarkness, the deepest lines of her face are carved into slashes winging from her nose, cut between her eyebrows. He barely recognizes her.

"What's inside the case isn't as important as who wants the case," Jaantzen says.

"Zacharia," says Julieta. "Levi. Thala, the Demosgas."

"The Alliance."

Julieta sucks a sharp breath through her teeth.

"Sit with me, Willem," she says, leading him to a marble bench beneath a clear spot in the canopy, any potentially visible stars washed from the sky by the brightness of the first moon. "Tell me."

"Acheta had an Alliance agent with him last night. We think that's how he knew about the case."

"Is the agent still alive?"

"Yes."

Julieta sighs. "I don't know if that's better. I'm sorry I involved you in this."

"Coeur involved us both." He lets that sit a moment before he shifts to face her. "And I come to my favor. I don't feel safe in Cobalt Tower. I need certain things to be moved somewhere safe. Discreetly."

"What exactly are we talking about, Willem."

That is the question, isn't it?

He's been debating whether to involve Julieta, even before the attack last night that made it clear the creature needs to be out from under his roof. Since the beginning, their relationship has been one of carefully balanced half-truths, of the knowledge that they can trust each other as friends while keeping their secrets as needed.

This is not a secret he's ready to share.

"Some medical equipment. Supplies. Things I'd rather the Alliance not find if they decide to attack again." They'll be moving the Alliance agent, of course. But he and his team can handle that.

"Where?"

"Outside of the city. I'm still deciding."

Julieta squeezes his arm. "I'll see what I can do."

"I'll have Toshiyo get in touch with specifications."

"Yes, of course. I wish you'd come to me immediately, Willem. What are you going to do about the Alliance agent?"

"That's under control."

"You should have killed her when you first found her and made it look like Acheta did it. But we're beyond that, aren't we?" Julieta waves a hand. "I'm sure you're bolstering your defenses, but speak with Calanthe about your legal rights against the Alliance." She takes an abrupt breath, perhaps at the thought of bringing another child into the same tricky business that devoured her youngest daughter.

"Have you spoken with Geum-ja about any of this?" Julieta asks.

The thought has crossed his mind. Chief Justice Geum-ja Leone has useful connections within both New Sarjun's government and the Alliance. Dealing with international intrigue may not be in her job description, but she wouldn't miss an opportunity to be at the center of something so momentous.

Jaantzen trusts Leone to make connections, to broker business deals. Trusts her enough to walk into her home unarmed and eat at her table. But to give her this kind of leverage over him?

Jaantzen shakes his head. "I'm not sure I can trust her."

Julieta tilts her head back and closes her eyes a moment, the witch lights softening the lines of her face and making her for a moment appear the formidable woman he'd met all those years ago.

"Geum-ja is angry with you, Willem," she says finally, opening her eyes once more. "She wasn't pleased with the way you took initiative on getting rid of Levi, and she's extremely unhappy that Thala is back in Bulari. Tread carefully."

"I appreciate any advice you can give."

"Act fast and trust no one."

"I think we've bought a bit of time." Manu had messaged him near the end of dinner that things were taken care of for the moment.

"Be careful, Willem. And put your pride aside and learn." Julieta's gaze becomes steel. "If you don't, she'll eat you alive."

"Gramma!"

"Here, sweetheart," Julieta calls back, and Calanthe's oldest, Julian, comes barreling down the path to throw himself face-first into her lap.

"Careful with your grandma, Jules," Jaantzen says, but Julieta just laughs and strokes the boy's back.

"It's time for dessert!" Julian launches himself from his grandmother's lap as quickly as he landed, then grabs Julieta's hand in his pudgy fingers and pulls her to her feet. Jaantzen reaches to steady her — the boy is going to pull her off-balance, send her careening to fracture against the stones.

"I'm not made of glass, Willem," Julieta says with an amused smile.

Jaantzen doesn't let go of her arm. "Humor me," he says, and she pats a papery hand over his.

Julian races ahead to the door. "I found Gramma and Uncle Lillem," he calls. "It's time for dessert!"

No one answers.

"Momma?" Julian calls.

Adrenaline spikes through Jaantzen's chest; he leaves Julieta braced against the doorway, is through the dining room to the kitchen with his hand on his gun in a breath — though he doesn't draw it, not with the boy here.

And he doesn't need to.

Everyone is in the kitchen, safe, and transfixed by the news feed on the kitchen table. Phaera looks up when he bursts in and shakes her head in warning — she sees what he's reaching for — then detaches herself from the group. She smooths her palms down his arms; she's standing so close he can smell the almond and citrus of her cologne, feel her warmth through the fabric of his suit.

"Everything's fine, we should have answered," she murmurs.

His heart is still pumping adrenaline. "I overreacted." He buttons his suit jacket closed once more, fingers stiff.

"You didn't." He can't read the look she's giving him, but she squeezes his elbow as she slips past him. "Julieta, we're in the kitchen," she calls.

Jaantzen joins the others gathered around the news feed. Smoke and wreckage and the gaping broken facade of a building — he's seen that too often these past few days. But it's not Phaera's Lorelei or his Cobalt Tower. With the state the building is in, it takes him time to recognize those marble steps, now dotted with blanket-covered bodies.

The Alliance embassy.

Six dead, a reporter is saying, more injured, though the blast didn't go deep into the building, and it was mostly empty after hours. A terrorist attack, and the reporter is speculating on some of the usual suspects when the feed cuts to a clip of Deputy Chief of Mission Marquez ó Lauris, who's refusing to guess at a culprit until they have more information.

The reporters move on from the wreckage and begin throwing out theories as to how this will affect the trade deal negotiations. Alex swipes the feed away.

Julieta has joined them by now, and the look she gives Jaantzen says they're thinking the exact same thing: After the Alliance attacked him last night, he'll be at the top of the suspects list.

"We should go," says Jaantzen.

On another night that point would be contested — stay for dessert, for a cigar, for a nightcap — but tonight the earlier sense of festivity has been overtaken by dread. In a few moments the pleasantries have been exchanged and Jaantzen and Phaera are enclosed by silence in the back of Jaantzen's new Dulciana JX.

The silence lingers as the driver, Raim, pulls away from the curb. Light from passing buildings flickers through the windows to skim Phaera's pale cheek.

On the drive over, he'd kept things light. Last night she saw him at his worst — he'd nearly killed Acheta's lieutenant when he saw the bruises on Phaera's arm — yet today she has been kind, gracious. The playfulness of her earlier flirtations with him has faded, though, been replaced by a touch of wariness. Or perhaps it's only a preoccupation that has nothing to do with him.

After all.

She called him this morning, didn't she? Came to Calanthe's with him?

Is sitting here with her arm brushing against his, even though she has plenty of space?

"Are you all right?" she asks finally, breaking the silence.

"Fine." Jaantzen clears his throat. "You?"

She laughs sadly and leans back, the black tips of her magenta bob feathering over her shoulders.

"Thank you," she says.

Jaantzen frowns at her. "For?"

"I know what you did yesterday, getting rid of Acheta. I know that wasn't just for me, but thank you. For all of us."

"Don't thank me yet. I did let Blackheart back into the wild."

"I was . . ." She laughs again, turns her face to the front of the spinner; streetlamps flash the outline of her profile. "I didn't know what was going to happen. I thought, Acheta won't kill me if I go to him. Probably. At least not until he gets his money, but maybe he would have. And Sjel might have killed Jae, or Sina, or . . . The threats he was making—"

"Acheta's gone."

"I thought, if I get in that spinner, I may never come back. And it might not do a damn thing to save the people who work for me. I thought, even if I had paid him, he'd just want me to pay him again and again, and eventually I won't have what he wants and he'll kill me anyway. And everyone else I love."

"Acheta's gone," Jaantzen says again, more firmly.

She finally turns to meet his gaze. "I know. I just can't shake the feeling that I should have done something different."

"You did fine."

She doesn't answer; he doesn't know if she believes him. "What did Acheta want at the tower?"

"What did Oriol tell you?"

A muscle twitches in her cheek. She's trying to decide if he's going to lie to her.

"He said Acheta and some of his crew broke in and shot the place up, and they didn't get beyond the lobby," she says finally, and Jaantzen relaxes. Good to know Oriol's holding to the public story, even if he's now officially on Phaera's payroll. "Acheta knew you weren't there, so I assume he was looking for something else."

"It doesn't matter," he says out of habit, and her eyes

flash. "I mean, it does. But it's gotten complicated. What I can tell you is that Acheta was working with the Alliance, whether he knew it or not."

"The Alliance." She takes a sharp breath. "Does it have anything to do with the bombing tonight?"

Jaantzen can't think of how it would, but that doesn't mean a damned thing. "Not that I'm aware of."

She's silent, and after a few long breaths she slips her hand into his. It's such an unexpectedly comfortable gesture that he stares at their hands a moment, pale and dark, unsure how to respond.

"Let me know how I can help," Phaera says finally.

"Just stay safe. Is Oriol working out?"

"I tried to give him the night off, but he's doing some sort of training thing with my security staff. Thank you for letting him go, he's a gem."

"Oriol's never been mine to let go." Jaantzen's beginning to recognize the buildings around them with a sinking feeling; they're just blocks from Phaera's apartment. "I'm sorry I can't tell you more."

He expects an argument, a lecture, but Phaera merely straightens in her seat.

"I don't expect you to spill all your secrets to me," she says with a tired smile. The spinner has come to a stop in front of her building. "And I'm not giving you the keys to my vault anytime soon. At least literally, I mean." Phaera winks, lashes light as a butterfly's wing against her cheek. "Metaphorically speaking, I don't suppose you'd like to come up for a nightcap?"

Jaantzen's mouth opens, shuts again. Phaera laughs.

"Good night, Jaantzen." She squeezes his hand and begins to let go; he keeps his fingers tangled tight in hers. An intrigued tilt of her head — she wasn't expecting that — and he lets the forward pull of her gravity draw him towards her. Her lips part, she's inexplicably not pulling back, and for a tantalizing moment he tastes only the whiskey on her breath.

He closes the distance for the briefest, gentlest of kisses; it lasts three slow heartbeats before her fingernails scrape along his jawline and she presses in, her lips so hungry and sweet his throat aches. Then her fingers trail down his lapel, over his thigh, and she's gone, the driver, Raim, holding the door open for her.

"Good night?" she says again, making it a question this time, the arch of her eyebrow an invitation.

It takes every screaming fiber of his being to give her the answer he must. "Good night, Phaera."

He can't read Phaera's smile as she steps away. "I'll call you," she says. The apartment guard greets her, and with a glance over her shoulder she disappears inside.

2

STARLA

The cuff around Starla's wrist is going *off*, vibrating in sharp bursts that drag her from her sleep. She fumbles at it until it stops, then reaches for her comm, heart pounding. Small paws knead her shoulder, annoyed at the disturbance.

It's early and she's exhausted. She spent the first half of the night shutting down panic attacks, until she finally drank two of the lagers Manu left in her fridge last week and drifted into uneasy sleep.

In her dreams the alien kept turning mundane situations into nightmares. She'd turn from the grocery store counter or from rehydrating dinner to find it flapping towards her, claws outstretched. The little bastard even managed to ruin a dream about Professor Sam Amrith by shredding him to bits in front of her before Starla's subconscious had had a chance to get properly inappropriate.

She thumbs on her comm. She's missed five messages from Oriol, which explains why the last part of her dream was just the creature taking her wrist in its fangs and shaking her.

The messages get increasingly anxious, asking if she's heard from Manu, until finally:

Is Manu there?

He wasn't there when she went to bed. But she slips her legs out from under a cat — Mango, by the coarseness of her fur — and pads out into the hallway to see if Manu let himself in in the middle of the night.

There's just enough ambient glow from the city that she can make her way down the hallway without turning on the lights. She does a double take at the two glinting beer bottles on the counter before she remembers she left them there herself.

Which means he should be at home with Oriol, or at work with Jaantzen, and either way, Oriol shouldn't be messaging her. The low, thrumming panic that has plagued her all night rekindles in her chest.

When she turns on the living room lights, she thinks, she's going to find Manu sprawled on her couch in his shirt-sleeves, one arm flung over his eyes to block out the light of the city, nose twitching in his sleep as Pepper's tail flicks back and forth across it.

She turns on the lights.

Her apartment is empty.

No and I haven't heard from him, she types. What's going on?

She doesn't wait for Oriol to answer. Adrenaline has pushed all sleepiness from her mind. She checks the levels on the cats' feeder, pulls on clothes, and splashes water over her face, raking damp fingers and a palmful of product through her hair in an attempt to mitigate the fact that she went to bed with it wet. Lens inserted into her eye. A swipe of mascara, because it's been a rough week and she looks like it, then she's out the door with a protein bar in one hand and her comm in the other.

It buzzes and she triple-blinks her lens on.

He didn't come home last night. Not answering messages. No one knows where he is.

Heading to the tower.

She palms her moto out of its dock and the engine purrs to life.

Toshiyo is awake already, or she never went to sleep — Starla would believe either one. She's crosslegged on a chair in the fourth-floor conference room, a bowl of oatmeal and fruit untouched at one elbow, a coffee carafe empty at the other. Starla watches her a moment from the door. An algorithm is running on the conference table in front of her, flipping through images, sorting them into piles. The faces of brown- and black-skinned men slip from the queue next to her and appear in front of Toshiyo. Everyone else vanishes.

They're images of death, Starla realizes with a lurch, every single one a morgue shot or crime scene photo. Toshiyo's paging through them with an impassive expression: dozens of battered, bloody faces, and none of them Manu's.

Starla hesitates in the doorway before she realizes what she's doing: studying Toshiyo for some sign that she's about to fall apart. But, "Tae never treated me like I was made of glass," Toshiyo had told Starla. "And neither do you."

Everyone else may treat Toshiyo like she'll break at any moment, but Starla's not about to start just because an Alliance agent stalked Toshiyo through the dark of her own home two nights ago and nearly put a bullet in her head. Starla knocks on the doorway and Toshiyo blinks at her wearily. A live edge of energy hums behind her bloodshot eyes.

"From the morgue," Toshiyo signs, her normally rapid-fire fingerspelling sluggish. Maybe it's the bandages around her forearms and left hand, maybe it's lack of sleep, or — her pupils are enormous — maybe it's something she's taking. "I already went through . . ." Toshiyo's fingers still as a new face appears on her screen. Her lips part in fear.

Starla leans over her shoulder. The face has Manu's cheekbones, his lips, the line of his jaw, though most of the top half of the head is either missing or blackened from some explosion. Starla reaches past Toshiyo's frozen shoulder to call up the identifying information: weight (too heavy), height (too short), what he was wearing (a delivery driver's jumpsuit), how he died (his truck colliding with a maglev train).

Starla swipes the horrifying image away. "It's not him," she signs to Toshiyo. "Where else have you looked?" Because surely she hadn't started with the morgues.

"Police records. Hospitals and clinics," Toshiyo says aloud, her words crawling across the bottom of Starla's lens. "But most don't list their unidentifieds right away, and the police might not have put him in the system if they arrested him."

Of course, those are only the public places that Manu might have disappeared to. Blackheart, what's left of the Dry Creek crew, some upstart crew who thought they were being clever — anyone with a grudge could have taken him.

The desk in front of Toshiyo blinks to let her know her parade of dead men has finished, and would she like to run the search again?

"I have an AI checking surveillance footage all over the city, but it hasn't turned up anything yet," Toshiyo says.

"Does Jaantzen know?"

Toshiyo doesn't answer, just turns her attention past Starla to the door. Oriol's arrived. He doesn't look like he slept, either.

"I don't think he's in the morgue, and he's not in a hospital or in jail that I can tell," Toshiyo says.

Oriol collapses into the chair on Toshiyo's other side and begins to swipe through her discarded files, pausing, ashen, at the one who looks so much like Manu.

"It's not him," Toshiyo says. She exits the program and the desk goes blank, Oriol's hands hovering over the spot where the face of the too-familiar-looking dead man had been. "He's not any of those, I checked." She turns to Starla. "Jaantzen knows," she signs; Starla had almost forgotten she'd asked the question. "He's upstairs making calls."

Starla nods and stands. "Keep looking," she signs to Toshiyo, then jerks her chin at the door for Oriol to follow her.

"Where was he last?" she asks Oriol in the lift.

"He said he had a meeting." Oriol begins the sentence in USL, but gives up by the end in his distraction. His words scroll along the bottom of her lens. "I was out late at the Lorelei, and he never came home. He's not answering messages. Do you know who he was meeting?"

Starla shakes her head. She wants to tell him things will be fine, but he looks like hell and they'd both know she was lying. She has no way of knowing how things will turn out.

She just brushes a hand down his arm instead, squeezing his muscled forearm in a way she hopes is comforting; he doesn't react to the touch.

The lift opens in Jaantzen's penthouse suite, where

Starla's godfather is sitting at his conference table, speaking with someone Starla doesn't recognize. Starla doesn't catch the last of the conversation as he signs off and turns to them. He rises to greet them.

"Oriol — "

"Where the fuck did he go last night?" Oriol asks Jaantzen, and Starla straightens at Oriol's words on her lens. She can't tell by his expression if it's venom, exhaustion, or fear.

His tone must be aggressive, by the sharp look Jaantzen gives him. "Have a seat," Jaantzen says evenly.

Oriol doesn't move. "You sent him to meet with someone," he says. "Who."

"We needed to deliver a message to the Alliance. Manu was taking care of it." A muscle tightens in Jaantzen's jaw. "That's what we know."

Oriol's expression darkens. "You sent him to talk to the Alliance?"

"I didn't send him anywhere, he was doing his job. Sit down."

"He was at the embassy last night? When the bomb went off?"

A flash of pain crosses Jaantzen's face. "I don't know. Oriol, sit down."

Jaantzen hasn't moved, but Oriol flinches back as though shaking him off. Starla's not used to this Oriol: that furious angle to his easygoing shoulders, that muscle tight in his normally smiling jaw, those tendons roping in his forearms as his hands close to fists.

That fire burning in his eyes.

It occurs to her that it's not anger at Jaantzen in particular, just another facet of the fear, the worry. Still, Starla puts a hand on his arm before he does anything stupid. He flicks her an irritated glare; the ease with which he breaks her grip is casual, professional.

"We're all trying to find him," she signs; she's purposefully at the edge of his vision, where he'll have to break his death glare on Jaantzen to understand her. A muscle twitches his cheek and he turns.

"What," he snaps.

"We're all trying to find him," she signs again. "Sit down. Let's think this through."

She's not sure he'll listen to her any more than he did Jaantzen, but he finally stalks past Jaantzen into the living room, though he doesn't sit, just stands there with fingers clawed into the back of the couch nearest the kitchen. Starla spells "Coeur" behind his back with a raised eyebrow to Jaantzen.

"I spoke with Coeur," Jaantzen signs, but he's speaking aloud, too, and Oriol whips back around. "She put out a search."

"Is she searching her own torture chambers?" Oriol asks.

"No." Jaantzen's flaring nostrils are the first sign of his frustration. He crosses back to the conference table and taps to open a channel. "Toshiyo, I need you here."

"He's met with the Alliance deputy chief before," Starla signs to Jaantzen. "Have you called him?"

"I haven't gotten through to ó Lauris," Jaantzen says and signs, hands precise as he concentrates on two languages at once. "I've been trying him all morning. He won't take my calls."

"I'll go."

"Oriol, I don't think that's a good — "

"I'm a fucking decorated Alliance war hero." Oriol's lips are barely moving, his jaw clenched so tight. "I'm still an

Arquellian citizen. I can get a meeting with my ambassador. If he was at the embassy — "

"We don't know he was at the embassy," Jaantzen says.

"*You* don't know?"

Jaantzen's gone still; Starla can feel the tension crackling in the air between the two men.

"Oriol," Jaantzen says. "I don't have a tracker on him."

Oriol's good leg has shifted back a few inches — the stance seems reflexive to Starla, not intentional — but his fists are balled and Starla can't tell if he's waiting for an excuse to snap or preparing to defend himself. Jaantzen looks like he's planning out his next steps across broken glass. Starla moves closer, ready to step in again if she can. And ready to fight Oriol if she has to.

But Jaantzen just lifts his hands. "We're wasting time. Go to the embassy and see if you can get ó Lauris to talk to you," he says and signs. His gaze flickers to meet Starla's and she nods. "Take Starla, and be careful."

"Not to step in whatever you're negotiating?" Oriol growls. "Whatever's so goddamn important that — "

"No," Jaantzen says, expression hard. "Be careful, Mr. Sina. For Manu's sake. For your sake."

And Oriol's jaw sets. The way his shoulders straighten, that upward flick of his chin: He's accepting an order. Maybe it's a reflex, maybe he's getting himself back under control. But Starla relaxes.

The lights flicker as the lift arrives with Toshiyo. Oriol squeezes her shoulder as he and Starla take her place, and she studies them both, obviously scenting the lingering air of violence in the room.

She doesn't ask.

"What did you need, boss?" Toshiyo asks.

"Show me what you've found so far," Jaantzen says, rubbing a hand over the back of his neck.

Toshiyo nods and slumps into a chair at his conference table, calling up her account.

"Be careful," Jaantzen signs to Starla as the lift doors shut.

Starla punches in the code to the garage before Oriol can touch a button. "I'll drive," she signs. "You can make calls if you need." That's not the reason she wants to drive — no way in hell is she letting him at the controls with how volatile he is. But after a moment he nods.

"Straight to the embassy?" Starla asks; she's led them to her favorite spinner, an earlier model silver Magnata coupe with an aftermarket weapons system and some special modifications she's made to the navigation.

"Let's start there," Oriol says. He wedges himself into the passenger seat like a tight-wound spring, comm in hand. "Hey, Hallelujah, it's Sina, got a question for you," he says, and she realizes he's opened a line to someone else. She turns her attention to driving.

Outside it's bright despite the dust kicked up in the winds, and the spinner's windows dim automatically to cut the glare. Not a full-on dust storm, but she does a mental inventory of the supplies she's packed the Magnata with. Definitely dust masks in here, at least four. She'll need to order a set of real desert-grade masks if she can convince Jaantzen to let her head north to Redrock, though, along with . . . She goes down the mental checklist once more, lets it distract her from where Manu could be, from the litany of worst-case scenarios trying to stampede through her brain.

She has to think he'll be fine, they'll find him. If she doesn't, she'll lose it right here. And then where will they all be?

She ignores the scrawling text of Oriol's calls and distracts herself with driving — now in queue to turn left into the government district — so she almost doesn't see it when Toshiyo's message cuts through with blinking urgency:

SULILA HOSPITAL FINGERS

Toshiyo's sent a map; Starla doesn't need it.

She wrenches the controls to the right, pulling out of the queue and gunning the spinner through the intersection just as the lights change.

"Oh, J Juric," the receptionist says as Starla catches up with Oriol; he was out the door before she'd docked the spinner. The receptionist looks relieved to have found the patient, and Starla doesn't blame her. Oriol's holding himself as calmly as possible, but every muscle on his lean frame seems poised to snap. "And you're family?"

The receptionist glances up at him with a frown; Oriol and Manu are night and day to brothers is probably what she's thinking. If not for their skin tone, for Oriol's Arquellian accent.

"He's my — my husband," Oriol says, and Starla tries to hide her surprise; in all the years she's known them, neither man has ever used that word. If the receptionist notices Oriol's hesitation, she decides to ignore it.

"We already informed the family," she tells him.

Starla blinks at the words on her lens, almost dismissing them as a bad transcription. But Oriol's also staring at the woman in confusion.

Starla raps on the counter. "What do you mean?" she signs. "What family?" There's no way the receptionist meant Jaantzen and Starla, and Oriol obviously didn't get a call, which means they called the wrong person. Which means anyone could be on their way to finish the job the bomb started, masquerading as family to get close to Manu when he's most vulnerable.

The receptionist glances between Starla and Oriol; at a sharp nudge from Starla's elbow, Oriol repeats her question. The receptionist's startled gaze flickers to someone behind them before she catches herself. Starla doesn't need to turn to guess who the receptionist was looking at. She remembers the layout of the room, the old man sitting on a bench near the door. She'd marked and immediately ignored him when she came in.

The old man. Is he family? Or enemy.

The nurse is squinting down at her monitor. "Are you on the list? Oh, I'm sorry. You're not," she says, though she hasn't asked either of their names. "His father said he had no more living family."

His father?

"I need to speak with his doctor," Oriol says. And he hasn't shifted an inch, hasn't made a move towards her, but whatever he put in his tone makes the receptionist decide in that moment that arguing with him is beyond her pay grade. She turns and says something over her shoulder, too soft for Starla's lens to catch.

"Wait over there," she finally tells them.

Starla thanks the poor woman and drags Oriol after her, sinking into a threadbare chair next to the door to the hospital ward and immediately turning her attention to study the man across the lobby. Beside her, Oriol is doing the same thing. And by his stunned expression she can tell he sees what she does.

It's uncanny. It's like looking at Manu in another thirty

years: the shape of the jaw, the nose, the cheekbones are right, though this old man's been wrung dry, chewed up, and spit out without even a hint of laughter in those eyes.

When she first walked into the hospital, she'd thought he seemed familiar. Now, studying his face, she doesn't understand how she hadn't seen the father-son resemblance from the beginning.

Though she hadn't been looking for it then — why would she?

Manu always said his father was dead.

It's only a few minutes, but long enough for the constant drumming of Oriol's fingers against his prosthetic thigh in her peripheral vision to get on her nerves, before the door swings open and a slim, dark woman with a complicated twist of skinny braids and a Sulila insignia embroidered on her coat enters the waiting room. She studies Oriol with an expression Starla can't read, then crosses to greet them.

"You're the husband," she says.

"Oriol Sina." Oriol rises a touch too fast to shake her hand, then motions to Starla. "Starla. She's a friend."

The doctor's hand is slim and cool; she settles gingerly on a chair across from them and, after a moment, Oriol sits down again, too.

"I'm Dr. Alzuabi," the doctor says — it's hardly what Starla's lens transcribes, but she can read a name tag just fine. "I've been working with the bombing victims. Mr. Juric was brought in late last night."

"How is he?"

"We're treating him for a concussion and pulmonary contusion," she says, her expression neutral. "He's currently in a coma. But you understand, with the political nature of this, I can't let anyone back who isn't family." She holds up a hand as Oriol straightens. "You're not in the system. You don't have any proof, do you? That you are who you say you are?"

Oriol scrubs a hand over the blond stubble on his jaw. "He's got a birthmark on his ribcage, lower right," he says finally. "Bullet scar on his left hip. The scarring on his left arm, that goes all the way up. You do a scan on his leg you'll find it was broke in three places about ten years ago."

The doctor's expression tightens; she's already seen all that. Her gaze flickers to Starla.

"I don't know who this man is," says Dr. Alzuabi. "But I know he's been tortured. The fact that you can list out his injuries and birthmark might mean you know him intimately. But this isn't the first time the Alliance has come to see one of my patients — though it's the first time they've tried the 'we're married' line."

She glances between Oriol and Starla, then begins to stand. "I'm sorry."

Starla elbows Oriol, makes Gia's namesign.

"Wait," says Oriol. "Do you know Giaconda Áte and Tevi Sharaf? They're Sulila doctors?"

Dr. Alzuabi hesitates, settles back on the edge of her chair. She nods slowly.

"Gia and Manu are old friends. Call her. She'll tell you who I am."

Dr. Alzuabi studies him a moment. The grief in Oriol's eyes is pure, naked.

She takes a deep breath. "And his father?"

"First time I ever saw the man was today," Oriol says. "But I've seen his handiwork. And I suppose you have, too. Upper back?"

Dr. Alzuabi's hard expression doesn't change, but Starla can't keep the surprise off her face this time. She's seen those scars, pale lines faded by years. She glances across the lobby; the old man is watching them as though he senses their attention, a bitter twist to his mouth, a smoldering rage in his eyes when they meet hers.

"He's been very insistent," says Dr. Alzuabi. "He wants to see his son."

"Let Manu make that choice for himself when he's awake."

A sharp nod, and Dr. Alzuabi stands. "You can come back, Mr. Sina. But your friend — " She looks at Starla, brows drawing together as she puzzles how to make the request. As though Starla hasn't obviously been following the conversation for the last few minutes. Dr. Alzuabi turns back to Oriol instead. "Only you."

"I'll wait out here," Starla signs to Oriol, then taps her gauntlet to let him know she has more for him. She doesn't trust him to understand USL for the rest of what she has to say.

She sends her message to his comm. His jaw tightens as he reads.

Next time you're pissed at Manu, take it up with him, not us. You're not the only one who loves him.

Before he can respond, she rises and steps in for a fierce embrace. After a moment's hesitation, his arms wrap around her in return.

"Tell Jaantzen I'm sorry," he signs when she lets go. She claps him on the shoulder, then settles back onto the waiting room chair, ankle crossed over knee, trading glares with the bitter old man across the lobby.

3

_____

CHO

The sign outside the shop reads Hallelujah It's Fixed! A cartoon choir of angels floats above it.

Somewhere else and the sign might be ridiculous, but here, next to the rest of the classy shops on the B level of Geordi Jimenez Space Terminal, it manages to look slightly cheeky. The door is flanked by a pair of picture windows where repaired electronics are neatly displayed, everything from VR jacks and home entertainment sets to small kitchen appliances and printers and domestic bots.

A young tourist couple walk by and share a smile at the sign, peer through the window. Detective Timo Cho gives them a nod as he pushes through the door, which the taller of the pair returns, though the shorter doesn't seem to notice.

Hallelujah Oni is sitting where he always is: behind the counter-slash-workbench that presides over the rear of the space. Louis does his major repair jobs in the back room of the shop after hours, but he's always got a small project going where he can sit and watch browsers when his door's unlocked. Today he's operating on one of the mister drones the city might use during outdoor festivals to monitor the crowd while keeping them cool in the Bulari heat.

Louis looks up and breaks into a wide grin. "Ah, Timo, *mon ami,* come in, come in." He sets his tools carefully aside, then steps around the counter to clasp Cho's arms. He, of course, doesn't act surprised when his hand meets the unyielding metal of Cho's right bicep.

He does frown at whatever he sees in Cho's face. "Bad day? The embassy?"

"I'm not involved with that." Cho gins up a smile and is rewarded by a grin from Louis — the man's always a good mood lifter.

Cho needs that, because yes. Bad day. He's out of the office this morning because he needed to blow off steam, and he spent most of the train ride to the terminal stewing. For the second time in a month, he'd had a closed-book perp in his interrogation room when Major Ngara interrupted to say it turns out the guy's innocent.

Throw the cage open, let the rat back out into the city.

This particular rat should be locked up right now on trafficking charges, but apparently he has a guardian angel with a say in the police department's budget — whether the contributions are on the books or off. Bulari's government is packed with people who think they can tell the BPD to look the other way. Even when it comes to stopping crime.

Cho could tell Major Ngara didn't like letting the guy go any more than Cho did, but he'd liked it even less when Cho blew up at him about it. So Cho decided to split. Run some errands. If he's not going to be allowed to do his job, he doesn't need to be in the office, right?

Eight more months.

Retirement's a cottonwood grove on the desert horizon, and Cho's getting thirstier by the day.

"What trouble did you bring me?" Louis asks, circling back to the far side of the workbench.

"It's always trouble, isn't it?" Cho says. He tugs the glove off his right hand and makes a fist. The pinky on his prosthetic arm sticks straight out, as it has for almost a month. Louis frowns and leans in to see, then reaches out his own right hand, pinky extended. He hooks his pinky around Cho's, dark smoky brown around gleaming chrome.

Louis looks deep into Cho's eyes.

"I can fix it," he says solemnly. "I promise."

Cho barks a laugh, and Louis breaks into a wide grin before he lets go. "Come, come, come sit," he says, waving Cho to a chair.

"If you have time," Cho says. "It looks like you're in the middle of something."

"I think it is an easy fix," Louis says. Cho hangs his jacket on the coat rack beside the door as Louis delicately clears space on the workbench.

Cho rolls his sleeve up to the elbow, shoving the fabric up to expose the smooth, painted gray plating of his forearm.

"This won't hurt a bit," says Louis, a little chuckle at his own joke. Some models are pressure-sensitive, giving haptic feedback even in areas that aren't critical for mobility, like the interior or exterior surfaces of the arm. Cho's prosthetic is bargain-basement, but it's the best he can afford unless he finally joins the club and starts taking kickbacks. Then he'd be able to afford more than just a new arm.

Nobody talks about it openly, of course, but a guy like his old partner doesn't get a shiny new spinner every year on his BPD salary alone.

Louis pops off the plate covering Cho's forearm and gets to work removing the wrist shielding. It's never bothered

Cho, seeing the wiry innards of his arm exposed like this. When he lost his arm, he was young enough still to think it was cool to be half robot, and he never did develop any sense of self-consciousness about it. Though he was grateful when he stopped having growth spurts and didn't have to keep going into debt to the mining corp for a new model.

Louis settles a pair of heads-up spectacles on his lean brown nose and turns them on. Colors glow in his dark irises; on this side of the lens, Cho can catch only a glint of what Louis is seeing.

"Has business been good?" Cho asks. "Or has the fighting scared people away?"

"Oh, plenty are scared, but I always have a backlog, you know? Business goes up, business goes down, but I've got too many loyal customers to let me sit on my thumbs for long.

"Sounds like it's time to raise your rates."

Louis laughs at that. "I do just fine for myself."

He uses a long, skinny tool to press the switch near Cho's elbow, and suddenly even the low-end haptics in Cho's fingers and palm go dark. His subconscious casts about reflexively for the missing bits of himself. Cho ignores the sensation. Feels weird every night when he takes it off to sleep, too.

"I don't suppose you're any closer to cleaning up the fighting with Dry Creek?" Louis asks.

"Not my department," Cho says. It might have been, once, but lately he's been stuck picking up scraps like it was his first month on the job. That's what happens when you push back against orders from on high, which is why Cho didn't let himself stick around the office to get riled today. He doesn't need to get taught that lesson twice.

Once upon a time, he kept asking questions even after

the upper-ups told him to stop. Then he'd found himself at the receiving end of a message in a dark alley. After he'd come home from the hospital, he'd been unceremoniously demoted. Moral of the story: Questions get you killed.

Louis is testing electrical connections, precise taps of his long, thin instrument causing Cho's fingers to curl and uncurl — thumb, index, middle, ring, but not the pinky. Louis makes a little pleased noise that could mean he's diagnosed the problem, or at least ruled something out.

"What's the word on the street?" Cho asks. He may have limits on what he can investigate professionally, but he's still recreationally curious.

"Ah, yes, the good word." Louis begins disconnecting wires in Cho's wrist with steady fingers and a wicked-looking set of needle-nose pliers. "You've heard about the miraculous death and rebirth of our Lady of the Black Heart?" Louis glances up with a delicate eyebrow rise.

It takes Cho a second to parse that, mostly because he can't believe the words coming out of Louis's mouth. Blackheart — Thala Coeur — died? And then came back? Cho shakes his head. "I've been out of the loop."

"Not worth keeping track of bad news," Louis says agreeably, going back to his work. "Seems Dry Creek had something to do with her disappearance. And our lady's vengeance is all-consuming."

"Wait, she's here? In Bulari?" That can't possibly be true.

"There you go," Louis says with a smile, and whether he's answering Cho's query or excited over the fact that his prodding has finally made Cho's pinky move, no outsider can tell. Cho ponders the implications silently, frustration churning in his gut. Visiting Hallelujah Oni is like being a recovering alcoholic and stepping inside a bar — all that heady, toxic information on draft and he can't do anything with it anymore.

"She and Jaantzen still have that beef?" he asks Louis, because he can't help himself. But Louis is humming an old song Cho recognizes but can't quite name. Either Louis doesn't know or he doesn't care to say. Cho's learned long ago not to ask twice. If Louis wanted you told, he'd've done it the first time.

Cho takes a new tack. "Bodies going to stop showing up once she's burned down Dry Creek?"

Louis meets Cho's gaze over the top of his heads-up device. "Hope so. Didn't think you were interested anymore."

Louis's tone is dispassionate, but there's something just below the surface, a note of warning, maybe. Louis is a source that goes both ways, and Cho's starting to get the impression that his questions have tripped a wire.

"Not my thing anymore," Cho says. "But it's hard not to be curious."

"Of course."

Louis returns to his work with the force of concentration he gets when every ounce of attention is focused on a particularly tricky problem. Cho watches in silence as Louis roots around in his wrist, humming softly. A faint spark and sizzle, and a triumphant grin flashes Louis's teeth. He hits the switch in Cho's elbow to turn the arm back on. A familiar rush of sensation plugs back into that missing area of Cho's brain. He makes a fist; the hand closes, every finger falling perfectly in line.

"Don't look too close at Blackheart and she won't look too close at you," Louis says suddenly, and the always-present twinkle of humor in his eye is gone. He snaps the wrist shielding and forearm plate back into place.

"Thanks, Louis," Cho says soberly, and Louis just nods and begins to clear up his workbench. "How much do I owe you?"

"On the house, *mon ami*," Louis says with a smile. "Bring me a trickier problem next time or I'll have to start paying you for the pleasure of your visits."

Cho's nearly back to his apartment for lunch when he gets the call from his partner, Ossandre Samson. "Where the hell are you?" she asks. "Ngara needs us at the embassy. I'm leaving right now."

"He asked for us personally?" Cho asks. "Or is this an all-hands-on-deck sort of thing."

"He asked for us," Samson says. There's a hint of cautious excitement in her voice, and Cho can't blame her. When she joined the Bulari Police Department a year ago, she was bright-eyed and ready to fight crime. Then she was saddled with Cho and his departmental baggage, which meant she hasn't gotten a shot at solving anything more interesting than the Case of the Tourist Who Needed Directions.

She never acts like she resents it, though she's got to be counting down the remaining months to his retirement as eagerly as he is.

"I'll meet you there," Cho says, and cuts the line.

Samson may be ready to wash away the disappointment of losing this afternoon's perp, but Cho isn't so optimistic.

It takes a few minutes to reach the embassy, where the techs are painting the shattered scene with scanner drones and shoe rubber. In the cafe across the road, Major Ngara's set up a field office. He's deep in conversation with someone in an official Alliance uniform, and it'll take Samson another five minutes to get here from the department.

Cho's got some time to poke around.

The damage is impressive. The front steps of the grand Alliance embassy building are rubble, and the techs are going to be sorting through piles of dust for days looking for any shards of evidence. He heard on the news feeds that the destruction didn't reach deep into the building, but from the outside, the entire embassy appears demolished.

The bodies have been removed, either shipped to the morgue for further study or to the hospital to see if the pieces can be put back together. Closer to the gaping facade of the embassy, a tech is mapping blood spatters into a hand unit. The dead and wounded have probably already been added to that little hologram of horrors for detectives to walk through over and over again later.

Cho doesn't miss that part of working the good cases.

The closest tech straightens to attention when the security shield flickers to let Cho through, like she's wondering if she needs to salute. He knows he's met her before, but her name — Essie, Su-Lin, something — currently escapes him.

He realizes too late that the man beside her isn't a tech. It's his old partner, Detective Arman Falk. He's a fine-featured man with perfect teeth and skin like midnight, and he's firmly in the camp of people in the Bulari Police Department who Timo Cho thinks can go to hell.

"What's the word?" Cho asks the new tech, ignoring Falk. A pair of deep lines appear between the kid's thick black eyebrows.

She starts to answer, but Falk beats her to the punch.

"The word is Major Ngara's set up shop in the cafe across the way," he says. "He's probably waiting for you."

The new tech gives Cho a curious look, then lifts her

golden-brown gaze to follow one of the drones to the building across the road, where it pauses in its preset scan pattern to examine a spray of chips in the plaster. It's trading lasers with a partner back on the steps; herald motes of the afternoon dust storm glimmer faintly in the narrow beams.

"Thanks, Falk," Cho says, then smiles at the new tech. "I hope you're getting good data."

"We are, def," she says. Her accent is charmingly deep Fingers. She glances at Falk, then back at her comm. She'll get the lowdown on Cho later.

He can sense Falk glaring at him even though the man hasn't moved. The new tech hasn't done anything to deserve being caught up in an office spat between two grown men.

And anyway, he can see Samson coming around the corner.

Cho winks at the young tech. "Gotta run, the world needs saved."

He ignores whatever Falk is muttering behind him.

Samson reaches the cafe before he does. Next to the lanky Major Ngara, she looks even shorter and stouter, her straight brown hair scraped back in a brief ponytail. She turns to see him descending what's left of the steps and Ngara turns as well, disapproval clouding his red-brown face.

"Good of you to join us," is all he says. "I wanted to brief you both on the angles we've been investigating. None of the usual anti-Alliance groups are turning up early leads, so we're starting to expand our suspect list to consider the local crews."

Cho's spine straightens. He spent almost two decades working the organized crime angle for the BPD before getting knocked back down to his current street cop status. The kids working that beat these days may know the current players, but vendettas and alliances in Bulari run deep. They'll need someone with the historical knowledge to read the patterns of what's going on today. They'll need someone like Timo Cho, and his mind's already spinning.

Hallelujah Oni's words from earlier echo in his head: "You've heard about the miraculous death and rebirth of our Lady of the Black Heart?"

Blackheart had lived at the embassy for three months before being granted asylum on Indira — and knowing her, that was three months longer than she needed to develop a grudge. If Coeur's back in town, she may be clearing up old scores.

"I'd be happy to help, Major," he says. "In fact, I — "

"Good." Ngara taps at the tablet in his hand and Cho's comm chimes with an incoming file. "We need someone to interview the victims."

Cho narrowly keeps his jaw from dropping. "The victims?"

"You have a problem with that?" The set of Ngara's scowl says he's still very, very pissed about Cho blowing up at him this morning. So that's what this is all about. Not the very real institutional knowledge and intel Cho could actually bring to this damn case — no. Ngara called him here personally as punishment for getting out of line.

Ngara's still glaring at him, waiting for an answer.

Does Cho have a problem with interviewing the victims? That's a job for an intern or an AI — it's barely even a job for Samson the rookie. Beside him, Samson clears her throat. The look she's shooting him says *Don't you fucking dare jeopardize my career.*

"No, sir," Cho says.

"Good. Anything else to add?"

He could share what he's just learned about Blackheart, but why? Surely the organized crime unit already knows she's back — if not, they'll find out soon enough.

"Nothing, sir," Cho says. "Just happy to do our part."

"Thank you, Detective."

Neither he nor Samson say anything until they're a few blocks away from the embassy, then she lets out a curse under her breath. "Sorry, man," she says. "I was really thinking — "

"It's fine," he says. "Eight more months and you'll be rid of me *and* these shit jobs." He calls the list up onto his lens as he walks, scanning angrily through the names and faces. "This is ridiculous. None of these people know anything about the bomb. Ngara might as well have told us to go round up stray dogs."

"Who knows?" Samson says. "Maybe we'll find the lead that breaks the case open."

"You keep that optimism as long as you can, kid. It's the only thing that'll see you through — "

Cho stops in his tracks. Samson's shoulder hits his and she catches herself before she stumbles.

"What is it?"

He fumbles to pause the list, then flips back a few ident cards to that all-too-familiar face.

He's spent ten years thinking about what he'd say if he ever got a chance to question the guy who delivered that message in that dark alley. But it was wishful thinking — the guy's one of those untouchables the department simply stopped investigating after Coeur was ousted from power.

One of those protected by orders from on high.

Manu Juric. Willem Jaantzen's man.

Cho may never see him in an interrogation room, but

he's about to get a chance to talk with him face to face after all.

"I might have some actual police work for us to do," he says, and Samson's face lights up. He smiles grimly. "Let's go."

4

———————

JAANTZEN

The Alliance agent's found a pair of house trousers and a tank top in the room's wardrobe, and now she's going through a series of exercises, lunges and pirouettes that leave her panting. Her black hair is tied back in a choppy ponytail. The yellow hue of the artificial lights gleam off the sheen of sweat covering her light-brown skin.

Jaantzen watches her a moment through the one-way-view security shield, Giaconda Áte at his elbow.

The two floors of apartments below Jaantzen's penthouse in Cobalt Tower are almost entirely unoccupied. Starla has one of the apartments, though she tends to stay in her own place on Nidaly Square. A neighboring apartment was originally set aside for Toshiyo, but Jaantzen doesn't think she's ever slept there — she has a bunk set up somewhere in her warren of an office. The others are empty unless he has guests, expected or not.

The Alliance agent is being kept in one of the studios meant for less-welcome guests. It's simply furnished with chairs, a table, and a bed that are all bolted to the floor. There's a private bathroom and a kitchenette complete with a stash of instant dinners, a rehydrator, water, tea, and no sharp objects. The original front door was replaced by a security shield that allows watchers to keep an eye on whoever is inside.

Two soldiers flank the agent's door, watching her with expressions of pure fury; they lost friends in the attack two nights ago. Beside Jaantzen, Gia's expression is unreadable. The Alliance woman is lucky Gia's student Elian is going to survive the bullet she put in his gut.

Jaantzen touches a button and the forcefield becomes transparent. The Alliance operative spins in place and freezes. She might be scared, she might be defiant — it's hard to tell. Her face is half-smothered under bandages.

"Good afternoon," Jaantzen says politely.

Her nostrils flare; she doesn't answer.

"The doctor is here to check on your injury."

"It's fine. I already checked it." Her drawl's thoroughly Arquellian. It's the first time Jaantzen has heard her speak, besides what he heard while listening to Toshiyo's feed two nights ago. But he hadn't been paying attention to the sound of her voice then. He'd been racing against time to reach Toshiyo.

"We're making arrangements to return you to your handlers," Jaantzen says, and she shoots him a one-eyed glare. "And we want to make sure you're in good condition. Please sit at the table with your arms over the markings."

The woman's shoulders straighten. "Fine. I'll play along," she says. "You don't need to — "

"There are harder ways." Jaantzen adds a razor's edge of politeness to his voice.

The woman looks at first like she'll argue more, but finally she sits, laying her forearms over the indicated places with a disgruntled sigh that says *This is all so unnecessary.*

Jaantzen presses a button in the entryway control panel and cuffs fold out of the table, snap into place.

He drops the forcefield, but even with the agent's arms bound, the two soldiers aim their stun carbines, advancing slowly to cover Jaantzen.

Gia waits until they've deemed their captive secure before she sits at the woman's left side and begins methodically to unpack her med kit: swabs, bandages, a suture kit, salve. The woman stares at every item Gia lays out as though expecting scalpels, pliers, drills.

Jaantzen sits across from Gia and the woman's attention shifts to him. "You killed five of my people," he says evenly. Five families he spoke with yesterday. Five funerals he'll be attending. "Shot a doctor and left him to die. I don't know what you call it where you're from, but from here it looks like a bunch of New Sarjunian citizens murdered at the hands of an Alliance agent, the week both our governments are negotiating a touchy trade deal."

He lets that sink in a moment. She stares at him, steel-eyed.

"At least, that's what my government will see." He drops the society gleam from his accent. "Only to me it looks like some off-worlder thought she could walk into my city, shoot up my home, and walk out with what's mine." He meets Gia's gaze and the woman's attention shifts between them — she's caught the silver glint of Gia's bandage scissors. She leans back as far as she can in her chair, struggling to keep them both in the field of vision of her remaining eye. Her fingernails scrabble involuntarily against the table.

"Makes me look weak," Jaantzen says conversationally. "Makes others think they can try me. Course, there are time-honored ways to remind people to keep their hands to themselves."

The woman swallows hard, clears her throat. "I'm an Alliance — "

"An Alliance agent. I know. Go ahead," he says to Gia, who murmurs a "Hold still" as she seizes the woman's chin in her strong fingers. She slices through the bandage wrapped around the agent's skull. The woman gasps, then actually does go still as she realizes what Gia's doing. Gia sets the scissors far out of reach, then peels at the edges of the bandage, businesslike; it comes away soaked in blood. The Alliance agent is trying to calm herself with short, terrified breaths.

"The only reason you're alive right now is because you make a good pawn in an international game of chess," Jaantzen says, accent polished once more. "If you were who you told Acheta you were — one of Coeur's crew from Arquelle — you'd be dead already. Or at least on the slow road there."

He leans in close, forcing her gaze to meet his; she stinks of adrenaline sweat and blood. "Don't mistake my civility for weakness. There are other much less comfortable places I could keep you while we negotiate with your handlers."

"This is going to sting," Gia says, swabbing at the stitched wounds. The woman's breath goes heavy with pain. Gia's not being excessively rough, but she's nowhere close to gentle. Jaantzen leans back to let her work.

Gia has a fine hand for stitching a wound back together, Jaantzen knows that firsthand. But she hadn't bothered here. She'd just run the automatic suture machine over the gashes the night of the attack without caring what it would look like when she was done.

And the eye . . .

"I need to get to a real doctor," the woman says, and Gia

lifts an eyebrow but continues working. "There might still be time to save my eye."

"There was nothing to do for your eye," says Gia. Jaantzen wonders if that was true.

There's certainly nothing to do for it now, clotted black with blood and still seeping gore. Gia swabs at the wound one last time. The woman's hands ball into fists, but she doesn't cry out.

"How do you know?" she says through clenched teeth. "My doctors — "

"I'm a real doctor," Gia says. "I train doctors, actually. The medic you shot in the hallway?" The woman tries to turn towards her voice, but Gia's strong fingers hold her chin steady. "You remember, you shot him in the stomach and left him to die? He was one of my students."

The woman stares straight ahead, tight-lipped.

"Sorry about your eye," Gia says. "Hazards of the job, I guess." She places a clean pad back over the ruined socket, then begins to bandage the rest of the lacerations on the woman's face. "Good thing you all get such good hazard pay."

That eye fluttering closed, that jutting of the jaw to keep it firm — it could be a reaction to pain but for the accompanying slump of the shoulders. It's brief, but it's there: despair.

She doesn't believe anyone's coming for her.

Now there's something he can use to get her to cooperate.

"Doesn't look like there's any infection," Gia says. She meets Jaantzen's gaze. From the razor claws of the creature, she means. He relaxes a fraction.

The woman straightens. "What was that thing."

"What were you expecting?" he asks in return, and her

lips shut tight. Jaantzen pushes himself back from the table; Gia has finished packing her supplies. "Let us know if you need anything. It might be a few days before we can get you back to your handlers." Her good eye flashes fear; it's not of him.

"Something for the pain," she says.

"What were you sent to get?" Jaantzen asks. Her jaw clamps shut tight and he stands, buttoning his suit jacket. "Or don't you know?"

"Don't forget to unlock me," the woman calls when he reaches the entry, and he pauses with his hand on the controls.

Jaantzen glances between the two guards who followed him out, their stun carbines still trained on the Alliance woman. He's been part of crews before where you barely knew the person next to you, let alone trusted them. Where you never knew who would stab you in the back for your share, your rank, or because somebody up above you both wanted you gone.

He doesn't operate like that, keeping his people fighting each other for scraps while he's the biggest rat on the scrap heap. He's built a crew on loyalty, not fear. Camaraderie, not competition. These two guards? The woman on his left lost her cousin two nights ago. They both lost comrades in arms. Friends.

"You going to unlock me?" the Alliance woman asks again, a note of fear in her voice.

"Whenever you two feel ready to release her," Jaantzen says to his soldiers.

He engages the forcefield, ensuring it's keyed to him alone. A little discomfort could soften her up, but he doesn't need to pit the pain of his grieving crew against his orders not to touch her.

He heads for the lift, not the stairs, and when he pushes the button, Gia gives him a look. "It's two flights," she says. "It's good for you."

"Another day."

That sigh: He's in for a lecture.

"Your knee's worse, isn't it?"

Jaantzen doesn't answer, but Gia apparently doesn't need him to.

"I spoke to Dr. Ko. He says you never made an appointment."

"I thought that kind of information was private."

"I'm meddlesome," Gia says. "You need to get that fixed sooner rather than later."

"I'll give him a call."

"Do it today, boss."

He glances at her, surprised — it's been years since she called him boss — but he doesn't comment on the slip. She doesn't seem to notice.

"I can't afford to be laid up," he says instead.

"You can't afford to ignore it." The lift door opens and Gia takes a deep breath. "Do you have a minute?"

"Of course."

So his knee isn't the only thing on her mind; she follows him into the lift, expression troubled.

"Thank you for coming today," he says as the doors slide open a moment later in the living room of his penthouse.

"Just doing my part to make sure Manu and that Alliance asshole aren't going to be the epicenter of some alien plague." She sighs. "The Alliance asshole, at least. I assume they're keeping an eye on Manu's arm at the hospital."

"Will you go see him?"

Gia shakes her head, twists of her black hair moving

gently around her dark cheeks. "Too many people there I don't want to see." She tries to say it lightly, but he can hear the pain in her voice. "Has he woken up yet?"

"Once, Starla said. Oriol's with him now."

"I thought I was going to get a chance to catch up with him this week, once things calmed down. Grab a drink. You know, old times." Gia's jaw clenches. "Things never calm down, do they?"

"How much longer will you be in town?"

"I should head home. Tevi — well." She smiles ruefully at Jaantzen. "I keep thinking Tevi just needs a chance to meet you both and he'll come around. But it's been — god, I don't even want to think."

"It's been ten years," Jaantzen says, and she takes a deep breath, lets it out slow.

Ten years since Gia came home from Maribi Station with Tevi Sharaf and his grand plans to challenge the Sulila indenture system, educate doctors who can help the people. To Tevi, Jaantzen was a symbol of everything that was wrong with Bulari, and Gia's employment with Jaantzen made him uncomfortable. Jaantzen had been happy to see her go on to her next phase of life, and she's seemed more at peace the few times he's seen her. But those times have grown farther and farther apart.

"I should have made a better effort," she says. "But now . . ."

"He'll be all right," Jaantzen says, and Gia gives him a skeptical look.

"I don't know that," she says. "Which means you definitely don't know that."

"He's survived worse." That's not a comforting fact, either.

Gia swears under her breath. "How many lives does that bastard have?"

"Hopefully a few more."

"I hope so, too, boss."

The second time that word has slipped out. Jaantzen studies her.

"I'm sorry," he says, and a line sketches itself between her brows. "I wish I hadn't had to call you."

"Anytime," she says, puzzled.

He shakes his head. "No. Not anytime. Gia, does Tevi even know you're here?"

She doesn't look away; he can see her formulating her answer. "I told him a friend needed help," she says finally. "I didn't tell him it was you."

"Then go home. Take Elian. Tell Tevi the truth."

"And leave you without a doctor? What you're cooking up, you're going to need me again sooner or later."

"We'll manage. We've been managing."

"You need me."

He allows himself a half smile. "Always. But your students need you more."

Gia takes a deep breath, then crosses her arms. "Elian won't be ready to move for a few days."

"Of course."

"And I'll want to see Manu when — " She clears her throat, almost hiding the break in her voice. "But I'll talk to Tevi."

He hesitates, not sure if what he's about to suggest will give her something to keep her busy, or open a whole new excuse for her to stay. "If you need something to do, Toshiyo will need help readying the creature for transport."

"Where are you taking it?"

"Julieta is helping me find a place."

Gia gnaws on her lip, thinking. "A friend of mine's been trying to sell her dad's property. Out by us in the Maraka Valley? Nobody wants it — too far from anywhere, and it's not good ranchland. And what she tells me, it's built like a fortress." A twitch of a smile. "Let's just say he was our kinda guy."

"A criminal?" Jaantzen asks pointedly.

The smile fades. "Paranoid. I brought up buying it with Tevi, but he didn't really get the appeal of a bunch of bunkers and landmines."

The Maraka Valley is difficult to get to. It's almost two hours north of Bulari, but that kind of distance might be good. And if the place is already built with defense in mind . . .

"Send me the details."

"Sure thing," she says, catching herself just before another "boss" crosses her lips. "I'll go check on Tosh."

"Thank you."

"Call Dr. Ko about your knee."

Jaantzen sighs. "I will."

Gia gives him a lopsided smile, then lets herself out through the door to the stairwell.

When the door closes behind her, Jaantzen settles in at his conference table. He has dozens of mundane messages relating to his businesses, but they're not the biggest problem on his plate at the moment. No, that's a tie between the Alliance agent locked to a table two floors down and the alien creature she was sent to steal. Getting the creature out from under his roof will help him breathe easy again — but of course, it can't stay secret forever. When this comes out, Coeur and the Demosgas will have to be handled very carefully. Not to mention the people of New

Sarjun, the press, and everyone else who will be frothing at the bit to find out what's going on.

Willem Jaantzen never wanted fame, nor the notoriety he's enjoyed instead. That notoriety has faded over the years, from those early tabloid headlines and breathless exposés when his battles with Coeur made the news, and these days he's a has-been. He likes it that way.

A few stories have popped up since the night Sjel was arrested, and one intrepid reporter called to ask about his connection to Phaera D after the night he was seen at the Devil's Table. A few days ago he was more worried about keeping that hidden for Phaera's sake, but now he's come to understand her flair for a good story. She'll probably relish the chance to spin a press-making story about a new paramour with a dark past.

He wonders how good she'll be at spinning the "aliens walk among us" story.

A vid call ripples through the conference table, and with a sigh he remembers he has a third problem vying for his attention at the moment. With everything else going on, he'd nearly forgotten Julieta's warning from last night.

Chief Justice Geum-ja Leone's smile is bright when he answers the call. From the background he can see she's in her chambers at the Supreme Court, her small, boxy frame bolstered by the imposing desk and ornate wall hangings.

He's found himself on her bad side before, and it's usually required a bit of groveling to get back in her good graces. A favor performed, maybe. A nice gift. Nothing he can't manage — he pushes aside the flash of irritation. Two nights ago he asked Calanthe Yang to make his case to Leone and the others, but he also made it clear that Acheta was a dead man whether they gave permission or not. Leone hadn't liked Acheta, Jaantzen is fairly certain. But she does like control — and Jaantzen hadn't given her that respect.

Time to do penance and keep the peace.

"Madame Justice," he says. "You look well."

"I thought I might have gotten a call from you earlier." There's a note of reproach under her words. "Before you made up your mind on certain things."

"I had to act fast in the interest of maintaining peace." He inclines his head. "I wish I'd had more time to discuss matters with you."

"Next time." Leone's smile is sharp; it's an order, not a nicety.

"We should discuss the new equilibrium," he says. She'll be just as angry about his choice to restore Coeur as she was about his decision to take care of Acheta. "Will you join me for dinner at the Jungle tonight. I have it on good authority that the chef's special is to be duck confit." Or at least it will be if she agrees to the meeting; it's a favorite of hers.

"That sounds delicious, but I couldn't possibly impose, Willem. Let me entertain, I insist." Her smile brightens again, a hesitation in it so brief it barely registers. "I have a friend I'd like to introduce you to. Are you free tomorrow night?"

The request isn't out of the ordinary; Leone is always introducing him to new people, her network a web of connections made and favors owed. But coming as it does now, it feels like a trap.

"Anyone I've heard of?" Jaantzen asks.

"You'll know his name — or at least his work. Say yes, Willem. It could be a good opportunity for you."

He inclines his head, gracious. "Then I look forward to it."

The connection cuts, her hologram fading from the conference table. Frowning, Jaantzen opens up a channel.

"Toshiyo? I need everything you have from Geum-ja Leone's surveillance feeds."

If this is a trap, he's not walking in blind.

5

———

ORIOL

Oriol wakes with a start to see someone sitting across the hospital room, near the door. He'd dozed off sometime in the afternoon; his stiff neck screams in agony. It takes him a moment to recognize Simca Anahoy, with her thick black braid, her high cheekbones and laughing eyes, her neon yellow jacket trimmed with electric-blue sequins.

He can tell she's armed, but her weapon's holstered and under her jacket, and she raises her hands as though to reassure him. "Simca," she says. "We jumped out of a plane together last week?"

"I know, I remember." Oriol scrubs a hand across his face. Was it only last week when he and Simca and Ximena Nayar parachuted in to Julieta Yang's greenhouse to rescue Jaantzen and Starla? Coming home to Bulari was supposed to be his vacation.

"I mean, I figured," she says. "You just looked like you were about to come up punching."

"You surprised me is all."

Simca slips off the stool and crosses to the other side of Manu's hospital bed. "How is he? No one will tell me. I mean, they're obviously not happy I'm here, but one of the nurses recognized me and asked for a picture, so one of the security guards did, too, and now I think they're feeling awkward about throwing me out. Have they told you anything?"

Right. This one's the talkative Anahoy.

"He was awake for a moment a few hours ago," Oriol says. Not that he'd gotten a chance to see much of that; he'd been ushered out of the room in seconds. "His lungs were injured in the blast and he has a concussion, but the doctor seems to think he'll pull through."

Simca smooths a glitter-manicured thumb over Manu's forehead, light as a bird. The room thrums with hospital beeps and whirs, the restless non-silence of monitors and autodoc bots running their patterns, that antiseptic stench, and Manu's raspy breathing through the mask over his nose and mouth.

His eyes are closed, his cheekbone bruised under dark skin, a bandage over his temple and ear. Tubes are plugged into his veins, but not as many as Oriol had expected to see. His chest is gently rising and falling in sleep under the faded hospital blanket, oblivious to Oriol's hand in his, to Simca's touch.

She lifts her hands. "Do you speak USL?" she signs.

"Go easy on me," Oriol says aloud.

"Starla has one of us assigned here at all times," Simca signs, going slow. "So if you need to get out for a minute or sleep or whatever, you don't have to worry."

"Thank you," he signs, and she shrugs — they're not doing this for him.

"We're still learning about the bomb," she signs. "But we don't think it was aimed at him. Wrong place, wrong time."

Somehow that's worse. All the dangerous shit Manu's gotten himself into over the years, and this is the thing that takes him out? Wrong place, wrong time?

Oriol acknowledges the thought, lets it go — forces it to go. This is *not* the thing that takes Manu out. It's just another story they'll share later, back home and healthy. It's just another "Remember when."

"Has his dad tried to come back?" Oriol asks aloud, and Simca gives him a curious look.

"His *dad* dad?" Her hands slip into her pockets; she doesn't care if they're overheard for this part. "I didn't know his old man was still around, did they call him? I guess they could look Manu's last name up, it's not like it's common." She shrugs. "No. I mean, not that I know. Was he here?"

"When I arrived."

"Oh. He comes back, do I let him in? Or no."

"Not until we get the word otherwise from Manu."

Simca gives Manu a sad smile. "Copy that."

And she catches her breath. Oriol notices the change in the autodoc bots' pattern before he hears Manu's breathing shift, rasping through the mask.

Manu comes to not with a flicker of eyelashes but with a violent start this time, machines blaring warnings around them. He claws at the mask on his face. Simca grabs his left arm as Oriol grabs his right, Manu's wild eyes searching the room but not finding Oriol's face even as Oriol calls his name over and over.

And Manu slumps back. A readout from the autodoc bots explains the sedative dose.

One of the nurses from before is through the door a moment later. "We need the room, please," he says, more than once before Oriol forces himself through the door and into the hallway.

He collapses into one of the chairs just outside Manu's door, and Simca leans across from him, hands in neon pockets and shoulders propped against the wall.

"He gonna be okay?" she asks.

Oriol nods reflexively; he has to believe it. "The autodocs got him smooth. Sulila doctors are the best. He'll be fine." His words are rote.

The corner of Simca's mouth tugs down; he wonders if she doesn't believe him, if she knows better, if she's humoring him. Before he has a chance to ask, though, an orderly walks through and does a double take at her. He walks past a few steps, then stops and turns back. "Simca Anahoy?"

Simca smiles, gracious.

"Wow, I can't believe it." He pulls out his comm. "I know this is — but my granddaughter would be so . . . Would you take a still with me?"

"Course." Simca's grin is genuine as she holds up a victory sign to the man's comm.

The orderly starts to turn away, then sees Oriol. "Oh! And you're — "

"No," says Oriol, unfriendly, and the orderly glances back at Simca and hurries down the hall.

"I'm what?" Oriol growls to Simca after he's gone.

She laughs. "Oh my god, your fight vid from Herran's? Oriol, it's all over the place. If you're ever looking for another gig I can talk to my manager — "

"I'm not," Oriol says sharply. But he accepts her comm when she hands it to him and watches the first few seconds of him fighting with Acheta's lieutenant on the floor of Herran's casino two nights ago. He thumbs it off when the man scores his first punch. Oriol can still feel the ache in his jaw; he doesn't need to see it happen again.

Doesn't need to see the streams of comments flowing across the vid.

"How do I take this down?"

"Man, you can't," Simca says. "But don't worry. People will lose interest in a couple of days. It's ridiculously hard to keep them engaged, let me tell you."

Oriol closes his eyes, tilts his head back against the wall, inbreath, outbreath. He's barely listening once Simca's moved on from her theory of the rate of fan attention decay to explaining some of the weirder publicity stunts her manager pulled to get her traction in the pro wrestling circuits in her early days.

After what feels like hours but is probably only a few minutes, the door to Manu's room opens and the nurse tells Oriol he can come back in, the doctor is on her way.

Simca stops her story as carelessly as she started it and gives Oriol an encouraging smile as he rises from the chair; that smile becomes sharper when the nurse looks like he's about to tell her to leave. She takes Oriol's place in the chair in the hallway instead.

The bed has been raised slightly, the mask is gone, and Manu's face lights up as Oriol crosses to the far side of the bed. Oriol takes Manu's hand. It's cool and dry; the copper lacquer on his nails is chipped.

"I thought I saw you before." Manu's voice is rasping, harsh. "Thought I heard you."

"I been here," Oriol answers. "They just keep kicking me out so they can save your life."

Manu laughs, a faint and awful sound. "Understandable." His expression sobers. He tries to raise his hands and winces, then lowers his voice instead. "I got the message through, right? What's going on with that woman?" He grimaces and is fingerspelling in Oriol's hand: *A-L-L-I-A-N-C*

"Mr. Juric?" They both turn towards the voice coming from the doorway: the doctor. "I'm Dr. Alzuabi. I've been taking care of the embassy bombing victims."

Manu's hand goes limp into Oriol's, and he breaks into a tired grin. "Oh, hey," he says with surprise. "You're a doctor, I didn't know you were a doctor."

Dr. Alzuabi glances at Oriol, her jaw set uncomfortably. "You never asked what I did," she says. "And since you apparently spend a lot of time with doctors, I'm surprised you haven't developed a radar for people who can stitch you back up."

"You two have met?" Oriol asks. Dr. Alzuabi has been acting strangely towards him this entire time, but he thought it had to do with his forced presence, his invocation of the notorious Dr. Giaconda Áte. He'd been too preoccupied to suss it out beyond that.

"She tried to pick me up at a bar when you were gone," Manu says. Oriol blinks; that wasn't what he expected to hear.

"You seemed receptive." Dr. Alzuabi turns brusquely to examine the readouts from the autodoc bots.

"I was, then," Manu says. "I thought you were going to wait for me."

Dr. Alzuabi's frowning at the readout, though whether it's at what she sees there or at Manu's comment, Oriol's not sure. "No guy's worth waiting for after a twenty-four-hour shift." The frown on her face is definitely about Manu's stats. She's tapping at her screen, giving him only a fraction of her attention.

Manu squeezes Oriol's hand, mouths *Sorry*. "Am I going to live or not?"

"I think she's gonna have to amputate your smart-ass gland," Oriol says.

"It's too late," Manu says. "Already metastasized."

"You're going to live. You were close enough to the blast origin to have overpressurized your lungs, but I'm more worried about the concussion you suffered when you were thrown down the steps. I want to keep you overnight for observation."

"I'd rather go home."

"You need to stay on oxygen for now."

"So send me home with some."

Dr. Alzuabi turns to face him. "Mr. Juric. You're obviously accustomed to injury and I'm sure you think you know your own body. Humor me."

Oriol squeezes Manu's hand before he can answer. "Simca's outside," he tells him. "Starla's been here. I'm not going anywhere." You're protected, he means. He doesn't like the idea of Manu being so exposed here, either, but he's watched Manu push himself past his limits only to crash harder too many times. "Listen to the woman with the Sulila training."

Manu's eyes close, slowly reopen. "Sulila train all of you to be hard-asses?" he says finally. His tone is light, but his hand in Oriol's is tense.

"Yes. It saves lives." Dr. Alzuabi smiles grimly. "I'll tell Dr. Áte you said that next time I see her."

Manu's laugh turns into a cough. "She knows."

"Now." The look on Dr. Alzuabi's face says she has more business. "What happened to your arm?"

"Moto accident," Manu lies automatically, and Dr. Alzuabi shakes her head.

"The new injury?" She points to Manu's right upper arm, where two nights ago, Toshiyo's demon clawed Manu good. The hospital staff had cleaned and rebandaged the wound after Oriol's original first aid and Gia's careful stitches.

Manu winks at Dr. Alzuabi, winces. "You start asking that question about every scrape and you'll be here all night."

She gives him a level look over the top of her heads-up display. "I'm here all night anyway. And if there's a wild animal out there attacking people, I should report it."

"No wild animals." Manu smiles at her and holds it until she finally sighs and turns back to the monitor.

"I'll be back in a few hours and we can talk about when you get to go home." She turns her attention to Oriol. "Do you need anything?"

"Just to stay here, ma'am. And let my friend in the hallway alone. And whoever else might come to take her place."

Dr. Alzuabi takes a deep breath but doesn't argue. When she leaves, Oriol and Manu are left with the humming of the machines, the faint beeps of the autodoc bots, but at least Manu's breath comes normal. No more of the slow, terrifying, mask-intensified breathing Oriol has been listening to for most of the day.

Manu takes a deep breath. "Sorry," he says.

"Was the bomb your fault?"

"No, I meant . . ." He waves a hand at the door, at the doctor's stand.

"About Alzuabi? I'm not expecting you to sit around your apartment and wait for me when I leave, Manu. I've told you that."

"Still."

"Don't." Oriol smiles wryly. "And she's right. Maybe

you should cultivate more relationships with medical professionals."

"This is my last time in a hospital. I promise."

Manu's smile is light, but Oriol can't appreciate the joke. Because he knows there will be a next time. He knows how close the last few times have gotten. Theirs isn't a story that ends with them doddering around an old folks' facility complaining about how slow the new server is with the coffee refills, and the thought stabs him through the chest like always.

Who knows how many years they have left — and he's spent so fucking many of them away.

He realizes how tight his grip has become on Manu's hand. Forces it to relax.

"Is anyone else here?" Manu asks.

"Just Starla and Simca. That's it, so far." Of course Jaantzen can't come, and as far as Oriol knows, Simca was the first shift Starla set.

Oh. Except.

"Your father?"

Manu's smile fades. He says nothing.

"He came to see you. The hospital called him when they ID'd you."

Manu's jaw clenches. "Where is he now?"

"He hasn't been back," Oriol says, and Manu breathes again. "I asked Alzuabi to let you decide if you wanted to see him." Manu doesn't look at him, and Oriol figures it won't be any easier to ask this next question later. Might as well take advantage of the fact that neither one of them can get much more emotionally exhausted.

"You told me he was dead," Oriol says. "Did you really think that? Or did you know he was alive this whole time? No judgement, just asking."

Manu stares at the door. "I'm sorry."

"You got nothing to be sorry about, it was none of my business."

"How did he look?" Manu asks after a moment.

Desperate to see his son. "Old and angry."

"How did you know it was him?"

"Hospital told me." Though if Oriol'd met that man on the street, if he'd been paying more attention when he walked in, he would've guessed in an instant. He'd been an older, more vicious version of Manu, but he had the same expressions, the same features, the same . . . everything.

Manu breathes in sharply. "Does he. Do I . . . look like him?"

Oriol squeezes Manu's hand. You're a mirror image, just happy. "Barely," he lies. "Hey. I may have told the hospital I was your husband."

Manu laughs, a dry cough. "That the only way to get back to see me?"

"Sure," Oriol says, because it's true but also because in the moment he simply hadn't known a word for a person whose orbit he hasn't left for twenty years, no matter how long or how far their bodies have been apart. "Anyway."

Oriol takes a deep breath. There's never a good time, is there? But the important things, they're not about timing. They're about taking advantage of momentum to say what needs to be said, do what needs to be done. This kind of conversation is like a knife fight. You don't force a stab or parry, you let the organic ebb and flow guide you to the right action.

"Anyway," Oriol says again, letting the momentum lead him. "It felt good."

The steady beep and whir of the machines cuts into the silence.

"It felt good to kick out my dad?" Manu's joking, but he's gone utterly, deathly still.

"Not that."

Oriol can feel Manu's heartbeat in his wrist, steady against his fingertips; meanwhile Oriol's own is spiking, beating rapid in his throat like he's just swallowed a hummingbird. His thoughts, calm and collected even in the midst of a firefight, swirl chaotically through his mind.

"I know we've always said it doesn't make a difference," Oriol says, his mouth dry, "but, anyway, it got me thinking." He's unable to find the second half to that sentence, letting it hang bright and unfinished in the air between them. Oh, *fuck*, what is he doing?

Manu's quiet a breath while the autodoc bots chatter around them.

"Okay," Manu says finally.

"Okay? Is that a yeah, or?"

"Yeah." Manu's hand tightens as he pulls Oriol down for a kiss. "It's a yeah."

"Okay."

Something loosens deep in Oriol's chest, sets itself free and light and airy like a feather on the wind. He can't stop grinning.

Holy shit.

6

STARLA

The shattered glass regen-tank-turned-alien-aquarium in Medbay 2 has been cleaned up and replaced by a surreal collection of exercise equipment, children's toys, old quilts, cushions, and a tub filled with water. Until they can figure out exactly what the little guy prefers, they're trying everything.

This morning it seems to prefer shredding a stuffed snake and arranging bits of fluff in precise rows around its nest.

Starla stands in the medbay's antechamber. She's been watching it through the one-way window, though she can tell it knows she's there. It stays facing her no matter where on the other side of the wall she's standing, though it hasn't actually looked up at her once.

Can it see her despite the one-way glass? Can it hear her movements? Does it have an organ to sense heat, infrared, the waves transmitted by Starla's wearable tech?

Who the hell knows.

Well, Sam might. Only Starla can't involve him in any

of this — so she's been trying to avoid him altogether, despite his several attempts to see her again.

Despite worries about her ability to keep any living thing alive, Toshiyo has thrown herself into understanding the creature. Since they learned Manu was going to be all right, she's spent every waking moment with it. Maybe she's getting somewhere with understanding it, maybe she appreciates the distraction of trying to devise a way to transport it out of Cobalt Tower, or maybe she simply doesn't want to be alone. More speculation, since Toshiyo for some reason isn't around to ask.

And even if she were, no one here talks about what's bothering them.

It's starting to drive Starla up the wall.

When they transformed the medbay into a comfy cage for the newly amphibious creature, they moved the second tank, with the embryo, into the antechamber. Starla turns to study it. What was the size of a black-eyed pea last week is now the size of a chicken egg, and through the translucent shell it's possible to see the shape of knobby elbows, a twitching tail, leathery wings.

A low thrum of panic shivers through her chest. What the hell are they going to do with two of these?

She glances back through the one-way glass, and the creature tilts its wide, flat, bat-like face towards her. It . . . smiles?

The lights flicker and Starla turns to the door. Toshiyo is back, one hand on the light controls, the other arm filled with groceries. She sets them down on the table beside the door with a wince; her left hand and forearms are still bandaged.

"I'm trying to figure out what he eats," Toshiyo signs,

then starts pulling things out of her bag: radishes, berries, a paper-wrapped fish.

Starla tilts her head, examining the groceries. They're not from the kitchen that caters to Cobalt Tower. They're from the market around the corner. She raps a knuckle on the table to get Toshiyo's attention.

"You went out?" She stops herself from adding, By yourself?

"Sure," Toshiyo says with a shrug, like she leaves the tower and wanders around Bulari on her own all the time. Starla's seen the entry and exit logs for the past few months. She knows how infrequently Toshiyo goes out alone in normal circumstances, let alone after the trauma of a few nights ago. She makes a mental note to flag Toshiyo's sign-outs, then shakes her head.

Toshiyo's fine.

It's Starla who's freaking out about her.

"Yesterday Lucky seemed to like fish the best, but the kitchen was out," Toshiyo signs. "And I figured I could use a walk."

"Lucky?" Having this thing in their lives hardly seems like a stroke of luck.

Toshiyo shrugs. "Gotta call little buddy something. What's up?"

"I came to see if you'd heard anything more from Ximena's contact up at Redrock," Starla signs.

Toshiyo shakes her head. "I've pinged them a few times — pretending to be Ximena like you said — but I haven't heard anything back."

"Maybe they found out Ximena's dead."

"Maybe *they're* dead." Toshiyo begins digging into the groceries, her next words scrolling across Starla's lens. "Did you know the area around Redrock is officially a satellite blackout zone? I can't get any aerial visual of the site to confirm the images Ximena's contact sent us. How much work was left on that old satellite we were restoring, do you remember?"

Back in ancient history — a time last week that Starla can barely remember between Coeur coming back to life, the shoot-out at Julieta Yang's, the appearance of the alien, and the attack on Cobalt Tower — she and Toshiyo had kept themselves busy with a pet project. Restoring an old surveillance satellite Toshiyo had spotted in a list of interesting inventory the Arquellian gunrunner Absolon Chevalier had passed to Starla.

"We're pretty close," Starla signs. "I'll mess with it this afternoon and see what else we're missing."

"I told you it'd come in handy."

"It wasn't me that needed convincing." Jaantzen has an unhealthy distaste for clutter and tinkering. Mostly Starla's stopped trying to get his buy-in for her and Toshiyo's side projects — it only seems to raise his blood pressure.

"We'll need to get it launched. Manu knows that salvage operator, right? The one who flew the night . . ." She trails off with a little twirl of the fingers: *You know what night I mean.*

Right. The salvage operator who's been running odd jobs for Manu for the past week can probably be tasked to put a satellite in orbit for them — or at least he'll know someone who can. Though if anything worse had happened to Manu, she's not sure how they'd find this guy. Or any of Manu's motley network of contacts.

I've got it taken care of, he says, and there's another thing no one ever questions.

That's gotta change.

Toshiyo picks up the paper-wrapped fish and begins to

pick at the knotted string holding it together. "Do you think I should cut it up?"

Starla shrugs and flips out a blade to cut the string, then pockets it again before Toshiyo thinks it's an offer to use it for culinary purposes — she doesn't need her good utility knife stinking like fish. Toshiyo leaves the fish lying on its wrapping, then grabs the bunch of radishes.

"We can start with this," she signs. She palms the biolock to open the medbay and the creature whirls to show its flat, bat-like face to them as the door opens. The force-field Starla set up to keep it secure while Toshiyo feeds it is down, she realizes with horror. Toshiyo either doesn't notice or she left it down by design.

The creature — Lucky, sure — bares its teeth at them out of apparent reflex when the door opens, then widens its mouth in a caricature of a smile and hops over to Toshiyo, scrabbling on the tile floor with clawed feet, wings spread like it's about to attack. Or like a toddler who wants a hug. Starla takes a step back, putting a hand on the electric barb on her belt.

Toshiyo catches her attention and tosses her a radish. "Feed him," Toshiyo signs, then dangles one by its leaves. Lucky snaps it off in one bite, wobbling its head back and forth as it chews.

It turns expectantly to Starla. She fights her urge to run. Holds the radish out between two fingers.

Lucky scampers over and bites it daintily, taking care not to get its gnashing teeth too close to her fingers.

"He likes you," Toshiyo signs, delighted.

"Does it like anyone else?"

"No, but he hasn't attacked anyone since Manu and the Alliance woman. He was just high-strung then."

And protecting Toshiyo.

Speaking of protecting Toshiyo. "I thought we set up a forcefield?" Starla signs. "It shouldn't be wandering loose like this."

"He's fine," Toshiyo signs.

"At least keep the medbay door closed." Lucky may seem friendly to Toshiyo at the moment, but even the most normal of pets can turn. And they don't know the first thing about . . . this. Let alone how it's going to react when they try to transport it away from Cobalt Tower.

At least they know Lucky likes radishes. Hopefully they can use that to lure it into whatever carrying case they devise.

Toshiyo hands the bundle of radishes to Starla, then turns her back on the creature and begins to clean the fish in the sink.

Starla can't imagine turning her back on the creature, though it's just munching radishes now, contentedly swaying back and forth as though it can feel some mellow internal dance beat.

Actually.

Starla pulls out her comm and picks something with a beat that reminds her of how it's swaying. Ayisha Amadule's latest hit. She flicks the audio over to Toshiyo. "Play that," she signs.

Toshiyo looks skeptical, but plays it, so lightly that Starla can't feel it at all. Lucky tilts its head at Toshiyo a moment, then changes the rhythm of its swaying. Starla moves her shoulders along with its rhythm and her memory of the beat; it watches her with empty black eyes before its mouth opens wide and toothy in what she's starting to think of as a grin.

Toshiyo finishes up at the sink and lays the fish out on a tray, then sets it on the floor. The creature scrabbles over to it, dance abandoned to dive in face-first with such messy gusto that Toshiyo takes a step back, eyes wide. Starla touches her elbow and guides her through the medbay door, then hits the forcefield.

"I've been thinking about the serum everyone wants," Toshiyo signs once they're separated from Lucky once more. "We think it comes from its venom sacs, so there must be some way to get to it. I've been reading about milking snakes for their venom, and it seems like an option. But I'd want to make sure Lucky's fine with it first."

"How do you make sure of that?"

Toshiyo shrugs.

"Maybe it's not a matter of milking it," Starla signs. "The Dawn had enough serum to turn some of their people into supersoldiers, but they didn't have an unlimited supply. They were trying to replicate it when they ran out. Maybe they removed the sacs."

Toshiyo expression clouds. "And killed our little buddy's cousins?"

God, the chill that comes over Starla at the thought that there are multiple more out there.

Starla sighs. "Keep working on the transport — Julieta said she'll be ready to move tomorrow." Starla for one will sleep better at night knowing their little alien is secured somewhere far out of reach of the Alliance. Plus, Gia's friend's booby-trap-ridden compound out in the Maraka Valley sounds fun.

Starla pauses in the doorway, watching as Toshiyo goes back to sorting through the rest of the groceries. Her mouth is moving faintly, though Starla's lens isn't transcribing it. Starla almost asks her to repeat herself until she realizes Toshiyo's toe is tapping to the same rhythm the creature has started swaying to again. She must be singing along with the new Ayisha song.

Toshiyo knows the words to pop music?

It's worth a shot.

Starla raps her knuckles on the doorframe and Toshiyo glances up, surprised to still see her there. "I'm going out with the girls tonight," Starla signs. "Want to come?"

Toshiyo goes still, frowning at Starla.

"It's just me and Leti and Simca," Starla signs. "It'll be fun."

Toshiyo cracks the ring fingers of both hands and Starla waits, wondering if she pushed too far, if she shouldn't have asked. She flexes her fingers, about to offer Toshiyo an out, when —

"Sure, sounds fun," Toshiyo signs. "Let me know what time, I'll figure out something to wear." She smiles broadly at Starla, then digs back into the grocery bags.

Starla lets herself out, closes the door behind her.

Well.

This oughta be interesting.

7

MANU

Manu aches all over, the insides of his eyelids are sandpaper, and the only thing he wants more than to not be in pain is to not be in a hospital room.

It's been a steady stream of nurses and doctors. Dr. Alzuabi has mercifully gone home, and although the man who replaced her is gruffer and far more suspicious of Manu's complement of unauthorized guards, at least Manu doesn't feel quite as awkward about the fact that he hit on his doctor last week.

He was kept through the night, but despite Dr. Alzuabi's promise to cut him loose in the morning, the new Sulila hard-ass, Dr. Than, is delaying signoff.

"If he's not back in thirty minutes I'm pulling IVs myself," Manu says.

Oriol looks up from his book. "Give him an hour and I'll help you."

"Forty-five."

"We're not negotiating cab fare, babe. This is your health. Just relax. Read something. Meditate. We'll be out of here in a minute."

"You've been saying that all morning." Manu manages a weak smile — he's trying to have a conversation, not a fight, but with each passing moment his frustration kicks into a higher gear. Every word is coming out accidentally barbed.

"You start pulling IVs without a doctor signoff and the autodoc bots'll be on you like piranhas."

"You'll fight them off for me, though, right?" Manu forces his smile into something more genuine.

Oriol relaxes and thumbs his book back on. "It'll be epic."

"Like that fight at Herran's?"

Oriol's gaze snaps up from his book, and Manu grins for real this time.

"Simca showed me while you were sleeping," he says. "Very impressive."

Oriol just shakes his head and goes back to reading. It's something about the history of science, Manu'll ask him to explain it again next time he's ready to sleep.

He's not sleepy now, though, and he's definitely not in the mood to meditate.

Manu goes back to brooding.

There's so much to do, and he's stuck helpless in this room while everyone around him speeds past him into unknown danger. At least he's marginally confident he's staved off another attack by the Alliance for the time being. He saw ó Lauris on the news — a rush of relief that the man had survived the bombing — and received an unsigned note earlier this morning. It read, *I was very sorry to hear. I delivered your message.*

Which means the Alliance knows Jaantzen has footage of their agent shooting unarmed New Sarjunian civilians. Manu had reached out to Jaantzen and was told not to worry about it, that Jaantzen was taking care of things.

Which is exactly what Manu should be doing.

Instead he's staring at the ceiling, unable to form a coherent thought through the incessant beeping of the equipment around him.

"Twenty more minutes," he says.

Oriol sighs, but before he can answer there's a knock on the door and an orderly steps in. The man flicks a nervous glance at Oriol that twitches the corner of Manu's mouth into a smile.

"Mr. Juric, you have visitors. Your father? He's been calling to ask if you are awake."

Manu's smile fades. Oriol lowers his book and Manu frowns at him. Is this the first time his father has come back? Or just the first time he's hearing about it. Oriol's expression is unreadable. Manu's always wondered: Is it better to never have known your father, or to know him as a monster?

Some people can't let go of the past, spending their lives in its grip, playing threads out over and over as though they could gain some control over what's already happened.

Not Manu. He prefers for the past to stay dead and buried.

He gets unexpected flashes of memory, sometimes — who doesn't? Mostly they're things he'd rather forget, like the way his cousin Siggy's face waned gray in their teenage years. Like images of it bloodspattered and lifeless before she made it to twenty. Like the more memorable fights with his father, Manu reeling star-eyed and split-lipped from a backhand into a carefully stacked pile of his grandmother's junk hoard, his grandmother yelling at them to stop before they broke something.

Less frequently, there are flash memories of joy: skimming cash from Grandma's corner store, playing hooky from school with Siggy, late nights kicking balls in the middle of the hardpacked dirt streets of Carama Town, the earth beneath bare feet still warm from the long-set sun.

Grief or joy, though, those times are long gone.

Manu heard about it when his grandmother died old and decrepit, heard somebody finally shot Siggy's father over a debt, and he hasn't paid any attention to news from back home since.

And now his father's here.

He'd rather've been told his visitor was Blackheart. And it very well could have been, now that Jaantzen —

He clenches his teeth to feel the stab of pain in his injured jaw.

Those are thoughts that need to stay buried, too.

"Babe?"

The orderly's watching him. Oriol's watching him. Manu realizes with a start that he doesn't know how long he's been caught in thought.

"Tell him to fuck off," Manu says, and the orderly's eyebrows shoot up. Manu almost feels bad for him. He remembers what a bitter old asshole his father could be when he didn't get his way. Old scars twitch.

The orderly is still waiting in the doorway, and it takes Manu's exhausted mind too long to remember why.

"You said visitors," Manu says. "Who else?"

"A detective who's been making the rounds. If you're feeling well enough? I can tell him — "

"It's fine."

A detective? Manu's not wanted for anything that he knows of, so this is probably related to the embassy bombing. Either way, if they were going to arrest him they wouldn't be asking his permission — which means at least this will be an interesting puzzle to keep his mind busy.

"Send him in."

The orderly slips out and Oriol leans forward, frowning at the monitor at the foot of Manu's bed.

"You think I should have seen him?" Manu asks.

"No." Oriol taps a sequence of buttons. "Right now your stress levels are about to set off the autodoc bots again." Concern is etched in his golden eyes. "You want me to let them go? They're going to give you something to — "

"I'm fine," Manu snaps. "I don't need something to make me even more helpless."

"Sure." Oriol's expression becomes unreadable again; he presses a final button, then sits back. The doors to the autodoc bots' docks slide shut with a click.

And the door to the hospital room swings back open. The orderly leads in the police.

The man in the faded brown suit is tall, with well-lined, weathered skin, his salt-and-pepper hair still thick and leaning towards unruly. His right hand is covered in a black glove, his elbow tucked close and tight to his ribs. He's backed by a woman who's closer to Starla's age, late twenties maybe, with a short brown ponytail, stocky stature, and sharp brown eyes that take in everything.

She stands like military, but *he's* got that syrupy detective vibe, that casual way he leans in the doorway like he possesses this place and has all the time in the world for you to tell him what he wants to know. Manu's had plenty of run-ins with men like him, or at least he did years ago. Since the civil war, he mostly hasn't needed to attract that kind of attention. And due to Jaantzen being on the winning side, everything from beforehand that could have warranted police attention was conveniently given a pass.

"I'm Detective Timo Cho, and this is my partner, Officer Ossandre Samson," says the man. "We have some questions about the bombing at the embassy. May we come in?"

"Course," Manu says. Cho. Something about that name tugs at his memory, but the pain and drugs aren't letting much through. He settles against the pillows, making himself comfortable. "C'mon in."

"We'll need the room," Cho says to the orderly and Oriol.

The orderly nods and leaves; Oriol thumbs his book off and lays it aside, then unfolds lazily and follows the orderly to the door, but not out. He shuts the door and crosses muscular arms over his chest.

"You, too, Mr. . . ."

"Sina," says Oriol. "And I'm not going anywhere."

"You're his lawyer?" Cho gives him a once-over.

"He need one?" Oriol lounges against the door looking nothing like a lawyer.

"My husband," Manu says. The word's surprisingly easy to say. "What can we help you with?"

Cho settles onto the stool to Manu's left, deciding to ignore Oriol for the moment. His partner stands back, watching Oriol warily. Oriol gives her a warm smile which she reflexively returns before smoothing her face back into a street cop scowl once more.

"What were you doing at the Alliance embassy two nights ago?" Cho asks. There's a live wire of energy behind the question, though the detective's hiding it well.

"Passing through," Manu says. "Good coffee that part of town, thought I'd grab one on my way home." He's sure there's video evidence that he was inside the embassy, but doesn't know if the Bulari Police Department would have that. The real question is whether this guy is ferreting out a particular angle involving Manu, or if he's just doing the rounds.

"Home from where?"

"Having a cup of tea with a friend. You think I did it?"

"We're interviewing all the victims, Mr. Juric," says Samson quickly, and Manu catches Cho's wince. An old hand's chagrin that his rookie partner gave information away; the man's body language says he's far more comfortable than she is at interviewing suspects.

"We're covering every angle," Cho says.

"I wish I could help," Manu says. "I didn't notice anything out of the ordinary, but I'd be happy to tell you everything I remember."

"In my experience, men like you don't remember much."

Ah. So he does know who Manu is.

"Concussion'll do that to you," Manu says.

"And they tend to get away with more. Can you think of anyone who might want to kill you, Mr. Juric?"

Manu's been waiting for this; he lets surprise show. "Me?"

"I imagine in your line of work, you make enemies."

Oriol lets out a laugh. "I don't think you've spent much time in the restaurant supply industry," he says; Cho's partner smiles at him before she catches herself.

But Cho's not smiling. "Can you think of anyone who might have had a grudge against you?"

"Man, I've got nothing but friends."

"And quite the record."

"Do I?"

A humorless smile. Cho is definitely used to this game.

"Grudges can last for decades, Mr. Juric. Even after someone's spent time off-planet."

Manu's professionally relaxed now, and he's not going to let Cho invoke Coeur to crack him. Still, something deep inside him snarls, primal and angry; he shoves it back down.

It probably wasn't her, he's been telling himself that all day. Bombing the embassy is theatrical, but not thoroughly vicious enough for Blackheart. And she'd probably have a better reason than a ten-year-old grudge if she was going to goad the system into interplanetary war. No way she's bored enough yet with Dry Creek to keep her busy.

Cho's just dowsing, Manu thinks, seeing if he can strike a rich vein. There's a lot of unsavory business in Manu's past, but as far as he can tell, his official record is all speculation. There's an evidence problem, a crooked cop problem, and definitely a witness problem.

Cho may know who Manu is, but he doesn't have anything on him.

And Manu's not going to let him get under his skin.

"Sorry to waste your time, Detective Cho," Manu says. "But I didn't have anything to do with that bomb. I'm not in any terrorist groups, even if you did think I'd be stupid enough to blow myself up."

"We don't think you're with a terrorist group, Mr. Juric. But we're looking into all the possibilities. There are other reasons things explode in this city."

Something sharp and deadly shivers just beneath the surface of his words, slipping away so fast Manu isn't sure at first that he heard it. Now the officer is watching him impassively, almost bored, no hint of the emotion lying beneath the facade.

He didn't just recognize Manu's name on the list. Something about this interview is personal.

Manu wracks his pain-addled brain again for this man's face. Comes up blank.

"I just have a few questions," Cho says, releasing a camera drone from his palm without bothering to ask permission. It hovers in the air between them, recording a hologram of everything in the room. It's probably against Sulila Corporation's charter with New Sarjun, what with monitors displaying potentially sensitive patient information. If Manu complains to the staff, they'll throw him out.

More interesting, though, is that Cho didn't want the first part of the interview on the official record. Manu wonders why.

"Can you walk me through your evening two nights ago, Mr. Juric?"

Manu looks past him to Oriol, who's already on his comm. "Can you —"

"I'm calling her."

"I'll be happy to answer more of your questions when my lawyer gets here." Manu pushes the call button beside his bed, then smiles at Cho ruefully. "Pain meds starting to wear off."

Cho gives him a tight smile and holds out his right hand stiffly; the drone lands in his gloved palm and blinks off.

"We can talk later," Cho says. "When you're feeling better. Maybe you could come down to the station to give a statement."

Manu smiles at him. "Let's keep in touch." He nods at Officer Samson. "Nice to meet you both."

Oriol melts out of his lean to open the door for the officers, then shuts it behind them. "Been wondering if they'd show," he says quietly.

"Me, too."

Manu's not wanted for anything — he would've seen it come up as he keeps tabs on the BPD's internal communications and, also, has a friend on the inside who's always been willing to pass him information. But his name showing up in a Bulari hospital would definitely set off some flags.

Being here is a stupid mistake.

"You think they're just sniffing around?" Oriol asks.

"Could be." But something in Cho's manner suggested a history, and Manu needs to find out what exactly that history is. He frowns, something edging at his attention. "You think Dr. Than really needs me around for observation?"

A muscle in Oriol's cheek tightens as he realizes what Manu's asking. "I think you're right."

That he's just been kept under observation until the officers had a chance to make all their rounds.

Manu swears so violently the autodoc bots float back into action in a solicitous flurry. Oriol swats one out of the way before it injects Manu, then types something into the monitor at the foot of Manu's bed, sending them beeping in protest back to their docks.

That long-precarious avalanche of frustration comes crashing down. Manu can't do a thing to help here, but that's not even the worst of it. No, his decision to go see ó Lauris at the embassy rather than catching him at home or setting up a meeting elsewhere has put his name on a list of victims and attracted the attention of the Bulari Police Department — at the worst possible time for Jaantzen.

Solving problems is the only thing he was ever good at, but this time he's made things worse.

Manu tries to lever himself into a better seated position with another savage curse, pain searing through his right arm where Toshiyo's hell-beast slashed him, his lower back aching from lying down so long. But nothing else feels too out of place. He hopes that's a good sign, and not just a sign that he's on too many meds to feel the extent of his injuries.

Oriol swipes away the monitor. "What do you need?"

"To get the fuck out of here." Manu's been trying to stay cheerful, but he's over this, and he's with one of the few people he can lower his facade for. He lets his exhaustion show and it feels fucking good not to have to act.

"I'll get it done."

"And I need to talk to the man."

Oriol's shaking his head. "It can wait. You're going home with me."

"I need to get my contacts. Starla was asking me about a pilot. Tosh needs — "

"They don't need you to take care of everything," Oriol says, gaze steel.

But it's the only goddamned thing that's going to make him feel himself again.

8

JAANTZEN

Somewhere from the neighborhood around Chief Justice Geum-ja Leone's home he can smell smoke, a faint hint of it threading through the night. Too sulfurous, too poisonous to be someone cooking an evening meal. He stops on Leone's broad front steps to take it in and the hint is gone as soon as it came, drifting away on the wind.

Jaantzen pushes the feeling of unease back down where it came from. Toshiyo has been keeping an eye on Leone's surveillance feeds today, and she identified the man who arrived just before Jaantzen as a political consultant. Going into a meeting with Leone and her politician friends should be no different from going into a meeting with an underworld rival, he tells himself. They won't be negotiating with muscle and overt threats, of course, but with subtext and influence.

There's no reason not to feel calm.

Jaantzen mounts the wide marble steps. His driver, Raim, will wait; he'll be Jaantzen's man outside in case anything happens. Toshiyo will be his eyes on the security feed, where she's noticed nothing out of the usual over the past few days.

Leone isn't a physical danger to him, but he'll have to tread carefully if he wants to stay on her good side. She sits at the heart of an incredible web of connections in Bulari's business and political communities, and access to that network has been a huge boon to Jaantzen over the past decade. Many of her contacts have become his own over the years, but still. Leone is too powerful a connection to sever. He'll do what it takes to stay in her good graces.

"Willem!" Leone greets him at the door, lotion-soft hands taking his, pulling him down for a kiss on the cheek; he stands with her perfume clinging to his lapel. She takes his coat and hangs it on the tree beside the door. "It was so good of you to come."

Jaantzen dials his smile in to match her own, then pulls a slim box from his pocket. "Thank you for having me, Madame Justice."

Her eyes light up — Leone could never refuse a gift — and then widen in honest delight when she sees the ruby-studded bracelet. "You shouldn't have!"

"A token of gratitude for your support over the past few days," Jaantzen says smoothly. "It's just as compatible with your home's security as your original cuff, but I thought some days you might want something more interesting than plain gold."

She smiles fondly at him, then tucks the box into the pocket of her voluminous green velvet dress. "Perhaps you can show me how to set it up after we've met my guest." But she doesn't make a move to lead him out of the entryway. Her smile fades to concern. "How are you? I was so sorry to hear what happened."

"I'll recover. Phaera and the Lorelei will recover. And the rest of us can breathe a little bit easier knowing Acheta isn't out terrorizing people."

A frown of disapproval; she's not going to argue that, but she's not happy about it.

"Thala." She straightens. "I want you to speak to her for me. Welcome her back. Tell her I would be interested in catching up when she's ready."

"Of course." Jaantzen suspects he'll be caught in the middle of people wanting to get messages to Coeur for a while before anyone else gets up the nerve to approach her on their own.

But Leone doesn't just want to extend pleasantries to Coeur. "I wish we'd had a chance to talk before you made your decision," she says, a note of reproach in her voice. "I understand you had to move quickly, but it seemed hasty."

"It was well thought out," Jaantzen says.

"Tell me seriously, Willem. How will she be any better than Levi Acheta?"

This won't be the last time he'll be asked this question, he's well aware. He could say that this Thala Coeur seems like a different woman than the one he fought to the ground and sent into exile a decade ago. That her rise to power and fall from grace, her time in exile, her near death at the hands of the Dry Creek crew and the Dawn cult, the loss of her sister — that all these things have changed her. But he's not entirely sure he believes that himself.

"She'll be no less vicious than him when crossed," Jaantzen says. "But she'll pick her battles more carefully, and take offense less easily."

Leone purses her lips. "That's not reassuring, Willem."

"It's not meant to be. We set loose a jaguar to clear out

the wild dogs running in Dry Creek. Coeur's still a monster, but I have a plan to keep her attention once she's destroyed that crew."

"And her old grievances?"

That's what Leone's worried about, of course. That Blackheart will turn her claws on the people who orchestrated her downfall ten years ago once she's done devouring the Dry Creek crew.

"You have my word," he says. "Treat this as an opportunity for a clean slate, and she'll do the same."

Leone's mouth turns down as she considers that, then she finally nods.

"Shall we?" Her entryway is all grand opulence, the glossy marble tiles patterned in black-white-gray and padded by thick, rich rugs, the massive staircase of carved Indiran oak rising to the balcony of the second floor, the walls hung with obscure and massive pieces of art.

It's the sort of home Jaantzen saw in dramas about posh Arquellian aristocrats as a child in the orphanage, and he hadn't thought such people lived on New Sarjun until he first came here as Julieta's guest. Leone's sitting room is every bit as stylish as the entryway, though more intimate and decorated in maroons and golds as if out of a dynasty drama.

A man is already there, perched on the low settee. He's dressed well, but not like a socialite off to a dinner party. His suit is designed to impress with professionalism. And just enough sophistication to let Jaantzen and Leone know that whatever it is he does, he's very, very successful at it.

"Willem, I want you to meet Tomás Vahid. You may have heard his name around? He's the man behind our success in the prime minister's race."

Vahid rises, setting his drink down on the coffee table, holding out a hand. He's dark-skinned, with dreadlocks wound thickly at the base of his neck and strong, square features. He gives Jaantzen a wolfish smile. "It's a pleasure to meet you."

"Likewise," Jaantzen says. Leone's smile is secretive and cool.

Jaantzen settles himself in the bronzed leather armchair to the left of the settee, his back to the wall so the doors to the dining room, entryway, and kitchen are all in easy view. "A drink, Willem?" Leone waves her butler out of the kitchen.

"Whatever you're having."

He's regarding Vahid levelly, indulging his curiosity and wondering at what moment the man's sunny disposition will begin to waver under his gaze. It doesn't; he assumes Vahid's dealt with plenty of dangerous people in his career. Jaantzen doesn't recognize the name, but he does remember the last race for prime minister and how the current man, de Grazal, had been lagging far behind the popular incumbent until a series of scandals had rocketed de Grazal to easy victory.

The man behind *our* success, Leone had said. Jaantzen wonders just how big a role Leone herself played in bringing down the last prime minister and propping up a newcomer in his place.

Wonders just how far her reach extends.

"Tomás has been running winning political campaigns for decades," Leone tells him. "And he's been a personal friend for even longer. In fact I don't know where I would be without him." The benevolent smile she grants Vahid is returned with the perfect amount of deference.

"You're too kind," he says.

The butler returns with glasses and a bottle of red wine he unseals and uncorks at the table; Jaantzen recognizes it as the one he gifted Leone last time he came to a dinner party, complete to the scuff on the label.

"I thought you'd want to try it, too," Leone says with a smile.

"I would love to."

It could be a gesture meant to put him at ease by offering him a glass of wine he knows he can trust. Or she could be telling him she distrusts his gift and wants him to drink it with her, though that's less likely — they were on perfectly good terms the last time he was here, as far as he knows.

Most likely it's a third option. That there's a new tension between them since he went behind her back to take care of Acheta, and she wants him to know she knows it. Otherwise she would have made him a drink as usual, and he would have enjoyed it without worry that Chief Justice Geum-ja Leone was planning on poisoning him in her own home.

"To our gracious host." He lifts his glass. "May her reign be long."

"To our host," Vahid echoes, and Leone clinks her glass with his and takes a long, fearless sip.

"Willem, I've been thinking," Leone says. "About what you want to do next."

"Next?"

"Next. You have another twenty good years at the top of your game before you're a little old thing like me, thinking about retirement. What will you do with those years? Install refrigerators and alarm systems? You could use your talents for more than that."

"I could go into politics, you mean." Jaantzen turns to Vahid, studying the political consultant once more. Whatever game they're playing here, let Vahid and Leone see him as willing until he can figure it out. "Are you going to off the new prime minister so soon?"

Vahid just smiles. "I'm still on retainer for him, Mr. Jaantzen. But even if I wasn't, I have a certain level of loyalty to my past clients. I think you'll appreciate that." He glances at Leone, who gives him a magnanimous nod; she's gotten used to granting permission to speak in her presence over the years. "And you'll forgive me, Mr. Jaantzen, but prime minister is a leap for someone with no political experience." Vahid says it easy, but his shoulders are tight; he's testing the waters.

"I should certainly hope so," Jaantzen says. Vahid relaxes imperceptibly. "I'd like to think there's a certain level of competency in our leadership."

"I mostly wanted to get to know you tonight. See if you're interested at all."

"In running for a public office." Jaantzen turns his attention back to Leone. "Is that the idea."

Leone leans forward, hands clasped. "I've been thinking about you lately, Willem. You have such a promising business resume, but I'm starting to wonder. Is that all you have your sights on? You're an adept networker. You have the attention of a great many powerful people."

There's a blade buried under those words, but Jaantzen pretends not to hear it. His intention has never been to challenge Leone for her circle of influence — he's always used the people he found in his orbit to get done what needed to be done. Once Julieta introduced him to Leone, his world expanded to include her network of businesspeople and politicians, financiers, diplomats. He'd built relationships with them — the business deal in Jet Park he's brokering with Mizal Seti, the terraforming business now with Aiax and Lhasa Demosga, the financing he's taken from Teo Lordeur. And certainly he would count some of them among his friends. Teo, for example, was recently willing to put himself in physical danger to lay the trap for Acheta.

And, of course, his relationship with one of Leone's favorite up-and-coming protégés, Phaera D, is veering into territory far beyond friendship.

He hadn't set out to undermine her circle. But perhaps Leone thought she was supposed to be the only one at the center of a web.

"Imagine the power," Vahid is saying. "And where would you want that power? Because let me tell you, I wouldn't want the job of prime minister or mayor. Too much pressure, way too much public spotlight, and not enough reward. Everyone has their own level of power they want."

Jaantzen raises an eyebrow at him, and the man flinches before he catches himself.

"Go on," says Jaantzen.

"You strike me as the kind of man who wants influence without the constant spotlight and scandals, is that right? The kind of man who likes to do useful things. Who — if you were interested in running for politics — would want a position where you can actually get work done."

"Something like?"

"I rely heavily on my relationships with certain members of the parliament," Leone says. "A dear friend of mine is retiring at the end of this year, and I think you would be perfectly suited for the role."

Ah, so be under Leone's thumb. It's unspoken, but it's there: She'll groom him into the position, but he'll be her new man in the parliament. With more power than he could achieve on his own, but at her beck and call.

Though, whispers a voice in the back of his mind, how much longer can the old woman live?

"Parliament is stocked with career politicians who've never worked a day in their lives," says Vahid. "They don't own businesses, so they're thinking about how a trade agreement with the Alliance will line their pockets, not help real business owners."

It's a line calculated perfectly to Jaantzen, and he appreciates the effort. And, to be honest, he wouldn't mind sitting alone sometime with Vahid and hashing this out. But with as much as Leone is trying to put him at ease, he can sense just how thin the ice is between them right now. She brought him here not to make him apologize with threats or shame, as he was half expecting. Her power play is to offer him a position, a next step in his career. To remind him that she has true influence and she's willing to share it with him if he agrees to be her thrall.

This offer is intriguing, but if he says yes, he owes Leone — and if he continues a relationship with Vahid behind her back, he'll exacerbate the situation between them. The way she's approaching him, Jaantzen can still believe there's a chance to salvage this relationship, ease Leone's pride.

But he's not about to walk into a trap.

"I'll have to spend time thinking about it," he says finally.

"I think we could do great things together," she says brightly. "You really should consider it. But at least we've planted the seed."

Vahid seems to sense that his time is up. He drains the

rest of his drink, then stands to shake Jaantzen's hand. "Mr. Jaantzen, I look forward to our next conversation."

Jaantzen pours himself another splash of wine while he's waiting for Leone to see Vahid out, thinking over what just happened. He can hear them talking; from the tone it sounds like light banter. He can't tell if Leone thinks this went well or not, but he is starting to feel more confident that he can smooth out the wrinkle between them.

Finally the door shuts and he hears the steady click of Leone's heels as she comes back. She stops in the doorway, smiling down at him like a proud mother; the back of his neck itches. "I do hope you're thinking about what Tomás said. This could be a good opportunity for you."

"I'm interested in the possibilities," he says carefully.

"I've always appreciated how deliberate you are with your plans."

Is that another barb? A subtle reminder that she considers his going around her back to reinstall Coeur not a forgetful slip, but a deliberate snub?

Jaantzen lifts the bottle. "More wine?"

"Please." As Jaantzen pours, Leone settles back into her seat. "Thank you. I had another reason I wanted to ask you here tonight." She sits back, swirling the liquid in her glass, light catching in it like rubies. "I've been having some trouble getting cooperation from a certain defense lawyer. I was wondering if you could send someone by to straighten him out."

She smiles at him like she's just invited him to the theater, and Jaantzen takes another long sip of wine, letting it roll over his tongue: rich copper and oak. He lets the flavors linger, playing the moments leading up to this over in his mind. He's hunting for the sound bites — has he said anything in her presence so far that could be incriminating?

Everything about Coeur, of course, because it hadn't crossed his mind that she would be recording this meeting until he understood where things were going with Vahid.

For a brief moment during that conversation, he'd thought she truly saw potential in him. But — no. Even if she's not simply asking this favor in hopes of catching a sound bite for leverage in the case of a future political appointment, she wants to remind him that she still thinks of him as her errand boy. Just like she did all those years ago during the civil war with Coeur.

Saying yes to Vahid would have been a navigable trap. Saying yes to this favor is a life sentence.

He chooses his words carefully.

"I'm not in that business, Madame Justice," he says.

She swirls wine in her glass. "What business, Willem?"

The business of taking orders from you — he'd love to say it, but he bites his tongue and sets his wine glass down. The fact that she asked for clarification makes him certain she is recording.

"Thank you for your time," he says, rising. "And I appreciate the introduction to Vahid. I'll be thinking about your offer."

She doesn't join him, and Jaantzen knows for certain she's heard his subtext loud and clear. He came here tonight hoping to find a way to smooth things over as equals, but she'll only be satisfied if he's on her leash. Whatever amends he was hoping to make tonight, he's made things far, far worse.

Leone settles back in her chair, imperious. "Is that all, Willem?"

"I'll be in touch soon." He kisses the back of her hand and shows himself out.

Outside, the night air is a cooling balm, though the

nearby acrid smoke has intensified; it claws at the back of his throat as he tries to take a deep breath and free himself from the lingering strands of Leone's web. He has a deep, certain feeling that he miscalculated tonight, but he can't quite put his finger on how. He had planned to walk in with a gift and an apology, make some motions about passing future decisions by her, and leave with their relationship smoothed over.

Instead, she'd pushed him to do a job he couldn't accept, not without accepting a choke collar, too.

Maybe his miscalculation was in thinking things could go back to how they were before.

He forces himself to walk normally, to greet Raim calmly when his driver opens the door, to keep his expression smooth and even.

Whatever comes next won't be a simple turf war, solved by soldiering up and tearing the enemy down. Whatever comes next will require him to master an unfamiliar game.

There's a message waiting on his comm. Phaera.

How was your evening?

Disastrous in ways he's not yet certain how to parse. In ways he's not even sure how to see — but that's not something you type. He hesitates at sending a response when he sees that her note was from nearly an hour ago. But despite the hour, it's probably not too late in Phaera's world. And he could use her insight.

Interesting. Are you still up?

Her response is immediate: *Doing inventory at the Table.*

Would you rather go out for a drink?

Seconds tick by. The wait is excruciating.

Come on by, I own an entire bar.

From one woman's turf to another's. But if he's going to

speak frankly with her about what happened here tonight, he wants to be certain no one is listening in.

So do I, he responds.

Another long pause, then Phaera's next message appears.

I'll see you at the Jungle in 30.

9

———

JAANTZEN

Phaera's exiting a taxi in front of the Jungle when he arrives. She's wearing a long-sleeved sapphire blouse, real silk by the way the light pools in the drapes of the fabric. Slits in the sleeves reveal slices of pale forearm and flashes of gold cuffs; the neckline smooths over her collarbones but drapes low between her shoulder blades. Her white trousers hug the toned lines of her calves, thighs, hips. Her strappy gold heels gleam.

Jaantzen is grateful he dressed well for his meeting with Leone.

"You can let me out here," he instructs his driver. Raim glances at him. Normally Jaantzen would have him dock around back.

"Sir?"

"It's fine, Raim," Jaantzen says, and the man pulls over behind Phaera's taxi. Jaantzen doesn't get out until Raim has done his scans, then crosses to open Jaantzen's door. Phaera's on the sidewalk, waiting, Raim having said something to her as he exited the spinner.

"You don't strike me as the sort of man who waits for

someone else to open doors for him," Phaera says when he joins her.

Not following protocol gets people killed, but that's not the best conversation opener. And it's also not entirely true; tonight he skipped full protocol for the pride of walking through his own front door with Phaera D on his arm.

"That doesn't strike me as the sort of thing you wear to do inventory," he says instead.

"Of course not. This is what I keep at the office in case a handsome man asks me out for a drink on short notice."

"Does that happen often?"

"I'm hoping it'll start happening more."

"I'll let any handsome men I meet know their service is required."

Phaera laughs and threads her arm through his. "I'm very picky."

The facade of the Jungle is understatedly garish, cream-colored vivistone molded to look like carved marble, vines constantly shifting around the columns, leaves unfurling and fading back, flowers blooming. The neon green holographic sign scrawls *The Jungle* in the air like handwriting,

There's a crowd formed in the lobby, people who are hoping for a table without a reservation. Jaantzen catches snatches of foreign accents and languages, tourists who are checking a trip to his restaurant off their Bulari must-do list.

The Jungle started as a whim, a joke from Manu that if Jaantzen was going to get into the restaurant supply business he might as well improve the quality of their local lunch options, a comment from Julieta that she had a few *Monstera deliciosa* plants outgrowing her greenhouse that could use a good home.

The seed was planted, and as Jaantzen met more people in the restaurant business, he soon found the right connections. In the end, some perfect alchemy brought him his head chef at the same time that the front-of-house manager at another fine dining establishment left her job.

He largely stayed out of the design except to insist on certain safety and privacy features that made the Jungle an immediate hit with people who had discreet business to conduct. He keeps out of the day-to-day running of it, too, unless he notices something in the regular reports he wants to comment on.

And, to be honest, he rarely comes here now unless he has someone he wants to impress.

Tae would have loved this place.

He lets the thought float on.

A flash of light, and Phaera pushes firmly yet graciously past a woman with a heart-shaped face and a camera drone painted with the logo of some celebrity chat show Jaantzen is only vaguely aware of. A reporter waiting for a table of her own? Or just hanging out in the lobby hoping to catch a glimpse of someone famous out to dinner?

Phaera's turning heads in her outfit, and getting more than one look of recognition. Her face has been on the feeds more these past few days after the business with Acheta. Jaantzen, on the other hand, does his best to stay out of the news cycles, which means the stray glances he gets from those paying attention to Phaera are tinged with curiosity.

Jaantzen greets the host with a warm handshake; the man has been the face of the Jungle for almost a decade. Jaantzen leans in. "Get the reporter out of here," he murmurs, and the host nods sharply.

Then Jaantzen holds out his arm to lead Phaera through the door marked only with the outline of a flower done in sizzling gold.

Anyone can get a reservation to eat at the Jungle or drink

at the bar by the lobby. Few have an invitation to the Golden Orchid room. Tonight, despite the crowds in the lobby, the Golden Orchid is quiet and sparsely populated. Jaantzen greets a few people he knows as they enter, then takes a seat at the end of the bar. Despite the bartender speaking with a patron nearby, all Jaantzen can hear is the soft ambient music.

In the Golden Orchid, conversations don't carry and staff are thoroughly vetted. It's swept for bugs daily. It's one of the few places outside Cobalt Tower that he feels comfortable holding private conversations.

Phaera orders one of the bartender's signatures and Jaantzen orders a whiskey. In the light of the bar she's glowing. He hadn't noticed her earrings before now, delicate gold-colored chains that shimmer against the backdrop of her magenta hair. Each chain is tipped with a simple faux-pearl drop.

She catches him looking and brushes a fingertip over one. "From my mother," she says, then clinks glasses with him. "Now. You said you had an interesting evening, and I don't have any scintillating stories about counting liquor bottles, so why don't you go first?"

"Leone asked me to come see her." He pitches his voice low, though he doesn't need to.

Ice clinks in Phaera's glass as she raises it. "That does sound interesting. What did she want?"

"To rein me back in." He describes Leone's displeasure at the way he handled Acheta and Coeur, the meeting with Vahid the political advisor, Leone's insinuation that she needed someone to do her bidding in the parliament.

"Would you consider it?" Phaera asks when he finishes.

"Running for office? I have more than enough on my plate." But in truth, the conversation with Vahid had sparked some interest he hadn't realized was there. Some sense of "Wouldn't it be interesting if." Phaera is watching him with a knowing look.

"I hadn't thought about it before tonight," Jaantzen says. "I'm not sure what it would accomplish."

"Right now it sounds like it would accomplish turning you into Leone's puppet."

"I agree."

"You should think about it," she says, and he frowns at her. "Not taking Leone's offer, but think about who's going to be in power once Leone and her friends start shuffling off to nursing homes. And" — she tilts her head playfully — "think about how you want to pass off that power when Starla's generation is taking charge."

"I think you're calling me old," Jaantzen says.

"I hope not," she says, laughing. "I'm right there with you. Listen, Jaantzen, now is the time for both of us to start thinking about what happens when Leone and Julieta and the Lordeurs and all the rest are gone. When you and — god help us — Lhasa Demosga and Mizal Seti are the wise old voices and influences around here. Who's going to be at the center of that web of power?"

She takes another sip and recrosses her legs; her calf brushes against his.

"And if it's you," she continues carefully, "what will you do with that power? Will you be Leone, desperately trying to maintain control? Because in the casino business it's the same. You have oldtimers like Herran Tarri who think they'll always be in charge even though they wore out their influence years ago. Then there's Cavy, who's mentoring the younger generation, like me and Ayisha, trying to help us grow while he stays relevant."

"Leone isn't an oldtimer who's worn out her influence," Jaantzen says.

She laughs. "I know she's not Tarri — that old coot is a pain in the ass, and I don't care who knows I think that. Worst he can do is tell everyone in earshot that I'm a conniving bitch, even though nobody's listening to him now." She takes a sip; light sparkles in her eyes. "But Leone? Make her feel like she has your respect, then do your own thing. But definitely don't mess with her."

"I'm afraid I already have."

"What do you mean?"

Jaantzen has been debating telling her. "Before I left, Leone asked me a favor. To 'straighten out' a defense lawyer for her."

Phaera's jaw drops, the unconscious rhythm of her leg moving against his stops. But she doesn't draw away. He stays perfectly still; maybe she just hasn't noticed she's still touching him, and he won't remind her.

"You mean . . ."

"I told her no."

"Has she asked you for something like that before?"

"Not for a decade." The last time was just after the civil war — a BPD detective was asking too many questions about who'd been behind the campaign to get rid of Coeur, apparently hadn't understood that the war was over. Leone had gotten the man demoted, then she'd asked Jaantzen to give him a more physical reminder that the time for asking questions was over. Manu had taken care of it.

Jaantzen's watching Phaera carefully, but she seems to be relaxing. Maybe her shock was more about Leone asking than about the reminder of who he really is. He'd like to remind her of that as little as possible.

"My guess is she wanted to have something on me if I did run for office. Some way to control me."

"Or she wanted you to know just what she thinks of you." Phaera says it with venom. "To keep you in your place. She does love to do that."

"What do you mean?"

"Just her little barbs." Her tone shifts to mimic Leone's syrupy drawl. "'How's your little business going, darling? Can you grab a tray from the kitchen, dear? Where would you be without me, sweetheart?'" Phaera smiles like it's nothing, but fire smolders behind her eyes. She tries to quench it with a long drink, and the subtle movement of her leg against his starts up again.

"Why do you keep coming around her?"

Phaera laughs. "I suspect the same reason you do. She's good for business. And not everyone in Empress Leone's court is so shitty. You were there."

Were.

The reality has been sinking in all night.

"I doubt I'll be invited back after tonight."

"If that's all she does, you'll be lucky. She tried to kick you back down, and you told her no. To her face." Phaera takes a deep breath. "You need to start shoring up your allies, and be ready if she decides to go on the offensive. Can you count on the Yangs?"

Jaantzen nods. Julieta and Leone have run in the same circle for years, but he wouldn't count the two friends.

"And you mentioned something about a business deal with Aiax and Lhasa?" Phaera doesn't quite manage to keep her distaste for the Demosga siblings out of her tone. "How much do you actually trust them?"

"I've known Aiax for a long time. He's not easily

swayed. But Leone could put pressure on him that I can't match."

"Then shore up your relationship before she does. Aiax is insufferable, but he won't go against his word. See if you can get some ink on a contract and put his money on the line."

"Same with Mizal," Jaantzen says. "Though I have much less faith in him."

"He's probably also mad at you for Coeur," Phaera says. "Let me talk to him. I've had an idea about getting Jet Park businesses to join the casino district's business association, I've been wanting to run it by you both. I'll give him a call tomorrow. What about Teo Lordeur?"

"I did business with Teo and his sister way before I ever met Leone," Jaantzen says. "He's with me."

"And let me talk to Cavy and Ayisha," Phaera says. "They don't know you, but they appreciate good people." Before he can protest that characterization, she's moving on. "We need to be prepared for Leone to play dirty. Have media people on standby. Start digging for leverage of our own. Do you know if she has anything on you?"

"You don't have to get involved in this."

Phaera gives him a rueful smile. "I already am. Anyway, she acts like she plucked me out of the ranks of the middle classes and made me who I am. Like I'm a case study of how she can make or break someone." She shakes her head. "I hear a lot of interesting rumors in my line of work that could make for good leverage against her if true. You might ask your man what he's heard, too." Her expression becomes serious. "How is he? Sina told me he'd come home from the hospital."

"I haven't been able to see him yet." Jaantzen clears his throat. "But Oriol tells me he's going to be fine. I'm going to try to keep him out of the office for as long as possible."

"I bet he goes stir-crazy if he's not working, though. I understand that, I'm a terrible patient."

"You've barely sat still through a drink."

She laughs and drains the rest of her glass.

"Another?" At the other end of the bar, the bartender is watching them for his sign.

"I can't," she says. "I have a breakfast meeting, and it's already after midnight." She presses a button on her gold cuff.

"Let me give you a ride home."

"I already called a cab. Gotta support the union." She slips off her stool, her thigh sliding along his. "Let's do this again soon."

Ah, yes. There's the other thing he should probably talk to her about.

"Phaera, I'm not sure we should be seen together," he says. "If Leone is planning anything, I don't want that to affect you."

She's standing so close. He hasn't yet gotten up from the stool, and with her heels they're eye to eye. She leans in for a kiss, gentle, her palm smooth on his cheek, no perfume but the warmth of her hair, the faint citrus and cardamom from the kitchen at the Devil's Table. He forces himself to relax — no one is watching them here.

"Promise me something, Jaantzen," she murmurs in his ear. Her breath on his skin is electric. "Let me decide what risks I'm willing to take. If you're done with me, that's fine. But don't push me back to protect me."

He breathes deep, cataloguing every scent. "I promise."

Phaera smiles and takes his hand, pulling him to his feet. "Walk me out to the curb, my car is here. Oh — I almost forgot. I worked with a killer woman last year in the PR campaign to shut down that Arquellian casino chain. She's whip smart and doesn't mind fighting dirty. Letizia Diamante — I can put you in touch."

Jaantzen laughs. "You've worked with Ms. Diamante?" What a small world.

"You know her?"

"Not personally." Jaantzen pulls out his comm and begins composing a text to Starla. "But it *is* girls' night."

10

STARLA

Starla's so deep in concentration that when her gauntlet buzzes she nearly stabs herself in the cornea with her eyeliner pen. She triple-blinks her lens on as she moves to the right eye, expecting Simca and getting Jaantzen:

Please ask Leti to schedule a meeting with me at her earliest convenience.

Starla finishes the line on her lid and frowns at herself in the mirror. The blue's a bit garish, actually — she twists the cap of the pen, dialing the pigment on her lash line back a few shades to something more silvery and pale. Definitely better. She types on her gauntlet.

Sure. Why?

Will explain later. Have a fun night.

Have a fun night? Like now she won't spend it stressing about what Jaantzen suddenly needs a PR shark like Leti for. Her fingers hover over her gauntlet, but she decides against prying just as another message comes through. Toshiyo, this time:

Do you have a minute? I need another set of hands. In the conference room.

*B*E *RIGHT THERE.*

For once she actually isn't running late. She'd figured giving herself adequate time to prepare for girls' night would help her feel more polished before she ran out the door, but she's just wasted it trying several thousand different shades of makeup and changing her mind about her dress and still not being one hundred percent happy with the final effect.

Turns out she's better off dashing out the door in a hurry — it's not like Simca and Leti care. And now that she's met Sam she definitely doesn't care what guys think about her choice of lipstick tonight.

Starla grabs a pair of bioleather flats from the shelf, wraps a whip belt around her waist, and checks the karambit Oriol gave her that's now strapped around her upper thigh. She's still pretty amateur with it, at least when compared to Oriol. But it's something she can wear with this dress.

Toshiyo is poking around the innards of the satellite when Starla arrives at the conference room on the fourth floor. The same innards that Starla *just* got put back together today. Starla raps in the doorway.

"What's going on?" Starla signs.

"Connection keeps going out," Toshiyo says aloud, hands occupied with a solar cell. "Can you tighten that bolt?"

Starla leans over the chair beside Toshiyo and tightens one bolt, then another as they reattach the cell. Finally Toshiyo sits back. "Thank you," she signs.

"No problem. Was that it?"

"Yep." Toshiyo hits the switch, then turns back to her login on the conference table to check the connection. She taps a black-lacquered nail on Yes when her screen asks if she wants to run the diagnostic again. "Fiftieth time's the charm."

"Next time let's buy one of these direct from the Alliance rather than steal it," Starla signs.

"We didn't steal it."

"*We* didn't. Absolon probably did."

"You don't learn anything fun buying things direct." Toshiyo grins, her expression turning to surprise as she finally registers Starla's outfit. "Are you going on a date?"

"Girls' night with Simca and Leti?" Starla lifts an eyebrow.

"Right! I'm sorry."

"Do you still want to come?"

Toshiyo's mouth quirks to the side as she glances at the conference table. The status bar shows her diagnostics program is now 0.1 percent done with its routine.

"Gimme a sec to change."

———

There's a line around the block to get into Kuli Xa, but one of the benefits of being friends with fan-favorite wrestler Simca Anahoy and PR shark Letizia Diamante is that one of them always knows somebody. Tonight Leti's chatting up the bouncer, a good-looking woman whose shoulders and biceps could be carved out of stone. Leti's done up in her version of casual, lime-green shirtsleeves rolled back over dark forearms, tailored silver vest and trousers pressed sharp. She spots Starla in the crowd and waves, then says something that makes the bouncer laugh.

The bouncer smiles at Starla and Toshiyo and keys all of them through the forcefield.

"You're flirting our way in now?" Starla signs to Leti with a grin as soon as they're out of sight of the bouncer.

Leti laughs. "No, my firm does the club's marketing," she signs back. "She was just cute." She glances back at Toshiyo expectantly. "Who's your friend?"

"Toshiyo Ravi," Toshiyo spells it and gives her name-sign. She somehow conjured up an outfit Starla's never seen her in before: a short black skirt and slouchy black lace top that covers the bandages on her forearms. "I know Starla from . . ." Toshiyo looks at Starla, not sure how to finish; of course, she doesn't know how much Leti knows.

"She works for Jaantzen," Starla signs. "Is Simca here?"

"She was grabbing us a table."

And sure enough, there's Simca holding down the fort at a reasonably well-lit table where they can all talk, wearing a long-sleeved minidress in a neon yellow that pops against her brown skin, her black braids wound around her crown. She waves and they head over.

Kuli Xa is made up of almost a dozen different rooms throughout an old warehouse, each room themed and decorated, each thrumming with a different beat. Simca's staked out a table in the Vermillion Room, blood-red faux leather and glossy red tables, all gleaming in the light. The walls are painted sunset orange and sketched over with projected lines. Toshiyo's eyes widen as they enter.

"The Vermillion Cliffs," she signs, pointing to the projections. "That's out by where I grew up." Now that she's pointed it out, the projected lines could be a stylized cliff face, the colors slowly shifting as though with the setting of the sun.

Leti looks curious. "You grew up in Ruby Basin?" she signs. "My grandparents lived there when they first immigrated. Indenture."

Toshiyo shrugs. "Everyone's story, out there."

"Looks gorgeous," Leti signs. "Would you go back?"

Toshiyo cracks the ring fingers of both hands.

Starla grabs her arm. "Let's get a drink." She waves across the room to Simca to ask if she needs anything. "I'm buying. Toshiyo?"

They settle in at the booth around Simca, drinks in hand. Simca greets Toshiyo with a hug that Toshiyo awkwardly returns — what would be out of place back at Cobalt Tower seems normal here. The rules of girls' night.

"When you were late I thought you decided to ditch us and go out with that professor," Simca teases.

Starla gives her a mock hurt look. "We were finishing something up."

"What professor?" Leti leans in.

"No one," Starla answers; she feels a pang of guilt at this morning's unreturned message. But she doesn't have time for a distraction, or a clue about how to date someone like him when she's Willem Jaantzen's goddaughter. "No talk about guys tonight. Or girls," she signs to Leti.

Leti winks. "You missed real excitement last time," she signs to Toshiyo. "This shard pusher? Melted in the middle of the dance floor."

Simca's watching Toshiyo like she's ready to dive in and help, but Toshiyo seems to follow — her eyes go wide.

"The Brujería?" She spells it out. "I forgot you guys were there. With the weird shard, like — "

She glances at Starla and presses her hands flat to the table; Starla wonders when was the last time Toshiyo talked to anyone who wasn't crew.

"Jaantzen bought this building in Jet Park that was crawling with a shard operation. They were cooking up the same sort of stuff that pusher took last week."

Simca's eyes go wide. "What? El didn't tell me any of that."

"He didn't want to worry you," Toshiyo signs, relaxing once more. Her mixture of USL and rapid fingerspelling trails inelegantly behind the natural signing of the other three women. "You had a big match that week."

Simca tilts her head at Toshiyo. "He told you that?"

Toshiyo gives a one-shouldered shrug. "Sure, he drove me over. We talked about a lot of stuff."

"Like work stuff?"

"Some?" The tips of her ears are turning red. "No talking about guys, that's the rule?"

Leti laughs, then turns back to Starla. "How big was the operation?"

But Simca's waving her question away. "Hold on. *Hold on.*" She leans in to Toshiyo, eyes mischievous. "What else did you guys talk about?"

"I don't remember — no, wait. I had just finished reading a book he loaned me. I told him I liked it."

Simca's grinning. "My brother loans you *books?*"

Starla smacks Simca in the shoulder. "Drop it," she signs. "And you're not allowed to say a word to El."

Simca laughs. "I'm sorry, Toshiyo — I'm just beyond delighted that my brother acts like a normal human sometimes. Not another word from me."

"Good," Leti signs. She downs her drink and tips the glass at the ring of empties on the table. "You ladies ready to dance?"

Toshiyo's brows draw together in alarm, but Starla smiles at her. "It'll be fine," she says. "No one's watching you, you can just hang out with me."

Toshiyo still looks wary, but not as much as she did when Starla first suggested girls' night to her. Starla doesn't think she's ever seen Toshiyo with a drink in her system, and at least some of her looseness might be coming from that. But the easy banter with Simca and Leti has also helped put her at ease. Maybe tonight's been good for her. It's definitely helping Starla's shoulders unwind from the permanent knot they've been in lately.

They're getting up from the table when a pair of security guards, a man and a woman, come walking over. Leti greets them with a smile but gets scowls in return. Starla triple-blinks her lens on — she normally keeps it off in places like this to avoid the constant snatches of gibberish chatter popping up in her field of vision.

" — going to have to ask you ladies to come with us."

"What's going on?" Simca asks aloud. She glances at Starla, who motions for her to interpret.

"We don't want to make a scene," says the woman guard. "Just come with us."

The man reaches to take Starla's arm and she breaks the grip and steps back. "Don't touch me," she signs. "What is this all about?"

The man glances between her and Simca, who's spoken Starla's words aloud. "You really don't want us to go into this here," he says to Starla. He grabs for her arm again, and Starla blocks, furious.

"I said don't touch me."

He reaches for the electric barb on his hip, and Leti steps between them, hands out, calming, saying something to the guards, though her accent is so thick Starla's lens never transcribes it, even when there's no noise interference.

Simca's positioned herself between everyone as well as she can to interpret for Starla and Leti, but she's also poised for a fight, shoulders loose and muscles taut. Starla's fingertips brush her thigh, the warm metal of the karambit's handle just below the hem of her skirt.

"You want to make a scene?" the woman guard asks. She points at Starla. "We had a report of somebody matching your description selling shard. Come with us, or we're calling the police. Or we can search you here."

The man grabs Starla's arms again, wrenching them behind her like he's going to cuff her.

She stamps on his insole and then whirls, breaking his grip and driving her elbow into his throat, throwing him back against the edge of the table. Her fingers are around the handle of her karambit when Simca is suddenly there beside her, gripping her wrist. Simca shakes her head.

Behind them, Leti is incandescent with rage, going off on the woman guard with a flurry of accompanying rude gestures as the woman shouts back at her.

"We're on the VIP list," Simca shouts over Leti, pointing at her. "Maybe you don't know who this woman is, but the owner of this club definitely does, and she's going to be pissed that you ruined her night."

For the first time, the guard looks like she's reconsidering.

"You wait," Simca orders, then taps Leti on the shoulder. "Why don't you get in touch with the owner," she signs and says aloud.

Leti touches her lime-green cuff and it begins to glow as she enters the number. Before she can send her message, the guard holds up her hands.

"Why don't you ladies finish up here for the night," she says. Behind them, her partner has staggered back to his feet, his hand pressed against his lower back where Starla rammed it into the edge of the table.

Leti looks like she's going to argue, but then she pushes

past the woman, Simca following. Starla motions Toshiyo after Simca, then flips the guards a rude gesture as she takes up the rear.

Out on the street, the evening air is cool, but Starla's blood is boiling. Leti is already on her comm, typing furiously. Simca is yelling something at the guards behind them.

Finally, Toshiyo raises her hands tentatively. "I've never gotten kicked out of a club," she signs after a minute. "Is this what girls' night is always like?"

Starla blinks at her, not quite sure if she's joking until Simca breaks into a grin. Leti throws her head back, laughing.

"It's not all melted drug dealers," Simca signs. She flashes a smile. "Wanna go get kicked out of another bar?"

Starla's having trouble taking this so lightly. "Somebody was messing with us. With me in particular."

"So they're messing with you. Somebody recognized you."

Starla spins to look around them, but after the initial flurry of excitement, everyone in line has gone back to their own interpersonal dramas. She does catch a lingering glance from one woman, a blond with a pointed chin and a sultry pantsuit. The woman puts out her cigarette and turns to go back inside when she sees Starla's attention. Starla frowns after her. She'd been sitting in the Vermillion Room when they came in, hadn't she?

Toshiyo is tapping her elbow, and Starla tears her attention away from the woman.

"Did you want to go somewhere else?"

Toshiyo may be looser after one drink, but Starla's wound tighter than ever after the accusation and the fight in the Kuli Xa. This is the second time in less than a week that she's been targeted outside of normal work activities — this may not have been an attempt on her life, but the instant the guard laid hands on her, she'd fought to kill. If Simca hadn't been there she might have done some real damage to the man.

Maybe it was just a prank. But her adrenaline is through the roof nonetheless.

She tries to shake it off, makes a note to talk to Oriol about it the next time they train. Maybe his suggestion to meditate isn't a bad idea after all.

The others are all watching her, the night still poised on the knife's edge between good time and disaster. Starla's not going to be the one who ruins it.

"Where were you thinking of going?" Starla asks. She's only half paying attention to the place Leti's suggesting as she reaches into her purse for her lipstick — she doesn't actually care where they go so long as they make the drinks strong. She stiffens when her fingers brush against an unfamiliar shape; Leti's hands go still in concern.

With her heart thudding in her chest, Starla pulls open the mouth of her purse. Inside there's a stack of shard tabs, neatly packaged as though for sale. She angles the purse so Simca can see.

Simca's eyes widen. "If they had searched you, they would have found that."

Leti swears, sharp, angry lines. "This is more than a prank. They would have arrested you if they found that. Some asshole is trying to frame you."

That blond in the jumpsuit? Starla has no reason to think it's true, but her gut is screaming to find her, grab her, make her talk. Starla whirls to head back to the Kuli Xa, but Toshiyo catches her arm.

"If somebody planted that on you, I can find out who."

"How?" Leti asks, but Starla cuts in.

"Let's go," she signs to Toshiyo. "You two wanna come back to the tower and drink wine while we hack into Kuli Xa security footage?"

Leti's lips quirk to the side. "Sounds like a breach of client confidentiality, actually."

"What if it's in service to a new client?" Starla signs. "I'm supposed to ask you. You have some time tomorrow to meet with Jaantzen?"

A slow smile spreads over Leti's face.

"I've been waiting for you to ask me that for years," she signs. "Wine and surveillance footage it is."

11

————

CHO

Fifteen years ago, Timo Cho had a finger on the pulse of the crime organizations in Bulari: Blackheart, Willem Jaantzen, Sylla Mar, the Setis, the Demosgas, the Sendera Dathúil, all of them. He could read the bodies and the shootings and even the traffic patterns like tea leaves to get a sense of how power was shifting among them.

Back then, he might have been able to guess what it meant that Jaantzen's right-hand man was visiting the Alliance embassy the same week that Jaantzen's mortal enemy moved back into town. These days, Cho doesn't have all the pieces of the puzzle.

And anyway, it's none of his damn business.

In the old days, when Cho was chasing a lead he might stop by any number of bars on the way home, see if anyone was floating in their drink enough to share some intel in exchange for another round.

Tonight, he doesn't even know if the informants he used to cultivate still hang out at the bars he's walking past. Or if they're even still alive. He thinks about stopping anyway, the buzz of potential about this case a constant distortion around the edges of his mind, begging for his attention. Cho is champing at the bit to fall into old patterns.

But even if he did come up with sufficient cause to get Juric into an interrogation room to finish their interview, it'd only be ten minutes before Major Ngara came rushing in with orders to set him free.

Just another untouchable.

Cho forces himself to keep walking, past his old information wells, down the night-lit streets of the government district, into the train station to head home. It's almost midnight, and he's exhausted from the late night at the office.

Today he and Samson compiled two days of interviews into a report that nobody but them will ever read. A bunch of accounts from victims who don't know a damned thing. A woman sitting on the embassy steps waiting for her boyfriend to finish up his desk job inside. An old man having a smoke in his usual rest spot halfway between his doctor's office and apartment. A little girl whose mother had tragically stopped to take a call a few steps closer to where the bomb went off.

Even if any of the victims had known anything, the chances of getting a useful statement would have been next to nothing. Almost twenty-five years in the BPD and the one constant Cho can count on is that no one ever sees a thing in this town. Marching band could have a shoot-out in the street. A black hole could open up in the plaza. An entire apartment building could sprout wings and fly off, and he'd still get those carefully uninterested expressions, that polite Bularian one-shouldered shrug.

He saw those a lot when he was investigating the local

crime organizations. Local crew bombs a rival warehouse and nobody notices a thing. Blackheart waltzes back into the Fingers, and nobody's heard about it. Cho hadn't believed that one at first, even though he knows Hallelujah Oni to tell only truth. But he's verified it from other sources now.

Thala Coeur is back.

Cho can't keep from wondering who else in the department knows. If anyone's even bothering to ask about it, or if they've all been paid off not to.

That last thought may be cynical, but it's not without a root of truth.

Coeur'd been ousted after three years of the bloodiest fighting this city has ever seen, and when the whole thing was done, the BPD was ordered to put the past to bed. All his open cases suddenly — infuriatingly — shut, Cho had started following the money, trying to figure out what forces were moving behind the scenes. He'd figured it was safe enough to ask police-work questions now that Coeur was out of power.

It wasn't.

Manu Juric's put a lot of bodies in the morgue. Put more — like Cho — in the hospital. Maybe not lately, and maybe he and his boss are untouchable now, but a slow thought has been forming since Cho first saw that name on the list of victims: That name is a gift, and the question is how he's going to use it. For the first time in years he's on the scent of something truly interesting. Thala Coeur is back, and she has motivation to bomb the Alliance embassy — and to order a hit on Juric. And since the Alliance is involved, evidence is less likely to disappear, interviews are less likely to be interrupted, and Cho might actually be able to force some traction on a case. He might finally be able to serve some justice. Even to a guy like Juric.

He should let it go, but —

No. He should let it go.

"Beautiful night."

Cho turns, startled; he's been watching a pair of boys too young to be out this late dare each other to throw the emergency switch at the edge of the platform, didn't notice the woman walk up to him.

She's tall, wrapped in a dark coat with a hat pulled low over loose brown curls that veil her heart-shaped face. A spray of freckles brushes her cheeks. She's not looking at him, she's fiddling with her cuff, maybe to check the train's arrival time. He'd think she's ignoring him completely but for the way she shifts her weight, nervous.

Cho frowns at her. Goes back to watching the boys.

"It's the kind of night that makes you think about freedom," she says. She clears her throat and continues stronger; there's no one else around she could be talking to. "Some people get it, right? They can go wherever they want and nobody can touch them. But plenty of others don't have a choice. Maybe they're too scared to leave home, maybe they're dead. And whoever killed them, they get to keep walking the streets. You ever wonder why?"

She cranes her neck to peer down the tracks, watching for the train. "I used to spend a lot of time wondering, but it's not a mystery, is it? Some people have power, some people don't."

"Who are you?"

She turns finally to him. Her hazel eyes have that sharp edge of desperation, he sees it sometimes in the interrogation room. It's the face of someone who's talking to him because she doesn't have anything else to lose. "I saw you at the hospital," she says, low and fast. "Talking to Manu Juric."

That place at the back of Cho's neck which has been tingling all night shivers bright and sharp. "What were you doing there?"

"I was — " A shadow passes over her face. "I was going to do something stupid. I've talked to the police, and no one's done anything. I was desperate. Then I saw you and I thought, hey. Maybe the police care after all."

"Care about what?"

A faint line sketches itself between her brows at his question. "That he killed Naali?"

Cho blinks at her. "Naali *Hinoja?*" The woman is — was? — Coeur's lieutenant, running Coeur's operations here on New Sarjun while Coeur herself was in exile. Coeur being back in Bulari isn't strong enough motivation to link her to a hit on Juric. But if he killed her lieutenant, that's a completely different story.

The woman seems to mistake his surprise for disdain; a spark of anger lights up her eyes. "He killed her and Chase. I know who she was and what she did, but I loved her. I know none of you care that she's gone, but I can't believe you're just going to let a murderer walk free. You're all a disgrace." She whirls and stalks away, farther down the platform. A familiar vibration has begun to rumble through the station; the train is nearly here.

"Wait," Cho says, following after. He lowers his voice. "What do you want from me?"

She glares, equal parts fury and grief in her eyes. "Justice. He killed someone I loved and there's nothing I can do about it. And nothing you *will* do about it."

"What do you know?"

Light washes over the platform, the blinding glare of the

train's headlights followed by the stop-motion stutter of light bars along the side of each car flashing past.

The woman gnaws at her lip, deciding.

"What do you know?" Urgency sharpens Cho's tone; it's surely on his face as the train slows to a stop. The doors hiss open.

Her shoulders straighten suddenly and she leans close. "There was a witness," she whispers. She names a bar, her breath hot on his ear. "Be there in ten minutes. She won't wait."

She steps away; he catches her arm.

"What's your name?"

She pulls her arm free and for a moment he thinks she won't tell him. But, "Victoria," and she steps onto the train.

That bar is five blocks from here. She's turned in the doorway, watching him with accusing eyes, and Cho's frozen for a heartbeat between following her and chasing this lead that could give him something concrete to pin on Manu Juric.

The witness won't wait.

Cho curses and jogs for the stairs that lead out of the train station.

The bar is nothing special: shadowy booths, clear exits, the music a little too high and lights a little too low. He'd bet almost anything this is someplace the witness has been before. Not somewhere she spends a lot of time — not somewhere she's known. But somewhere she feels safe enough.

He grabs a seat at the bar and orders a cider, waiting. He didn't quite beat the clock, despite breaking into a run for the first time in years, and he can only hope the witness didn't disappear the minute the clock struck midnight.

There are two lone women in the bar: a leftover office worker still wearing her day-job suit, and a pale-skinned girl with a shaved head who's probably not old enough for the neon cocktail she's drinking way too fast. The older woman's drinking like a pro. The younger's drinking for courage. And at her glance, he knows he has her pegged right.

Cho pays for his cider and heads to one of the shadowy booths with a clear view of the exits, and after what looks like a deep breath for courage, the girl with the shaved head detaches herself from the bar and joins him. There's intensity and nerves in her body language, but no violence. She's just here to talk.

The girl doesn't hesitate once she makes her decision to join him, but she doesn't quite settle into her seat either. "You're the detective?" She's eying him like he might bite.

"Detective Timo Cho." Cho shows her his badge, and she relaxes just a touch. "I'm grateful for anything you're able to tell me." He figures she's not the type who wants to spend any more time here than she has to, so he gets right to the point. She gives him a curt nod.

"I know where they buried Naali and Chase," she says. "I seen it."

"Good, that's good," Cho says. He's trying to judge: Is she here for money? Out of fear? Out of a sense of justice or revenge, like the woman on the train platform? He hopes it's just money. It's by far the simplest, just the back and forth to come up with a price, and none of this jostling around with emotions trying to figure out what's got an informant spooked or who they're hoping you'll take down.

"Tell me what you saw."

It takes her a few false starts, but once she finally launches into the story, she hits her stride, her Fingers accent strong. They all start the same: situating in place and time, establishing a perfectly good reason to be loitering in an area and seeing things they shouldn't. He's had past partners — like Arman Falk — who try to rush past this part like it's not important, or who assume that all informants are lying about why they were there anyway so it doesn't matter what this one tells them. But Cho doesn't believe that. There's a lot to learn in how an informant sets up a story.

And in this case, the girl is giving him too many details about her friend whose apartment looks out on a little pedestrian plaza. "You know that korris place near Navarro's Grocery, the Oasis? He's got this table, my friend does, it's set up by the window, and sometimes you know, after dinner you sit and have a beer or whatever?"

She's trying too hard to set the scene — but whether she's nervous or lying Cho can't make out.

"So I'm sitting there, he's going to grab another beer, right? And I see Naali and that other guy walk in, the blond guy she runs with. Everybody knows her," she says with a nervous laugh. "I mean everybody who knows things." An indirect admission that she probably runs with a local crew. Could be valuable later.

"I think maybe she likes korris, but this isn't really her neighborhood, right? But then I seen *him* walk in." Now she twitches nervously, sweeps her gaze around the bar. The name's barely a whisper: "Juric."

"Alone?"

She blinks, scratching a sudden itch on her neck. "I knew you wouldn't believe me, so I got proof." She doesn't offer it in the moment, so Cho files it away to ask her about later.

"Then what did you see?"

"Nothing, not at first. But I heard gunshots, we had the window open, it was hot? And a woman screamed. Naali, I guess."

Gunshots and screams get reported in a neighborhood like that, and if it was a hot day just after dinnertime, plenty of folks would have noticed the same things this girl did. At least someone would have called it in, which means Cho should be able to find a record even if the police didn't head out to investigate. Assuming the girl's not lying.

"Some other guys showed up, and a few minutes later he left — "

"Juric?"

A sharp nod and sideways look; she doesn't like saying the name, or she's leaving him to fill in the gaps so she won't have to come up with so many lies. "He left, and then the guys left with a couple of big packages that could have been bodies." She clears her throat. "And so I followed them."

"The guys with the bodies," Cho confirms. "Why?"

She shrugs. "Because it was fucking huge, man," she says. "And I figured sometimes it pays to know something."

And she sits back at that. They're at the bargaining part of the evening.

"What do you want?" Cho asks.

"Twenty thousand."

Cho laughs; she scowls.

"Okay, kid. Here's how this is going to go. I'm not made of money, but you're right. If you deliver, this is valuable information. You have evidence Juric was there?"

She nods, a hand slipping unconsciously into her jacket pocket.

"Great. Give me that and tell me where the bodies are buried. I'll give you five hundred marks — "

"No way, man."

" — five hundred marks tonight, and if we find those bodies where you said they'd be, you come by the station tomorrow evening and we'll give you some more. Probably not twenty thousand more, but you'll get paid."

"One thousand tonight."

"Five hundred is literally all I have in my bank account at the moment, kid."

He keeps an easy smile, like, *You're getting a great deal*, and she glares at him, thinking. But he can tell she's not thinking that hard. She wants him to have this information, probably because somebody else — the woman on the train platform — is already paying her to talk to him. She's just getting greedy.

The girl finally removes her hand from her pocket and slides a data stick across the table to him. "Code is five two eight seven one."

Cho's comm detects it, the code gives him access. There's a single video file on it, and Cho plays it with the volume muted, the screen angled so only he can see it while the girl watches his face.

It's a surveillance camera, time-stamped two weeks ago. Three men are walking into the restaurant. The big guy in the back is Willem Jaantzen, Cho would know him anywhere, even in grainy surveillance footage. The older man beside him Cho doesn't know, but the lean man ranging in front of them with his left hand on his pistol is Juric. Cho speeds the footage. Jaantzen and Juric leave together a few minutes later, with no bodies in sight. But — there we go — another angle off the alley shows a trio of guys in janitor uniforms rolling out big garbage bins.

Not quite the packages the girl said in her story. And that blink when he asked if Juric was alone; she hadn't actually answered him, had she? She hasn't seen this footage, and Cho doesn't believe for a minute the girl actually saw this go down, unless she was too deep into her drug of choice to remember seeing Willem Fucking Jaantzen walk into the korris restaurant as well.

But if the footage is real and she legitimately knows where the bodies are, he can worry about the reliability of his "eyewitness" later.

"You said you saw them bury the bodies," he says. "Where?"

"Pull up your map," she says, and he sets the comm in front of her with the map open. She zooms in on a spot. Tags the location.

"There's a couple of cargo containers at the turnoff, all rusted out like a skeleton. The road dead-ends at some old mine in a canyon."

Cho swipes five hundred marks from his comm to hers, hoping like hell this will prove to be worth it. "Come see me at the station tomorrow night for the rest," he says, knowing there's a fifty-fifty chance she'll never cross that threshold, and she skulks off without another word. The cost is painful, but if her information is good, he's got a lead on a man everyone knows murdered and robbed his way to the top.

He wants to call Samson, tell her to meet him at the office right now, but he forces himself back to the train station. He hasn't been riding this high on a case in a decade, and he needs to take it slow. Look at the footage. Make sure there are actually bodies before anyone too high up gets wind.

Just because no one's investigating the murder of Naali Hinoja doesn't mean no one knows about it — it could just be kept under wraps. But if he can surface her body and this tape as part of an Alliance investigation?

Cho's smiling despite himself.

That's pure gold, right there.

That could lead to real justice.

12

JAANTZEN

Through the sandstone-and-glass lobby, past potted palms and tan couches and the elderly concierge who gives him that same friendly wave as always, up to the thirtieth floor. Jaantzen knocks on the door, waits. It's long enough that he almost knocks again before it finally opens.

Manu's wearing a black tank top and loose trousers, a stark white bandage wrapped around his right upper arm. He braces himself against the doorway.

"Hey," he says, holding out a hand; Jaantzen takes it carefully. "Thanks for coming."

"I'm sorry I didn't come see you at the hospital."

Manu just smiles. "Best you didn't, the place was crawling with cops. Come in."

Manu shuts the door behind them with a wince, sends home the bolts, then leads Jaantzen down the short hall to the living area. His apartment is airy, tall ceilings making the space feel bigger than it is. The hallway opens up to a couch and loveseat, both looking out the picture windows to the desert. The kitchen to the left is well equipped, though Jaantzen knows it doesn't get much use, and a dining table that could seat eight occupies the space to the right. It's currently shoved out of the way, dining chairs lined haphazardly against the walls to clear floor space. A door beyond the couches opens to a balcony set with a few brown-leafed plants, a table, and more chairs.

Jaantzen doesn't spend much time at Manu's apartment — his lieutenant's always at Cobalt Tower — but he's been here enough over the years to know it has two basic states. Spotless and barely lived-in when Manu's living here alone, and Oriol-strewn, like it is today: a baggy gray sweatshirt draped over the back of a chair, crutches propped in the corner, slippers left haphazardly in the middle of the hallway. Manu kicks the slippers out of the way with a wince of pain. Jaantzen glances into the bedroom off the hallway; it's a hurricane of clothes and rumpled bedding.

"I picked up some black bean ginger soup from Jade's," Jaantzen says. "I didn't expect you were doing much cooking."

"I'm not doing much eating, either," Manu says. He sinks slowly back onto the couch, where he's apparently been camping out. It's piled with pillows and blankets, his tablet within easy reach.

"You hungry now?" Jaantzen asks.

"Nah, man."

Jaantzen puts the soup containers into the refrigerator, then sits across from Manu on the loveseat.

"How are you feeling?"

"Been better. Give me a couple of days; it's just bruises."

Jaantzen smiles ruefully. "I'd give you all the time in the world if you'd just take it. How's your arm?"

"Tosh's hell-beast doesn't seem to have given me any alien plague yet," Manu says. "Are you checking in on her?"

"I am. She seems fine — she went out and got groceries for it yesterday."

Manu's eyebrows shoot high. "Like *out* out?"

"Out. She's determined it prefers radishes. And fish, which is going to be expensive." Jaantzen sighs. "And it likes music, particularly New Manilan ballads."

"That's nice. But do we know what it is yet?"

"No. Starla's started talking about going up to Redrock to find out more about the wrecked spacecraft."

Manu frowns. "I don't like that."

"I don't, either." It's one thing to have Starla taking risks here in Bulari where he can be there the instant something happens. But on the other side of the Jupari Desert? His stomach clenches at the thought. At the fear that it might well become necessary.

"We're moving it today," he says.

"Where to?"

"A tip from Gia — a friend of hers was having trouble selling property in the Maraka Valley. Apparently it's hard to get to and riddled with bunkers and booby traps."

Manu shakes his head. "And it's in the Maraka Valley. You ever met Maraka Valley people?"

"They keep to themselves. We'll fit right in."

"Just don't talk to the locals is all I'm saying. I don't know how Gia can stand it out there."

"She grew up in the country."

"Still."

Jaantzen hasn't had much reason to leave the city limits of Bulari — the city's massively sprawling, and if you're looking to get anywhere else civilized, you take a capsule train or hopper. No need to go wandering out in the desert in a private vehicle unless you're burying bodies or caching illegal goods.

Or hiding an alien creature for further study.

"I'll rest easier not having it under my roof," he says. "And I'll feel better about our next moves with the Alliance."

Manu nods slowly. "Deputy Chief ó Lauris didn't know anything about the attack, and he didn't know anything about Coeur. I got the impression he's pretty unhappy about Alliance special ops playing in his backyard without cluing him in. I think if we can convince him it's in the best interests of peace, he'll help us make a deal."

"Do you think he has the authority to rein in special ops?"

"Not the authority, but he has the influence. And the ear of the Alliance ambassador — she's been working her ass off to get this treaty through, and we have the ability to completely derail it. They'll tread carefully."

"Good." Jaantzen takes a deep breath. "Because we have another problem." He briefly recaps the events of the night before — Leone's offer, his refusal, his conversation with Phaera — and Manu lets out a low whistle.

"I have a meeting with Aiax and Lhasa today," Jaantzen says. "And with Starla's friend Leti tonight. Phaera's reaching out to her own contacts and looking for leverage. We'll need anything we can find."

"I'll see what I can dig up. What else can I do?"

"Just make some calls and get some rest," Jaantzen says. "I'll fill you in when I hear — "

An incoming call to Jaantzen's comm cuts him off, and at the name he frowns: Mizal Seti. Phaera wasn't going to talk to him until this afternoon, which means this conversation probably isn't a chat about how the Jet Park business district is shaping up.

Jaantzen sets the comm on Manu's coffee table, answers it warily. "Mizal. It's good to hear from you."

Manu leans back against the couch, staring up at the ceiling, hands clasped loosely in his lap.

"I want to say I'm shocked, Jaantzen," Mizal says. "But I don't even know where to start."

Manu catches Jaantzen's eye a second before turning his attention back to the ceiling. Jaantzen hadn't expected Mizal to simply roll over on Coeur reinstatement; it was a calculated risk that their partnership might devolve. Jaantzen isn't worried. Between his business arguments and Phaera's silver tongue, Mizal can be convinced to accept her.

"I assure you I thought this through," Jaantzen says. "Why don't we meet for dinner to talk more. This has the potential to be very beneficial to us both."

"Shard manufacturing?" Mizal asks, a note of derision in his voice. "I didn't think you were the sort."

Manu rolls his head to frown down at the comm. Jaantzen leans forward, elbows on knees, steepling his fingers over his lips.

"Shard manufacturing," Jaantzen says.

"In Jet Park? I thought you were shutting down the operation in that building you bought, but instead you were just clearing out the competition, then striking a deal with Thala Coeur." He spits out the name with fury. "I thought you were a man worth doing business with. I've defended you to people, I've said, 'Jaantzen? You don't know him like I do.' And you take advantage of my trust to cook shard in the very neighborhood I thought we were cleaning up together?" Mizal takes a breath, seething. "With the woman who *murdered my father?*"

"I'm happy to explain my decision about Coeur to you,"

Jaantzen says evenly. "But I suggest you explain why you're accusing me of manufacturing shard."

"It's all over the feeds, Jaantzen."

Manu levers himself upright, then reaches for his tablet with a wince, opens a search. Jaantzen can tell by the darkening expression on his lieutenant's face that what he sees isn't good.

"You were with me when we found the shard manufacturers in that building," Jaantzen says. "You saw me shut them down."

"I saw you murder the managers," Mizal says. "But shut it down? Shit, Jaantzen, I'm starting to wonder if you're no better than *her*."

"I suggest you rethink what you just said to me," Jaantzen says, voice low. Silence on the other end of the line; maybe Mizal's starting to realize his misstep. "Take some time, Mizal. Consider how long we've known each other. And consider if I'm a man you want as an enemy."

He cuts the line, realization settling in his gut like a cool, smooth stone. Leone didn't just go to Mizal privately to seed rumors and try to break up their business partnership. She aimed even lower than he expected.

Jaantzen lifts his chin to Manu. "Tell me."

Manu swipes the feed from the tablet onto the coffee table, and a news story begins to paint the lurid details: Local businessman Willem Jaantzen, long rumored to have a secretive and shady past, is now linked to shard manufacturing in Jet Park. And — in a shocking twist — he also owns the downtown business tower that was attacked two nights ago. Coincidence? Or another crooked link in the ongoing underworld drug war that's been wracking our city with violence? We'll continue to investigate.

"Leone moves fast," says Manu.

"She does." Jaantzen stands. "I need to start making calls."

"How's this going to affect your meeting with the Demosgas?"

"I'm sure it won't be a problem," Jaantzen says. "Get me leverage on Leone."

"I'll see what I can find." Manu swipes away the footage. "Give me a sec to get dressed, I'll come with you."

"You should rest."

Manu laughs bitterly. "When all this is done I'll go on vacation, I promise. Until then, I'm not lying around here while you need me." He begins to brace himself against the soft couch cushions, but Jaantzen reaches for Manu's good left arm to help haul his lean frame to his feet. Manu wavers, fingers clawed into Jaantzen's forearm for support; Jaantzen clasps Manu's shoulder until he's steady.

"When all this is done I'm sending you and Oriol to some Indiran beach if he has to drag you kicking and screaming," Jaantzen says. And at that, finally, the glint on Manu's hand that's been catching his eye for the past ten minutes clicks into place.

Jaantzen shifts so he can see Manu's left hand, still gripping Jaantzen's own forearm. There's a ring on his lieutenant's scarred fourth finger. Jaantzen blinks at it in surprise. Manu pats his arm and lets go, a smile tugging at the corner of his mouth.

"I'm getting sentimental in my old age," Manu says over his shoulder in explanation as he limps towards the bedroom.

"Officially sentimental?" Jaantzen calls after him.

"Working on the logistics. We'll let you know."

Manu's just past the kitchen when his own comm

chimes with an incoming call. Manu sighs and slumps against the counter, swiping open the connection there.

"Hey, Lo."

"Hey." Cobalt Tower's new Chief Operation Director's voice cuts through the apartment. "I'm sorry to bother you, but, ah, have you seen the news?"

"Just did."

"Okay, well. I'm starting to get calls from some of our tenants. I've been telling them it's all baseless allegations, and it'll be cleared up soon." A brief pause. "I'm not lying, am I?"

"You're not, def. It's all bullshit. Is anyone trying to rattle you?"

"RevanCo is being a pain. I reminded them they still have eighteen months on their lease, and that I can have our lawyer get in touch if they need somebody to explain the breach-of-contract penalty."

"Thanks, Lo. I'll be right in."

"You will not. I've got things under control, and you should be — "

"I'm fine. See you soon." He cuts the connection with a curse, then takes a deep breath and pushes himself back to his feet. "She's an amazing enforcer and I don't think she even knows how to load a gun," he says to Jaantzen with a wry smile. "Give me two minutes."

13

PHAERA

Phaera's footsteps echo sharply against the marble. She's dressed in a suit today, not one of the airy dresses she would normally wear to lunch with Leone, and whether it's the steel daggers of her heels or the look on her face, people in the courthouse hallways are getting out of her way.

Geum-ja Leone has been a mentor since they met at a fundraiser and Leone decided Phaera *simply must* start attending her own dinner parties. It had been an amazing personal success at the time. Securing an invitation to the fundraiser had been a stretch goal for Phaera — landing an invitation to Leone's exclusive gatherings? Beyond her wildest dreams.

And Phaera'd said yes, of course, though her heart raced for days before the first one. That feeling's an old friend by now. Every yes of her career has been said firmly and forcefully against a wall of terror, every step forward taken against that invisible hand dragging her back: Who do you think you are?

Phaera's secured meetings with names that make her

parents' jaws drop when she tells them and still make her own stomach flip with anxiety. She's charmed her way into parties where a single earring on any other guest equals the sum of her entire wardrobe. She's skipped meals to pay for her hair and nails to be up to snuff. She's learned to cultivate a wardrobe of timeless elegance rather than wasting her savings on the latest fashions. She's learned how to turn a snobbish comment about a cheap accent necklace into a charming conversation starter when she says it's a gift from her father.

And it's worked, each connection leading to the next, from curious sidelong *Who is she?* looks to gushing "You simply must meet!" introductions.

Geum-ja Leone has opened doors to Phaera — like so many of Phaera's connections before, and so many after. Yet somehow Leone has gotten the impression that the door she opened was Phaera's big break, rather than just another step on a long, hard-fought path.

Leone is powerful, and her usefulness hasn't dried up. She's been a constant font of new introductions and referrals; at least a dozen of the most recent new patrons of the Devil's Table are there because of Leone.

Phaera does owe her — but no more than she owes anyone else.

And no more than she owes herself for stepping up day after goddamned day.

Normally their catch-up lunches are planned weeks in advance to slot into both women's busy schedules. Normally they meet in Leone's favorite cafe near the courthouse, quaint and buzzy with ludicrously expensive food made by a famous chef who wastes his energy on presentation over taste. Today, though, Leone invited Phaera to her office at the last minute.

Invited her? Summoned her, really. And though Phaera's right on time, Leone makes her wait twenty minutes before calling her in.

Phaera wonders if she's supposed to feel intimidated.

The thing is, though, she's lived in a state of intimidation every day since she got fed up with waiting tables and decided that this low-class tramp was not only going to open her own casino, she was going to create the most exclusive experience in the entire city. And she was going to do it so well people wouldn't even remember where she came from.

You have to do a lot more than intimidate Phaera D if you want her to back down.

Phaera makes herself at home in the waiting room outside Leone's office and kills time sorting through the ever-growing pile of incoming messages, hiding any sign of frustration. The waiting room is grand, of course. The whole courthouse is a throwback to Indiran architecture and pompous statehood. The style is meant to make it seem important, but there's a whiff of *reaching* to it. Like the earliest settlers of New Sarjun were pulling a dress off the rack a few tiers above their price range in an effort to make the more established countries of the Durga System take them more seriously.

Good on them, Phaera thinks.

Finally the fresh-faced young secretary — is he even old enough to have graduated third levels? — calls Phaera in to Leone's office.

Phaera presses Record on her cuff, straightens her shoulders, and walks into the lion's den.

Geum-ja Leone stands to greet her with a hug and air kisses on both cheeks, a cloud of face powder and perfume. Phaera smiles warmly at her, studying the fine lines and deep crevasses of the old woman's face. She looks like everyone's grandmother, but Phaera has no illusions about how dangerous she can be.

Leone's imposing desk commands the room, but she waves Phaera into one of the plush, overstuffed chairs near the picture window before sitting in the other. Two girlfriends having a chat.

"It's wonderful to see the inside of your office," says Phaera. "Thank you for inviting me here."

"You were a darling to say yes on such short notice." Leone pours pale amber liquid from an antique teapot into the waiting pair of porcelain cups. She hands one to Phaera, who breathes in the steam appreciatively. There's a tray of cookies on the table, as well; both women ignore them.

"Phaera, sweetheart." Leone draws the pet name out. "I'm worried about you."

Thank god she's cutting to the chase, Phaera isn't in the mood for small talk. She takes a sip of tea: orange blossom and Indiran vanilla. "No need to worry about me, I've never been better. Business is wonderful, even after all of that mess with Acheta."

"I'm not talking about business." She gives Phaera a meaningful look. "Forgive me for meddling. I know you and Willem have been friendly, and he can be very charming. But I'm starting to hear rumors. Phaera, frankly, I thought you had more sense than to get involved with someone like him."

Phaera can't keep her surprised laughter in check. "I've heard that line before, Geum-ja. And as my mother can tell you, it's never been particularly effective. I know the two of you have had a disagreement recently, but Jaantzen . . ." She reaches for the right words. "He could be a valuable ally to you. I hope you can come to an understanding."

She gives Leone a *Here's some friendly advice* smile.

With any luck, Leone will be happy with the warning shot across Jaantzen's bow today and Phaera can talk sense into her. The allegations of shard manufacturing will hurt Jaantzen in the short term, but they won't stick for long. Phaera's hoping Leone can still be convinced to step down from her vendetta with her pride intact.

And failing that? Hopefully she can get Leone's guard down enough to get an incriminating sound bite.

"He told me about meeting with you and Tomás Vahid last night," Phaera says. "You have some experience backing political contenders? Jaantzen mentioned something about the prime minister's race. That was incredible work."

And also a highly illegal and unethical breach of her position if Leone *had* thrown her support behind a specific candidate. Phaera's hoping for proud acknowledgement of her role for the recording, but Leone only gives her a secret smile.

"I enjoy making connections between talented people," Leone says. Her mouth turns prim and disapproving. "But Jaantzen, well. I just don't think you know him like I do. I was aware of the shard, of course, but I thought he'd put all those dealings behind him. It's quite the stain on my reputation that I've invited someone to my parties who turned out to be so . . . *common*."

Phaera doesn't have a quick response that's not bitchy, so she just puts on her most genuine *I'm sorry you had a bad day* bartender face and waits.

"He told me he'd gotten out of that business, but apparently he's not a man of his word." Leone shakes her head sadly. "He's not good for you."

Phaera sets her teacup down and gives Leone a steady look. "With all due respect, ma'am, you are not my mother and it's been a long time since I was seventeen."

"I may not be your mother, but I can sympathize with her." Something in Leone's eyes changes, a malicious gleam kindling deep. "I'm sure it will be a shock to her to find out about your relationship with him, especially after the news that's come out today. And doesn't she have a weak heart?" Leone leans forward, solicitous. "How is she doing?"

Phaera's mouth goes dry; Leone's expression is concerned, but there's the play of a smile in her eyes. "She's doing very well, thank you for asking," Phaera says carefully, trying to hide her shock. "She'll be tickled to learn that the chief justice of the Supreme Court was asking after her health." She takes a sip of tea to wet her tongue.

"That's good to hear, dear," Leone says. She waves a hand and they're back to being girlfriends, like Leone hadn't just implicitly threatened Phaera's mother. And she hadn't — not verbally. Phaera plays that clip back to someone, they won't see the threat in Leone's body language, they'll just hear an old woman acting concerned.

"Now," Leone says. "I understand how charming a man like Willem can be — I've made bad decisions about men myself." Her girlish laugh grates down Phaera's spine. "I would just hate to see you get hurt."

"I've been around the block a few times," Phaera says. "I know how not to let myself get hurt."

"I'm not just talking about your feelings." An edge of frustration seeps into Leone's voice. Phaera certainly is making her work to get her warning across. "I'm worried about you getting mixed up with a man in his line of business. It's violent business, darling, and it breeds violent people. The stories I've heard about how he treated his poor ex-wife — "

"Geum-ja," Phaera snaps, because she'll be damned if

she's going to sit here and let Leone pour poison about Jaantzen being abusive into her ear. "That's enough."

Leone sits back as though slapped, though Phaera's not sure what else she expected. If she thought Phaera was the sort of woman who lets someone else talk shit about her man in front of her, she hasn't been paying much attention to her 'protégé.'

"Maybe the rumors about him are just that," Leone says, and her patronizing hands-out *Calm down* gesture is having the exact opposite effect on Phaera. "But once word gets out that you're being seen with a drug dealer, I can't imagine the effect it will have on your businesses."

That's something Phaera's been thinking about all day, of course. Not that she believes any of the allegations, but ever since she spoke with Jaantzen last night she's been ready for the moment Leone started dragging his name through the mud.

Of course, says the tiniest practical voice in the back of her head, what if he can't clear his name? And what if there's something worse — something true — that comes out later?

Phaera pushes the thought aside. She's not some seventeen-year-old bringing home a bad boy to test her mother's patience. She's a grown-ass woman who has spent the better part of two years considering making a play on Willem Jaantzen. She'd calculated the risks and rewards professionally and personally before her heart finally lost patience and snatched up the reins. She's made the right decision. And Geum-ja Leone is not going to sit here and tell her she's a fool.

"I'd just hate to see you throw away everything you worked so hard for," Leone says. "It's so easy to let little things slip. Permits, licenses — it's just so easy to miss a payment. Especially when you're distracted with someone like him." There's that malicious fire in Leone's eyes again. This isn't advice, it's a threat.

Phaera fights to keep the fury off her face, and by Leone's smug smile she can tell she's failing. Losing the Lorelei and the Devil's Table is Phaera's most common nightmare, but it's not her worst. She'd rather see everything she built burn to the ground than mortgage her soul to someone like Geum-ja Leone to keep it.

"I appreciate the concern," Phaera says sharply. "And I'm so sorry to cut this short, you know I'd love to stay and chat. But things are still rough at the Lorelei at the moment. They need me there."

Leone stands, all smiles, arms out for a hug. "I understand," she says as they exchange kisses. She steps back but doesn't quite let go, her fingers still clawed lightly around Phaera's shoulders, eyes searching Phaera's face. "Take care of yourself," Leone says, patting Phaera's arm. She pulls open the door.

The fresh-faced secretary is on his feet as soon as the door opens. "Madame Justice?" he says. "About your afternoon . . ." His glance at Phaera says he doesn't want to discuss it in front of her.

"Don't just stand there." Leone beckons him in. "Let's do talk again soon," she calls after Phaera.

"I'm sure we will."

Phaera takes a moment in the waiting room to compose herself before facing the gauntlet of the courthouse with this anger stamped all over her face. She knows she didn't walk out of that conversation with anything usable, just the knowledge that Geum-ja Leone isn't going to be dissuaded from her battle with Jaantzen.

And that by not denouncing him and groveling, Phaera has made herself, her family, and her businesses into targets.

She ignores the fear — she's dealt with bullies like Leone before — and is about to walk through the door when she realizes the secretary has left his desk open to Leone's schedule. Before she can overthink it, she snaps a still with her cuff and pushes out into the hallway with her heart thundering in her chest.

14

JAANTZEN

"It's rolling over for the Alliance is what it is." Aiax Demosga's voice booms through the speakers of Jaantzen's conference table. His hologram hovers to Jaantzen's right; his sister's hovers to the left. Lhasa Demosga sighs pointedly, but Aiax ignores her.

"And it's killing innovation. This trade agreement will make shipping food from Indira even cheaper than producing it here, so who's going to take a run at the food business? The margins are tight enough already without having to drive prices down to compete with Alliance companies."

"We know, Aiax." Lhasa gives Jaantzen a long-suffering look.

That's been the primary argument against the trade agreement from the start, that it makes it more profitable for Alliance companies to ship food to New Sarjun while reducing the ability of New Sarjunian producers to compete. The Alliance has argued that it will make food less expensive and more widely available on New Sarjun, solving chronic food shortages.

Of course, if Ximena's intel is true and the Alliance now has the ability to grow food out by Redrock Prison on northern New Sarjun, lowering the tariffs on Alliance food imports will give them incredible margins — without having to foot the bill for shipping from Indira.

Jaantzen's sure that information isn't on the negotiating table. Yet.

"The parliament's got a perfectly good bill drafted to make it cheaper for local companies to feed New Sarjun, but what do they do?" asks Aiax. "Stick their hands down the pants of Alliance corporations for kickbacks. This trade agreement goes through and the Alliance will get a monopoly and jack up their prices."

"We know, Aiax," Lhasa says sharply. "We all know."

"They did it to New Manila twenty years ago," Aiax says. "Choked out local food production and then used the food shortages to pressure them into joining the Alliance."

"I didn't know you were such a revolutionary," Lhasa says drily.

"Twenty thousand people died of starvation." Aiax jabs a finger at his camera; in the hologram it flares enormous and grainy. "I'm not saying I'm a revolutionary, but I understand why whoever planted that bomb did it. Good on them."

Jaantzen stiffens. "A lot of innocent people died in that explosion," Jaantzen says evenly, and Aiax waves a hand.

"I'm not saying it was the right thing to do, I'm saying I sympathize." And he makes a face. "Oh, shit. I'm sorry, Jaantzen, I forgot. How's your man doing?"

"He'll be all right."

"Good, good."

Lhasa clears her throat. "We're not here to talk politics."

"Business is politics," says Aiax. "Food is politics. Profit is politics. But no, we're here to talk Jaantzen's magical plan for growing food in the desert without a greenhouse."

Lhasa holds up a tablet; the data on the screen flickers badly in the hologram. "Which is what I've been reviewing while you've been pontificating."

Jaantzen cuts in before the siblings can start bickering once more. "First I want to clear the air about the news that came out earlier today." He had assumed that would come up at the beginning of the call, but Aiax had launched into his diatribe against the trade agreement as soon as the connection was made. Jaantzen's reasonably certain the Demosgas won't be bothered by any allegations against him, but they might prefer the optics of keeping their distance until there's no chance they'll be tainted.

He may lose a few clients for Admant Security because of the shard manufacturing allegations, and a few colleagues, like Mizal Seti, may panic and rush to break contracts rather than thinking things through. But if he plays his cards right and reminds key people that they've always trusted him and can continue to do so, these allegations won't be a death blow to his businesses.

Which means that Leone is starting with a warning.

"The shard?" Lhasa waves a hand. "Well, it's not true, is it? So what is there to discuss."

"They've said far worse about me," says Aiax. "And even if it was true, no one cares. Give it until tomorrow and it'll blow over."

"Glad to hear it."

"Now," says Aiax. He leans elbows on the table and steeples his fingers. "I read what you sent over. Why don't you elaborate on your little scheme. Crops growing right out under the sky, is that right?"

"It's unique, I'll give you that," Lhasa says. "And believe

me, I've read a million proposals about terraforming." Aiax and Lhasa share a look, and Jaantzen can guess at what's coming next. He's been wondering when they would broach this.

"And where did you get this information?" Aiax asks, all false casual. If Jaantzen didn't know better, he might not catch Aiax's tells. He and Lhasa were already aware there was a new potential terraforming technology on the market, since they'd been contacted weeks ago about purchasing it. It had slipped through their hands, and they have to be wondering how it ended up in Jaantzen's.

Of course, Oriol had been contracted to steal the plans before Aiax could buy them. My lieutenant's partner stole the plans out from under you, however, is not the answer Jaantzen will be giving.

"Bennion Zacharia," he says, and Aiax's eyes narrow at the name.

"I heard about some unpleasant business at Julieta's," he says.

"As I understand it, he hired Thala to steal the serum he needed to execute the plans he already had. She double-crossed him" — Lhasa huffs pointedly at that — "and I ended up acquiring both the serum and Thala. Zacharia tried to get it back, I killed him, and I acquired the plans. That's the short story."

The Demosga siblings share another look, and Lhasa nods. They believe him for now, and he'll make it worth their while to not ask again in the future. It's a good enough business opportunity that they could all benefit from it.

Lhasa sighs. "Aiax and I trust you," she says. "But we'll need some reassurance we're not going to regret going into business with *her*."

"I understand. For now you have my word that she

understands how lucrative this opportunity is, and she's committed. She also understands the scope — she can't do this without the rest of us. You can make your own assessment when we meet."

"Which will be when?" Lhasa asks. "Aiax, when are you coming planetside?"

"Later this week." He frowns at something to his left, hand reaching past the edge of the hologram to swipe at his calendar. "Three days from now, we could do dinner."

"That works for me," Jaantzen says.

Lhasa purses her lips. "I'll be frank, Willem. I don't think it's wise to involve her."

Jaantzen meets her gaze coolly. "She's part of the package. We're going to keep her busy, and we're going to keep her paid."

"We're in, Lhas," says Aiax. "We have a thousand hectares in the Moire Valley that would be perfect for experimenting. Nobody gets out there except satellites."

"I can take care of shielding."

Aiax lifts an eyebrow. "For a thousand hectares?"

"Yes." Jaantzen smiles at Aiax's expression. "Coeur's people will provide ground security."

Lhasa's lips flatten, but she doesn't comment. "One more thing, Willem. I understand the plans you sent over technically. But the serum? It's some sort of fertilizer?"

"Yes."

Lhasa holds his gaze a moment, then nods. "We can talk more when we meet in person."

"If this trade deal doesn't pass and flush our profits out an airlock." Aiax grins at him. "Looking forward to doing business with you, Jaantzen. And don't worry about the press — nobody'll care in a day or two. And if it seems like it's sticking? Throw them a more interesting bone."

Something like footage of an Alliance agent crashing through his lobby and shooting his unarmed people? There's a bone that could tear apart the trade agreement negotiations, too.

"I'll see what I can think up," Jaantzen says.

"Let me know if there's anything I can do to help." Aiax's face gets momentarily huge as he leans forward to switch off his hologram. Jaantzen reaches for his, but realizes that Lhasa is still watching him.

"Yes?"

Her dark eyes study him. "What does she have on you?" she asks, and his mind reels for which woman she could be talking about. Leone? Coeur? Phaera, even — he knows Lhasa and Phaera have never gotten on.

"I'm sorry?" he asks.

"Coeur," Lhasa says, and Jaantzen relaxes. It's ironic. After all these years, the one person who isn't currently increasing his stress levels is Thala Coeur.

"She has nothing on me," he says. "We've come to an understanding that I expect will be mutually beneficial."

"Fifteen years of trying to kill each other and you two just had a heart-to-heart?"

"It was a bit more complicated than that." And yet somehow this new relationship he has with Coeur feels refreshingly simple in a way he can't quite put into words. "I didn't think you would have a problem working with her."

Lhasa takes a sip of tea, studying him over the rim. "I don't. But I have a problem with going into business with two partners who don't have a solid foundation."

"Hold your judgement until we all meet in person," he says. "No agreement we make is valid until then."

"Fair enough." Lhasa tilts her head. "It's Leone, then."

The comment catches him off guard, and he blinks at Lhasa before responding. "What about her?" Jaantzen asks slowly.

"Someone's going through a lot of trouble to make your life hell right now. If it's not Blackheart, then my second guess is Leone."

"And why would that be."

"Because that's what she does." The bitterness on her face says it all.

"And you didn't want to say this in front of your brother?"

"He hasn't personally felt her leash tighten, so he thinks I'm too sensitive." Lhasa takes a short breath. "I'm sending through a file. I haven't been able to do anything with it, but maybe you can. And see if you can speak with a man named Orris Moss, you'll have a better chance of getting to him than I would. I'll see you in a few days." Her hologram vanishes; the holoprojector in his conference table sinks back into the faux marble.

A number of messages have come in while they were talking, and Lhasa Demosga's sits on top. It's a list of names, dates, crimes. The crimes range from petty theft to murder and extortion, and he doesn't see a pattern until he reads the sentences. Every one of these convicts, no matter how minor their crime, was sent to Redrock Prison.

He frowns down at the list, puzzling at that.

It's difficult for a New Sarjunian citizen to be sent to Redrock. The Alliance operates the prison in a concession in the uninhabited deserts of northern New Sarjun. It's filled with terrorists and pirates operating out of Durga's Belt, along with a few political prisoners from Indira or Corusca that the Alliance wants to secure far from home and their supporters.

There's no reason any of the crimes on this list should have flagged the perpetrators as international terrorists. Yet somehow they were all labeled that way and shipped north for the Alliance to deal with.

He opens the next file. Another list of dates, these ones matched with bank deposits.

Not *shipped* to the Alliance, then. *Sold.*

For the labor? Ximena said the terraforming operation required manual labor — she herself had siphoned off supplies from the main prison to feed the prisoners she claimed had been disappeared to go work there.

He forwards the files to Toshiyo with a note to find the owners of the bank accounts, and figure out who the hell Orris Moss is and why Lhasa wants him to find the man.

Instantly, another message blinks into his inbox. Subject: *Thought you should know*.

There's no message inside, only photos: Phaera, wearing the same outfit she was wearing last night when they met for drinks. But the man she's got her hands — and lips — all over isn't Jaantzen.

He's not proud that his first reaction is jealousy, but it blazes through him like a flame. He takes a sharp breath, letting his eyes close. Forcing himself to think. If anyone close to him had seen Phaera with another man last night, he would've heard about it in person. These images were sent to him anonymously, which means they're designed to get a reaction.

He can't afford to give anyone a reaction.

He turns his attention back to the images. She's wearing the exact same sapphire blouse, the same white trousers, but her heels are black instead of that blinding gold, and when he zooms in on her face he can make out gold hoops, not the delicate, faux-pearl-tipped chains she'd been wearing last night. Her fingernails, curling into the other man's hair, are painted the same magenta as her hair. He can't remember the last time he noticed her nails painted.

It *is* a very good outfit to keep around the office in case a handsome man asks you out for drinks.

Jaantzen swipes the images away, though the lingering feelings of jealousy don't disappear as quickly. He sits with them a moment, realizing what they mean. If he had any doubts that he'd let himself get in over his head with Phaera, they're gone now.

She put herself in his path, and for the past week he's been wondering if he should veer around her. If he should put a stop to his growing affection for her. If he's caught himself soon enough to back things off to a casual friendship.

Apparently it's far too late for that.

There's one decision off his chest, at least.

A sudden lightness sweeps through him at the realization. He'd let himself smile, but as the jealousy fades it's replaced by a nagging worry that has nothing to do with Phaera.

Someone is trying to manipulate his emotions as well as his reputation, and his money is on Leone. She's not content with shaking the foundations of his trust with his business partners, she's trying to crush the fragile new seeds of his relationship with Phaera, too.

More than that, however, she knows what Phaera was wearing last night. She knows Phaera and Jaantzen parted at the Jungle. His mind reaches instantly for the reporter who'd taken a photo of himself and Phaera when they arrived, and he tries to picture the woman's face: pointed chin and tawny, freckled skin. Hazel eyes, a short blue pixie cut.

He opens a channel to Toshiyo.

"Hey, boss. How fast do you think I am?"

Her voice sounds distant, tinny. In the background, he can hear a low rumble. Of course. She's not at her desk, she's driving with Starla and the alien creature out to the Maraka Valley.

"I wasn't calling about that."

She laughs. "I did find Orris Moss, though. He's a clerk used to work for Leone, but he's in prison now."

"Redrock?"

"No, the Palace."

Taufang-Set, otherwise known as the Crystal Palace, serves the area around Bulari. It's where Jaantzen would expert most of the names on the previous list would end up, not Redrock.

"What is he in for?"

"Gimme another couple of minutes, jeez. The connection out here isn't great."

"Find out how we can talk to him, and good work." Jaantzen sighs. "When you get back, can you go through the Jungle's front-door security footage from last night? I'm looking for a specific person. I think she might be a journalist, and if so, I want to know who she works for." He describes the woman.

A short pause. "Blue hair?"

"Yes. Why?"

"She sounds like the woman who slipped the shard into Starla's purse last night."

Ice spreads slow through his chest.

"What?"

"She was blond, though. But we caught her on the Kuli Xa's security cams, and if she was at the Jungle I'll find her."

"Someone slipped shard in Starla's purse."

A pause. "Sorry, boss. I figured you knew by now. We were at the Kuli Xa, and this woman planted the shard on Starla, then called security. We got kicked out."

Jaantzen isn't sure if he's more surprised by the story, or the "we."

"Find her. And find out what her connection is to Leone."

He cuts the call and pushes back from the conference table, shaping his fury into a weapon. Leone may be trying to shake the foundations of his business allegiances and relationships, and she may be targeting his daughter. But she's only fighting with rumor and allegation. As dangerous as her lies could be, they're just lies.

Lhasa has given him the seed of something true he can use against her.

And secrets never stay buried for long.

15

———

CHO

They're only a handful of kilometers past the last houses of Carama Town, but it feels like they're in the heart of the desert. It makes his skin crawl.

It's the sky, Cho thinks, vast and open and empty. It's the sand, he feels it gritty between his toes even though they've barely stepped out of the ORV that brought them here. It's the knowledge that if something happened, no one would ever find you.

And it's definitely the hot, sticky sun with no shade but what little you can find from the scraggly thorn trees.

"God, I love it out here," Ossandre Samson says. Cho's partner hops out of the ORV, kicking up a dust cloud around her boots as she spins to take it all in. "The rock formations are fascinating, don't you think? I've always loved the way the weather carves the sandstone, all these channels . . . ." She's studying the walls of the ravine, one hand up to shade her eyes. "Look at the quartz striations, it's incredible!"

"It reminds you of home?" Cho guesses. He actually can't remember the name of the podunk town where she's from, though he remembers it's somewhere to the south and has something to do with potatoes and onions.

Samson shakes her head. "Lavar is just rolling hills, and all you can see for miles around is greenhouses. I mean, basically it's flat and boring. Maybe that's why I like this so much."

Maybe Samson is attracted by the contrast to what she knows, but for Cho, these ravines feel more like an alien, uninhabited version of the Bulari he's lived his entire adult life in, all blind corners and crevices. Except at least in the city he knows what kind of dangers are lurking around them. Out here it's wild dogs and scorpions, and probably venomous reptiles? He has a vague memory of being warned about venomous reptiles in the desert the one time he came out here hiking years ago.

"We're not here for the nature," he says, partly to Samson and partly as a ward against any nature that might've seen them roll in and is getting curious about how they taste.

There'd been a pair of stacked, rusted-out cargo containers on the road, just where the informant said they would be. They marked the turnoff to a rocky track that heads off into a ravine. It's one of dozens of turnoffs on this road alone that could lead to anything and nothing at all: rundown farmsteads, decrepit factories, spent quarries, some cartel's manufacturing operation, horrifyingly empty wilderness.

This one dead-ends at a deserted mining claim, just like the girl said.

She didn't tell them where the bodies were buried, only that Jaantzen's cleanup crew brought them here. But since they know they're looking for digging, it doesn't take long to see the last place there was any activity. The constant desert wind has smoothed things over a bit, and in a few more days maybe they wouldn't even be able to see this much. Their timing is lucky.

While he unloads shovels and tarps from the back of the ORV, Samson unpacks a pair of forensic drones. She swears under her breath a moment as she tries to slave them to her comm — "No I am *not* going to update." — then lets out a cry of triumph, and the palm-sized drones spin into the air and begin their pattern.

"This is going to save us all kinds of digging," Cho says. "You're a goddess." Samson had sweet-talked the forensics team into letting her borrow the drones for training this morning, keeping Cho from having to explain to anyone just what they need them for until he knows for certain that something is going on. He's not interested in having whoever Major Ngara reports to shutting down his little investigation before it starts.

Samson squints at the hand terminal while the drones paint the area with their scanners, starting with the place that seems most disturbed. A 3D image of what's below the surface slowly appears on her comm, each onion-thin layer revealing a tiny bit more, detailed and excruciatingly slow.

"I'm not seeing any signs of human remains," Samson says after a few minutes. "Do you want me to start looking elsewhere? This seems awfully far down."

"How long have you known the name Willem Jaantzen?" Cho asks.

Samson glances up, then back down at her comm. "Since I started working in Bulari, I guess."

"And how many cases involving him have gone to trial?"

She's frowning like he's trying to trick her. "None?"

The only life within earshot has exoskeletons, scales, fangs, or a combination of all three, but Cho still finds himself looking over his shoulder. He pretends to adjust a windblown tarp to cover the move.

"Believe me, that man has done plenty that could land him behind bars. But he pays his taxes, he runs clean businesses, and he's never gotten caught. He's made too many people loyal to him over the years — either that or afraid of him. But having loyal friends and terrified enemies won't keep you out of jail if you're sloppy."

"And I take it he's not sloppy."

Cho shakes his head. "Maybe let's send one of them out to paint the rest of the area for surface disturbance, but do me a favor and go at least two meters down in any spot before calling it clean."

It's another two hours before they find what they're looking for about two dozen paces from the original disturbed spot: an anomaly in the earth that Cho and Samson nearly ignore before she realizes that the soil composition chart is throwing back an identical repetitive pattern of sand and rocks no matter how deep they go.

Thirty minutes of digging and Cho's shovel clinks against what turns out to be military-grade defensive shielding, probably salvaged off some sort of aircraft.

"Please please please don't be just some buried plane," Samson says.

"I don't think this area is big enough to bury a plane."

"Don't jinx it, Cho."

It's not a plane. Another hour of digging gets them to the edges, and with a final grunt, Cho and Samson lift the defensive shielding out of the hole they've dug, shoving it off to the side. He braces himself for the stench of decay, but he can smell only cool earth and taste only the salt of sweat.

And at their feet are a pair of human-sized forms swathed in slick black body bags.

"Jackpot," Cho says.

Waiting for Major Ngara in the desert is one of the hardest things Cho's ever done.

Well, next to convincing Ngara to drop whatever he was doing and drive out with a couple of forensic techs in the first place. But finally a cloud of dust appears in the distance, and Cho swipes a grimy, sweat-stiff sleeve over his drenched forehead and tries to make himself presentable.

He and Samson have finished digging out the hole, and they opened the body bags just enough to verify that they do indeed contain people who look a lot like Naali Hinoja and Chase Ratham. But other than that, they've done nothing to disturb the scene. Samson coughs into her sleeve as a cloud of dust from Ngara's ORV roils over them, then straightens to attention.

"Let me handle this," Cho says.

Ngara's first out of the ORV, waving at the forensic techs to stay in the vehicle until he has a handle on what's going on. "What the hell are you dragging me out into the desert for, Detective Cho." A sheen of sweat is already forming on his dark brow. Ngara strolls past them without waiting for an answer, stands at the foot of the grave with arms crossed. He scowls down at the body bags. "These had better be more bombing victims, since that's what you're supposed to be investigating."

"No, sir." Cho meets Ngara's disapproval evenly. "But they may be our clue to both motive and culprit."

A lifted eyebrow tempers Ngara's scowl. Cho goes on.

"Are you aware that Blackheart is back on New Sarjun? In Bulari?"

That lifted eyebrow shoots even higher. So that's a no.

"It's true, I've been asking around. She's been heading her crew again for the past few days. I'm not sure what brought her back, but it was soon after the murder of her lieutenant Naali Hinoja and Hinoja's partner Chase Ratham." Cho nods down at the body bags. "I believe we're looking at their bodies."

Ngara's watching him, skepticism slowly being replaced by realization.

"I have an eyewitness who claims the killer was Manu Juric, and video evidence that puts him at the scene of their death." That's a stretch, but if it's good enough to get this case going, Cho's sure they can connect the rest of the dots. "And you already know that he was one of the bombing victims."

A muscle twitches in Ngara's jaw. "You're saying Blackheart bombed the Alliance embassy as a hit on Juric in retaliation for Hinoja's murder."

"It's my working theory, yes."

"And you didn't bring this information to Falk, who's in charge of the investigation."

That flat tone, it's not quite reproach. Ngara knows why Cho didn't bring this to Falk, just like he knows why Cho didn't explain why he needed Ngara out in the desert over compromised office communication lines. Somebody with power went to great lengths to bury these two quietly, and they won't be pleased when they resurface.

Cho takes a deep breath. "If something like this comes out in the course of a joint investigation with the Alliance, it's harder to sweep it under the rug. Somebody made these bodies disappear once. I didn't want it to happen again."

"You're sure it's them?"

"Pretty sure. It looks like them — at least, what's left does."

Ngara's on a knife's edge of decision, Cho can see it in his face. Call it in, and stir up a shitstorm that could have huge repercussions on him personally? Or order Cho and Samson to pile the dirt back in and pretend none of this ever happened.

There's a third possibility Cho might have worried about if Ngara had arrived without the forensic techs in tow: He shoots them both and tosses their bodies down in the grave with Hinoja and Ratham.

Major Ngara glances over his shoulder at the forensic techs sitting in the ORV, then heaves a sigh and hoists himself into the pit, careful not to step on either of the bodies. He unseals the closest body bag, face pinched in anticipation of the stench.

"Fuck me," he says softly.

Both bodies are well-decayed — there was some sort of chemical in the body bags to speed up the process — but some things are still recognizable. Like the bullet holes punched through the female's white suit coat. And her distinctive hair, dyed flame red over dark roots.

"It's Hinoja," Cho says. It has to be.

Ngara nods with resignation, then seals the bag shut once more and stands, wiping his hands on his uniform trousers. He doesn't bother opening the second bag.

Cho holds out a hand to help him out of the pit, and Ngara waves to the forensic techs in the ORV. "Call backup and get started on this — nobody opens those bags," he yells to them, then turns to Cho and Samson. "I'll let our Alliance partners know about our new potential lead. Don't tell a soul who's in those bags and it might just work."

"Thank you, sir."

But Ngara's watching the forensic techs unload, jaw set like he's made the biggest mistake of his life.

"You better have a fucking good eyewitness," he says.

"I'll make sure this case is tight."

Ngara just shakes his head and opens up a channel back to the station. "Get me in touch with the Alliance lead," he says. "I've got something they're going to need to see."

16

JAANTZEN

The forcefield goes down and the Alliance woman stiffens, then looks curiously at Oriol standing in the doorway to her room.

Jaantzen leans into the monitor, studying her reaction. It doesn't seem like she recognizes Oriol. She wouldn't have seen him the other night, since he'd been busy trying to save Elian's life while the rest of them went after her and Toshiyo. And if she'd been briefed on Jaantzen's regular crew, Oriol may not have been included. Jaantzen's always wondered just how close a watch the Alliance has kept on Oriol in the years since he was discharged.

Whether or not she knows him, though, she recognizes training — therefore danger — in his bearing. She watches him warily.

Oriol waves back the guards. "Wait outside," he orders them.

Jaantzen takes a sharp breath, ready to open a channel to the guards and belay that order; he forces himself not to. Oriol knows what he's doing.

He doesn't like it, Oriol being alone in the room with

that woman. But Oriol's armed and fit, she's injured, and he's got a better chance of talking to her if she feels more comfortable. Which is why Jaantzen has taken himself out of the picture and is watching from the room next door.

Oriol *does* know what he's doing. For all his insistence that he's just a hired gun, he can play a good head game when he wants to — and he's shining it on strong now. Oriol's standing like a general, and at his accent and imperious order to the guards, the woman had instinctively assumed parade rest. Now a flicker of uncertainty crosses her face. Oriol may have a military bearing and Arquellian accent, but he's wearing casual civilian clothes.

"It's fine, at ease," Oriol drawls, which only seems to confuse her estimation of him even more. Her shoulders relax, but she doesn't move. Oriol lounges into one of the chairs at the dining table and smiles sadly at her. "So they got your eye."

Her back goes ramrod straight once more. "What was that thing?"

"The Alliance, I mean." Oriol raps knuckles on his prosthetic left thigh. "They got my leg — they get something from all of us in the end. But don't worry, they also have the best hardware around, and they take care of their own. This thing?" Oriol flexes his knee. "Incredible. I mean, my *leg* hurts sometimes, but nothing you can do about that. It's been gone for decades."

She frowns at him, but doesn't speak.

Oriol waves a hand at the bed. "It's all right, soldier. At ease. Sit down. An eye's not so bad. I've got one buddy with a fake eye you can't even tell. Like I said, Alliance tech is incredible."

A beat, and the woman's shoulders finally slump. She

sinks onto the edge of the bed, the expression on her face somewhere between jealousy and despair.

That was fast. The angle Oriol took was brilliant and brutal, and the woman's body language indicates he's already deep in her head. Oriol lost his leg in a covert operation, but it was during a legitimate war with New Manila, and he got a medical discharge with full benefits. He's happy and healthy and free. This woman lost an eye seeing something she wasn't supposed to see. She's not getting a medical discharge with benefits and a chance at a new life. She'll be lucky if the Alliance lets her live.

"What do you want." Her tone is bitter.

"Hey, I'm just here to talk. I'm Oriol."

She considers him a moment: the casual lounge, the charming good looks, the friendly smile.

"Tilde," she says finally.

Jaantzen lets out the breath he hadn't realized he was holding.

"You drew the short straw on this one, huh?" Oriol asks.

"Don't worry about me."

"Oh, I stopped worrying about the Alliance years ago." Oriol stretches out his legs, crosses his ankles, and leans an elbow on the table, one hand raking through his shaggy bronze hair. "Perks of a disability discharge with honors from a war nobody wants to remember. You get a good chunk of change and a shiny new leg every few years, but nobody wants to drag you out and 'honor you' for political theater all the time. Best outcome, really."

The Alliance woman — Tilde — is hanging on every word. He gives her another sad smile. "You probably figured you'd die young for the Alliance, right? I did. But then I got blown up, and it gave me a whole other life I'd never dreamed I could have. You, though, you know something you're not supposed to. If they let you live, it'll be in solitary somewhere. No human contact."

Her jaw clenches; she knows it.

"I mean, they didn't tell you you were here to find a fucked up bat monster, right?"

"What was that thing?"

"Standard briefing, right? Here's the dossiers on the bad guys, here's a bunch of vids on how this é Vega gal walks and talks, here's a bottle of hair dye, here's a nose job — you let them cut up your face for this, didn't you? Man, that's rough. And then what'd they tell you: Here's the layout, here's a photo of a silver case. Grab it and run."

Her lips press tight.

"They didn't prep you for what you'd actually find. Like they didn't think you'd come back." He raps fingertips on his thigh. "Tell me about it."

Jaantzen can see in her face that Oriol's got it right on the money. She doesn't know anything that could help them learn more about the creature, which is a pity. But she's more terrified of going home than staying here. That's something they can use.

"Figured." Oriol starts to stand. "Listen, Tilde. I'm here as a friend. And we both know that once Jaantzen gets you back to your handlers, you're never going to have a friendly conversation again — if you even see another human. But you don't wanna talk, you don't gotta."

He's almost to the door when she clears her throat.

"Wait," she says. "What are you offering me?"

Oriol smiles. "A way out. Think about if you got anything to offer me in return."

"Like."

"Like we both know how illegal your mission was." He raises his hands: *No judgement.* "Believe me, been there.

Done that. But ain't many who'll believe Willem Jaantzen over the Alliance special ops if he tries to make a case of it. If he had a recorded testimony from the guilty agent?" Oriol shrugs. "He'd be in a position to help you out."

Tilde leans forward, gaze locked on Oriol. "Help me out how."

"Listen, kid," Oriol says, expression serious. "You left Jaantzen with two options for negotiation with the Alliance here. Pass you back to your handlers, or use you as leverage. Your life and safety aren't leverage — we both know the Alliance doesn't give a shit if you're dead. So unless you give him something better to use, it's option one."

He hits the forcefield at the door and the woman pushes to her feet — the two guards train their stun carbines on her and she freezes. Slowly raises her hands.

"Okay," she says.

"Okay?"

"I'll talk. I'll tell you everything I know."

"Recorded."

She nods. "I want immunity. Some sort of . . ." Her hands circle helplessly, grasping for the word.

"We've got lawyers can help with that." Oriol smiles. "I'll be in touch, soldier."

He saunters out the door, and as soon as the forcefield's back in place, the woman sinks back to the bed, head in her hands.

Jaantzen reaches to turn the monitor off, then leans back in his chair. With her testimony they'll have a real bargaining chip to ward off another attack by the Alliance — without having to worry about her talking to the wrong people about the alien. Not that it matters quite so much now. Today, Toshiyo and Starla are out in the Maraka Valley, settling the thing into its new home. Toshiyo has scrubbed Cobalt Tower's systems of any record it was ever here, and Jaantzen is immensely relieved to no longer have it under his roof.

Now he can turn his full attention to dealing with Leone.

He's been poring over the files Lhasa Demosga gave him all morning, trying to find the missing link that connects the payments to Leone. Manu is looking into Leone's old law clerk, Orris Moss, but hasn't been able to contact him yet. Jaantzen hesitates, then shoots off a quick message asking about progress there. He's trying to avoid disrupting his lieutenant's rest at home as much as possible, but they don't have time to spare.

The door opens with a faint knock and Oriol leans in the doorway. He holds up a thumb and an eyebrow.

"Yes, thank you," Jaantzen says. "It seems like she's all in. Is that your sense?"

"Yeah." Oriol sighs. "She doesn't know shit about our demon friend, but the Alliance didn't just send her here to die. They figured she'd walk out of here with the case in hand — so either the Alliance didn't expect us to have gotten it out of the case, or they don't know about the aliens at all."

"I'd guess the former. How much time do you think this will buy us?"

"Hard to say. The special ops team won't stop coming after you, but they won't be as direct about it. Between the vid of her shooting unarmed guards and her testimony, that should get the embassy hot and bothered enough to put their foot down on whoever's in charge of special ops." Oriol shrugs, shoulders liquid. "For a minute, at least. We oughta get her talking before she changes her mind."

"I'll call Calanthe."

"It should be just Calanthe and me. You walk in the room, she's gonna clam up."

"I think you're right. But don't leave the guards outside this time, especially not with Calanthe."

"Course. I'll go get prepped." Oriol turns to go, but hesitates in the doorway, one hand on the frame. His fingers drum twice in thought before he finally turns back. His eyes are serious. "Hey. I don't want to make this a thing — I know there's a lot going on. But Manu should be at home. You couldn't give him another day to heal up?"

Jaantzen sits back, frowning. "Is he here?"

A faint furrow sketches itself between Oriol's brows. "He told me you needed him at the office."

"I told him to stay home." Jaantzen sighs and opens a connection to Lo é Njeri, who answers with a note of surprise in her voice; he can count the number of times they've spoken on one hand. "Ms. é Njeri, is Mr. Juric in his office?"

He hears the rustle of fabric on the other end of the line as she checks. "Yes?"

Jaantzen shares a look with Oriol.

"Thank you. Please join me there in ten minutes." Jaantzen cuts the call. "I'll take care of it," he says to Oriol. "Go get things ready for the interview."

Jaantzen heads down the hallway to the lifts, dialing Calanthe along the way.

17

JAANTZEN

Manu's office is furnished with austere attention to detail: a desk, a pair of chairs, matching lamps. There's art on the wall, an original Davica Siobhani etching and a triptych Manu bought from a street artist years ago featuring abstract views of the Bulari skyline in contrasting colors.

And Manu, bent over his desk and flipping through pages of data; he straightens when Jaantzen opens the door.

"Hey, boss," he says, leaning back from his desk and dimming the data. He pinches the bridge of his nose a moment, then blinks. "Just checking some traps. You remember a detective named Cho from back in the day?"

"Timo Cho." It's been a long time since Jaantzen's heard that name, but it's been kicking around his mind ever since Leone made her request that he take care of the defense attorney. "The one Leone needed a message sent to, after Coeur."

"That's the one. He's the one who came nosing around the hospital. I figured out why he was so familiar, but I'm still not sure if he was there to talk to me specifically, or if it was just coincidence he got stuck on victim interview duty. Figured it's better to know what he's up to, though. So I stuck a flea on his and his partner's accounts with the BPD system. It's cloning everything they do there and sending me a copy."

"Find anything interesting?"

"Not yet. My guess is he won't do any real work in the system. He's smart. He got the message about asking questions the first time it was told him."

Jaantzen doesn't know the extent to which Detective Timo Cho was on to Leone's conspiracy to oust Coeur back during the civil war. What he knows is, Cho got close enough to need a warning, but not to be removed entirely. He wasn't the only one who got such a warning back then — but his name is the one indelibly printed on Jaantzen's memory. He'd considered that job his last favor owed to Leone.

Interesting that the man would be surfacing now of all times.

"Keep an eye on him," Jaantzen says. "But do it from home. At least for the rest of the day."

"I don't think when I'm home. I convalesce." Manu kicks out his feet, steepling fingers over his abdomen. "What do you need?"

"For you to convalesce."

"You just pinged me about Orris Moss," Manu says, ignoring him. "Man's out of touch. Not in solitary, but he's being kept separate from anyone I know in the Palace. No visitors, no messages in or out. I've got a couple ideas I'm working on — and I'm digging into the files Lhasa sent."

"Toshiyo's looking at those files."

"Tosh is out in the desert with her hell-beast right now. I

figured I could lend a hand. How did Oriol do with the Alliance agent?"

"She'll record a confession. Manu. Everything is under control."

A flash of frustration crosses Manu's face. "It's not, though."

"You need rest."

Manu's nostrils flare. "Sure, but going home isn't going to help that. I haven't slept for a fucking week. Every time I close my eyes, it's nightmares about — " Manu's jaw clamps shut against whatever he was about to say.

Jaantzen waits silently, watching emotion war over his lieutenant's face before he gets control of himself once more.

"I'm just glad that bitch isn't under our roof anymore," Manu says after a moment. He straightens and wakes his desk; the light from the data casts his dark face in sickly shades. "I'd rather be here, being useful."

Something cold and tangled slowly knots below Jaantzen's ribcage. He knows Manu has been unhappy with every step along the path to reinstating Blackheart in her former territory. But if Jaantzen thought killing her was the best choice, he would have let his lieutenant put a bullet in her head back when they first found her chained up in Dry Creek.

Jaantzen doesn't doubt any of the decisions he's made in the past week when it comes to Thala Coeur, but he's realizing with the certainty of a slowly closing fist that he hasn't thought everything through.

"Manu," he says quietly. "I'm — "

Three taps on the door, and it opens. Lo é Njeri stands in the doorway, and the surprise on her freckled face says she's reading the tension in the room like a book.

"I can come back," she says.

"Yeah, Lo, now's not — "

"Thank you for coming, Ms. é Njeri," says Jaantzen. He and Manu need to have a conversation about Coeur, but he's waited far too long to take care of this business with Lo already. Jaantzen holds out a hand, and she straightens, brushes a short lock of burnt orange hair off her forehead, and takes his hand with the briefest of hesitations, false casual as though she comes face to face with Willem Jaantzen every day.

"It's nice to meet you in person," Jaantzen says.

"Likewise." Lo gives Manu a small *Are you all right?* frown, but he's all relaxed charm now, kicked back in his chair.

Jaantzen towers over Lo, so he sits in the chair farthest from the door to put her more at ease; she settles with faux calmness into the other, nervousness radiating from every fiber of her being. She's watching him expectantly.

"I rely on Manu," Jaantzen says. Lo's gaze snaps quick to Manu before she looks back at Jaantzen. Wariness clouds her clear face. "And he relies on you. I wanted to learn why."

He remembers her résumé from the pile of candidates they'd vetted ahead of time. In her application vid she'd had an earnest, hardworking vibe. Her family was well-off enough that she hadn't had to take an indenture to pay for her education, but just barely — her parents, struggling Arquellian immigrants, had fought hard for that. She'd taken longer than most to finish her degrees as a result, working odd jobs to earn the money to go back and pay for the next round of classes.

Jaantzen had appreciated that as much as her résumé.

Lo's frowning at him, waiting for him to ask her a question.

"When you applied for the job, you knew you would be working for me," Jaantzen says. "That didn't faze you?"

Lo's gaze doesn't waver. "I'd been applying for jobs for months. No one else would give me a shot — they told me I was too young, or I hadn't gone to the right schools. Or I had the wrong name." Her eyes flash at that. The Arquellian naming convention, of course, Lo, the daughter of Njeri. That sort of thing normally fades out after a few generations on New Sarjun as immigrant families marry and adopt new surnames to fit in better.

"So I gave this a shot," Lo says. "The work sounded interesting."

"Building management." Jaantzen says it drily.

Lo straightens, and Jaantzen catches a knowing smile from Manu. "I'm very good at what I do," she says seriously. "It's like . . . It's like a puzzle, right? All these moving parts, and it's not enough just to keep them moving. I want to make them better. Like job orders for maintenance work? You used to deal with them one at a time, but I had a program built to automate that. If you've got somebody coming to fix the plumbing in Admant's offices now, they can run a query that scans usage and last service times for every unit, and whatever comes back as likely in need of repairs is automatically bumped up to me for approval. Then — " She cuts herself off with a wince. "I'm boring you to tears."

"Not at all," says Jaantzen. "That's clever."

"She's got some alchemy she works with the invoicing system and payment plans, too," Manu says. "Hasn't been a late payment since she started."

"I set deadlines and I make follow-up calls," Lo says. "It's not magic."

"The event space on the sixteenth floor went from nearly empty to a significant source of revenue," says Jaantzen. "The constant turnover in the corner retail unit seems to be over for now. And my security chief was impressed by the way you handled the city inspectors after the incident a few days ago. She told me they obeyed your boundaries to the letter; she had expected to have to step in if they started wandering around."

"I have friends in the permitting department." Lo clears her throat. "I'm sorry, Mr. Jaantzen. What is this about?"

Jaantzen's gaze slides to Manu; a muscle clenches in his lieutenant's jaw. "You knew you'd be working for me," Jaantzen says to Lo. "I want to know why you said yes."

"I'm good at what I do," Lo says, not quite shortly. She's warming from her first timidity and Jaantzen is becoming just another of the many people she doesn't take shit from. Good. "I walked into the interview ready to be told no for the hundredth time by some stuffy office manager, and it's Manu sitting with his feet up on his desk, you know?" She smiles at Jaantzen like they're sharing a joke. "He poured me a shot of whiskey and said," — her accent goes from Bulari standard to a touch of the Fingers — "'Ms. é Njeri, I have a tenant who's chronically behind on rent, and another who has these ridiculous repair requests. What do I do about it.' So we sat and drank whiskey for a few hours and came up with a strategy."

"You didn't need a few hours for that strategy," Manu says.

"I needed the whiskey," Lo says to him without missing a beat. "And you even got a call, I remember, another interviewee had shown up, but you told the receptionist to send him home. Next thing I knew it was dinner and you said the job was mine if I wanted it."

She turns back to Jaantzen. "He wouldn't let me say yes that night," Lo says finally. "He told me, 'Go home, order yourself some takeout, and look up Willem Jaantzen. I'll call you tomorrow and see if you still want the job.'"

She's holding his gaze.

"And did you? Look me up?"

"Of course. I looked you both up." She gives Manu a pointed look. "You, I found nothing about." Manu winks. She turns back to Jaantzen. "I read about you. Where you came from, I mean." Jaantzen stills, but Lo's starting to smile. "I appreciated that you weren't just another rich guy who felt entitled to things you hadn't earned. And I read about some of the charities — those were really hard to find, by the way."

"They're not there for people to find." Jaantzen hides his surprise. But he supposes a few news stories must have gotten out — not everyone understands why a donor would want to remain anonymous.

"And anyway, I had to find out the name of whoever was doing Manu's hair," she says. "When Manu called the next day, he told me all about you. About the way you run a business. The way you treat your people."

"And you wanted to work for him," Jaantzen says.

Lo lifts her chin. "I wanted to work for you."

Jaantzen regards her a moment. She doesn't look away.

"Do you still?" he asks. "After what happened?"

"I'm upset." Her voice is matter-of-fact, but there's a touch of fear in her eyes at speaking the truth. "Everyone's upset, I've been fielding calls for two days about what the police are doing, what the security team's doing, if anything was stolen, if it's going to happen again. And that's before people started hearing rumors about you and shard — most of them didn't realize who actually owned this place. I've talked four businesses out of leaving already. I don't know what any of this is about, but I know enough to guess it isn't random."

She's searching his face like she's waiting for him to reassure her, but she's too smart to take any reassurance at face value.

"So, yes," says Lo. "I'm scared."

"The man who attacked the tower is dead," Jaantzen says, to see if she flinches. She does. Recovers herself. "That problem's been taken care of."

"And future problems?" Not even a glance at Manu at that, her gaze is level on Jaantzen, though he can make out the flutter of a heartbeat in the hollow of her throat, tension in the clasp of her hands. "You know how many people are relying on you — not the office space. But on your payroll?"

"Seventy-two."

Lo's chin lifts a fraction.

"There are always future problems, Ms. é Njeri, but my goal is to mitigate those to the best of my ability. That means having people I can trust at the most important levels of my organization. People who aren't afraid of hard work." He studies her. "Or me."

Lo's shoulders straighten.

"You can count on me, Mr. Jaantzen."

A long, weighted pause, and Jaantzen holds out a hand. Lo meets it this time without hesitation. Her palm is warm, her grasp firm.

"I know I can," he says. "Manu will likely ask you for help that's outside your job description. I may come to you directly. Please speak up immediately to either of us if you feel uncomfortable with a request." He holds her gaze until she nods. "But mainly I need your help managing the day-to-day of things that neither of us have time for at the moment. Manu has already handed off any duties he has related to managing Cobalt Tower or RKE?"

"Most of them," Lo says, a note of disapproval in her voice that Jaantzen appreciates.

"You'll be taking on the rest, thank you. I need his plate entirely clear for the time being."

Manu lets out a breath and leans forward, waking his desk once more. "Let's talk that over," he says. "Lo, you got a minute to catch me up on who's been at you about the shard thing?"

"Of course."

Jaantzen stands; she straightens, but he motions for her to stay seated. "Make sure he goes home after this," Jaantzen says. "I hear you're a very good enforcer."

A blush touches her cheeks. "I'll try my best."

"Oriol's in the building if you need backup."

He studies Manu from the doorway; the smile Manu gives him seems genuine, the lines of his face less pinched, his eyes less haunted than before Lo came in.

For the moment, at least. Always only for the moment.

18

———

MANU

He got the sense that someone was following him nearly ten minutes ago, a shadow in a hat pulled low that had made one too many of the same turns for it to be an accident. Manu stopped for longer than necessary at a street crossing to read the news holo, leaned a moment against a wall to compose a long response to a question from Lo, and watched both times as the figure lingered just out of his line of sight. And began following him again when he started to move.

It's late, fading to evening with a muddy glow from the hazy sky. Durga's a sickly pale disk whenever he catches a glimpse of the horizon through the skyscrapers. Everything is cast matte and dimensionless, and the man's features are impossible to discern in the shadow of his hat brim.

Manu walks past his apartment building, then turns down the alley just beyond and slips into a doorway, pressing back until he can feel warm metal against the length of his spine. He can use the evening shadows, too.

The figure walks tentatively around the corner, footsteps picking up with a muffled curse. The man thinks he lost Manu.

Manu counts the man's footsteps to the doorway — this isn't his first time at this game — and strikes lightning fast. Grabs right lapel with right hand, foot out to trip the man off-balance as Manu spins him into the wall, forearm across his windpipe, gun in his left hand and pressed against the figure's jaw before the other man can even cry out.

Beneath that low-pulled hat is a face so familiar it's like looking in the mirror.

His father's eyes are wide with terror.

Manu lets out a stream of profanity and shoves his gun back in its holster, releases his grip. He steps out of the doorway, straightening his jacket.

Halden Juric clears his throat experimentally, shoulder blades still pressed into the metal door as though he's afraid to move. He's staring at his son, wide-eyed.

The muffled sounds of the evening commute echo through the alleyway: A bus thrums past, a door slams shut with a metallic clang, a girl shouts after her mother.

Manu takes a deep breath, hunting for an opening line. "Sorry I never returned your call," he says. He's not. "I had a lot to catch up on."

"You're moving pretty good for a man who was just in a coma." Halden rubs his throat ruefully. "How're you feeling?"

"Fine." Manu bites the word out, but in truth, every place on his body hurts in one way or another, and the sudden movement kicked his faint, ever-present headache into high gear. His temple throbs and a dark, staticky blot pulses in time in the corner of his left eye. The main thing worrying him, though, is the fire licking at the lacerations from Toshiyo's hell-beast on his right bicep. He can have

Oriol check them over and stitch him back up tonight if he tore something open.

Halden is studying him with an intense expression, though Manu's got no fucking clue what he hopes to see.

"What do you want?" Manu finally asks.

"I tried to see you at the hospital." The corners of Halden's mouth turn down even farther in complaint. "They called me, but then they wouldn't let me back."

Manu shrugs. He should maybe say thanks for coming, offer some sort of apology for the trouble. All that comes out is, "Yeah, well."

His father's scowl twitches. "I was surprised to get the call, actually," he says — it's an accusation. "I thought you were dead. My only son." His voice breaks, is it an act? Maybe, but for the way Halden's face crumples briefly before he regains control.

A stab of guilt at that, but Manu pushes it away. He doesn't owe the old bastard anything.

"Your uncle is dead, your grandmother is dead. You're all I have left."

You don't have me, asshole. Manu can't quite get the words to come out, though. Nor can he get himself to say, Maybe if you weren't such a bastard, you'd have someone to care for you in your old age.

Halden straightens, and height-wise, Manu had him beat by a hand's width even before he left home. But back then, Halden'd still had enough muscle to be intimidating. Now he's just frail.

"I wanted to see you." Halden's voice is still deep and strong. "Face to face. You look good." He sets his hat straight on his head again and takes a step past Manu, keeping his distance as he goes.

And Manu should let him. Let him keep walking right

out of that alleyway and back to whatever hell he came from, away from whatever satisfaction he came here to get.

Manu curses under his breath.

"You want to grab a cup of coffee?" he says to his father's back. Manu wants whiskey and bed himself, but he's not watching liquor pass the lips of this asshole. And he's definitely not inviting him into his home.

Halden turns back slowly, a suspicious scowl. "If I'm not getting in the way of your plans tonight."

"I can change them."

His father's scowl softens; Manu knows he's seen the man smile, but he can't for the life of him remember what that looks like. "I would like a cup of coffee," Halden says finally.

"C'mon."

Manu leads them around the corner to Jade's. He'd been planning to order takeout here tonight anyway, and the waitress calls a surprised hello when he takes a booth instead of heading to the kitchen window like usual. And does a double take when she sees who he's with.

Oriol was lying through his teeth. There's more than a passing resemblance between himself and his father. It's like gazing into a strange mirror: This is who you'll be in another twenty-five years. Those angry lines around the mouth, that deep and angry furrow between the brows. That thin, judgmental press of the lips.

Halden looks bent, frail, and part of Manu wonders that he ever found this old man so terrifying.

Old scars twitch.

"Couple of coffees for here, black," he calls to the waitress. "You still take your coffee black?" Halden nods. "And number four for me, extra black bean sauce. To go. We won't be here long." That last is for his father as much as for the waitress.

Nobody stays to eat at Jade's, and the three hard metal booths away from the window are always empty though the kitchen window is constantly piled with takeaway orders. The place is rundown, but the cracked tiles on the floor are polished sparkling each morning before opening, and who cares what a place looks like when the chicken's this good.

The waitress sets a pair of coffees down in front of Manu and his father in the booth farthest from the window. Halden ignores the roiling steam to slurp his coffee black and scalding as ever.

"You come here a lot?" Halden asks, and Manu instantly wishes they'd gone somewhere else, though it doesn't matter. Halden's tracked him down once already; knowing his haunts won't make him any more or less likely to find him again. The only way now to get the man out of his life is to tell him to get gone. Hopefully a cup of coffee will be enough to satisfy his curiosity. And, to be honest, Manu's curiosity.

Manu lifts his mug and inhales coffee steam; his headache sharpens, and he sets the mug down with a clatter. His father is studying the web of scars on his left hand.

"I thought you were dead," Halden says again. "I thought, if you weren't you would have come back to see me by now. You would have come back to see your grandmother at least."

Knife's in and twisted — that didn't take long.

"I'm not." Manu presses his palms against the coffee mug until they burn. "Heard you took over the store? How's business?"

"Business is hard, but I'm keeping it running. I'd love to sell and retire but I'll probably work myself into my grave."

A pause, just enough to set Manu's jaw on edge. "Just like your grandmother. You should come see it, I've changed things up. It's real nice in there." Halden glances out at the busy downtown street with disdain. "That is, if you ever come to Carama Town anymore."

"Sometimes. For work."

"And what do you do?"

"Restaurant supply."

Halden gives a skeptical look at the place under Manu's jacket where he holsters his weapon, and Manu waits for the lecture. He doesn't have a particularly low profile among certain elements of this town, and at the very least, his cousin Siggy's boyfriend was a neighborhood kid. What Manu did to him after he killed Siggy must have reached back home.

If Halden had been looking for him at any time in the past twenty years, he would've found him. So was his refusal to do so fear of his own son? Fury that Manu left? Indifference?

Manu'd put money on the latter.

He realizes he's still waiting for a lecture from Halden, that old rant about how some people make an honest living while criminal lowlifes destroy the city and what does Manu think he's doing with his life skipping school? But instead of challenging him on his half truth about his job, his father just nods slowly. "Glad you're doing well for yourself."

"Thanks."

"Kids?"

"Nah."

"Married?"

"Yep."

"I want to meet her."

Manu clears his throat. "Him."

Halden blinks. "Oh. I want to meet him."

Manu tries to imagine Oriol in the same room as this man. Oriol'd probably play the good, deferential son-in-law. He'd probably keep Manu from snapping, but if there was even one wrong word, he'd make sure Halden Juric never got near Manu again.

Silver lining, there.

"Could be," Manu says, and regrets it immediately. "Where are you living?"

"Your grandmother's place."

Not a chance is Manu visiting him there.

Manu's been pressing his palms against the coffee mug long enough that they've stopped burning; the pain's just a dull throb. He lets go, smooths his hands down his thighs. "Listen. It was — " He stops himself from saying It was good to see you; he doesn't mean it. As if on cue, the waitress gives him a thumbs-up; his order's ready. "Thanks for reaching out. I'll be in touch if I want to see you again, but I've got a lot going on right now."

"It would mean a lot to me if you came out to the shop."

"We'll see."

Manu starts to stand and his father reaches to take his hand. Manu breaks his grip reflexively and with more force than he should have; his own untouched coffee sloshes across the top of the table. The kitchen goes quiet a moment before pans begin to clang once more.

"We'll see," Manu says again, firm.

"I'm your father." Halden's probably going for stern but it comes out like a threat. And it's enough to remind Manu he's not dealing with some frail old man.

Manu leans in close, letting decades of fury sharpen the edges of his growl. "You didn't give a shit about me back then. You didn't give a shit about Siggy. And if I decide to give a shit about you now, it's going to be on my own terms. Stay the fuck away from me until I say otherwise."

He swipes marks from his comm to cover the tab, gives the waitress a tight smile, and stalks from Jade's with order in hand and that dark stain in the corner of his eye pulsing ever larger.

19

______

JAANTZEN

"If it's true Leone took bribes to ship these people to Redrock, I can't say I'm surprised," Calanthe Yang says; she's frowning down at the tablet in her hands, the lists of names and dates Lhasa Demosga gave to Jaantzen. They've taken after-dinner drinks to the couches, the remains of their meal still sitting out on the conference table. Phaera's done something with the lighting to make the penthouse feel more intimate, dimming the lights around the edges of the room so that the couches are a pool of warmth against a backdrop of the moody glow of the dying sunset, the glittering lights of the city, the slowly kindling witch lights floating in the hydroponic garden that slashes through the penthouse floor.

This little gathering may look like a charming dinner party; it's not. It's a war meeting.

"Everybody gets kickbacks," Calanthe continues. She hands the tablet to Letizia Diamante, who sits to her left. "The trouble is that this was a while ago, back when she was a city judge. I mean it's still illegal, she can still be prosecuted for it. But is it going to take her down? Or will it just be some long-ago scandal? Like I said, everyone takes kickbacks."

"From the Alliance?" Phaera asks. She pours Calanthe more tea; the rest of them — Phaera, Jaantzen, Leti, and Sebastian, Leti's interpreter — are drinking brandy.

"Well, no." Calanthe takes a sip. "That won't go over well."

Leti sets the tablet aside. "An old crime can always become a current scandal," she signs. "It's just a matter of making it relevant again."

"How so?" Jaantzen signs and says. He's trying to use USL as much as possible, despite the presence of the interpreter, but his mental energy is taxed by this business with Leone.

"I have a reporter friend, he's incredible at these sorts of human interest stories," signs Leti. "These cases may have been ten years ago, but that's plenty of time for kids to grow up, have their own babies, get married. All with their parent still unjustly behind bars. That's real heart-wrenching stuff. Send me these names and I'll tip my friend off to the story."

"The story may be more current than we think," Phaera says. "I met with Leone yesterday and caught a glimpse of her planner. She had a meeting scheduled with the warden at Redrock Prison after me." She looks at Calanthe. "I snapped a photo of it."

"The human interest angle might get people to care," says Calanthe. "But the meat of the story is going to be *why*. What does the Alliance need with more prisoners?"

Most likely to work the terraforming operation — but Jaantzen's not ready to share his ideas on that question aloud. He turns to Leti. "Do you know an investigative journalist, as well?"

"The best. If there's a story there, she'll find it."

"Good, thank you."

"Of course," Leti signs. "This is all a long game, though. Once I have a story, I can give it legs — but until then I'm not doing my reporters any favors if I let rumors leak early."

"I understand."

"We'll all work as fast as we can," says Calanthe. "But it's a long game on my end, too — especially if we want to accomplish this without tipping her off. Leone's had plenty of time to plan her angle for attacking you, but you don't have that luxury."

That's the crux of the problem. If they want any chance of making their attack bulletproof, they need time to gather evidence and put the pieces in place. Meanwhile, Leone is buffeting them with her storm of knives. He can't afford to let her force him into an unready reaction, but he might bleed to death by a thousand cuts before he has a solid case to throw at her.

"We need to talk about managing the damage Leone's doing to you, as well," Leti signs; apparently they're on the same page. "The shard allegations? What are you doing about those?"

Jaantzen's been hoping it will blow over, really — Aiax Demosga's advice echoes in his mind. "Throwing them a more interesting bone," Jaantzen says. "It's not influencing anyone who matters."

Leti shakes her head. "All the news stories say you couldn't be reached for comment, which is another way of saying you're guilty. Who's handling your media requests now?"

"We're handling it internally." Actually, he told Lo é Njeri not to respond at all — which, Leti's right, might as well be an admission of guilt in a certain light. Perhaps he's been remiss in ignoring what to him seems like a minor attack. Jaantzen and his crew have dealt with these sorts of things their own way for years, and he's falling back into old habits rather than adapting to Leone's game.

He does have one tried-and-true strategy for success, though: hiring the best people in the business and letting them do their jobs.

"I'll forward any media requests to you," he tells Leti.

"Good. We'll take care of it." Leti clinks her glass against his and drains it. "I'm going to get back and reach out to those reporters. Thank you for dinner, it was a pleasure to finally meet you."

"Likewise," Jaantzen signs back. "I've heard so much about you."

Leti laughs. "Not bad, I hope." She hasn't asked where Starla is, which means Starla probably already told her she wouldn't be at the meeting. Tonight, Starla's driving back from the desert, after helping Toshiyo get the creature settled into its new, more secure home. Jaantzen's been shoving aside worry about them all day.

"I should probably go, too," Calanthe says. She pats her taut belly. "Put us both to bed."

It's been a long day for her; she was already at Cobalt Tower when he invited her to stay for dinner to meet with Leti and Phaera. She and Oriol spent the afternoon moving the Alliance agent to a secure safehouse and getting her testimony on vid and arranging for her to get sanctuary if she does agree to testify against the Alliance in court. It's one more thing off his plate, one step closer to being free of his worry about the Alliance coming after the alien creature or the agent, either one.

He can only hope it will be enough.

"I'm sorry to ask so much of you at the moment,"

Jaantzen says to Calanthe. He stands and helps her to her feet.

Calanthe just waves a hand. "You have no idea how terrified everyone can be of a pregnant woman. This is the perfect time to do a job that requires being intimidating." She turns to Leti. "It was a pleasure meeting you," she signs roughly.

"I'll help you clean up," Phaera says as they walk the others to the lift; in her expression it's clear that she has more to talk about with him.

She's not alone. As the other three make to leave in a flurry of handshakes and air kisses, Calanthe leans close. "I thought you should know, Willem," she says, voice low. "When I made my rounds to sell your plan for Acheta to the others, more than a few commented on how happy they were with your initiative, and how displeased they'd been with Leone's inaction."

She's watching him steadily to see how that lands.

"Meaning?"

"That you're talking tonight like you just want to weather Leone's storm, but you should set your sights higher. You have the support for a change in leadership." She gives him a secretive smile. "I'm only planting seeds."

He studies her a moment. She's the spitting image of her mother as a younger woman, that same razor edge of clever ambition wrapped in an elegant dress.

"And I'll need someone who can navigate politics and government."

Calanthe's smile sharpens. "Naturally."

"We'll talk. Give my love to your mother."

"I will." She inclines her head to him, then trades kisses with Phaera. "I'll be in touch," she says as the lift doors closed.

Phaera gives him a curious look once they're alone. "What was that about?"

"Ms. Yang seems to think I have enough support to dethrone Leone and take her place." It feels more natural than he anticipated to say the words aloud.

"I told you as much the other night at the Jungle." Phaera slips out of her heels and leaves them next to the couch, tossing her jacket casually over the back before going to clear plates from the dining table. The zipper down the back of her maroon sheath dress is studded with tiny crystals that catch the light as she moves.

"Leave those," Jaantzen says. "Someone else will take care of them."

"I don't mind. And Calanthe's right."

She doesn't expound, and so he joins her in stacking dishes on the kitchen counter, lost in thought. The moody lighting Phaera set to make their after-dinner conversation on the couches more comfortable now feels strangely confining, limiting his attention to the room around them. When he's not working he often leaves it dark, the windows so clear they're invisible, the room lit by the glow of the city, the wash of the moon, the glimmer of the witch lights in the garden swath, Bulari glittering like gemstones below.

"You should host more," Phaera says after they've worked in companionable silence a moment. "You have an incredible space for it."

"Maybe," he says. It never seems like the right time, and it occurs to Jaantzen that he doesn't remember the last time he thought of that table as anything but a place to do work. It seats twelve, and tonight with Phaera, Calanthe, Leti, and her interpreter, it was filled with laughter and joking despite the grimness that brought them all together. Maybe he'll consider it once things are normal again.

"Something small to start," Phaera's saying. "Teo Lordeur? Julieta and Calanthe? I could ask Cavy and Ayisha. We could even invite the Demosgas. Aiax isn't that bad if I've had enough to drink."

He frowns at her, realizing this isn't, in fact, a change of subject.

"A dinner party," he says.

"A dinner party." She smiles slyly and tops their glasses off with another splash of brandy, then leans against the back of the couch, watching him load dishes in the sanitizer. She hands him his glass when he's done; her fingers brush against his. He sips, then sets his glass on the kitchen island and settles on one of the stools. Phaera perches on the back of the couch once more.

"When I went to see Leone yesterday, she tried to get me to break things off with you," she says lightly. "She sounded like my mother when I was a girl: I thought you had more sense, you should have more respect for yourself, he's no good for you."

Jaantzen's chest tightens — Leone's not wrong. He's had the same thoughts running through his head.

"In all fairness, your mother might still say that when she finds out," he says. He's trying to match her casual tone, but this conversation isn't relaxing him. He takes a sip of brandy to cover his unease. From what little he's gleaned about Phaera's mother, he assumes she won't be pleased to learn about him. What Leone thinks of him may not matter to Phaera, but he knows she's close with her parents.

Her arms cross tight over her ribs, a pale slash across the dark wine of her dress. Her casual demeanor slips; there's real fear in her eyes.

"She threatened my mother, Jaantzen," she says, and he can see the effort it's taking Phaera to say that calmly.

Jaantzen frowns at that. "What exactly did she say?"

"Leone said, 'Doesn't she have a bad heart? What do you think will happen when she gets a shock like learning you're seeing a drug dealer.'" Phaera lifts her chin, a challenge. "You think I'm overreacting? I know what it sounds like."

"I don't think you're overreacting," Jaantzen says quietly. "She's not clumsy. If she made you feel threatened, she intended it."

Phaera's shoulders relax a touch; she swirls the brandy around its glass. Captured light kindles gold at the heart of the liquid.

"You should ask your parents to leave town for a while."

"It won't come to that."

"It may. Think about where they could go, Phaera."

She nods, finally. "I have an aunt near Alusina."

That's plenty far — nearly on the other side of New Sarjun, and much closer to the southern pole than Bulari.

"It's a beautiful time of the year to visit, I hear."

"I'll talk to them." She sighs, and that tinge of fear is washed away by her frustration. "I don't know what I'll tell them."

"She's trying to get under both our skins," Jaantzen says. He clears his throat; he's been debating telling her this. "Someone sent me a photo this morning. Of you, wearing the outfit you had on when we met at the Jungle, but different earrings and shoes. You were with someone else. Tall, curly black hair. He had a beard." Heat's creeping up the back of his neck; he ignores it.

"That would have been over a year ago," Phaera says, she shakes her head in disbelief. "Which means she's been saving leverage on me for at least that long. What else does she have on me?"

"Do you have any ideas?" For him that list is long, though most of what he did working with Leone during the civil war implicates her, too. But he probably isn't thinking of everything, despite racking his brain for the last few days. "You don't need to tell me, but you should think hard about what she might be able to hold over you."

"I can't think of anything. But she's manufacturing things about you. There's no reason she couldn't do that to me, too."

"Then I suggest you make certain your affairs are as clean as possible," he says, regretting the wording the instant it's out.

Phaera quirks an eyebrow at him.

"Your business, your debts," he says quickly. "Your professional relationships."

"I will," she says. She's finished her brandy; he didn't notice when. But now she crosses the room to set it beside his still-full glass on the kitchen island. She's not quite touching him, but she's so close he can feel her warmth. She gives him a playful smile. "I will see to my affairs."

He still has people out there in the night. Manu should be comfortably at home with Oriol, but Starla and Toshiyo are on the road back from the Maraka Valley. Meanwhile, Leone is planning her next move, and the gears of the Alliance are grinding slowly towards him.

"You've probably had a long day," he says. He should stand, put some distance between them; he doesn't.

"And you probably still have work to do."

He can feel her breath on his cheek. "It's late."

"You're right." She smiles, mischievous. "It *is* too late to be working." Her fingertips brush across his lapel, the faint scrape of her nails on the back of his neck, thumb along his jawline, and she's fully inside his defenses, stepping one leg over his to press her body in as she kisses him, other hand slipping beneath his suit jacket to spread heat like a salve along still-bruised ribs. He palms her hips as they kiss, lets his hands trace her curves. The tiny, rough line of crystals on her zipper appears under his fingertips; he follows that trail of stars up the length of her spine to the nape of her neck. The zipper pull is smooth in his fingers.

A chime slices through the moment.

It's just his comm, not the lift, but still Jaantzen straightens like a thief caught in the act. It chimes again with another message and Phaera breaks the kiss gently. Her lips brush his jaw and she laughs in resignation, hot breath across his earlobe.

"Give me a second." Jaantzen calls up the message on the countertop. It's from Starla, brief and reassuring. She and Toshiyo are back safe, everything went well. The knot of unease he's been carrying between his shoulder blades loosens.

I can come by and brief you if you're still up.

Phaera's reading the message, too. She smiles sadly and steps back, leaving a cool ache the length of his body in all the places they'd been touching, a rueful dab of a finger at the corner of her mouth.

"Always work," she says.

Starla's back, she's all right, and anything she has to tell him can wait until tomorrow. Jaantzen's fingers pause over a reply.

"I should get home," Phaera says. She's already slipped her heels back on, takes her jacket from the back of the couch and turns with a smile. "Good night, Jaantzen."

He hits Send:

Let's talk in the morning.

Jaantzen swipes the counter and the penthouse's security to Do Not Disturb. Phaera's already heading to the lift, but he closes the space between them and catches her fingers in his, pulls her back to him. Her shoulders come to rest against his chest like a missing piece of himself falling into place. His free arm circles her waist.

"No," he murmurs into the curve of her neck. He barely notices the rustle of fabric as her jacket pools at their feet, only how her smile presses the warmth of her cheek into his.

20

———

CHO

The Bulari Police Department's downtown office is impressive and historic on the outside, and when it's bustling with people, it's easy to ignore the cracks in the granite columns, the peeling paint on the walls, the warped doorframes that let drifts of gritty sand in to coat the tile floors.

Look too close during the day and everything comes off as threadbare and dingy. But at night, with your footsteps echoing like ghosts, the oppressive weight of the place has nothing to do with the feeling that the building's going to collapse in the next earthquake.

It's a wearing place to spend your days — or nights, if, like Detective Timo Cho, you're trying to hide the fact that you're working an illicit murder investigation.

He's staked out the least malfunctioning investigations cube on the second floor and is picking apart the seams of this case. There's an assortment of greasy takeout containers on the side table, which Samson acquired long enough ago that Cho's stomach is starting to rumble again. He peels back the lid of the nearest one and gives an experimental sniff. The congealed curry was much more appealing at lunch.

The informant never came back to get the second half of her money, and that's not sitting well with Cho. Maybe she picked up a day job and doesn't have time to make it in. Maybe she spent the money he already gave her on the real good stuff and she's dazed up in some drug house. Maybe she could handle meeting a cop in the bar but is too nervous to show up to the police station itself. Maybe she knows she'll be caught out in a lie.

Or maybe Willem Jaantzen heard the news and she's found herself a desert grave, too.

Cho hopes against hell it's not the last option. Partly for his own safety, and partly because this case against Juric isn't going to stick with just the bodies and the footage of him walking into the restaurant. Cho knows for sure someone else saw what happened in that restaurant. He's watched the vid over and over to see the owner of the Oasis, Ajesh Paiman, walking in to his own restaurant all arm in arm with Jaantzen. Buddies. If one of the restaurant staff didn't see what happened, Paiman probably did.

Man like that's probably in Jaantzen's pocket, though. Cho starts nosing around the Oasis, Jaantzen will know about the investigation in a heartbeat. And Cho's second reminder to stop asking questions won't be as friendly as the first.

The bodies haven't officially been logged in to the system — Cho fought for that, and Major Ngara agreed. The BPD's system is far too compromised, this place leaks like a sieve. So far it's just Cho, Samson, Ngara, the Alliance lead, and the coroner who know the actual identities of the bodies that were brought in today. The forensic techs who did the scene of the burial might have a guess as to what was going on, but the names Naali Hinoja and Chase Ratham were never uttered in their hearing, and the body bags were kept firmly sealed until Cho and Samson were alone with the coroner.

Cho's reasonably sure he can trust Ngara and the coroner. It's not likely that the Alliance is working with Willem Jaantzen. And Samson's probably fine — she hasn't been around long enough for someone to get their claws in her. He hopes.

He's got to keep this under the radar.

Cho's hunched over the scenario desk, running the hologram mock-up the coroner's tech sent over, based on the wound patterns: Two figures matching Hinoja's and Ratham's stats sit at a table. A unisex blank steps up behind a figure labeled 2 — Ratham — and shoots him once in the back of the head from less than a pace away. The shooter then fires three rounds into the figure labeled 1 — Hinoja — as she tries to stand. The shooter isn't labeled, but the height stats match Juric better than Jaantzen.

Cho has found a floor plan of the restaurant and has plugged in a dozen variables a dozen ways — the kitchen is the most likely point of attack. Hinoja and Ratham would have been watching the front doors, which means anyone walking through there wouldn't have a chance to get behind Ratham. But they'd expect people coming in and out of the kitchen, and that could allow someone just enough time to get close and fire off those shots before Hinoja or Ratham could react.

The second possibility is that Hinoja and Ratham knew the shooter well enough to turn their backs, which isn't likely if Juric made the hit.

If either victim — after all his years working this city, Cho is having trouble thinking of these two as "victims" —

was armed, they didn't have time to draw and they weren't buried with their weapons. He's been scouring snapshots of the restaurant from review sites and he found something that looks like a weapons safe behind the front desk. From what he can tell, the Oasis is normally hopping during dinner. Even in this town, *someone* will report a shoot-out in the middle of the dinner rush, which means the restaurant was probably deliberately empty for the meeting.

Classic, Jaantzen and Hinoja sitting down in a known meeting spot to create an alliance or hash out a disagreement. Cho would bet anything that Hinoja's and Ratham's weapons were in that safe.

He needs to get inside that restaurant.

Without getting himself on Jaantzen's hit list.

He's got the volume cranked up on the scenario desk — something about the way the crack of the bullet through the speakers hits his sternum helps put him in the scene — and at first he thinks he's hearing an echo of the gunshots.

But, no. He hears the footsteps again, from the hallway outside the investigations cubes, a sharp dress-shoe clack that definitely isn't the janitor. The footsteps stop outside his cube and Cho's heart rate spikes — he'd thought he was alone in the building. Cho swipes at the scenario, the plates on his metal fingertips not quite catching the first time. He curses. Swipes again.

The bodies flicker into black just as Arman Falk pushes the door open.

Cho slides his left hand down his thigh to dry the sweat. "Try knocking," he says angrily. "I was working."

"What are you doing here so late?"

"Just caught up on the victim interviews and thought I'd stick around a few more . . . minutes." Cho hadn't actually noticed the time until Falk said something. He'd thought it was just pushing up on dinner, but that hour's been and gone. No wonder he's starving.

"How is there possibly something that interesting in your victim interviews?" Falk's lounging in the doorway like he owns it, like Cho will need to ask his blessing if he wants to leave the investigation cube. He was like this when they were partners, too, doling out information about the case you're both working like he's doing you a favor, like you'll owe him after.

There's something about the way Falk's watching him, that *Gotcha* grin. It could be he's simply caught wind of some bodies brought in from the desert and is hunting for intel.

Or Falk knows who the bodies are.

Which means whoever bankrolls Falk's shiny dress-shoe collection and new-spinner-each-year habit knows.

"What are *you* doing here?" Cho asks, reaching for anger to cover the feeling of being caught in the act.

"Actual police work. I read through your interviews. Nothing interesting there."

Cho shrugs. No shit.

"Except for one name. You had the chance to learn something, but you didn't press — you're losing your touch." The corners of Falk's mouth tilt up at a vicious angle. "Manu Juric?"

"You know guys like him don't talk," Cho says. "You're not thinking it was a hit?"

"Did it feel good?" Falk asks, and Cho frowns, not understanding. "Standing over him like that? Having the upper hand?"

Cho refocuses on Falk, slow realization dawning — he's not just here to throw barbs about Cho losing his touch. "What do you mean?"

"After what Juric did to you?"

Cho's mouth goes dry; Falk's grin sharpens.

Cho hasn't told a soul who it was that put him in the hospital ten years ago, back when he and Falk were still partners. Before he got demoted. He'd paid for his lesson about asking questions with flesh, and it had stuck. Do you have a name? they'd asked. Do you want to press charges? But he's always maintained he didn't see who it was. Lying through his teeth just like every other witness who refused to testify. Like every other witness he'd ever cajoled and cursed.

No, he never told a soul about Juric.

So how the hell does Falk know?

"What are you getting into this time, Timo?" Falk asks, his tone threading the line perfectly between curiosity and threat.

Cho's metal fingers clack in the code that'll wipe the scenario desk without saving his work — that's hours lost, but it's all locked away in his head. "I'm starving," he says. "Can't believe it got this late; thanks for checking in on me."

He reboots the desk just to make sure — it comes up empty — then dumps the leftover lunch containers in the bin beside the door. Falk jerks back as curry splashes on the wall beside his awfully nice slacks.

"G'night," Cho says, and shoves past Falk so hard the impact jars through his metal humerus and goes deep, aching, into his shoulder socket.

Cho doesn't go home.

He tries the bar where he met the informant last night. He tries another two that seem likely spots someone like her might spend time. Then, finally, he grabs a greasy wrap stuffed with sweet potato and shredded lamb that tastes like it's two days gone but has a combination of spices that unexpectedly remind him of a dish his father used to make.

He eats it on the train platform, watching for a mysterious brunette who doesn't show, then sinks against the lean rail of the empty train car to watch the lights of the city flash by.

It's three blocks after he disembarks before he suspects he's being followed, five before he knows for sure, and when he finally has a chance to surreptitiously check, it's her.

He turns when he reaches the corner shop at the end of the empty block, and she stops, nervous, then gives him a brave smile and keeps walking towards him. A delivery van rolls by and the street's silent once more but for the hard soles of her boots against the sidewalk.

"I suppose I'm not as clever as I think I am," she says with the ghost of a smile. In the light spilling out of the corner shop he can see dark-red lipstick and hazel eyes against golden skin that's a half-dozen shades paler than her curls.

"I was looking for you earlier," Cho says.

"Did you meet with the girl?"

"I did. I gave her half the money, but she never came back for the other half."

Her little frown deepens, but she doesn't look overly concerned. "She's flighty. I'm sure she'll be back to see you at some point. I take it you found them."

"The bodies," he says, testing to see if she's avoiding the word. She flinches.

"The bodies," she agrees, a tightness to her mouth, a sadness to her eyes. She straightens quickly. "Can we go somewhere to talk?"

Cho turns in a slow circle like he's trying to find a place for them to go. He's lived here twenty years. He knows what's on offer: the deli counter at this corner store, an all-night coffee shop where druggies go to get out of the weather, a dingy bar even he doesn't want to set foot inside.

"There's not much around," he says.

"You live in the neighborhood?" She pulls her coat tighter. "I just want to get off the street."

And he doesn't want to bring her back to his apartment, but the alternative is walking another few dozen blocks through inhospitable streets or getting back on the train. He suddenly wonders how she got here, how she's getting home. If she'll be safe.

"So long as you don't mind the mess," Cho says. And it's two blocks until they're through the door of his rundown building, keying into his shitty little apartment, where several days' worth of dishes are stacked on the coffee table and the sink's piled with molding mugs.

"Have a seat."

"Thank you." She sits gingerly on the edge of his blanket-covered couch, turning her head to take in the room. He almost expects her to ask if he's just moved in — he basically lives out of boxes, with nothing on the walls — but she doesn't comment on the decor. After he retires, he thinks, he's going to have to do something about this place.

Or find a hobby that keeps him away as much as his job does currently. "Cider?"

"Please."

He circles his right thumb and forefinger to pop open two ciders, his metal thumb sans glove forming a perfect bottle-opening ledge. Sets one bottle in front of his visitor.

The woman isn't sneaking furtive glances at his hand like most do; she tilts her chin to the side, examining it.

Without his glove, his bare metal fingers look skeletal. Every one is mismatched salvage Louis Oni sold him cheap, in a range of grays from brushed steel to gunmetal. His ring finger is a warm bronze. Cho stopped noticing a long time ago.

"What happened?" To your arm, she means. It's what that question always means.

"Mining accident," he says, and normally that's all the conversation he gets. Everyone and her brother knows someone who's lost a limb in a New Sarjunian mine.

"Detective is a second career, then?"

Cho just laughs. "No, I was twelve when it happened. I was working off my parents' indenture after, you know." He waves his hand in a way that means *The usual*. There are plenty of orphans on New Sarjun; everyone knows what *The usual* is. "I was just in the wrong place at the wrong time. Good news is Blacklode Corp forgave the indenture after that."

Next question he generally gets is if it still hurts after all these years, but the woman looks down at her own hands. "I found out why you're so interested in him." Her gaze meets his. "In Manu Juric."

A chill shivers through him for the second time this night. Cho has always wondered who in the department leaked his activities to the people who sent Juric after him; now he'd bet anything it was Falk, the man all but told him that tonight. And though Cho hasn't told anyone in the department who put him in the hospital, it's probably common enough knowledge in the criminal underground of Bulari. If this woman was involved with Naali — and he suspects she was — then she'd probably know.

"Victoria, right?"

She nods sharply.

"You know why I want to take Juric down," he says. "Why do you?"

"I cared about Naali," she says. "Naali and I — " She looks away, and something about this sweet-young-thing act is starting to rub him just wrong enough to notice. He's not sure yet if it's that she's acting awfully innocent for someone who apparently spent time with Naali Hinoja's crowd, or if he doesn't quite believe she is who she says she is.

"I couldn't let her death go unpunished," she finishes.

"You ran with her crew?" Cho asks, and Victoria looks offended.

"Of course not. But I was a friend. She was like a sister to me."

"Well, Victoria," — he puts the slightest hint of disbelief on her name — "if we're going to take Juric down, we need more than bodies and a vid to make it stick. It's enough to bring him in for questioning, but you know he won't talk. We need something definitive. An eyewitness."

"I'll try to track the girl back down."

"She didn't see it happen, she just saw Juric go into the restaurant." If she even saw that — Cho still has his doubts. "I need someone who witnessed the murder."

She doesn't even hesitate. "Talk to Ajesh Paiman, the owner of the Oasis."

"He and Jaantzen are friends," Cho says. "He won't talk."

She laughs. "Ajesh is neutral, and he made a lot of money off being a safe place for enemies to meet up. Until Jaantzen ordered a hit in his restaurant. Ajesh is ruined, now. I'll get him to talk."

"What's in it for you?"

"I get to see the man who killed Naali taken down." She

leans forward. "And you get revenge on the man who cost you your career."

Cho frowns at her. "And just who are you?"

"Does it matter, if I help you put a killer behind bars?"

Cho wants to say it does. That if he's going to do police work, it's going to be clean. Most of his colleagues, they wouldn't be sitting here having this moral argument with themselves. Sometimes he suspects that the only way anyone actually gets arrested is when a cop makes a deal with someone even shadier than the perp. Victoria's offering him a deal he's seen so many of his fellow officers make: take the information, don't look too close at where it comes from.

He takes a sip of his cider, trying to tell himself the method still matters as much as the results.

Amusement tugs at her lips; the expression's a glitch in the sweet-young-thing persona, a hint of truth behind the hologram. Or — not a glitch, Cho realizes. It's a recalculation of her little act. Victoria gives him a wry smile and takes a long draw of the cider; when she sets the bottle down, her posture is different. Relaxed. The vulnerable young woman he let into his apartment is completely gone.

"No more bullshit, Detective Cho," she says. "You need an eyewitness, and I'm delivering one on a silver platter. Ajesh Paiman saw the whole thing go down, and he'll tell you everything he knows. Do you want that or not?"

"In exchange for?"

Victoria's eyes gleam. "For doing your job. You can take this opportunity to put a killer away, or you can slink off to retirement knowing you missed your shot. But at least your morals will still be shiny and new." She takes another pull on the cider. "Fat lot of good that does for the next person who goes down to Juric's gun. Not to mention whoever else he might hand over to you."

"A guy like that doesn't talk."

"Not about Jaantzen, obviously. But he's a loose thread — start tugging on him and you'll see who else he's connected to."

The thought's been in the back of Cho's mind. Now that the Alliance is involved, they'll keep digging until they get to the truth about who bombed their embassy. If they start investigating the angle that Manu Juric killed Naali Hinoja and Chase Ratham, and their embassy got blown up because of it, there's nothing people like Falk will be able to do to stop it. An investigation like that gets going, no telling what other trash might get swept up.

Cho swears under his breath; Victoria smiles.

"What else do you need to bring Juric in?" she asks, like it's a foregone conclusion that he'll work with her.

It is.

Cho takes a long pull on his cider, forcing himself to think. They have the bodies, and the video evidence that Juric was there. What he's seen so far of the graveside evidence is good, and who knows what else they'll find once he gets into the Oasis. The original witness has vanished, but she wouldn't have held up under questioning anyway. Ngara will sign off on bringing in Ajesh Paiman, and with the Alliance on their side, they can offer more than corrupt police protection for Paiman and his family. They can offer Alliance sanctuary, new identities, a better life somewhere away from all this mess.

That could sweeten the pot and allow Paiman to testify openly — and it will definitely remove the usual eyewitness problem they have in these sorts of cases, where people back out at the last minute, or skip town, or turn up dead.

Coming as it does as part of the Alliance investigation into the bombing, this is an opportunity that Cho can't miss.

The last big break of his career — hell, the only break of his career. Before this it's been nothing but dead ends and frustrations, thwarted at every turn. He lets this woman walk out of here and he's throwing away his one chance to make a real difference.

Does he really care who she is? Right now, she wants what he wants.

He's not going to throw that away.

"Get me Paiman and we'll talk," he says.

21

MANU

Foot traffic along Anjali Lumaban is picking up. It's not yet sticky hot, the morning breeze from the south cooling things a touch, though in an hour no one will be out in the full sun unless they have to be. Right now, old folks are walking laps on the promenade, young couples are parked on statue steps, and a few food vendors are on the prowl.

Anjali Lumaban Boulevard is one of Bulari's rare tree-lined avenues, with a broad center promenade for pedestrians. Tree aloes and fan palms march in stately rows, interspersed with ornate wrought iron lampposts. The road, currently clogged with delivery trucks and electric mopeds, runs on either side of the park, but the pedestrian promenade is paved and elegant. And very out of place among the rest of the slums of Carama Town.

An artist has done the Durga System in scale throughout the whole plaza, Durga at the far end, glittering in bronze, delicate arcs tracing orbits around her through paving stones with colorful glass planets embedded in them. Manu walks slowly towards her, past the mother-of-pearl ice planet, Bixia Yuanjin, its trio of inhabited moons studded into the pavement around it, past the spray of scattered copper nuggets that is Durga's Belt. New Sarjun is next, banded around the belly with jasper to signify the Jupari Desert.

He stops at the jade-green disk that is Indira.

It's everyone's home planet, Manu supposes. Every person on this plaza, the panhandlers, the mimes and street vendors selling baubles, the old men strolling arm in arm, the teenagers playing hooky from jobs or school and smoking at the foot of the statue of Anjali Lumaban. Everyone here can trace their ancestors back to this little green-gray speck in the Durga System. And the *Ark Matsya* before, and ancient Earth before that.

Some residents of New Sarjun arrived more recently than others, of course. Deputy Chief of Mission Marquez ó Lauris may have lived on New Sarjun for decades, but his loyalties still lie on waterlogged Indira. Manu tilts his head to stare at the jade disk, scattered with stylized blue and white swirls, glittering chips sparking in the sunlight.

"He's alone," says Toshiyo in Manu's ear. A pair of her beetle drones are specks overhead; Oriol is lounging on a bench near Durga.

Ó Lauris is just another old man out for a stroll, reading as he walks, groceries in a bag on his elbow from the weekly street fair at the far end of the pedestrian plaza. He slows as he approaches the jade disk of Indira; no one else is within a dozen meters.

"Thank you for meeting me, Mr. Juric," ó Lauris says. "It's good to see you well."

Manu studies him a moment — he seems to honestly mean it — then looks back down at the jade disk. "Do you miss it?"

"Some things," ó Lauris says. "Certain foods. Seasons. I feel like I've lost whole years here, not realizing how swiftly time is passing. It always catches me off guard to find we've completed another circuit around our star — you don't feel the rhythm of it in your bones."

"We have seasons. There's the dust-storm season, the parched-wind season, the scorpion-mite breeding season." Manu cracks a smile. "And don't forget those five hours in spring when the desert's blooming."

"Spring is lovely here."

"Blink and you miss it." Manu shifts, scanning the plaza; it's business as usual all around them. "How long have you been in Bulari?"

Ó Lauris smiles, but it's half-hearted. He looks exhausted, with a thin hum buzzing beneath his placid surface like he's running on stimulants rather than sleep. "Twenty-five years. Have you ever been to Indira?"

"Not yet."

"When you go, let me know. I can make some introductions."

Manu looks back at that. The offer seems genuine. "Thank you."

Ó Lauris's half-hearted smile fades. "I've been instructed to deliver a message," he says. "'The Alliance does not negotiate with terrorists.'"

"I meet any terrorists, I'll let them know," Manu says. "You could've told me that over a call."

"Mr. Juric, I do suggest that your employer take the Alliance seriously. The people who are in charge of these things aren't easy to reason with. I understand the footage you have looks very bad for us if it comes out. But your credibility is crumbling, whether the news is true or not."

"I appreciate the warning, Deputy Chief."

Ó Lauris shifts his groceries, making his own scan of the plaza. If he notices Oriol surreptitiously watching them, he doesn't show it. "I asked you here in hopes that we could exchange information," he says after a moment. "I have been on your planet for . . ." He looks Manu up and down, calculating. "More than half of your life. It has never been an easy post. I arrived here mere months before the Alliance's missteps in New Manila flared into an all-out war. As you can imagine, your government had a lot of hard questions for the Alliance embassy about that affair. The protests were quite impressive."

"I remember."

"When we weren't on the verge of being thrown out of Bulari by New Sarjunian protesters, we were about to be pulled for safety reasons by our government when Bulari got too violent. Each time, I fought to stay."

Ó Lauris turns back to Manu. "I've served under seven ambassadors. I've worked with three prime ministers. Four mayors. And now, after twenty-five years, our governments have the best relationship we've ever had. My patience, my hard work, is paying off — but this peace between our governments is a folded paper house, and someone on my side is juggling fire."

"I take it you've been asking questions about Blackheart."

"I've been asking questions about Blackheart." Ó Lauris sighs. "Stop me if I've got this wrong. But our side stole something highly irregular from New Sarjun, and Thala Coeur stole it back and brought it home. From what I can gather, somehow your employer acquired both Coeur and the item, which is why my lot sent in a covert agent. Obviously the agent didn't manage to kill Coeur, and I'm assuming they didn't manage to recover what they sought."

Ó Lauris searches Manu's face for confirmation. The corners of his mouth pull down. "I've been around long enough to know when something's gotten out of the box that can't be put back in."

"And what do you plan to do about it?"

"My colleagues don't understand Bulari. They think they're dealing with a common criminal who happens to own a nice office building, and who won't be missed if they take him out. Forgive me, Mr. Juric, but if that were the case, my job would be so much easier."

It's not a joke, and Manu doesn't smile. Deputy Chief of Mission Marquez ó Lauris runs an efficient operation. If removing the obstacle that is Jaantzen and his crew was as easy as filing burrs off a gear, ó Lauris would have had it done.

The fact that he's here telling Manu about his frustrations could be a sign that he intends to work with them. Or it could mean he's trying to ascertain the extent of the damage control he'll have to do.

The slow fury that's been banked in Manu's gut all week fans to life at the thought. Manu's getting tired of these games. Tired of trying to convince the rest of the world to leave his corner of it — his people — alone. He should stay the diplomat, treading carefully to make sure that the option that doesn't end in all-out destruction is the first on the table. But every fiber of his being is screaming to burn it all down to the ground.

"I'd like you to see something," Manu says, and from her aerie back at Cobalt Tower, Toshiyo sends to ó Lauris the vid of the Alliance agent's confession. Ó Lauris blinks in surprise at the incoming message, and his left eye mists silver as it plays. He scowls; it deepens.

"Killing me and mine may make your job easier," Manu

says when ó Lauris's eye clears; he keeps his tone light. "But your problem's gone way beyond that, now."

"Tell me you haven't filed for amnesty yet," ó Lauris says.

"Not yet. But the pieces are in place, and she's being kept somewhere safe. If anything happens to Jaantzen . . ."

"I can kiss my precious peace goodbye. We understand each other, Mr. Juric."

"Good. Spread the word."

"I will. Tell me. What is the nature of this thing Thala Coeur stole? Am I trying to contain a weapon? A new technology?"

Manu considers the question, not sure how to answer.

"In the wrong hands, it could be a weapon," he says carefully. "In the right, it might save lives. Either way, it's going to change the world as we know it once the secret gets out."

Ó Lauris's lips thin. "When it's time for the secret to get out, I hope you and I can work together on the logistics."

"I hope so, too. I'll be in touch."

Manu inclines his head, and they continue on their separate ways, ó Lauris strolling off like he hasn't a care, Manu firmly pushing back against the feeling that the entire world is about to come crashing down around them. Ó Lauris isn't on their side, but he'll do what it takes to keep the peace. And so long as Manu can keep him believing that attacking Jaantzen again will be a disaster, the man might be an ally.

"Bout time, this sun's a killer," Oriol says; he appears at Manu's elbow as Manu approaches the cab stand.

"He knows," Manu tells him. "Not about the hell-beast itself, but about what happened to — *shit.*"

Concern sparks in Oriol's golden eyes.

Manu bites back another curse. In this business with ó Lauris, he'd nearly been able to distract himself from the next task at hand — but now it comes back, crushing like a vise. He squeezes his eyes closed a moment, pinches the bridge of his nose, and when he opens his eyes again the now-familiar dark stain in the corner of his vision is back.

"He knows what happened to Coeur," Manu says.

"Back to the office?" Oriol says. He opens the door of the first cab at the stand, holds it for Manu. "Or maybe take the afternoon off?"

Manu shakes his head and slips inside. "I'm meeting the man near the Tamarind for lunch. You can drop me off, I'll get a ride back to the tower with him." He gives the address to the driver, who lurches away from the curb and into traffic in a wake of horn honking and curses.

Oriol gives him a long look. "Lunch meeting with who?" It's rare for Jaantzen to meet with any of his crew outside the tower unless someone else is involved.

Manu considers lying. He wishes briefly that he'd just told Oriol to take his own cab back to Phaera — but, no. He may not want a fight, but Oriol deserves to know.

"We're meeting *her*," Manu says finally.

Manu's waiting for the argument, the anger, but Oriol's relaxed facade doesn't crack. "Does the man know?"

Manu frowns at him. "Know what? He's the one set up the meeting."

"Does he know how much this is costing you."

The words are a knife through his ribs, searing and sharp.

"He knows," Manu says shortly.

A muscle clenches in Oriol's jaw. "Does he care?"

The air inside the cab is stifling, sunbaked and so thick Manu's practically choking; his lungs suddenly ache with the effort to breathe. He cracks the window, protocol be damned.

"Oriol," Manu says when he can breathe again. "I don't need you to make shit harder for me. I need you to have my back."

Fury flares in Oriol's eyes. "What do you think I'm doing?"

Manu doesn't have an answer for that. He slumps against the seat, closing his eyes, trying to remember a single bit of what Oriol's ever taught him for meditative breathing. Inbreath. Outbreath. *Fuckfuckfuck.*

Oriol's hand slips into his, warm. Not gripping, not asking — just there.

"I have to do this," Manu says finally without opening his eyes, and the hand in his gives a gentle squeeze, slips away. Around them, the traffic of Bulari is a cacophony. Oriol doesn't answer.

22

JAANTZEN

A knock on the window of the Dulciana and Manu opens the door to the back seat; a wash of dry heat from the baking afternoon hits Jaantzen as Manu slips inside. He's late, just a touch, but that's not what has Jaantzen worried. Manu looks like hell: cheeks hollow, a grayish cast to his dark skin. He apparently booked time this morning to freshen up his look, but his manicure is a matte black that drinks in the light and the highlights in his fresh-cut hair have been dyed back to natural. His pupils are sharp as pins.

"What's wrong?" Jaantzen asks.

"I'm fine."

"You're not."

A muscle jumps in Manu's jaw, but his shoulders relax, he rolls his neck. A deep breath and the tension drains from his face; when he opens his eyes he almost looks normal.

"That better?" Manu asks.

That wasn't what Jaantzen had been trying to say. "Manu — "

"You been to the Bronze Room since?" Manu asks, clearly going for a change of subject.

Jaantzen studies him, considering. At another time he would, should, push. Make it clear that he's worried about his lieutenant's mental health, not his appearance going into this meeting. If they had time to get into it, he would — but they're due inside. Maybe letting Manu distract himself is the right move.

"I have been," Jaantzen finally says. "You?"

"Nope."

The Dulciana is parked across the street from the Bronze Room, a dingy bar in neutral territory whose battered exterior doesn't invite curious visitors — and Jaantzen's spent his wait for Manu lost in memory. Twenty years ago, the place exploding around him, Teo and Tara Lordeur diving to the floor while the terrible lounge singer wailed terror into his mic. And — in the middle of the chaos — one fresh-faced hitman whose aim was mere inches too low for the bullet to take.

He doesn't think Coeur understood the irony in her choice of meeting locations, but in a way, the Bronze Room is the perfect place to begin a new chapter with her.

Beside him, Manu's frowning pensively at the bar's dented and stained door.

"I often think how glad I am I didn't kill you that day," Jaantzen says.

That gets a quirk of a smile; it doesn't stick.

"Same. Glad I was such a lousy shot."

"You got better."

"Happy I tried, though," Manu says. "It was a good way to meet people."

Jaantzen remembers staring into the eyes of the young man who'd just tried to kill him. Time had stood still in that adrenaline-clear moment, and something about the splashy artistry of the distraction, the playful spark in the kid's eyes as Jaantzen's fist tightened around his throat, the flash of his acid-green nails digging into Jaantzen's wrist, had given him pause.

If Manu hadn't tried to kill him with such panache, Jaantzen never would have met him, and his life would have been very different. As would Manu's, he supposes. The job Jaantzen ended up hiring Manu for had eventually introduced him to Oriol.

And introduced him to Coeur.

Jaantzen wonders if Manu would say yes to him today, knowing what that would put them all through in the end.

Manu's still frowning at the door to the bar; Jaantzen studies his face, not certain how to read what he sees there. Manu isn't buzzing with the restless energy he gets when he's preoccupied, he's not dragging with exhaustion or — necessarily — pain. He's leaning back against the seat, chin tilted up, legs stretched out, fingers laced over his abdomen. Manu closes his eyes and breathes deep as though steeling himself. Not to action. To make a decision.

A chill touches the back of Jaantzen's neck.

"Manu," he says quietly.

"I can count on one hand the number of people who give a shit what happens to me." Manu's eyes open again; he's still not looking at Jaantzen. "Oriol, Tosh, Starla. You."

Jaantzen lets him speak.

"I know you need me. But I can't do it." He stares at the doorway to the Bronze Room, shaking his head. "I'm sorry."

"You can't do what?" Jaantzen asks quietly; he almost can't hear his own voice over the blood rushing in his ears.

"Coeur, man." Manu shoves himself to a seated position with a wince, leans forward with elbows resting over knees, wrists dangling. "I can't fucking do it. Toshiyo has this place bugged to death, Starla's got people inside who can protect you better than I can, the shape I'm in. You're safe, and Blackheart won't touch you. But I can't go in there. I can't watch you make another goddamned deal with her."

Jaantzen takes a deep breath, realization melting the edge off the spike of ice in his gut: Manu's not leaving. Jaantzen knows this thing with Coeur has pushed him to the edge, he knows it has him slipping precariously, but it hasn't sent him tumbling down.

Not yet.

After Leone is dealt with, he's been thinking, he'll figure out what he can do to make things right with Manu. It's been on his list since the night he promised Ximena they would help rescue Coeur, but it's constantly being pushed down by more urgent demands. But he can see now, it can't wait. Oriol's been trying to tell him — dammit, *Manu's* been trying to tell him that for days.

They'll sit down and truly talk this through, Jaantzen tells himself.

After this meeting.

"It's fine," Jaantzen says. "El's already inside, I'll be safe. Go home. Get some rest. I'll see you tomorrow morning."

Manu shakes his head. "I'll wait here."

Jaantzen hits the button to open the Dulciana's privacy window to the man in the driver's seat. "Raim, take Manu home. El will give me a ride back."

Manu starts to protest, but Jaantzen cuts him off. "Go home. Rest. Don't make me have Toshiyo change your security codes to keep you out of your office."

Another quirk of a smile; Jaantzen takes it tentatively as a good sign.

"I'm staying here," Manu says firmly. "I just can't fucking sit across from her again and pretend I'm fine."

Jaantzen takes a deep breath. "All right," he says. He catches Raim's eye; the other man nods. "I'll see you both in a few minutes."

Manu sinks back against the seat, an exhaustion that goes deeper than physical.

After this meeting, Jaantzen will make everything right.

The interior of the Bronze Room hasn't changed at all since the day Manu tried to kill him: Metal tables and layers of threadbare rugs and shadows in every corner made up of stains and cigarette smoke and ancient fryer grease. A tilted stage in one corner gathering obsolete wiring and discarded posters like cobwebs. A bar stocked with labels Jaantzen hasn't been able to stomach for decades, encircled by the not-so-discreet groove of a security shield on the ceiling that the bartender can activate if things get rowdy.

The Bronze Room's bar is empty but for El and the bartender.

The floor is empty but for Blackheart.

Coeur raises her bottle as Jaantzen enters, her gaze sliding past him to where Manu should be at his side. Her face registers surprise but she doesn't comment.

She's brought her new lieutenant, Aden Damyati. Jaantzen recognizes the man, though he's never met him in person. Damyati was pivotal in welcoming Coeur back to her crew, and the position of lieutenant is a fine reward — but Jaantzen wonders how much Damyati's presence is for his protection and input, and how much is Coeur's careful political dance to reassure him and the others that just because she made an alliance with Willem Jaantzen, she's not his puppet.

Manu would know, he'd be able to read it somehow in

Damyati's body language. Jaantzen pushes the thought aside, signs for El to stay in his position.

Damyati stands to greet him with a handshake, but Coeur doesn't bother to get up. Her cane is propped against the table, and from the pinched lines of her face, she's still in pain. "Damyati, Jaantzen," she says, waving a gloved hand around the table in some semblance of introduction. "You've been making waves, Willem. How'd all that bullshit get started? I hope you don't think it was me, I don't get my hands dirty with rumors."

"I'm well aware of that. It was Leone."

Coeur laughs. She's gotten her missing incisor replaced; it's blood red and sharp.

"Her guard dog's acting out, yeah?" And she leans back in her chair with a grin. Jaantzen doesn't bother answering — the bartender is coming by to take orders. Coeur orders another lager and Damyati begs off. Jaantzen orders the only decent whiskey the Bronze Room carries.

When the girl comes back with the drinks, Coeur lifts her fresh bottle to Jaantzen and takes a swig. "To pissing off Leone."

"So far it hasn't been worth celebrating," Jaantzen says.

"I was gonna let bygones be bygones with her, but if she's going to come off the ropes fighting dirty, I'll have to reconsider."

Jaantzen frowns at her. "She hasn't come after you."

"She's coming after a business partner, though." Coeur graces Jaantzen with a lazy smile, predator's gleam back in her eyes. "Right?"

He's not sure if Coeur is just testing him, prodding to find the limits of his tolerance rather than actually planning to involve herself in this business with Leone. He decides to let it go.

"Aiax will be coming down for dinner in two days," he says. "I hope you can join us."

She shrugs a bony shoulder. "Course."

"I spoke with Lhasa and Aiax yesterday. I'll provide the plans and the tech security, they have a thousand hectares of land in the Moire Valley and the technicians who can implement the operation. We'll need ground security from you."

"How many people?"

"I'm thinking six to start, round-the-clock watch — three shifts in pairs. You could swap them out with another team if you want, one week on, one week off. Depending on how many people you can trust to keep this quiet."

Coeur's gaze turns on Aden Damyati, who nods slowly. "I'll come up with a list," he says.

"It's not just security jobs," Jaantzen says. "When this gets going we'll need workers. Administrators. Warehouse employees. A lot of good jobs for people in your territory. They'll pay well, of course, and you'll both get your cut."

If Coeur wants to secure her place back at the head of her territory without fighting every last person in it, demonstrating that she can bring lasting change and prosperity is the key. For all of Coeur's viciousness and petty backstabbing, she's always been a visionary, looking ten steps beyond in order to carve out the best advantage for herself and the people loyal to her.

Trick to working with her is not to be the one she carves.

Jaantzen can see in her eyes that she understands the value of what he's offering her. And Damyati — Jaantzen's learned everything he can about him in the last few days. A fighting man who pays more attention than you give him credit for, who can see beyond the immediate actions of now. Jaantzen doesn't know Damyati well enough to understand his motivations, but the biggest problem with Coeur will be to convince her this operation is too big for her to double-cross everyone and try to run on her own — and that her share of the pie will be bigger and better if they all work together.

"The thousand hectares is for us to experiment on to start," he says. "But the Demosgas have infrastructure in place to scale rapidly. This will be bigger than anything you or I have ever done."

That gleam in her eye; she sees it.

"Beyond the logistics, the biggest hurdle we're facing is the trade agreement with the Alliance. If it passes, that's lower profits. Lhasa's already working on it."

"Demosgas aren't the only ones who think that deal is bad for business," Coeur says; her tone snags at Jaantzen's attention.

"That bomb at the embassy," he says slowly. "Was it you?"

Coeur shakes her head. "I got something better planned for those bastards." A slow smile spreads across her face as she catches his look. "I'm kidding, Willem."

Jaantzen doesn't smile.

"Fine, fine. We're doing serious. Then I got a question for you. The serum. You need it to make the terraforming plans work, and I happen to know you have just one of the two cases I stole from the Alliance, since you blew up the other one with Zacharia around it. Is it enough?"

"We're working on a way to manufacture it," Jaantzen says. Let her think — let everyone think — that the cases themselves contained whatever serum the terraforming plans call for. Now that Toshiyo's creature is happily ensconced in its new desert lair, hopefully they'll have the breathing room to figure out exactly what the serum is and how to get a consistent supply of it.

Coeur lifts an eyebrow; she sees through his reassurances. "And here everybody is worrying I'll be the weakest link."

Jaantzen isn't sure if she's baiting him on purpose or just falling into her usual patterns. Probably the latter, because she leans back and takes a long swig of her beer.

"I wanted to let you know you've got a more immediate problem, though," she says. "Some detective is starting to look after Naali and Chase. Guy named Cho. He's found the bodies, and likes Juric for the man who put them in the ground."

Jaantzen takes a sip of his whiskey, considering. It's not the first time bodies have come back from the desert, though with everything else Leone's thrown his way in the last few days, he can't believe the timing is coincidental.

"How do you know?" he asks Coeur.

She smiles. "Snitch who told the police came to me, too. Thought she'd get a double payday, but her story was bullshit. I know you didn't have Naali killed, why the fuck would you have done that? She was just feeding out a line."

"Do you know who gave her the information?"

Coeur smiles slowly. "I couldn't get her to tell me a name."

Jaantzen sighs. "I don't suppose there's a chance I can speak with her."

"You know I don't keep shit like that around." Coeur takes a swig of her beer. "She did give me a description. Woman, maybe around forty, real fit. Curly brown hair, brown skin, freckles. About my height."

"From Bulari?"

"The girl thought so, but she'd never seen her before.

Said she talked sweet, all girlfriend-to-girlfriend, but the girl still seemed more scared of her than me."

"Do you know her? Or is she a new player in town?"

"Fuck if I would know," Coeur says.

Beside her, Damyati shrugs. "We've been asking around. No leads yet."

"I'd ask the guy who owns the restaurant, personally." Coeur smiles coldly. "I could swing by on the way home if you want."

"I'll handle Ajesh, Thala," Jaantzen says. "Thank you."

Jaantzen sincerely hopes it wasn't Ajesh Paiman or any of his family who leaked that information; he's always liked the man. But even if Ajesh talked, Jaantzen isn't letting Coeur anywhere near him. Jaantzen can clean up his messes himself.

And if Ajesh talked, he hadn't decided to out of the blue — or without someone leaning on him. The "reporter" snapping photos of him and Phaera at the Jungle. The blond woman who slipped shard into Starla's purse. The woman who fed the girl the intel about the Oasis. It could be multiple people — but the most reasonable explanation is usually the simplest.

Leone.

"Leone knew Acheta killed Naali and Chase," Jaantzen says. "He bragged about it to everyone the night he did it. Did he tell Leone where they were buried? Or is someone else in your crew working with her?"

"If they are, fuck them. Bitch drove me out of Bulari."

"Leone didn't drive you out." Jaantzen shifts forward slightly, locking his eyes on hers. "I did."

Coeur's gaze is steady on his a long moment before she lets out a laugh and polishes off her lager. "Fuck you, too, Willem," she says lightly.

Aden Damyati clears his throat. "It was Acheta," he says to Jaantzen.

"How do you know?"

Damyati tips his head. "He figured you'd deal with the mess he left, so he had your cleanup crew followed. By me. I grew up in the desert, I'm good at getting around out there without being noticed. I saw where they were buried, and I only told Acheta. He might have told Sjel, but nobody else in the crew knew."

Which means Leone was collecting leverage on Jaantzen even before he'd made plans to deal with Acheta. He casts back to the night of that dinner party, trying to remember Leone's reaction to Acheta's arrival. She'd seemed displeased, but still cordial. She could have been unhappy with him for the *way* he killed Hinoja, not the act itself. Or she could have been putting on an act for them all.

"Gods that boy was an idiot," Coeur says. "So Leone's coming after you with guns blazing because you killed her new pet. What are we doing about it?"

"We?"

"If she's at you, it's only a matter of time before she's at me." Coeur folds her gloved hands gingerly over each other on the table. "She's pulling out all the stops because she's scared. She's not going to be content taking you down a peg, Willem, she's looking to cut off your arms and legs and leave you bleeding in the desert for the wolves."

She slides something across the table to him: a disposable holoplayer. "And the bitch thinks I'm one of her wolves."

Jaantzen presses Play. The image is of him and Leone in her entry, from a few nights back — he was right, she had been recording him. "We set loose a jaguar to clear out the wild dogs running in Dry Creek," he's saying in the hologram. "Coeur's still a monster, but I have a plan to keep her attention once she's destroyed that crew."

"You gonna tell me that it sounds better in context?" Coeur says.

"No." Jaantzen watches it with a frown. "I'm sure nothing else I said about you that night was any more complimentary."

Coeur shrugs. "You've said worse than this to my face."

"And I'm sure I will again."

"I don't care what you say about me. I care that Geum-ja Leone thinks I'm her puppet. Like all she has to do is bait me with a fucking vid and I'll come after you." Coeur smiles, slow. "Like I don't have some good shit on her, too."

"Such as."

"The things she thought she could pull when I was mayor. Bribery, embezzlement, extortion." Coeur shakes her head in mock sadness.

"The usual, then."

"Not quite the usual. When she was a city judge, she got kickbacks for changing the sentences of certain prisoners."

"Selling them to the Alliance to work at Redrock?"

Coeur blinks in surprise. That's a yes.

"Any of yours?" Jaantzen asks.

"Sending mine up was her favorite hobby."

There's a black viciousness in Coeur's eyes as she says it, and for the first time in days, Jaantzen allows himself a tentative spark of hope. Dealing with Leone isn't like ordering a hit on Acheta — he's been feeling in over his head. But Leone's broken the first rule of survival in Bulari: Don't fuck with Thala Coeur.

"I've been digging into this. I have a reporter working on

the story, and lawyers putting together a case against her," Jaantzen says. "Send me what you have."

Her expression darkens, and he's sure she's about to argue when Damyati lays a hand on the table between them.

"Neither of us are going to beat Leone alone, but it can't look like we're working together." He looks to Coeur, who lifts her chin at him to continue. "I suggest we pool resources, but keep it quiet. She thinks she can use you to take down Jaantzen, or she wouldn't have sent you that vid. We keep her thinking that way, we'll have an in."

Coeur frowns at Damyati, considering, then grins. Her red-lacquered incisor shines; Jaantzen wonders if she chose the color to remind her crew of the triumphant, fresh-blooded smile she used to wear after a victory in the ring.

"I'll get you the information," Coeur says. "And I'll see if anybody wants to talk to a reporter or a lawyer. What else do you need?"

"Do you know a man named Orris Moss?"

Coeur looks to Damyati, who shakes his head.

"He used to work for Leone and could be pivotal to making this case, but he's locked up at Taufang-Set. We haven't been able to get to him."

"I'll see what I can do."

"Thank you." Jaantzen stands, shaking Damyati's hand and inclining his head to Coeur. "I'll be in touch."

El follows him out the door, keeping an eye on Coeur and Damyati as they leave. What a strange world in which he doesn't worry about turning his back on her. Where he actually trusts that she'll keep her word when it comes to supplying him with the information about Leone he asked for, and the ground security to manage the farming operation. That she'll keep her word about not harming any of his people.

Physically, at least.

Any more than she already has.

Preparing himself for the meeting with Coeur had been surprisingly easy. Steeling himself for the conversation he needs to have with Manu is taking more effort.

He turns to El. "Get back to the tower and help Starla finalize things there. Manu and I will meet you . . ."

The back seat of the Dulciana is empty.

"Manu wanted me to tell you when we were done," El says. "He was listening in on Toshiyo's feed. He went to take care of things at the Oasis."

The way El says it, he has no clue what Manu meant by "take care of things at the Oasis." El had been sitting at the bar for backup, not listening in on the conversation Jaantzen was having with Coeur.

Jaantzen clenches his jaw not to let his frustration show in front of El. "I'll meet you back at the tower."

He slides in the back seat of the Dulciana and opens a new message.

Do you need backup?

He gets no answer.

"We'll be picking Mr. Juric up at the Oasis," he tells Raim. "Quickly, please."

23

MANU

The restaurant is dark through the windows, the tables empty, but the side door to the alleyway's unlocked, and so Manu pushes it open carefully, listening for voices and hearing nothing but a faint shuffling and clanging in the kitchen. It doesn't sound like cooking, it doesn't smell like dinner preparations.

Everything about the Oasis feels wrong.

Everything about this situation feels wrong.

When he decided he couldn't go into the Bronze Room with Coeur, he wasn't planning on listening in, either. Coeur's lazy drawl, the too-comfortable way Jaantzen spoke with her — it all grated on him. But he knew Toshiyo would have the feed, and he already had one of her bugs in his ear. He'd asked her to patch him in and she had. Had pushed the vid from El's location through to his comm so Manu could match words with body language. Maybe he couldn't force himself to walk into the room, but he could at least do that.

The fact that the bodies had become unburied didn't shock him, but Leone's woman pinning it on him is an interesting choice. Why not Jaantzen himself? It feels like a game, all these indirect attacks. Is Leone going for subtle? Or is her goal to slowly pick off Jaantzen's support to leave the man exposed and alone so she can finish him last?

That's not happening.

If the BPD has the bodies, they might know where Hinoja and Chase were done. But if they'd started nosing around the Oasis, Manu would have heard about it from Ajesh and Mirana. They've been friends of Jaantzen's for a decade, they've been treated well. The police shouldn't be able to get a thing out of the Paimans.

But something's gone wrong.

Manu doesn't call out. He unbuttons his jacket and slips into the short hall to the kitchen, locking the door behind him. The hallway's stacked with boxes, claustrophobic. He brushes past a rack hung with aprons, a water-refilling station, and into the doorway to the kitchen.

The kitchen's tight for the crew that usually works it, Mirana Paiman and her two daughters, but usually it's humming with sizzling pans and bright with chopped vegetables and laughter. Today the lights are dim, the ovens off, and Mirana is emptying the safe beside the stove, her back to him. She's sweeping the contents without care into a bag, her movements hurried, clumsy. She's alone.

"Hey, Mirana," Manu says, leaning one shoulder against the doorway.

She shrieks and straightens, then spins to face him, snatching up a chef's knife from the counter and holding it in front of her with both hands. When she sees it's Manu, the tip drops almost instinctively. And rises again, resolve hardening the lines of her mouth, fear quickening her breath.

Manu keeps his casual lean, gun hand free; his right

shoulder burns where the hell-beast swiped him. "Where's Ajesh?"

"Please go." Mirana's voice is pitched high and tight. It seems unnaturally loud in the silent kitchen.

"You alone?" Manu asks, and she grips the knife tighter. A tear glints bright in the corner of her left eye. "I'm not going to hurt you. Where's Ajesh."

"He's out." It's barely a whisper.

"He's out where?" Manu doesn't move, but she flinches away. "Talking to the police?"

Mirana lets out a hoarse sob and an involuntary step back, bumping against the counter and sending a stack of metal ramekins tipping to the tile floor. They scatter and roll. Her attention never wavers from Manu.

"Who are you running from, Mirana?" Manu tilts his head, studying her. "Me?"

"Please, Manu," she sobs. "Please just go." The tip of the knife wavers; her hands are shaking violently.

"Listen." He comes off the lean, hands empty and raised. "I need you to put down the knife so we can have a conversation. I'm not here to hurt you. And if I was, that knife's not going to stop me, yeah?"

She takes a sharp, shallow breath. He knows that didn't come off as reassuring, but he's not trying to be. Not until he knows exactly why she and her husband are throwing him to the police.

"Don't make me take the knife, Mirana," Manu says quietly, and the decision comes in the slump of her shoulders, the resigned clench of her jaw. Mirana slowly lowers the knife, sets it on the counter by the stove. Her hand rests just beside it.

"Okay, good." Manu lowers his hands, but stays in the

doorway. "You alone here? Anyone else I need to know about? I've had enough surprises this week already."

Her fingers twitch towards the knife. "I'm alone," she whispers.

"Thank you. Ajesh is in talking to the police?"

She nods, and he settles back into a lean to calm her down, left shoulder this time to spare the stitches on his right. He's not as worried about speed; she's not lying about being alone, and she's not going to attack him unless he makes the first move. The alley door's locked behind him. He has a clear line of sight through the kitchen to the front door.

He's probably standing in the exact same spot Acheta was when he waited for Naali and Chase to settle in so he could murder them.

"So he's talking to the police," Manu says. "Sometimes you have to do that. What's he telling them?"

"About those two that were killed," Mirana says finally.

"He's telling them I pulled the trigger, yeah?" Manu asks. The hand that's not itching to grab the knife flies to cover the hollow of her throat. "It's okay, Mirana, I just need to know."

Her chin dips, a nod.

"Why?"

Another hoarse sob, and a tear spills out, traces the strong line of her nose, comes to rest in the corner of her mouth. Both arms fold over her chest, the knife forgotten. She's terrified, and it's not of him. Not of Jaantzen. Slow certainty settles in Manu's gut. Ajesh Paiman and his family have been friends with Jaantzen for years. Jaantzen's taken care of them. There's not enough money in the system to turn Ajesh.

A man like that's got a far more effective lever.

"Where are your girls?" Manu asks gently, and the tears flow free.

Mirana braces herself on the counter with one hand, the other covering her face as she cries, and Manu takes one step forward, another. Reaches to squeeze her upper arm and she doesn't flinch. She melts as he puts his arms around her, sobbing into his shoulder. She smells like cumin, lavender, sage, and fear.

She doesn't let herself go long, pushes herself free self-consciously and turns away to blow her nose on a napkin, wipe her eyes on her sleeve. Her shoulders rise, fall as she composes herself. Manu slides the chef's knife unobtrusively out of her reach.

"Tell me," Manu says to her back, and Mirana takes a deep breath before she turns around.

The fear's gone; it's just fury now.

"The girls were out shopping yesterday," she says, voice hoarse, she's talking fast, now. "They didn't come home when they said they would, but at first I wasn't worried. Then a woman came in. She said Ajesh needed to go see the police about those two that were killed, and that he should tell them you and Mr. Jaantzen came to meet them, and that you shot them both. Ajesh said no, we don't know anything about that, and she said — " That hand's at her throat again, clawed tight. It takes her a few breaths before she can speak without crying.

Manu hands her another napkin, she dabs it at her leaking eyes.

"She said she had the girls, that she would kill them if we didn't do what she said. I'm so sorry."

"She give you a specific cop to talk to? Or just in general."

A sharp nod. "Detective Cho."

Huh. The guy's definitely not on Leone's payroll. Which means he's got another agenda, or he's being played. Manu can worry about that next.

"Thanks, Mirana. No one will know you told me, it's easy to find out who's on what cases, okay? And don't worry about me or the man, we'll be fine. I'm going to show you a picture."

She nods and he reaches for his comm, opens a set of stills from the security footage Toshiyo had sent him: the blond in the jumpsuit, the reporter with the short blue hair. The same woman, with the heart-shaped face, tawny skin, hazel eyes, spray of freckles.

"Is this her?" he asks.

Two breaths, and the hand pressed to her throat relaxes, her fingers toying with the charm on her necklace. Mirana frowns down at the picture. "She had black hair. But yeah." Hope fills her eyes. "You know who she is?"

"What else do you know about her?"

"She sounded local. She — " Mirana squeezes her eyes shut, thinking. "She had a . . . scar? Just below her left eye. I'm sorry."

"Where were your girls shopping? Surquillo Market? Okay. Mirana." He waits until she's looking at him. "Do everything she says until you hear from me. Don't breathe a word I was here, not to Ajesh, not to anybody." He jerks his chin at the safe she's emptying. "You running from me?"

She takes a sharp breath. "I knew you'd find out," she whispers.

"Good. Run. Stay scared. Scared of me, scared of her, scared for your girls." He points to the stand mixer on the counter. "This needs fixed, where do you take it?"

She frowns. "What?"

"You need to get a message to me, take it to a place in

Geordi's called Hallelujah It's Fixed. Tell Louis, he'll pass it on. You understand? Good."

He slides the chef's knife back towards her; she doesn't reach for it. "Stay scared, Mirana. And lock your alley door."

Her voice catches him in the doorway. "Manu, I'm so sorry."

He gives her a one-shouldered shrug but doesn't answer. Shouldn't've entertained Jaantzen and Hinoja and Coeur and the Lordeurs and all the rest so many years, but there's no taking that back now. And for all Manu knows, Ajesh and Mirana hadn't had much choice of clientele in the beginning anyway.

He lets himself out, hears the bolt click into place as he walks down the alleyway.

Opens up a channel back home.

"Tosh. That woman you've been seeing on the security feeds. Tell me you know who she is."

He can almost hear Toshiyo's grin. "I've got some good news for you," she says. "And the boss is parked outside the alley to pick you up. I'll see you in a few."

24

JAANTZEN

A glowing panel in the back of the Dulciana's driver's seat pulses softly; Aiax Demosga is requesting a connection. Jaantzen puts it through, voice only.

"Aiax, thank you for calling. I just left our mutual friend; she's prepared to hold up her end of the bargain and is looking forward to the meeting. When — "

"Meeting's off," Aiax cuts in, an edge of anger in his voice. "For the moment, at least. Looks like you're poison right now, Jaantzen."

Of course. Wasn't it only a matter of time before these shifting sands caught the Demosgas, too?

"Go on," Jaantzen says.

"I just got off the line with a certain chief justice who apparently has it out for you. What did you do to her?"

"What did she say to you?"

"That if I knew what was good for my business, I'd stay away from you."

"Is that so."

Leone's early blows to his reputation had soured business relationships with people like Mizal Seti who weren't able to separate fact from fiction. Jaantzen has expected Leone to continue chipping away at his support, but apparently she's no longer content to destabilize him through indirect attacks and subtle barbs. Now she's contacting his associates directly. But did she contact Aiax particularly? Or is she on a general campaign.

"She made it sound like she was just concerned about your reputation tarnishing mine, but I can read between the lines," says Aiax. "She's blacklisted you. If I ever want her support again, I can't be connected with you." Jaantzen hears Aiax shift on the other end of the line.

"Do you think she suspects we're working together?"

"I don't think so — she's just spreading the word. I get the impression your social calendar is going to be empty for a while."

So she's blacklisted him and is making sure everyone in her circle knows about it. Destabilizing his support, yes — but not because business owners like Aiax believe her allegations against him, or would prefer to work with Leone. She's not giving them any choice.

Jaantzen can use that.

"You've never struck me as the sort of person who lets someone else make his business decisions," Jaantzen says, tone mild but words meant to dig and twist — remind Aiax what control he's signing away to Geum-ja Leone.

"You think I like this? I need her. And not just to grease the wheels every once in a while — she's got me by the balls, Jaantzen." Aiax bites out a profane curse. "You know how things are. You need a little help, you ask your friends. And then they know too much about your business and they fuck you over."

So Leone isn't just suggesting Aiax comply with her order to shun Jaantzen — she's blackmailing him. She might have tried that with Jaantzen in the first place, but it's not likely she has anything on him yet that won't also take her down. It's why all her attacks have been circumspect so far, eating away at his supports rather than targeting him directly.

If she's pulling the blackmail card on the Demosgas, she may be using it on others. She's pulling out every stop she has in her quest to destroy Jaantzen. If she succeeds, though, she's going to have quite the collection of discontents on her hands.

Especially if Jaantzen has any say in the matter.

"She's so certain she owns you," he says, and Aiax lets out another curse. "That's not how I treat my colleagues, you know that, Aiax."

"Well, Leone's in charge, not you."

But Calanthe's words from last night are slipping through his memory: *You have the support for a change in leadership.*

"Have some faith," Jaantzen says.

Silence on the other end of the line, then Aiax laughs bitterly. "I want to believe that. But there's no taking care of Leone. Whatever it is you did to piss her off, you better make it right. Get back with us when you have." Aiax cuts the connection. Jaantzen lets out a fury of curse words.

This needs to end.

He sends a message to Teo Lordeur, but he doubts he'll get a response. Leone's tightening around them like a noose, drawing them all into a war just like ten years ago with Coeur. Only this time, she and Jaantzen aren't fighting on the same side.

But he's seen how she fights. He and his crew were primarily on the ground, handling the physical fight against Coeur. But Leone had been waging psychological and financial battle, too. Coeur hadn't been ousted from her position of mayor just because she ran out of soldiers — she'd lost in the court of public and business opinion.

For Jaantzen, it doesn't matter much what the public thinks of him. His business deals are made one-on-one with people like Aiax who have known him for years and aren't going to be swayed by rumors — even if they are vulnerable to blackmail.

Leone, on the other hand, relies a great deal on public opinion. Push it too much in the direction of disapproval — say, let the world know she's been selling New Sarjunian citizens to the hated Alliance prison — and she could lose her position.

Assuming they can bring it all together in time.

Jaantzen leans back against the seat and catches a whiff of citrus and cardamom, Phaera's scent still imprinted on the jacket he'd worn the night before. Despite how little sleep they'd gotten, she'd been out the door early this morning, and today's unfolded without much time for him to reflect on the lines they crossed last night.

Though maybe there were no lines. After all, Leone had already targeted Phaera because of him; last night didn't put her any more squarely in Leone's crosshairs.

And no one had died — he'd gotten Starla's report of no issues, and after her long day in the desert, she'd been perfectly happy to wait until morning to fill him in. He'd spent a night without holding every thread of his world tight, and it hadn't unraveled without him there to watch it close.

Or so it seems.

Jaantzen can't help but feel like he's overlooked something. If he'd gone over the pieces once more last night rather than allowing himself to slip, maybe he would have caught the missing puzzle piece before Leone made today's calls. Maybe he would have found the clue that would help him finish this thing once and for all.

Or maybe a man needs an hour — or several hours — where he doesn't feel hunted and reeling with the need to maintain control.

He breathes deep, banishing last night from his memory.

Leone has issued general warnings to the Demosgas and Lordeurs, she's stripped away Jaantzen's support from fair-weather partners like Seti. She's been deeply personal in her attempts to get Phaera and Coeur to turn. She's making direct attacks on his crew by trying to frame Manu for the murders of Naali Hinoja and Chase Ratham.

So far there's only one person he hasn't heard anything from.

He makes the call.

"Yes, Willem?"

Julieta Yang sounds wrong, like she's ill, or she's just woken up from a nap. Something soft and instrumental is playing behind her voice; Jaantzen is trying to place it. The song doesn't sound quite like the New Manilan ballads Julieta prefers, those soulful, husky female vocals on the verge of tears. He knows he's heard it before though — something about it tastes electric and raw and scrapes at his memory.

"Julieta. Where are you?"

"I'm visiting a friend." There's a note in her voice, it could be annoyance at his timing but for that small quaver. "I'll call you back when I'm free."

"Julieta — "

"Willem," she hisses. "Run."

Before he can answer, he hears her cry out — it sounds

like anger, not pain. The rustling of fabric, another cry —
pain, this time — and a slamming door.

"Julieta!"

For an agonizing moment there's silence on the other
end of the line. He checks the connection, but it hasn't
been cut.

Someone on the other end of the line takes a breath.

"Hello, Willem."

Geum-ja Leone.

Dread is a cold, polished stone beneath his ribcage.

"What a pleasant surprise," says Leone. He can hear the
click of her footsteps on tile. "I hope you're well?"

"Where's Julieta."

"She's visiting for lunch. It's so pleasant, isn't it? Having
lunch with old friends. Oh! Though I expect you have
fewer people willing to call themselves your friend these
days."

"Not when you're threatening them, no." Jaantzen
pushes back worry about Julieta, forces himself to think
calmly. Leone won't physically harm her, he tells himself.
She's just trying to scare him. "I thought you'd be happy
threatening blackmail, though. Not attacking such an 'old
friend' as Julieta."

"I'm beginning to suspect she's not my friend," Leone
says coldly. "Now. What did you want to tell her? I can pass
along your message."

"My message is for you. Call off your dogs. Let's work
this out like adults. I've apologized for making a decision
that affects us all without consulting you first, and although
I don't regret my actions, I do regret making you an enemy.
But I'm not going to play games with you, Geum-ja. You're
spreading my name around and threatening our mutual
colleagues. Call off your dogs, or I will act."

"You'll act, Willem? I'm not a Thala Coeur who can just be swept out of existence without a second thought. I have real strength, real power. Making me your enemy has real consequences."

"I'm well aware."

"I don't think you understand," Leone says. In the background, he hears a heavy thud and muffled shouting. Leone sighs and her footsteps resume. "I've already won."

She's pushed away his support, she's threatened his people. She's shown him that despite how solid he'd thought his business partnerships were, she can shred them to pieces. She's now got her claws into his oldest, dearest friend.

But if she thinks that's enough to send Willem Jaantzen quietly into the night, she doesn't know him at all.

Not like she thinks she does.

"Let Julieta go, Geum-ja. You and I, we can talk."

Leone laughs, offended. "You make me out to be some kind of monster! We're just having lunch. And anyway, I don't think there's anything to work out between us. I think it's time for you to leave. You're not wanted here anymore."

"*I* should leave." He doesn't bother keeping the anger from his voice.

"You have no allies, Willem. There's no one left in the city who will work with you. Your reputation is shattered — or, should I say, your reputation is finally out in the open. The whole world is seeing you for who you truly are, no more facade, no more of your tricks."

"I've never tried to hide who I am."

"Haven't you? That's not what others will think. You have no support. Even now, people are pulling out. From your security business, the restaurant supply, all of it. No one will work with you. No one will give money to a company associated with your name." A pause, and he can hear the smile enter her voice. "I can help you. I can connect you with a buyer for your businesses, which will give you enough to cut your losses and leave the city. You can start over elsewhere. No reason for you and your people to suffer any more than you already have."

Jaantzen laughs aloud, honestly shocked by the audacity of her suggestion. Every person on his payroll, every one of their families who set their table with a solid paycheck rather than an indenture stipend. And he's just going to cut them loose to Leone.

"If you want to have a conversation, let's talk," Jaantzen says. "But I'm not discussing this while you hold Julieta hostage."

"Hostage?" He can hear the feigned surprise in her voice. "I'll admit I invited her over for lunch with clouded intentions. But, you see, the Bulari Police Department gave me a call and asked if I could help. It seems she was behind a grisly assassination a few weeks ago. They've followed the money, and found she paid you and Mr. Juric to kill Naali Hinoja for her. It's such a shame."

Fear spikes through Jaantzen's chest.

"They may have turned a blind eye all these years to her side business, but they won't turn a blind eye to murder," Leone continues. "Though I'd hate to see her locked up, poor old thing. She's become so frail lately."

"Leone. Let her go."

"I'm making you an offer," Leone says. "Sell off your interests here and leave town. Then I'm certain the police will realize they made a horrible mistake. Willem, don't make poor Julieta suffer because of your pride. Neither of us know just how much she can take."

"If you lay a hand on her — "

"I won't have to. Let me know your decision soon, Willem. Don't make Julieta spend the night in a cell."

The line goes dead.

For the second time today, there's a knock on the window to the Dulciana and the door opens — only three people's prints bypass the locks, beside his: Manu's, Starla's, and Raim's.

Manu slips into the seat.

Jaantzen holds up a finger and makes another call; the wait is excruciating as the connection request cycles, then — "Sorry, Willem, Julian is being a nightmare today. But my god, there's *gold* in those files you forwarded from Thala."

"Calanthe. Leone is having your mother arrested."

In the seat beside him, Manu straightens.

There's a long pause. "Willem . . ."

"She's trying to frame Manu for Naali Hinoja's murder, and she's claiming your mother paid for the whole thing."

A sharp breath; an unholy curse.

"You need time to make this case. Letizia needs time to pull together the story. We can't let her force our hand, Calanthe. What else do you need from me?"

She sighs. "We have a paper trail, but I need to talk to someone who knows. This Orris Moss guy Lhasa mentioned. One of the Redrock prisoners if we could possibly get access."

"We'll get you Orris Moss."

"Thank you. The amnesty deal for the Alliance agent. When am I filing that?"

Jaantzen glances at Manu, who shakes his head. Apparently they don't yet need to play that particular card.

"I'll let you know. Get to your mother. Let me know what I can do to help."

On the other end of the line, Calanthe takes a sharp breath. "I'll bring her home."

Jaantzen cuts the connection and closes his eyes briefly, trying to clear his head. "Ajesh?" he asks Manu.

"At the BPD right now testifying that I did Naali and Chase."

"And that Julieta ordered it."

"That won't stick for long."

"It won't have to." Jaantzen swears under his breath. "How did she get to Ajesh?"

Manu flicks an image from his comm onto the panel in front of Jaantzen. The woman who's been plaguing their steps for the last few days — even in this security still, she's got a faint smile in her hazel eyes. Like she's daring them to catch her at her game.

"Her."

25

PHAERA

"It's just a few weeks," Phaera says; her mother, Marjani, is giving her a skeptical look. "You always say how much you like Alusina this time of year — and when's the last time you saw Auntie Dahla?"

Her mother arches a suspicious eyebrow.

Phaera's been at this for the better part of an hour, and she's honestly not sure how many other ways there are to try convincing her mother to get out of Bulari without outright telling her that the highest officer in the planet's judicial system has threatened her life.

They're in an airy cafe in the Tamarind, on the park blocks where the original busy road was torn out and replanted to create a stunning slice of green in the city. Towering eucalyptus and oak, fan palm and tree aloe. Meandering paths cutting through the park, and shops and cafes lining either side. They're at her mother's favorite table at her favorite cafe. Lunch is a hearty vegetable tagine over couscous, and her mother ordered them a gorgeous vinho verde. Phaera hasn't had more than a few sips.

It's a gorgeous day; all Phaera can feel is creeping dread.

Her mother is not listening.

Oriol is tucked discreetly at a nearby table, sipping tea; he looks like he's ignoring them, but for the way his body angles towards them. She could tell he disapproved of a lunch out with her mother, but he hadn't outright tried to stop her.

Her initial irritation with Jaantzen at assigning her a bodyguard had waned quickly, once she realized that Oriol wasn't going to put her under glass like some rare breed of fragile flower. He telegraphs his disapproval, but he doesn't step in unless he's truly worried. Which means Phaera has actually started listening to him rather than assuming every reaction is an overreaction. She's not about to live her life in a constant state of red alert like Jaantzen and Manu — but having Oriol around for a gut check and an extra set of eyes has been surprisingly reassuring.

He catches her eye, then goes back to idly scanning the park.

"The lavender festival's going on right now," Phaera says. "When's the last time you saw the lavender festival?"

Her mother's suspicious expression doesn't change as she takes a sip of her wine, light catching like peridot in the glass. Phaera's trying far too hard to make this sale, and she learned all her best sales tactics from her mother in the first place. There's no pulling the wool over this woman's eyes.

"What's wrong, sweetheart?" Marjani asks.

Phaera gives her a chagrined look. "You're impossible to shop for, you know that? So I thought I'd give you and Daddy a trip for an early anniversary present — but I didn't want to just spring it on you. You're not making it easy."

Her mother's smile is genuine, and Phaera takes a quick breath of relief.

"That's so sweet of you!"

"I know Daddy's been traveling so much for work, and you haven't been feeling well. Let me treat you both. Tell me you'll go see the lavender."

"I'll have to talk to your father when he gets home tonight."

Phaera waves a hand. "Let me call him. He'll say yes if he knows you want to go."

Marjani purses her lips. "Well . . . let me think about it."

"What's there to think about, Mama? Clear blue skies, lovely cool days, no dust storms? I bet if I call your doctor he'll say you should be in Alusina yesterday."

Marjani's gaze narrows; Phaera's trying too hard again. Dammit.

When she met Jaantzen that night at the Jungle, she had half expected this to blow over. Expected a few words of apology would be enough to make Leone calm down, but she's not letting go. She hasn't said another word to Phaera, but with how methodically she's working to bring Jaantzen down, Phaera suspects it's only a matter of time. Especially once Jaantzen's counterattack comes out in full force.

Phaera won't rest easily until her parents are far from here.

"Don't you need help around the Lorelei?" Marjani says. "When your father's back home we can come by and give you a hand."

"The Lorelei's fine, Mama. I have plenty of people helping me."

"I still can't believe it." Her mother takes another sip of her wine; she's nearly done with her second glass, though she's barely touched her food. Phaera's been forcing herself to eat even though she doesn't feel hungry, even though she can't taste anything. She realized this morning how much weight she's lost in the past week — she can't afford to keep forgetting meals if she's going to stay alert.

"It's fine, they caught the ones who did it," Phaera says. "I was looking at tickets to Alusina, and there's a flight leaving tomorrow morning. Daddy can have a nice night at home, then you can whisk him off on vacation. It will be sweet."

Her mother waves a hand. "When I was growing up, no one shot up stores! Now I don't even feel safe going downtown anymore. Did you see the news about the business tower that was bombed?"

"It wasn't bombed, if we're talking about Cobalt Tower," Phaera says.

"And now they're bombing the embassy? Of course, from what I'm reading, it's not innocent people like you, dear." Her mother leans in on this, voice hushed and conspiratorial. She's always enjoyed scandal, and milking Phaera for gossip from a very different world is one of her favorite parts of their lunches together. "The man who owns that tower, apparently he's some sort of drug kingpin."

Phaera sighs. "Willem Jaantzen's not a drug kingpin, Mama. I know him."

The look Marjani gives her is one part intrigued, one part concerned. "You know *of* him?"

"I know him personally."

After how well she got to know him last night, that bland statement feels like salacious innuendo. Phaera takes too quick a sip of her wine to distract herself from some of her choicer memories. Is she blushing? Dear lord, she's blushing. "I'll give Auntie Dahla a call — "

"I know sometimes the people you meet in your business do things a little . . . differently," Marjani says. "But you need to be careful who you're spending time with. The stories they tell about some of the people running this city, I don't want you mixed up with anyone like that."

"You'd be surprised, Mama. Now — "

"I know, I know," Marjani says. "I just worry that you're a little too trusting. I don't want you to get mixed up with the wrong people."

"Don't worry." Phaera sets down her wine glass a little too sharply. "I'm very picky about who I spend my time with."

"Phaera, it's one thing to be involved with the gambling. But drugs?"

"I'm not involved with drugs, Mama. And neither is Jaantzen."

"But everything they're saying about him in the news?" Her mother shakes her head. "Why would they be saying it if it wasn't true?"

"You remember last year, when that Arquellian company paid a PR agency to say all those things about me?"

"But that was all lies. I know you."

"And I know him." Phaera takes a deep breath. Maybe it's time to have this conversation after all. "We're actually quite good friends." Here she is, a grown woman in her fifties, struggling to figure out how to tell her mother about a man. "Actually — thank you."

The busser is setting down the after-lunch tea this restaurant has as its specialty, an herbal digestif. Phaera forces a smile, as much grateful for the distraction as annoyed at the interruption.

It's not the same woman who'd been bussing earlier, but they're having a late lunch and — Phaera can't help but have one eye on the operation of the restaurant — the shifts have changed as they sat here. Though it seems like their server is the one staying through the afternoon lull, so Phaera doesn't feel bad lingering — they're not keeping anyone. Probably the busser is just coming on shift.

"You're welcome," the woman says, and there's something in her expression that snags at Phaera's attention — it's like she knows something Phaera doesn't, like she's in on some joke Phaera wouldn't understand.

The woman winks one hazel eye and turns away to deliver another pair of teacups a few tables over. Oriol catches Phaera's attention, that faint sketch of a line between his brows asking if everything's all right.

It's nothing, Phaera thinks, but . . .

But it's not. Maybe she's spent the last week in a heightened state of vigilance and it's making her see danger everywhere. Or maybe it's honed her ability to sense when something's off. She cuts her gaze to the busser's back and Oriol nods. Swipes marks onto the table to cover his tab and unfolds lazily, like he's finally done with his tea and is ready for a stroll around the park blocks.

Marjani has seen the whole interaction with Oriol. "Do you know that man?"

Phaera frowns at her mother, trying to decide if it will worry her less or more to know her daughter now has a bodyguard following her every hour of the day.

"Let me buy you tickets to Alusina," she says instead. She cups her hands around the teacup — she loves the rustic clay cups this restaurant uses, every interior glazed in a different rainbow hue, every exterior left rough. But the rough clay under her palms isn't glowing with the heat of the tea, it's cool to the touch. The tea inside is just lukewarm. Easier to drink down quickly, Phaera thinks, and her mother takes a long, thirsty draw from hers.

"No!" Phaera grabs her mother's wrist; the clay cup shatters to pavement, its glazed interior cracking open in brilliant blue shards.

"Phaera!" Marjani stares at her in shock. "What was that for?"

Phaera doesn't quite know, but she suddenly feels exposed, worried that she's made a terrible mistake bringing her mother here. What has she done?

Their server is at their table in a second to see if there's anything he can do, and the busser — the real busser — comes over to sweep up the shards.

"It's fine, I'm so sorry," Phaera says. She settles their tab, feeling flustered and a shade embarrassed. Oriol hasn't come back, so he must still be trailing the woman who brought them their tea. Probably just following her to the break room, finding nothing but that she's here early for tonight's shift.

"Let's go for a walk," she says to her mother; she can't handle the worry on Marjani's face. "I'm still a little stressed from everything that happened last week. We'll go for a little stroll around the park and we can talk more about Alusina."

She can tell her mother doesn't believe her, but Marjani gathers her purse and starts to get to her feet.

Her forehead wrinkles in pain; her hand clutches at the edge of the table.

"Mama? What is it?"

Marjani doesn't answer — maybe she can't, one hand flies to clutch her chest as she drops back into her chair, her breath coming ragged, wheezing like her throat is constricted.

Phaera rushes to her mother's side as Marjani slides out of her chair. She catches her mother in her arms, helps her lie down on the floor, holds her head as she starts to convulse. "Get help!" she yells to the stunned staff. "Get help!"

26

JAANTZEN

An array of security stills are lined up on the conference table in front of Toshiyo. The "reporter" at the Jungle wearing a frumpy suit and a blue pixie cut. The blond woman in the sultry jumpsuit who'd slipped shard into Starla's purse at the Kuli Xa. A gambler in a silver evening gown, auburn hair pinned up in intricate braids, drinking at the high rollers' bar at the Lorelei.

And a commuter on a train platform standing next to Detective Timo Cho: Loose brown curls and a high-necked coat obscure her features, but when Toshiyo zooms in, it's definitely the same woman. Tawny skin and heart-shaped face with a spray of freckles.

"Who is she?" Jaantzen asks.

"Her name is Victoria Tierren, and she's on Leone's payroll." Toshiyo pulls up an ident card; in this photo, Tierren's hair is bleached blond and bobbed at a severe angle. "I've found her meeting with Leone, mostly at Leone's house after dark. I'm going back through the security footage to figure out how long — but it's been almost nightly for two weeks now."

"Two weeks?" Jaantzen frowns at that.

"The first time was the night of the last dinner party, after everyone had gone home." Toshiyo swipes through a stream of data, pounces on the image she's scanning for. It's a grainy surveillance shot of Leone's back garden. The chief justice is holding court with a pair of figures: the heart-faced woman, and Acheta.

Manu leans in, enlarging the image. "Well, shit."

"I wonder what Acheta offered Leone." Jaantzen leans back, rolling his neck to ease the tension between his shoulder blades. Leone has been building a trap for him since before he even realized he'd upset her, which means she's felt threatened by him for a while. Just as she felt threatened by Coeur a decade ago. Back then, though, Coeur had burned bridges with everyone who might have supported her in her fight against Leone. Jaantzen's bridges are still there, if shaky. Leone's having to do the burning herself.

She's doing her damnedest.

When he looks at the penthouse around him, nothing's outwardly changed. But although it's still filled with his belongings, his home already feels like a distant memory. Almost all of his early life was spent without reliable shelter or food. He was too wary to sleep a full night even when he did find a place of his own, too distrusting to eat at the tables of others, every friendship a tightrope with no net. Until he met Starla's parents, Raj and Lasadi Dusai. Julieta. And, eventually, Tae.

In a way, it was easier. When a situation blew up in his face, he could grab his meager belongings, slip away into the night, steal unattended takeout from a food courier, and settle down in the next empty warehouse he found.

Building an empire provided its own form of security. And it came with its own unique set of vulnerabilities.

Willem Jaantzen can't simply vanish into the night, not anymore.

"Tell me you tracked her down," he says to Toshiyo, who flashes him a smile.

She rakes her curtain of black hair over one shoulder and leans over the desk to call up a new screen. "I eventually started following that detective to see who was feeding him information, and I found her." She taps the image of the brunette on the train platform. "She was at his apartment last night, and there were few enough people out that it was relatively easy to follow her back to this address."

Toshiyo pulls up a map on a new screen, where a pin marks a house in a residential neighborhood near Surquillo Market. She touches it to bring up a hologram of the townhouse there. "The house is listed as condemned, but she's been in and out for the past two weeks. And yesterday she wasn't alone."

Another still, and this time the woman has two teenaged girls with her. Manu swears under his breath; he knows them just as well as Jaantzen does. Ajesh and Mirana Paiman's daughters.

"She's gone in and out since, but the girls haven't."

"Is she there now?" Jaantzen asks.

Toshiyo shakes her head. "She left about an hour ago. Starla already called El and Simca — they're downstairs suiting up."

Waiting on his call.

Jaantzen shares a look with Manu.

"She works for Leone and she's got an impressive wig collection," says Manu. "What else do we know about her, Tosh?"

"Not much. Her ident card didn't show up anywhere before two weeks ago, so I don't know if she's new to town, new to this identity, or both. She doesn't seem to have an arrest record, and all I can tell now is that she's wandering around stirring up trouble." She shrugs. "Probably best to assume she's dangerous."

Manu nods slowly. "We need those girls," he says. "The BPD's case against me and Julieta falls apart without Ajesh's testimony. Plus . . ."

"Ajesh is a friend," Jaantzen says. He nods to Toshiyo. "Do it."

"Copy that." She hits a button on the desk and switches on her ops screen. "Green light, guys."

HEADING OUT, Starla messages back.

"Be careful," Jaantzen says unnecessarily.

OF COURSE.

Manu clears his throat, settles back in his chair, one ankle crossed over the other knee. It's a pose Jaantzen's learned means he has something to say, and that Jaantzen probably won't like it.

He nods for Manu to go ahead.

"Without Ajesh's testimony, the case against Julieta and me falls apart," Manu says again. "But they're still looking in the completely wrong direction. We need to point them towards the truth."

"And how do you suggest we do that?"

"The lead detective. Cho. He's sharp, but he's asking the wrong questions. He got close to sniffing Leone out ten years ago — my sense is that he actually cares about finding the truth. So we show him where to look. He's been Leone's tool; he could be ours instead."

Jaantzen can see where this is going; he doesn't like it.

"I can talk to him," Manu says. "He needs to know who's pulling his strings."

"Then we find a way to tell him that doesn't expose you to the possibility of arrest."

"Tosh, where is he right now?"

Toshiyo glances sidelong at Jaantzen, then sighs. A clatter of black-lacquered fingernails against her desk and she pulls up more surveillance footage. Cho, walking down the street with shoulders hunched and frequent glances back; the man looks hunted.

"He just left the office," Toshiyo says. "I'd guess he's headed home for the night."

"I agree that he could be an asset," Jaantzen says. "But we'll find a safer way to send him that message."

"You know I'll be more convincing than any note. And nowhere is safer than out in public. Tosh, you've got me, yeah?"

Toshiyo cracks both her ring fingers but doesn't answer.

"The police have Julieta," Manu says. "I know Calanthe is doing what she can to get her out, but this could speed up the process. Every minute she's in there . . ."

Jaantzen shakes his head. "Calanthe is doing her job."

"And I'm trying to do mine." A muscle jumps in Manu's jaw. "I brought his attention on us in the first place when he was interviewing victims. Let me fix this."

"You didn't bring his attention to us. Leone did."

"I'm the one who — "

"Stop."

Jaantzen locks his gaze on Manu's. Twenty years has taught him to trust that his lieutenant knows what he's doing. But it's also taught him that Manu's biggest blind spot is himself. Oriol is a balancing force, when he's around, and Jaantzen's normally better about watching out for

Manu when Oriol's not — but this time he failed. He let himself get distracted, by Leone, by Acheta, by the constant barrage of small cuts the last few weeks have brought.

By Phaera.

In a heartbeat, in a different time, Jaantzen would tell Manu no. That they don't need this. That they can come up with another plan a few days from now, when they've all had a chance to recover in relative safety.

But Leone has them in her sights, and every move Jaantzen is plotting against her requires time to work. Every move except for this one.

Jaantzen nods solemnly to Manu. "Toshiyo?"

Toshiyo sighs unhappily. "I can track you," she says to Manu. "And I'll run a filter on the BPD chatter so I can warn you if he calls for backup. But." She sweeps a hand at the desk; tags labeled Starla, El, and Simca are on their way through the maze of Bulari to Tierren's house.

"They're your first priority," Manu says. "I won't take any chances."

Toshiyo's lips thin. Manu puts both feet on the ground and shifts forward to tuck a strand of her hair behind her ear; she doesn't look at him.

"You have two hours," Jaantzen says to him. "Then meet Starla at the safehouse. Those girls will need to see someone they know."

"I'll be there."

"And so will we. Toshiyo, status?"

"They'll be there in five," she says; her tone is flat, she's retreating into the job. She opens a side screen, data flowing at the click of a few keystrokes. "I'll get that filter going on the BPD chatter."

"Thank you."

Manu squeezes her shoulder and stands. "I'll be fine,"

he tells her. She doesn't look up. "Don't worry. I'll see you in — "

A call chimes on Jaantzen's comm and they all start; Jaantzen's surprise turns to fear as he sees the name.

"Oriol. What is it."

Jaantzen can hear voices in the background, sirens.

"Phaera's mom," Oriol says. "She's at the Old City hospital, she had some sort of seizure. Maybe poisoned. We're here with her now."

"What do you mean, poisoned?" Jaantzen asks, and Manu and Toshiyo both look at him in concern. He swipes the call to the conference table so they can hear. "Phaera's mother," he says in explanation to them.

"They were having lunch and a woman snuck in dressed like a busser, served them tea. Phaera didn't drink it, but her mother did."

"Did you see who did it?" Jaantzen asks. He taps the photos that are still laid out in front of Toshiyo. "Send him these," he signs to her.

"Yeah," Oriol says. "I followed her, but lost her near Surquillo Market."

"I'm sending you some stills," Toshiyo says. "Is that her?"

A pause as Oriol receives the images. "Yep."

"She's been popping up all over the place," Toshiyo says. "We think she works for Leone, and that she's currently holding a couple of girls hostage — Starla and the Anahoys are on their way to find her."

Another pause. "Why?"

Toshiyo glances up at Jaantzen. Of course, Oriol doesn't know yet about Julieta and the murder charges.

"It's complicated," Jaantzen says.

"They need help? I can call Jae Bakshi to spot me."

Jaantzen racks his brain a moment for the name: the head of security at the Lorelei. They don't know how dangerous this woman is. Is she more likely to try to finish what she started with Phaera? Or to head back to her apartment and surprise Starla?

"Stay with Phaera," Jaantzen says.

"Copy that. Tell them she's fast, she moves like she can fight. Manu with you?"

"I'm here," Manu says.

"Good." Oriol pauses like he wants to say something more. "I'll keep you updated."

"I'll see you tonight," Manu answers.

"Keep 'em safe, Tosh," Oriol says, then cuts the connection.

A moment later Manu's comm chimes. "'Don't do anything stupid,'" he reads out loud. A faint smile tugs at the corner of his mouth.

"Did you two get a psychic connection to go with those rings?" Toshiyo asks.

"Guess so." Manu squeezes her shoulder again and she finally gives him a smile. "I won't do anything stupid," he says with a nod at Jaantzen. "I'll see you both in two hours at the safehouse."

The lift doors hiss shut behind him, the little dots on Toshiyo's map are approaching the flag, and Jaantzen can't force himself to sit and watch. A quiet fury is singing in his veins. Not that Leone's attacking him, but that she has the audacity to put innocent people in her sights. Julieta. Starla. Manu. Phaera's mother. This is his fight, not theirs.

Phaera's mother isn't the last straw, because there has been no moment in which Willem Jaantzen wasn't going to fight Leone tooth and claw for his freedom.

But until today, he might not have aimed to destroy her.

He scrubs a hand over the back of his neck, thinking. Toshiyo takes a sharp breath in and looks over her shoulder. He's been hovering, watching Starla and El and Simca close in on the unknown.

"Call her, okay?" Toshiyo swivels her chair to face him. "If she can't answer, she won't, but then she'll just call you back like a normal human. She doesn't think it's your fault — and I know you don't believe me, but just stop brooding and call her. You're making me crazy."

Jaantzen blinks at her, surprised. "My apologies."

"Just call her, boss. She wants to hear from you. I promise." Toshiyo turns back to her screens. "We've got two minutes."

Jaantzen takes a deep breath, then walks to the end of the penthouse's garden to give Toshiyo her breathing room before putting through a connection to Phaera's comm.

She answers immediately.

"Oriol called," Jaantzen says, feeling like he needs to explain. "How is she?"

"Stable," says Phaera. "Out of immediate danger. They're keeping her now to see what kind of permanent damage she might have." She murmurs something to someone, receives an answer and thanks them. "To her heart. God, I was trying to convince her to leave town — if I'd been able to talk her into it earlier . . ."

"What do they think was the cause?"

"They're saying it was shock. I tried to tell them about the tea, but they haven't been able to find anything in her tests."

"They're overlooking something."

"Or I overreacted and scared her, and gave my own mother a heart attack."

"It's not your fault," Jaantzen says firmly. It's his fault.

She takes a ragged breath; she's not answering, maybe she can't.

"Who is there with you?"

"Just Oriol." She clears her throat, and in his mind's eye he can picture her straightening her shoulders, lifting her chin. "Willem, I know — " She cuts herself off.

"What is it?"

"Never mind. I know you have a lot on your plate."

"Phaera, if you want me to — "

"You're busy." She's telling herself that, not him.

He listens a moment to her silence; it's slowly dawning on him what she's trying to ask. "Do you want me there?"

"Yes." The fact that she doesn't hesitate sings through him. But just because she wants him there doesn't mean it's a good idea.

"You're sure."

Now there's a pause, maybe she's thinking through the potential press fallout of having Willem Jaantzen show up at her mother's hospital bed, maybe she's simply thinking about how to have the awkward conversation with her mother about who Jaantzen is.

"Please," Phaera says finally.

Jaantzen glances back into the conference room; Toshiyo catches his eye. "They're in," she signs.

"I can be there in an hour."

"Thank you. Jaantzen?"

"Yes?"

"We need to end this," Phaera says. "I need to go to Leone, see if I can talk to her."

"Phaera, listen to me," Jaantzen says. "The only way this ends tonight is with a bullet, but that loses me what few allies I still have, and ensures I never occupy a public place in this city again." Leone is trying her hardest to make that happen on her own, but he could do it just as quickly — and with more finality — if he turned to violence here. "We have a plan, but it needs time to develop if it's going to hit home. Don't let her force our hand."

On the other end of the line Phaera curses under her breath, but doesn't answer. Across the room, Toshiyo has sunk into ops mode, a steady flurry of information processed and commands given, the world and the people around her becoming nothing but data she can find patterns in. Starla and the Anahoys are in good hands; he can't do anything for them that Toshiyo isn't already doing.

"We will end this," Jaantzen says calmly. "But on our terms — not hers."

Three heartbeats; he's not sure she heard him.

Then, "All right," Phaera murmurs.

"I'll be there as soon as I can."

"Thank you."

The place where her voice was goes dead, and Jaantzen feels the silence like a physical loss. He understands Phaera's impulse — he wants to come down decisive and brutal, wants to deal with Leone like he had planned to deal with Acheta, like he would deal with someone like Coeur. But Leone is on a different level entirely, and he needs to play her game.

Of course, politics and public relations aren't her only tools. Her seat may protect her from a direct physical attack, but she's more than willing to stoop to physical violence and threat when she wants to. Her woman, Tierren, is kidnapping children on her orders. Poisoning old women. What else will Leone be willing to do?

Across the room, Toshiyo stiffens. Cocks her head like something's caught her attention but she's not yet put her finger on what it is.

"El, stand by," she says. She turns to a screen on her right, trailing her hands through the images streaming there until she spots the one she wants, plucks it out, and swipes it wide, then away before Jaantzen can see whatever it is she sees.

"Simca, cover the door," Toshiyo snaps. "Starla, get them out of there. She's coming back."

27

STARLA

The neighborhood around Surquillo Market is one of those rare pockets of Bulari that isn't either glaringly affluent or heartbreakingly rundown. The well-patched streets are lined with modest rows of townhouses jammed shoulder to shoulder, ranging the gamut from shabbily loved to meticulously restored. Starla maneuvers the silver Magnata two-seater slowly to avoid both potholes and kids playing in the street, rolling up behind El's battered blue Bierat Tegu.

The condemned townhouse they're looking for fits right in with its neighbors but for cracked and crumbling front steps and the city-issue trespassing deterrents to keep squatters out: bulletproof stasis wrap over the windows, a motion web in the doorway, signs announcing alarm systems that are probably no longer operational.

Those deterrents didn't stop Tierren; Toshiyo suspected she's been using the back door. And sure enough, the motion web over the sideyard gate is shorted out, the back door is locked but unprotected. Easy enough to break into with the right equipment.

Inside, the place is empty. Furniture gone, appliances torn out, floorboards missing in the living room and treads pulled off the stairs to the second floor. The stairs to the basement are intact. There's no trace that someone's been living here for the past two weeks.

"I'm guessing basement," Starla signs to El and Simca. Dragging a pair of uncooperative teenagers up a set of broken stairs to the second floor seems like too much hassle. "Simca, run upstairs to be sure. El, with me."

One of Toshiyo's drones sweeps down the basement stairs in front of Starla, illuminating the way — and confirming her suspicions. While the main floor is all but destroyed, the basement has obviously been lived in. It's a single open room with a bathroom tucked in one corner and a closet along the far wall. Bedding is shoved into the corner, food wrappers litter the floor. Starla breathes shallow against the musty, stale air — something smells faintly of decay.

Starla is about to step into the room when El catches her arm. Her heart rate spikes and she scans for the trap. But he's pointing to a shelf above the bed.

A perfect row of severed heads.

Starla plays her light over them, horror turning to relief: They're just head-shaped forms, each topped with a wig. Brunette curls, black braids, blue pixie. Starla recognizes the blond updo from when she first saw Tierren at the Kuli Xa. She glances back at El, whose jaw is tight with unease.

"She's sleeping in the basement," he says on the ops channel; his words scroll across Starla's lens. "Sim?"

"Nothing up here."

COVER THE DOOR, Starla types to her.

COPY.

Starla turns slowly, taking in the room. The girls aren't

here. At least, they're not anywhere Starla can see them. The state the room is in, though, it's hard to see anything. The wigs are the only objects that have been treated with care — everything else is strewn haphazardly about. Clothes lying in drifts around the room, shoes in mismatched piles, scavenged electronics shoved into corners. The bed is just a pile of stained cushions with a few ripped blankets thrown over the top.

I NEED A SCAN, she types to Toshiyo, and a moment later one of Toshiyo's drones flickers in Starla's peripheral vision. It washes the area in red light.

Starla blinks out snapshots, sending it all back to Toshiyo so they can analyze it later. It doesn't look like a place someone lives, it's a base of operations. No identifiers, no personal comforts, no mementos. The woman definitely sleeps here, but she doesn't live here full time. Does she have another apartment in the city? Is she from off-planet? Does she live outside Bulari?

El begins running his hands along the walls, searches through the bathroom. Starla carefully shifts the bedding, looking for a trapdoor hidden beneath the grimy cushions. She doesn't find a trapdoor, but her fingers brush against something small and hard shoved between the cushions and the wall. She tugs it out. Another shoe.

Starla's about to toss it on a nearby pile when she realizes it's smaller than the others strewn about the room. It's practical, sturdy — the sort of thing someone might wear if they were on their feet all day in a kitchen.

It's bloody.

Starla takes a snapshot.

PROBABLY ONE OF THEIR SHOES, she types.

They have to be here.

Something about this place is tugging at Starla's attention, and she turns in her crouch, scanning the room again. She's not the tidiest person, but living in this chaos, every day? The thought makes her cringe. Every inch of space covered except — ah. That's it.

The closet. The entire room is a messy jumble, the closet rail stuffed so tightly that garments that have fallen off the hangars are still suspended by the press of clothes around them. Debris is piled beside the closet door, but the floor of the closet has only a single coat tossed onto it.

SCAN THE CLOSET, Starla types to Toshiyo, and the drone soars out of the bathroom and over to where Starla is standing. But now that Starla knows it's there, she can feel the staticky hum of cheap security electronics pricking against her skin. She kneels, running her hands around the floor until she feels the indentation, fits her thumbnail in the groove, and pushes it aside to reveal a handhold. Hinges are flush with the floor in the back, nearly invisible.

FORCEFIELD, Toshiyo writes back. SIGNATURE PATTERN IS OFF-THE-SHELF. TRACES OF HEAT BEHIND IT.

And there's the controls, just to the left of the door, covered by another panel that slides away when Starla digs her nail into the slight indentation. She recognizes the model instantly — she replaces a lot of these for clients who have done DIY security jobs and now want something more . . . well, robust isn't the word. When they want something that will actually work.

A unit like this won't keep out a thief who knows its infamous weakness, but it probably does just fine to keep a pair of girls in place. Starla types the factory reset code from memory, and in the two-second delay as it reboots, she slips the tip of her knife behind the faceplate and twists. A spark and the sharp scent of scorched wiring as the unit powers back up and instantly shorts.

The crackle of low-grade static humming against her skin disappears, and Starla pulls the trapdoor up. The faint scent of decay becomes stronger, and for a moment Starla's breath quickens in fear of what she's about to find. The crawlspace below stretches out into black gloom beyond the square of light the trapdoor makes. Two teenaged girls are huddled together against the foundation wall, hands bound and gagged. The younger is lying with her head in the older's lap.

They're alive. Two pairs of dark, terrified eyes stare up at her.

"We're friends," Starla signs, and both pairs of eyes flicker over her shoulder — Starla glances back to see El interpreting. She lifts her chin to him. "Talk to them."

Starla lowers herself into the hole as words scroll across her lens: El being reassuring, Toshiyo relaying the news to Simca.

The cool darkness smells of earth and dust and fear, and even with Toshiyo's drone bathing the girls in light, Starla can't see more than the corner the girls are huddled against. The darkness could go on forever in the other directions, anything could be creeping around out there. What a terrifying place to be trapped and helpless.

Starla pushes the thought aside and pulls her knife from her boot. She reaches for the younger girl's bound hands — she's all matted black hair and tearstained cheeks. She thrashes out of Starla's reach.

"I'm not going to hurt you," Starla signs, but she slips the knife back into her boot and catches a handful of the girl's hair, working the knot of her gag loose instead. The girl begins jabbering hysterically at her the instant it's out, but Starla's lens is transcribing nonsense. She glances up at

El. He's frowning at the girl as though trying to make out what she's saying.

"We're friends," he says. "We're here to take you back home."

While the girl's distracted by El, Starla slices through the bonds around her wrists. She grabs the girl's scrawny waist and wrestles her kicking up to El. One bare heel connects with Starla's ribs, the impact dulled through her vest. Starla narrowly ducks as the girl's other foot comes swinging by her head.

As she turns back to the older girl, the corner of her lens flickers red.

Her lens is still transcribing gibberish from the younger sister, so Starla blinks the transcription off so she can read the message Toshiyo is trying to send through.

SIMCA COVER THE DOOR. STARLA GET THEM OUT OF THERE. SHE'S COMING BACK.

ALMOST DONE HERE, Starla types.

Starla quickly cuts through the older girl's bonds and gag — she's more cooperative than her sister — and the girl immediately begins trying to tell her something. Starla looks up at El.

"The woman, she told them if they try to escape, she'll kill their parents," he signs.

Ah. That explains it.

"Your parents are safe," Starla signs — the girl watches El as he interprets. "But the woman who kidnapped you is coming back. We need to leave."

She helps the girl to her feet and boosts her out of the hole. El grabs her arms and pulls her the rest of the way, then gives Starla a hand as she hauls herself back out, leaving the scent of decaying flesh behind.

The younger girl is unsteady on bare feet, but she can

walk all right. The older girl takes a step and falls — there's something wrong with her foot. The instep is swollen and red, like a cut that got infected. In the better light, Starla can see how bloodied and bruised she is. Knuckles raw and fingernails broken, she must have tried to fight back.

Starla pulls the girl's arm over her shoulder and tucks an arm around her waist; she's trembling with cold, fear, exhaustion. They're almost out the door when the girl flinches and looks at the ceiling, hand flying to her mouth to stifle a cry.

"Gunshots," signs El.

GO OUT THE FRONT. Simca's command sears across Starla's lens. Then another message, garbled, which cuts off. El's face twists in fear.

Starla releases the older girl and hands her off to El. "Get them safe." And she sprints up the stairs towards the back door.

Simca's pinned down in the doorway, bullets chewing into the doorframe whenever she tries to lean out and fire back.

"Just one," she signs to Starla. She yanks a stun grenade from her belt and flings it around the corner; Starla feels the concussion in her chest as it makes impact. It's not deadly, which makes it a better choice for the middle of a residential neighborhood, but if a person's too near when it goes off, it'll knock them unconscious.

It wasn't close enough in this case. The woman's still on her feet — Starla peeks out the doorway and squeezes off a shot at the woman in the yard, just as she stumbles back around the corner. Back towards the front of the house, where El will be leaving with the girls.

"Help El," Starla signs to Simca, then gives chase after Tierren.

But Tierren doesn't head towards the front entrance — she must know she's outnumbered and isn't willing to fight for the girls. Instead, she throws her leg over a moto that's parked in the sideyard and guns it through the flimsy gate.

Starla chases after her, vaulting the splintered pieces of gate and sprinting towards the Magnata. She tears away from the curb, not caring this time about potholes in the road. The kids that were playing ball earlier have already darted out of the way of Tierren on her moto.

Starla swerves around the corner to follow Tierren to the right — but there's no one on the street ahead of her.

Left next alley.

Toshiyo's directions flash onto Starla's lens, and Starla yanks the controls to the left, skidding into a narrow alley that's just barely wide enough for the Magnata. She flinches as she squeezes between a recycler chute and a stack of crates; sparks fly from the Magnata's wheelwell. Ahead of her, Tierren banks to the right and out into a busy street. Starla follows, narrowly catching a gap in the traffic — behind her, a delivery truck swerves to miss her and jackknifes across the street.

Starla guns it, weaving through traffic to catch up with the woman, but on her moto Tierren can catch gaps Starla isn't able to make. Toshiyo's directions flicker on her lens — *right, left* — keeping her always one step behind the woman until —

Right into Surq.

Dammit.

Starla skids the Magnata to a stop in front of the south entrance to Surquillo Market, ignoring the angrily gesturing people around her as she throws the spinner into park and leaves it blocking the pathway. Not as many people seem to care as might otherwise — most are still staring in shock after the woman on the moto who plowed through the crowd and into the market's crush of people and food stalls and banners.

I lost her, Toshiyo writes. *Do you have visual?*

Starla doesn't take the time to answer. She sprints after Tierren, pushing past bystanders. She can see the trail of chaos Tierren's causing up ahead on her moto, but Starla's on foot and the crowds are slowing her down. One intersection, another, and Starla no longer has visual. She pushes through another knot of shoppers and soon sees why: Tierren's moto is tipped into a juice bar stall at a four-way intersection. Now that Tierren's on foot, Starla can't see the chaos of the moto running through the crowd. A few stalls away, stairs lead to the upper and lower levels of the market.

"Where did she go," Starla asks the owner of the juice bar, an older woman who's gesturing wildly to a younger man at the damage the moto caused to her stall. And either they don't understand her or they didn't see, because the old woman and the young man point in opposite directions.

Starla spins again, scanning for anything that seems out of place. Any sign of where Tierren might be.

She could be hiding anywhere.

She could be *heading* anywhere.

Starla stops with a growl of frustration. *Tell me those girls parents are safe*, she types to Toshiyo.

Yes. In hiding. E&S on way to safehouse.

At least there's that.

On my way.

28

JAANTZEN

"Willem Jaantzen, here to see Marjani Harris," Phaera says to the clinic's receptionist, and the young man's gaze spears Jaantzen with surprise. His fingers hover over his desk, and not for the first time, Jaantzen thinks he's made a terrible mistake coming here.

This clinic is worlds apart from the emergency triage center at the Sulila hospital in the Fingers. You need money in your account to be admitted, for one — they're not in the business of offering payment plans and chasing down defaulted loans. That's clear from the lobby, which resembles a hotel more than a hospital, with tasteful furniture and walls made up of screens so realistic it's nearly impossible to tell you're not looking through a window out onto an Indiran ocean.

The receptionist is still staring at him.

Jaantzen is making trouble for Phaera and her mother by being here — not the same trouble he would have made for Manu if he'd come to the Sulila hospital, but trouble nonetheless. Though, maybe all the damage he can do has been done. The tabloids may not have caught wind of their relationship yet, but there's really only one person who matters right now: Geum-ja Leone.

Leone already knows how much Phaera means to him.

And she's already using it against them.

Phaera clears her throat, steel in her gaze, and the receptionist catches himself, types Jaantzen's name into the visitor log. Jaantzen's skin crawls at the record.

"Thank you," Phaera says politely. Her fingertips brush Jaantzen's sleeve, inviting him to follow as she heads to the doors that lead to the patient rooms.

It's the first time she's touched him since he arrived, and the feeling lingers long after her hand is gone. He's been keeping a respectful distance despite the overwhelming desire to pull her close — she looks exhausted and scared, and it's tearing him apart. The hem of her blouse has come untucked, there's a smudge of black in the corner of her eye, the cuticle of one index finger is spotted with blood where she's been picking at it. He wants to take her hand to keep her from tearing at it more.

He has no right. He's the reason her mother was put in danger, that Phaera's been pushed to the edge of grief. He can't fix what happened, but he can put an end to Leone.

And he will.

"Thank you for coming," she says as she holds the door for him; he catches the faintest hint of her perfume as he passes. "My mother's just been moved to an observation ward."

He realizes he doesn't know the woman's name, and he grasps at what Phaera told the receptionist before it slips out of his memory.

"Marjani . . . Harris?" Jaantzen asks delicately.

She grants him a ghost of her normal carefree laugh. "Harris," she repeats with a faint smile.

"I had assumed your family name started with a D."

The smile fades. "My middle name is Dalvinia. Phaera Dalvinia — I think my mother was hoping for someone a little more flowery. I sound like I belong in Julieta's greenhouse." Her hand slips into his, squeezes, disappears. "Phaera D is what my grandpa always called me. Come on."

A doctor is waiting for them outside a closed door. If he recognizes Jaantzen's face or has been told his name, he doesn't give a sign.

"How is she?" Phaera asks.

"She's awake," the doctor says, a glance at both of them. "Though it's still too early to determine if there will be permanent damage."

Phaera flinches; Jaantzen smooths a hand down her back before he catches himself, but she doesn't move away. He leaves it resting against the curve of her spine. She shifts closer, just a fraction.

"And the cause?" Jaantzen asks.

"We've had a watch on her heart for years now," the doctor says. "It seemed like she was improving, but sometimes these things take a turn for the worse. It could have been a shock she had, or perhaps she overexerted herself. It's impossible to tell at this point."

"Could she have been poisoned?" Jaantzen asks.

The doctor slides Phaera a look that's almost disappointed. "We've done a blood test, but we found nothing. Trust me, we're not leaving any avenue unexplored."

By the way he says it, he's had this conversation with Phaera more than once. That admonishment in his voice says *I see you've involved someone else in your conspiracy theory.*

"You found nothing in the tea sample I brought?" Phaera asks.

The doctor shakes his head with a sigh. "Your mother wasn't poisoned, Ms. Harris. She has a weak heart and got a shock."

"I'm sure you've been thorough," Jaantzen says before Phaera can answer. She's practically vibrating with rage under his hand. A sense of unease is creeping over him: that inability to find anything. Maybe there's nothing there, maybe it's impossible to trace.

Or maybe Phaera's mother isn't safe here, either.

The doctor turns to Phaera. "We'll monitor your mother overnight. If you have any other questions?"

"Just one," Jaantzen says. "How soon can she be moved?"

Phaera searches his gaze a moment, then nods. She doesn't feel good about this place, either.

"Oh, no." The doctor is shaking his head, hands up to caution them. "I wouldn't recommend that."

"You said she's stable," Phaera points out.

"I also said we should keep her for observation."

"And if she wants to go home?"

"I would recommend against it."

"But you can't stop us." Phaera straightens her shoulders. "Noted. Give us a minute, please."

The doctor opens his mouth to argue more, until he meets Jaantzen's gaze and decides against it. He turns with an expression that says he has better things to do, then stalks back down the hallway.

Phaera sinks onto the bench beside the door, hands knotted. "Oriol's in there, he's watching out for her." She glances down the hall after the doctor. "Do you think . . ."

"I don't know," Jaantzen says quietly. "But I don't trust anyone right now."

"Then where do we go?"

"We take her to Gia."

"Who?"

Of course — the events of the last week have created an artificial closeness, and he's begun to think of Phaera as always having been a part of his life even though they were merely acquaintances until recently. She fits so seamlessly, so comfortably, it's strange to think she doesn't know who Gia is. Or that he didn't actually know her family name until minutes ago.

He can't decide if that should feel like a good sign or if it should give him pause.

"A doctor I work with," Jaantzen says. "She has more faith in conspiracy theories and probably a better knowledge of the sorts of drugs you can use to — " He cuts himself off from saying to murder someone without a trace; he's talking about Phaera's mother, and she looks about ready to crack. "For this sort of thing. She and her husband run a clinic outside the city limits. They're both Sulila trained, and their equipment is state-of-the-art. Your mother will be cared for there, and she'll be safe."

"You don't think I'm overreacting about the tea?"

"Of course not. The woman who served it to you? She's connected to Leone, and we suspect she's been involved in other problems we've been having. Maybe she didn't poison the tea, but she wasn't there on accident. We need to move your mother somewhere Leone can't get to her."

Phaera nods and gets to her feet, expression fierce. "Thank you."

"Of course. Phaera." He tucks a strand of magenta hair behind her ear; she presses her cheek into his palm, smooths her hand over his. "Leone will pay for this."

Phaera takes a deep breath, steadying herself, then laces her fingers through his, lets both their hands fall to her side.

"Thank you," she says. Her lips find his before he can think to react; then she turns and pushes open the door, pulling him after her.

Marjani Harris is in a private room that's outfitted like a hotel but for the medical equipment surrounding her and Oriol lounging on a chair in the corner, reading a book. Marjani's got the news playing on a holo-display above the bed, but her eyes are closed; they flicker open at the sound of the door. Jaantzen freezes in the doorway, prepared to wait out on the benches in the hall — it hadn't occurred to him that Phaera wanted him to be more than emotional support for herself.

"I'll let your mother rest," he murmurs. Her fingers tighten around his.

"Come on, Jaantzen," she says, and a faint smile quirks her lips to the side. "No time like the present. Besides, she already knows."

Chilled dread settles to churn beneath his ribcage. Jaantzen takes a deep breath and follows Phaera.

"Mama?" Phaera's hand slips from his as she crosses to her mother. "How are you feeling?"

Phaera's mother doesn't answer; she's frowning past her daughter at Jaantzen, disapproval furrowing her brow. This is already going so well. Jaantzen catches Oriol's eye across the room. The other man lifts his chin in greeting.

"Be ready," Jaantzen signs to him. "We're taking her to Gia."

Oriol gives him a thumbs-up and slips his book into his thigh pocket.

Phaera is beckoning him to her mother's bedside. "Don't just stand in the door, Jaantzen," she says. "Come meet my mother, Marjani. Mama, this is Willem Jaantzen, and I hope you remember we already had a whole conversation about not believing what you see on the news."

Marjani Harris gives her daughter a skeptical look that's an exact mirror of Phaera's own, but she takes Jaantzen's hand when he offers it.

"It's nice to meet you," Jaantzen says. Her hand is ice-cold. "I wish it was in better circumstances."

"This old heart," Marjani says. "I'm sorry Phaera made you go to all the trouble of a visit; I've been in and out of this clinic for years. Though it's nice to have such charming company this time." She winks at Oriol, who laughs.

"Willem's the one who introduced me to Oriol," Phaera says, and that gets Jaantzen an appraising look. Marjani's expression softens; the comment seems to bring Jaantzen up in her estimation, rather than pulling Oriol down. That's a good sign.

"Then I suppose I should thank you," Marjani says finally. "I worry about her."

Jaantzen pats Marjani's hand and releases it, letting it rest gently back at her side. "She's very capable of taking care of herself," he says. "But a little insurance never hurts."

"I've thought for years she should have a bodyguard," Phaera's mother tells Jaantzen, leaning in conspiratorially. "But she doesn't listen to me. Nicely done."

"Mama." Phaera shakes her head, and Marjani gives Jaantzen a wink that catches him off guard. "We're not here to talk about my safety, we're talking about yours. Do you feel well enough to travel? I'd like to get a second opinion on your heart."

Marjani frowns at her. "I trust Doctor Ani, I've been coming here for years."

"Yes, but this time seemed different," Phaera says

smoothly. "Willem has a friend who's a specialist in this sort of thing. A Sulila-trained doctor at a private clinic."

"You'll be quite comfortable there," Jaantzen says, but her attention is no longer on him, her gaze has shifted past him to the holo-display on the ceiling, where the news is still playing quietly in the background.

Now the display is filled with an image of Cobalt Tower. He's been seeing it all week, the facade smoking and shattered — but this image is fresh. The facade is still scarred from the attack earlier this week, but the damage has been repaired, and Cobalt Tower is surrounded by BPD vans and assault teams.

This isn't B-roll, this is a livestream.

Marjani's eyebrows draw together. "Isn't that . . ."

Phaera shushes her and slides her finger up the volume bar.

" — at the heart of a conspiracy to destabilize the very fabric of our nation," the reporter is saying over the livestream. "The Bulari police have fanned through the city to serve warrants for those responsible for the tragic bombing at the Alliance embassy earlier this week." The footage cuts to the reporter at his desk; in the split screen, the image of Cobalt Tower is replaced by a rotating series of ident cards.

Marjani gasps.

Because Willem Jaantzen's face is front and center, marked with the words *Armed and dangerous*. Julieta now, followed by Manu. And Thala Coeur with her million-mark smile — so much for fooling Leone that they're not sharing information.

"The police have issued warrants for those at the heart of the conspiracy. Anyone who sees these perpetrators should call the police immediately. We go now to the

Supreme Court, where Chief Justice Geum-ja Leone is commenting on the heroic work the BPD has done in association with the Alliance to bring down this shocking conspiracy."

The footage cuts to Leone in full regalia, standing behind a podium on the steps of the Supreme Court building. She smiles at the camera, malevolent, and a chill brushes down Jaantzen's spine.

Phaera flicks off the display as Leone takes her first breath to speak. "Willem," she murmurs. "You have to go."

Jaantzen squeezes Marjani's hand briefly. "It was a pleasure to meet you, Ms. Harris. I hope you understand I need to leave." He gives her a faint smile; her earlier tentative warmth has melted and she's staring at him in shock. "As your daughter said, don't believe everything you see on the news."

Oriol has come up behind them, he claps Jaantzen on the shoulder, then starts fiddling with the monitor at the foot of Marjani's bed. "I've got things here," he murmurs. "I'll make sure they get safe to Gia's."

"Thank you."

"And I'll sweet-talk Ms. Marjani for you," he says with a wink at Phaera's mother. Marjani gives him a skeptical look.

When Oriol glances back at Jaantzen, his charming smile has faded. He takes a sharp breath, and Jaantzen cuts him off before he has to ask.

"He was out running an errand, with Toshiyo tracking him," Jaantzen says. "He should be at the safehouse by now. If he's not, I'll bring him home myself."

Oriol searches his gaze a moment, the only break in his Zen-like calm the bunched muscle in his jaw. He holds out a hand to Jaantzen. "I'll see you all out in the wasteland, then."

Jaantzen meets his grip. "Gia says the wasteland's quite nice." He can already hear the commotion starting in the hallway, voices calling to each other in panic. Jaantzen gives Marjani a last smile she doesn't return, then walks with Phaera to the doorway. He kisses her, not caring who's watching; she wraps her arms tightly around him. "Get her to safety," he murmurs into Phaera's hair. "Oriol knows where to go. I'll come find you."

"Good." She kisses him again, then releases him. "Go."

The Sulila hospital would have had armed security guards at every level, but this fancy clinic is staffed by people who can only frantically call the police. The doctor from earlier does an about-face and dives into an open door when he sees Jaantzen, and an orderly takes off running down the hall. No one here is going to do a thing to stop him leaving. After all, Willem Jaantzen should be considered armed and dangerous.

He gives every cowering person he sees a polite nod as he walks past. He's already pinged Raim to pick him up, and the black Dulciana JX is waiting when he arrives at the front doors. Jaantzen inclines his head to the receptionist, who's having a frantic whispered conversation with the police, then pulls out his own comm.

Toshiyo answers immediately.

"Is Manu there with you?" Jaantzen asks. Raim is pulling away from the curb as Jaantzen shuts the Dulciana's door.

"Not yet," Toshiyo says.

Fear wrenches Jaantzen's gut — Manu's errand shouldn't have taken this long.

"Send me his location. The rest of you, stay put."

29

MANU

Manu waits two stops on the train north from downtown Bulari before he slides into the seat across from Detective Timo Cho.

Cho's face blanches with fear.

"Relax," Manu says. "Just relax. Reach for your gun, reach for your comm, and this is going to end very poorly. You got me?"

Cho's chin jerks down in a nod.

"Good." Manu leans forward, hands clasped, elbows braced on knees. "Now listen. I'm not the guy you're looking for. I know they all say that. But somebody's building a web around both of us, and it's meant to catch you, too."

Cho's slowly relaxing, enough that he breaks eye contact with Manu, gaze darting around the train car. It's busy but not packed. Everybody's minding their own business, no attention paid to a pair of men in suits having a friendly conversation. Cho's holding a bag of takeout, and he sets it carefully down beside him — so he can keep his options open in case he decides going for his gun is the right move, Manu assumes.

He's not gonna do that yet. Not in a car full of people. Not unless Manu gives him the opening.

"Someone's building a web," Cho repeats, voice steady. "What do you mean?"

"Somebody's feeding you lies. Anything about this case feel off to you?"

Cho doesn't answer, but he's listening, eyes narrowed. The train comes to a stop; people wash out, wash in. Manu's got a view of the door, and it's all civilians.

"Let's take your eyewitness," Manu says conversationally when the train has started again. "Did he seem like he was under duress when you talked to him this morning?"

"I've interviewed a lot of witnesses. When somebody decides to testify against a killer like you, they're always terrified."

"Sure. I bet Ajesh is fucking petrified of me finding out he talked to you. But he's afraid of someone else more." Manu leans in; Cho flinches back. "I would ask him again once his daughters aren't being held hostage."

"Held hostage by who?"

"I'm not the detective, man." Manu shakes his head with a sigh, lounges back against the hard metal seat. Cho tenses like he thinks he has an opening and isn't sure whether or not to take it.

He doesn't take it.

"I don't know how you guys are always so out of the loop," Manu says. "But Levi Acheta's the one killed Naali. You ask anybody, that's what you're going to hear. The asshole was bragging about it to anybody who would listen."

"You're going to tell me he buried the bodies, too?"

"Nah, man. We did that. Me and the man were there to

meet with Naali, but Acheta didn't like that idea. So he made his play and sent us a message at the same time. Didn't seem polite to leave all of this in Ajesh's lap, so we took care of it."

"Concealing a homicide."

Manu shrugs. "Guilty, sure. But I didn't kill Naali, the man didn't kill her, and the whole damn world knows who really did. Somebody's trying to feed you a line, but it's not gonna be long enough to get your conviction. It's just gonna hang you, and tangle me up in the process."

The train slides to another stop. For a minute, Cho's face clouds with indecision, like he might walk away from this conversation. He doesn't. The train doors slide closed again.

More people have gotten on at this stop, but none come to sit near Manu and Cho — the tension between them is palpable, and seasoned commuters are instinctively choosing a safer part of the train car.

"I'm just supposed to believe you," Cho says when they're moving once more.

"Didn't figure you would. But I thought you might care enough about the truth to appreciate a heads-up. You're being steered in the wrong direction."

Emotion has been warring in Cho's face; something clicks into place and his jaw sets. A decision has been made.

"Manu Juric, you're under arrest for the murder of Naali Hinoja and Chase Ratham." Cho stands, swaying with the rhythm of the train. "Get up. I'm taking you in."

They're definitely attracting attention now. "Sit back down, man."

Cho draws his gun, pointing it at Manu's chest. "Bulari police," he calls; nervous voices sound up and down the train car. "Get up. You're under arrest."

Manu unfolds himself from the seat, hands raised. He props himself against the vertical handrail, the pressure between his shoulder blades steadying him as the train sways. "Did you listen to anything I just said?"

"Every word," Cho says. "But let's say you're right and I'm a fool for bringing you in on this when everyone can dispute it. I have enough evidence to keep you for now, and I'm sure we can find something you've done."

"They're setting you up, man," Manu says. A chime sounds; they're getting close to the next stop. "Just like before."

Cho's gaze narrows. "What do you mean?"

"They've got you asking questions again, only this time you're asking the wrong ones." The words land, Cho frowns at him. "Both of us, we're just pawns in a bigger game. You ask the questions, I deliver the messages. But we're both just playing a part."

"Your boss's game."

Manu shakes his head. "Back then, you were getting too close to the secrets of someone very important. She ordered you stopped, and now she's using you."

"Tell me who you're talking about."

"Not if I'm in cuffs, man."

They're rolling into the station. A pair of security guards are running towards the platform. Either Cho alerted them or the train AI noticed the commotion and called backup.

Dammit all.

Manu ducks and comes back up under Cho's arm, shoving the other man's shoulder to force him face-first onto the seat Manu'd just vacated and stripping the gun from his hand. Manu grabs a handful of Cho's coat to haul him back to his feet as the train comes to a stop, the detective's body between Manu and the security guards, gun to Cho's head.

"No hard feelings," Manu says in the detective's ear, then raises his voice to address the security guards. "Let us by or he's dead and you're next."

He doesn't need to say it twice. Both guards back off slowly — they were hoping to assist with an arrest, not deal with a hostage situation. But they've still got weapons, and there's no telling who else more impressive might have responded to the call.

"If you kill me, they'll hunt you to the ends of the system," Cho says through gritted teeth as Manu forces him towards the door.

"Don't do anything stupid and I won't have to."

"There are police on the way. Put the gun down and you can have your fair chance at justice like everyone else."

"You let them take me, you'll never find out who's playing you like a puppet," Manu says. "But that won't matter long, because I'm going in a cage over your dead body."

People are screaming around them, but Manu ignores that. Cho's breathing is coming shallow, but it's starting to smooth as he thinks through his options. Manu can sense it — Cho is afraid to die. He may not be afraid to take a bullet in the line of duty — especially if it means getting his man. Manu can respect that. But there's something else behind the fear in Cho's eyes.

He's not ready to die not knowing.

"Do you want your questions answered or not?" Manu asks.

Cho slowly raises his hands. "Do what he says," he shouts hoarsely. He lets Manu walk him off the train.

Manu jerks his chin at the security guards. "On board,"

he says, and they scramble past him onto the train car. The doors hiss closed. The train pulls away, a blur of wide-eyed faces watching through the window.

Manu slips Cho's gun into his pocket and grabs the man's arm, pushing through the crowd, up the stairs, out onto the street.

"Where are we going?" Cho asks.

"Keep walking and don't try anything, and you'll be fine," Manu says. "Can they track you?"

"I keep it turned off."

"You lying to me?"

"No."

Manu searches his face, then shoves Cho onto a streetcar just as it pulls away from the curb. He swipes marks for them both and deposits Cho in a seat across from the back door, away from prying eyes and ears. Manu braces himself against the rocking of the streetcar, but doesn't sit.

"I came to talk to you in good faith," Manu says.

"How was I supposed to know that?"

Manu shrugs. "Trust your gut, I guess. But you know that now because otherwise you'd be dead. We clear?"

Cho nods.

"Good. Like I was saying, I had nothing to do with Naali's murder, and neither did Julieta Yang. Your charges against us won't stick, and the person who's siccing you on us knows it. They're using you."

"Who."

"Chief Justice Geum-ja Leone."

He sees shock, then understanding warring in Cho's face. "She hired you . . ."

"She was behind getting rid of Coeur — the man was on her side, did the sort of work she couldn't get her hands dirty with. And when that was over, she had a few last jobs needed done. To keep her name out of everything."

"And I was asking too many questions."

"You were."

"And you — "

"I did my job." Manu sways with the motion. "I shut you down. In a way, you're welcome — if you'd found out the truth, you'd be dead."

Cho blanches at that. "I'm not going to thank you."

"Didn't expect you to."

"Who else is working with her in the department?"

Manu shrugs. "It's been a long time since the man took orders from Leone."

"Falk. My partner."

Manu nods slowly, remembering. "That sounds right." He can see that's not a surprise to Cho; Manu wonders how long he's suspected. No more time for chitchat, though — the streetcar is stopping.

"This is my stop. Look at who you trust, and leave me and mine alone."

Cho doesn't answer. Manu's feet hit pavement in a shopping district just shy of Jet Park, and he walks a few blocks the pace of the crowd, trying to loosen his stiff spine and blend in. Feels like a target is etched between his shoulder blades. After a few minutes, though, he finally starts to relax. Cho may have called backup to the train station or he may have been bluffing. Either way, it looks like Manu's good. He's clear.

He turns down an alley to get off the main drag, glancing over his shoulder to make sure no one is following him — and nearly colliding with someone who stepped out into his path.

"Excuse me," he says, registering her at the same time as

her right hand flies to the side of his neck. Her grip is soft and intimate as a lover ready for a kiss but for the sharp prick of a needle against his jugular. A knife is in her left hand, the tip poised a centimeter above his hipbone, a centimeter below the edge of his tactical vest. Viciously sharp and angled up.

Her eyes are a cool hazel, almost gray. A spray of freckles is scattered across her tawny skin, the ghost of a scar below her left eye. She smells of floral perfume and leather.

"Hi," Victoria Tierren says with a slow smile.

30

______

MANU

The prick of the needle against his throat pulses in time with his heartbeat; the woman's hand on his neck is rock steady, her fingers cool and dry.

"Move and I'll plunge this in," Tierren says quietly. "The whole thing will kill you, but a little will only knock you out until the police get here. Makes their job a whole lot easier, I suppose."

"Wouldn't want them to have to work too hard." Manu swallows, feels pain sharpening at the point of the needle at the motion. "Do I get a choice in dosage?"

"No."

"You're just still deciding."

"Strange that you think you're the one asking questions right now," Tierren says. For a moment, the sharp pain at his hip disappears as she reaches for the pistol in his shoulder holster, tucking it into the small of her back. The intensity of her gaze on his never wavers, the needle never moves. When she's disarmed him, the knife digs back into his belly.

The weight of Cho's pistol in his jacket pocket rests against his left side; he doesn't dare reach for it.

Tierren tilts her chin, studying him with a look of such alien curiosity in her expression that it reminds him of the hell-beast. "But you like to talk, don't you? It's why he relies on you."

"Seems to me you're here to talk," Manu says. "Or I don't think I'd still be on my feet."

The woman shrugs, shoulders liquid. "It's nice to meet you in person."

"You work for Leone."

The woman sighs pointedly, like Manu's not offering interesting-enough conversation. Her gaze flickers past him to the mouth of the alley. Footsteps are passing by, two women laughing as they walk, their voices muddied. Traffic is a distant hum that seems worlds away.

Not that it would matter if anyone looked into the alley. He and Tierren are standing so close Manu can feel her breath on his cheek, and all anyone would see is a man and a woman stealing an intimate moment. Her hand on his neck is a gentle caress but for the prick of the needle against his jugular; the knife pressed against his abdomen is hidden from the road. From behind, even the tilt of his head might seem more invitation than self-preservation.

"I've been hearing so much talk about you," she says once the footsteps have passed.

"And we've been talking about you," he answers. "You've been having fun feeding the BPD a story, haven't you. I'm impressed."

That doesn't get the flicker of satisfaction on her face he expected. She's a mercenary, and he's met hundreds in his life. Some, like Oriol, do their work efficiently and with as little mess as possible — Oriol would've hit him with a tranq dart from a dozen paces away rather than attempting what-ever this little game is. Others just don't feel like it's a job well-done unless some punches get thrown.

Still others thrive on toying with their targets — they concoct elaborate schemes and get off on the satisfaction of a trap well laid. On watching the moment the jaws snap shut.

Or they get off on the fear, the groveling.

Tierren doesn't seem to be here for any of that.

"Why do you stay with him?" she asks finally. "That's what I don't get."

He frowns at her. "Jaantzen?"

"Blackheart almost kills you once, shame on her. But twice?" Tierren laughs. "You need to find an employer who actually gives a shit about you."

"Someone like Leone?" Manu keeps his voice level, but his mind reels, searching for what she means. Twice?

"Kaboom." Tierren smiles, sly. "You didn't know? You didn't wonder why Jaantzen didn't come visit you in the hospital?" Her gaze sweeps past him once more as another set of footsteps pass the mouth of the alley. "Nice that he can still feel shame — I think Leone's long past that."

Manu wants to say, Coeur didn't set the bomb. He wants to say, And if she did, Jaantzen didn't know about it.

But he's having trouble forming those words of denial. Because it's absolutely the sort of thing Coeur would do, and absolutely the sort of knowledge Jaantzen would protect Manu from — and destroy himself with shame over.

A slow smile is forming on Tierren's lips as she watches him — and with an effort, Manu shoves the feeling of real-ization aside. That dizzying sense of pieces falling into place isn't epiphany; no one thinks clearly at knifepoint. Jaantzen didn't let Coeur try to kill him. Not the first time, not this time. No amount of adrenaline-spiked false-revelatory euphoria is going to make that true.

"They made the plans together," Tierren says, and now she's thoroughly reaching, the uncanny verisimilitude of her previous lie melting to glass.

Manu breathes deep against the prick of the needle.

Tierren's faint smile turns to a frown at whatever she sees on his face; she's a split second from deciding she's done talking.

Keep her talking.

"What proof do you have?" Manu asks, glossing betrayed denial into his voice. But she doesn't believe it; her eyes narrow as she studies him.

"Unwavering loyalty in the face of everything you've been through." The words are laced with scorn. "How sweet."

"It's worked so far," Manu says, and he's done talking. He relaxes, shoulders loose, breath steady, mind clear. She's obviously fast, but so is he — and she doesn't know he's still got Cho's gun.

Tierren's about to speak again, but another set of footsteps are passing on the street outside the alley. These don't continue past. They stop. Wait.

Tierren's gaze slides past Manu; she tilts her head to see whoever's stopped in the mouth of the alley. Manu's left hand creeps towards Cho's gun in his pocket. This doesn't change his plan to act. If it's the police, he'll take the full dose of whatever's in her syringe or her blade plunging into his gut before he'll let her knock him senseless so they can throw him in a cell.

Behind him, a pistol whines as it warms to the hand of its owner.

"Take another step and he's dead," she says conversationally to whoever's holding the gun. She digs the knife into Manu's belly. "Tell him."

But before he can ask who he's telling, the newcomer speaks. Rich and resonant, a voice Manu has trusted for twenty years.

"I'm the one you want, so no more games," Willem Jaantzen says. "Let him go, and I'll come with you to see Leone."

Tierren's eyes widen in astonishment; she shakes her head at Manu like they're sharing a moment. "Really?" she asks, turning her attention back to Jaantzen. "I think you're underestimating what Leone wants from you. She doesn't just want to take you down a peg, she wants to destroy you. Humiliate you."

"Let her. But let him go."

Tierren's studying him over Manu's shoulder. "She wants to turn you into an object lesson," she says. "Not quite flay you alive and nail your corpse to the temple doors, but when she's done you'll wish she had."

"She can do her worst. Let him go."

Tierren tilts her head, thinking. A lock of her ice-blond hair slips free and knifes past her cheekbone.

Keep her talking.

Manu's fingertips brush against his jacket pocket.

And the knife presses in hard, slicing pain above his hip. Manu gasps but doesn't move; the pressure from the needle sharpens against his throat.

"I can multitask, Juric." Tierren gives him a deadly smile. She twists the knife, fire searing into his flesh. A warm trickle of blood slips along the line of his hipbone.

"He's not the one you want." Jaantzen's voice is infinitely calm. The sole of his shoe scuffs against the pavement as he steps forward. "Let him go."

"Put down your gun."

"Release him first."

She laughs. "Not likely."

"Then I suppose we're at an impasse."

"An impasse where he dies."

"And so do you."

Tierren's smile quirks to the side, but it's not recklessly cocky, it's not fanatical. Maybe she only snared Manu to lay emotional landmines, or maybe she truly was planning on handing him over to the cops. Either way, she wasn't expecting Jaantzen. Manu can read her expression now: She's playing through her options to find the one where she gets out alive.

"Do you really think you can take us both?" Manu asks quietly. "Maybe you get that syringe empty before I can do anything. But he's got his sights trained on you."

"You don't know me," she says coolly.

"No. But I know him."

Something shifts in her expression, all playfulness gone. The sting at his neck turns to fire as the needle pierces his flesh for real; Manu flinches but she holds tight, increases the pressure on the knife blade.

"When I empty this syringe, his heart will stop in seconds," she says over his shoulder to Jaantzen. "There's an antidote, but you'll have to be fast." She turns her head to study Manu, and the searing pain of the knife above his hipbone vanishes to a dull ache. She rummages in her pocket, then presses something into his left hand: a warm metal cylinder. "Don't drop this," she says.

Before Manu can answer, she depresses the plunger and molten metal sears through his neck. She shoves him backwards, a foot behind his ankle to send him off-balance.

He stumbles on uneven pavement and adrenaline and the dizzying fire she's sent through his veins.

Manu fights to remember what he needs to do as time slows. Loosens fingers clenched tight around the metal cylinder in his hand — somewhere in the distance he hears it ringing against the pavement — and fumbles for the handle of Cho's pistol. His hand tightens around the grip, pulling it free and taking aim even as he's falling backwards, even as pain is blazing through his chest, even as darkness pulses around the edges of his vision.

Manu thinks he squeezes off two shots, maybe three before his legs give out beneath him.

He doesn't hit the ground.

Strong arms catch him from behind, lowering him gently, and Manu is vaguely aware of the pressure of the asphalt against his backbone and shoulder blades, of a dark, blurred shape scrambling in the alley for the vial of antidote that Manu dropped in order to grab the gun. A hand on his throat as he begins to convulse — Manu claws at it weakly, but the strong fingers are only grasping his chin, holding it steady. Something hisses against his neck, a sharp sting, and the scorching heat in his blood begins to cool. The feeling of being crushed subsides, and suddenly Manu can breathe again. He gasps down air, shaking. Jaantzen holds him steady.

"Dammit, Manu," Jaantzen says. "What the fuck were you thinking."

"Did I get her?" Manu isn't sure he's even said the words, his mouth is dry as a bone and his tongue is thick and sluggish.

"Talk to me," Jaantzen says. "Tell me what's going on."

"I think I'm okay." Manu can't tell — everything happened so fast, and with the relief that comes from no longer being crushed, he almost feels like he's flying. Light-headed with exhilaration. He forces himself to breathe. To think systematically through the chaotic symphony of sensations in his body.

"I think I'm all right," he says finally. "Did I get her?" He'd taken his chance. This woman who's been trying to destroy his family at every turn, he'd had his shot at removing that threat, and he took it. "Please tell me I — "

"Manu."

Manu forces himself to focus on Jaantzen's face.

"No."

Manu lets out a furious curse, disappointment almost as crushing as whatever poison Tierren pushed into his veins.

"I missed?"

"It doesn't matter." Jaantzen lets him lie back on the pavement; Manu feels hands probing beneath his jacket, gentle, professional. A faint pressure at his hip where Tierren's knife cut him, Jaantzen's fingers on the bloody fabric of his shirt.

"You're bleeding."

"It's just a scratch." But apparently Jaantzen doesn't believe him, because he tugs the hem of Manu's shirt free to see the wound; the heat of the day feels cold on Manu's bare skin.

"It doesn't look deep," Jaantzen says after a moment. "Can you move? We need to go."

Manu nods and Jaantzen helps him sit up, then pulls Manu's arm over his shoulder. Together they stand. Somewhere against the background fog permeating every sense comes the awareness of how badly Jaantzen is favoring his right knee, and Manu tries to push back, to relieve that burden, but when he does he stumbles, swearing.

Jaantzen's grip on his arm, around his waist, is ironclad.

31

STARLA

Starla doesn't make it a habit to disobey direct orders from her godfather, but his command to stay put at the safehouse while he hunts down Manu has pushed her almost to the edge. Tierren is still out there, and the more Starla examines the stills she took in the woman's lair, the more unnerving that fact is.

She wasn't the first resident of that basement — Toshiyo's examination of the footage in the weeks before Tierren showed up found an older man who used to come by. The last time he appears in the security feeds is entering the house. Tierren follows him in a few moments later.

It could be that he slipped out again; at night it's difficult to make much out in the low-res footage, but Starla doubts that. Studying the clutter in the stills makes her think it's not all a woman's; if the old man left, he didn't take his scant belongings.

Starla remembers the scent of decay from the crawlspace with a shiver.

Who the hell are they dealing with here?

If Starla had been faster back at the townhouse. If she'd

been on her moto instead of in the Magnata. If she'd had the confidence to take a shot in the market crowd.

If.

But she wasn't fast enough, agile enough, confident enough. Tierren got away. And now that she knows they found her hiding place once, she'll be even more careful next time.

This was their chance.

Starla must be making more noise pacing than she thought, because Toshiyo catches her eye. "You're scaring the girls," she signs.

Starla groans in frustration and drops into an armchair.

Most of her godfather's safehouses are bare-bones, sparsely furnished with whatever couch and table someone found on a street corner, but this apartment obviously used to be someone's home, before it was pulled into Jaantzen's service. Long enough ago for the decor to have fallen out of fashion. Matching pastel-peach couch and armchairs in the living room, baby-blue carpeting, a tech-free coffee table made of faux pearly orange glitter marble, garish color-blocked paintings on the walls.

The kitchen counters and dining table keep with the pearly orange glitter theme, the cabinets are the same pastel blue as the carpets. The interior design hasn't aged well, but the place is off the network, the cabinets are well stocked with rations and first aid supplies, and the shower works.

Toshiyo is curled in the corner of the couch; she bends over her hand terminal, a curtain of black hair hiding her face. The Anahoys and the Paiman girls are sitting around the kitchen table.

The girls have cleaned themselves up and changed into some of the old clothes that these places are always stocked with. The youngest is in a sweatshirt printed with a cartoon character Starla remembers some of her little cousins being into, while the oldest found a man's button-up shirt and a pair of star-print leggings. They're eating curried TVP Simca found in the cupboard, though the oldest has only picked at hers; her face is pinched and pale, her injured foot up in El's lap as he carefully cleans and bandages the infected cut. Her instep is angry red but there isn't any streaking — yet. They'll need to keep a close watch on that wound.

Neither of the girls have said much beyond asking about their parents, though they seem to be relaxing into the idea that Starla and her team really did rescue them. That they're safe, even if they're with strangers.

Something El says finally makes the older girl smile, and a bit of the pain smooths out of her face. He bends back over her foot, strands of his electric-blue hair escaping his pony-tail to brush over his strong cheekbones. The girl's expression shifts from wariness to shy intrigue.

Simca catches Starla's eye. "My brother, the hottie life-saver," she signs behind El's back with a grin. It vanishes and she straightens, attention past Starla to the front door. The two girls follow her gaze; on the couch, Toshiyo looks up with eyes wide.

Starla sits up straight, calls up the door's security feed on her lens. The decor may be decades old, but the security is cutting-edge — Starla's got a wide visual of the hall, plus biosignature and weapons scans.

Jaantzen and Manu. They're alone.

Relief floods through her.

Starla overrides the locks and throws open the door, pulling first Jaantzen, then Manu into a hug. They both look like hell, and she doesn't like the lack of strength in Manu's arms around her, the salt tracks on his dark temples, the faint tremble in his hands. She frowns at him with a raised eyebrow — *What's wrong* — but Manu just gives her a ginned-up smile, claps her on the shoulder, and strolls past her to greet the Paiman girls.

They're both calling his name and talking at once; Starla triple-blinks her lens off as it tries and fails to transcribe all the chaos. Whatever Manu says to them finally coaxes a smile out of the youngest girl.

Simca vacates her chair for him, and he settles in with a grin at the girls and something approximating his usual casual lounge. But Starla didn't miss the scent of sweat and adrenaline when she hugged him, the blood flecking the collar of his shirt, the way Jaantzen steadied him in the security feed just before Starla opened the door.

Jaantzen's still watching him like a hawk.

She squeezes her godfather's elbow to get his attention. "What's wrong?" she signs.

A muscle jumps in his jaw. "That woman?" he signs. "We ran into her."

A chill runs down Starla's spine. If she'd been faster. If —

She cuts that line of thought off with an angry breath. She wasn't. And beating herself up about it isn't going to help them right now.

"What happened?"

She has to repeat herself; Jaantzen's attention is glued to Manu.

"I'll tell you later," he signs.

He begins to turn away, but Starla catches his arm, shaking her head. "Tell me now. We need all the information you have." She snaps twice and El straightens, lifts his chin to her. She points to Manu's back. "Keep an eye on him, he's injured." El nods and shifts subtly to face Manu.

Simca's seen the order, too; she heads to the sink to fill a glass of water for him.

Jaantzen resists Starla's glare a few heartbeats before taking a deep breath and sinking into one of the pastel-peach armchairs. Starla does a quick scan through the security system — all clear — then perches on the couch beside Toshiyo, who's now sitting crosslegged and straight-backed, watching them.

"Are you all right?" Starla asks Jaantzen.

"I'm fine."

He's obviously not; she doesn't press.

Jaantzen's jaw sets. "She surprised him somehow. Toshiyo told me where he was and I found them." His lips thin and his palms press together; he's trying to figure out how to sign the next part. "She injected him with something, but gave us the . . . cure? So she could get away." He glances toward the dining room, where Manu's still talking with the girls; grief flickers over her godfather's normally stony face before he catches it.

Starla glances at Toshiyo. She's white as a ghost.

"Tierren injected Manu with poison," Starla clarifies, "but gave you the antidote to save his life. Why didn't she just kill him?"

"To buy time to get away."

"She didn't have to give you the real antidote, it would have still bought her time. Why?"

"Leone wants him alive," Toshiyo signs. "More leverage."

"If he's in jail, Leone can control you," Starla signs to Jaantzen. "If Tierren had killed him . . ."

She doesn't have to finish the thought. The grief in his eyes from before is back, only now it's tinged with rage.

"We'll take her down," Starla signs. She's not going to

miss if she gets a second shot at that woman. "Once we're settled again. Oriol just got in touch. He's on his way to Gia's with Phaera and her mother. We have the Paimans safe — El and Simca will take the girls to their parents and oversee the guard rotation. Lo's handling the police at the tower. Leti's already got her PR machine running. Calanthe told me she brought Julieta home and she has the Alliance agent somewhere safe. Two of mine will be with her at all times."

She raises her eyebrows at Jaantzen and he nods, he's following along. "What am I missing?" she asks.

He steeples fingers over lips, thinking. "The detective; Manu was able to deliver his message to him," he signs after a moment. "We may get some help there."

The knot in Starla's gut loosens the tiniest amount — they desperately need an ally on the other side of the law. "I'll make sure we follow up with him," she signs.

"That woman. Tierren. I need to know who she is."

"I'm working on it," signs Toshiyo. "We'll find her. Once we're all safe."

Jaantzen nods slowly; he still looks exhausted, but the ashen pallor to his rich brown skin is gone. His gaze locks on Starla's. "Let's go."

Starla claps twice as she gets to her feet and the group at the dining table turns towards her. She motions for Simca to interpret for the girls. "El and Simca will be taking you to your parents," she tells them. "You'll stay there until it's safe to go home."

"How long?" asks the older girl.

"We don't know, but you'll be safe there." She motions for Simca to stop interpreting; she doesn't care how young and traumatized these girls are, she's not trusting them with any more details than they need to know. "Tosh and

Jaantzen will head to the compound; El, meet us there when you can. Simca, I want you to keep an eye on the Paimans." She spears Manu with a look. "You I'm taking straight to Gia unless you tell me you need a doctor sooner."

A tinge of humor colors Manu's smile. "Waiting for Gia is probably fine."

"*Is* fine? Or is *probably* fine."

Manu's gaze sweeps the ceiling as he considers. "*Is* fine."

"Then let's go."

Starla turns to take in every person under her guard. Toshiyo already has her gadgets packed away and her satchel slung across her body; she's leaning forward and murmuring something to Jaantzen, who's listening with head tilted. Simca has tossed the remains of their meal kits into the recycler and is coaxing the younger Paiman girl to her feet while El helps the older girl stand.

"Do you need a hand?" Starla signs to Manu, and he gives her a slight warning shake of his head — it doesn't mean *No*, it means *Not yet*, and Starla's stomach flips as she wonders just how much Manu's hiding behind the charming grin he turns on the Paiman girls. But she lets him sit until the girls have said their goodbyes to him and been trundled out by El and Simca, then she lets him use her arm to haul himself to his feet. He drapes an arm heavily over her shoulders, breath coming fast; his skin is clammy but his heartbeat is strong.

And he laughs. Starla feels it thrum through her own chest and glances over to catch the tail end of what he's said. She blinks her lens back on. "What did you say?"

"I said Gia's gonna be pissed," Manu signs with his free hand. The corner of his mouth quirks to the side.

"I wouldn't worry about Gia," Jaantzen signs, trying for

a smile himself. "Oriol's there with Phaera's mother. He's going to murder you and me both."

Manu takes a deep sigh, shakes his head in mock sadness. "Well, it was nice knowing you all."

Jaantzen ghosts him a smile before he turns towards the door; from the angle, Manu probably can't see the moment Jaantzen's expression cracks with heartbreak, but Starla does. That terrible adrenaline of barely averted loss is stabbing through her own chest, too. She shares a look with Toshiyo; the other woman's lips are bloodless even as she's trying to smile at Manu's joke.

"We'll see you at the compound," Toshiyo finally signs, then threads her arm through Jaantzen's. "Let's get out of here, boss."

Somebody knocks like that after dark, it's either a girlfriend who's found out about another woman or a neighbor telling him the building's on fire. Timo Cho's been between girlfriends for a while now and he doesn't smell smoke, but if it's the latter, he'll probably be able to afford a better place with the insurance payout. So here's hoping.

Because the other option is it's someone sent to take care of the job Manu Juric started ten years ago.

He didn't go back to his office after the run-in with Juric, because for all Cho doesn't believe the man is telling him the whole truth, what Juric did say has knocked everything sideways.

"Somebody's feeding you lies. Anything about this case feel off to you?"

Little things about this case have seemed off since the beginning; now it's like Cho's looking at it all through warped glass. Whatever instinct he had to tell the difference between a solid lead and bullshit seems to have short-circuited.

So instead he spent the rest of the afternoon at home

going through files he hadn't cracked once since coming home from the hospital ten years ago.

Chief Justice Geum-ja Leone.

She fits neatly into the center of the mystery he'd been unraveling after Thala Coeur was ousted from New Sarjun. He won't take Juric's word for it, but the name gave him a place to start looking again. A point to start teasing out the threads that connect whatever happened ten years ago with why he's being manipulated today.

The knock's faltering, but it's not stopping.

"I'm coming," he yells to shut up the knocking; it doesn't work. And maybe he'd dozed off on the couch while he was thinking, so he drags himself to his feet, drags himself with even more effort out of the dreams he's been having in which he's trapped in an investigations cube, choking to death in the stale air, sugar-fine Jupari sand pouring through the cracks in the door and burying him alive, Falk laughing from the other side of the wall.

He shoves his pistol in his waistband and heads for the door to his apartment with threads of dream trailing sticky as caramel behind him.

Calls up the security camera beside the door, and a chill touches his spine. It's the woman. Victoria.

He thinks about letting her keep knocking, even if she is going to draw a crowd — he's not sure what game she's playing, and he knows he can't trust her. But even in the grainy, cheap feed of the ancient system he can see she's injured. The arm of her coat is red with blood.

Her eyelids flutter like she's about to pass out.

He shoots open the deadbolts and palms the biolock. She stares at him, eyes glassy with pain.

"What happened?" he asks.

"I didn't know where else to go," she says.

Her face is pinched and she's cradling her left arm. He can't tell what the injury is, but if it's soaked through her coat then she's lost a lot of blood.

He's not the only one assessing.

Her hazel gaze brushes over his bare stomach and chest, spends a brief moment considering the stump at his shoulder. The biomech interface there blinks in standby.

"You should go to the hospital," he says, to be the first one to speak.

She takes a shaky breath. "I can't. I don't have anyone else to turn to."

She looks like she's been through hell, and as much as Cho wants to tell her to wait outside, he'll call her a cab, he knows he's not going to send her off like this. She searches his face, the hope in her eyes fading to despair. She turns to leave.

"Wait."

Cho glances down the hall but doesn't see any open doors. Whatever her game is, he can't send her away like this. And anyway, if he plays his cards right, maybe she'll leave him with fewer questions once he's patched her back up. He beckons her in and shuts his door after. Resets his locks.

He waves her to the kitchen counter and clears aside yesterday's — no, two days ago's — dishes to make room. His prosthetic is lying on the floor beside the couch; Victoria glances over briefly at the click and whir when he fits it to the biomech plate and straps the harness across his chest. He flexes his fingers — smooth as butter, Hallelujah — then pulls his shirt off the back of a chair and starts on the buttons.

"Let's get your coat off," he says when he's decent.

She lets him help her out of her coat, hissing in pain as

he eases it off her left arm. He sets it carefully somewhere it won't stain his furniture, then turns back to assess the damage.

He hasn't seen her without the voluminous coat; in the fitted short-sleeved shirt she's lean and boyish, her arms and shoulders roped with muscle. She cradles her left arm close, huddling over it protectively. Black blood pools in the crook of her elbow from the bullet wound just above it. A drop gathers on her fingertips, stretches, falls to splash beside others on the floor.

"Sit down," he tells her. "We need to get that elevated."

Cho pulls his med kit down from above the stove and sprays a pair of gloves on himself over the trash can. He's tried to get blood out of the cracks and crevices of his prosthetic plenty of times in the past, and damned if he's doing it again today. He grabs a towel to put under her arm on the kitchen counter. Her light-brown face is ashen under the freckles.

"You should have gone straight to the hospital," he says, setting the med kit beside her arm.

"What happened with you and Juric?"

His mouth goes dry, and he busies himself with the med kit to hide his shock. She knows about Juric's visit today. "What do you mean?" he asks, trying to keep his tone even.

"Ten years ago," she clarifies. He can't read anything in her expression that says she means anything else. "I know he put you in the hospital, but I don't know why."

Relief floods through him, and Cho forces himself to relax. He straddles the stool beside her, pulls out a wad of cotton, and starts swabbing. "I asked too many questions."

"About what?"

"Blackheart." That's the short version, but until he

knows who she works for, he's not going to give her the long one.

The bullet went clean through — the exit wound's in the front, which means someone shot at her from behind. Nothing seems to be embedded in the wound, so he flushes it with sterilizers and local anesthesia. Considers the suture machine, decides against it. Her breath is coming quick; blood soaks the towels beneath her elbow. He sops at the wound again then grabs a new wad of cotton, has her hold it against the exit wound while he readies bandages.

"None of your colleagues helped you get back at him?" she asks.

"I didn't tell anyone who'd done it. I didn't know who I could trust."

"I'm amazed you stayed in the force."

Her eyes are locked on his now, and she seems to have forgotten entirely how much pain she's in. He presses another wad of cotton to the entry wound and begins to wrap bandages above her elbow. Her eyes close tight for a moment, her lips pressed together.

"That's not the whole story," Victoria eventually says through clenched teeth.

"Maybe not. But you haven't been telling me the whole story, either." Cho seals the bandage, then wets another wad of cotton to swab away the rest of the blood on Victoria's arm. "You should still go to the hospital. It doesn't look like it hit an artery, and the bandage should stop the bleeding, but I'm no doctor. And a professional can help make sure it doesn't scar."

Victoria flexes her arm gingerly, nostrils flaring at the movement. "No one cares if it scars."

Cho sloughs off his gloves into the trash and pours them each a glass of water. "So. What happened?"

She doesn't speak, instead pulls her comm out of her pocket and lays it on the counter between them. A short video clip: a pair of girls who look remarkably like the restaurant owner Cho was interviewing this morning. They're bloodied and barefoot and being handed into a battered Bierat four-door by a man with electric-blue hair.

"Who's he?" Cho doesn't need to ask who the girls are, Juric's comment from earlier still in his head: "I would ask him again once his daughters aren't being held hostage."

That flicker of a glance and he realizes he's made a mistake. He should have asked who the girls were. He wipes his palm down his thigh to dry the sudden sweat.

"El Anahoy," Victoria says. "He works for Jaantzen. He's trying to change your witness's testimony." And that's obvious — though would Jaantzen be holding the girls hostage to get Ajesh Paiman to tell lies about who really shot Naali Hinoja and Chase Ratham? Or to tell the truth?

And is Jaantzen the one who kidnapped them in the first place?

Does Cho trust the woman he let into his kitchen, or the man who beat him nearly to death ten years ago?

A chill touches the back of his neck.

"Send me some stills and I'll look into it," he says. "Jaantzen is slippery, but if there's anything to it I'll find out."

"I've met worse."

"Worse than Willem Jaantzen?"

"He's hardly the deadliest scorpion in this ditch," Victoria says. She smiles; it's unnerving.

Cho straightens, on edge. "I think it's time for you to go," he says. He stands and grabs her coat, but she stays seated at his kitchen counter. He holds out her coat. She doesn't take it. "Come by the station next time you have something for me."

Her eyebrows shoot up. "I'm trying to help."

"I don't know what you're trying to do."

"I told you. I just want to see Naali's killer — "

"Spare me. I don't know what your agenda is."

"I thought you didn't care so long as we took Juric out." She tilts her head, studying him. "Or have you changed your mind about that?"

"I haven't changed my mind. I'm just trying to understand what's going on. And I need space to think."

Because as much as he doesn't want to believe Juric, the man's warning keeps echoing through his mind. That whoever hired Juric to send him the message all those years ago is the same person who's playing him like a puppet now.

It could be Victoria, but in his experience people like her — like Juric — aren't calling the shots. They're the ones other people hire to keep their own hands clean.

"Who do you work for?" Cho asks finally.

She sighs and levers herself to her feet. He tenses as she closes the distance between them, but she turns her back to him, lets him help her right arm into her coat. The left arm is stiff with blood and bandage, so he settles the coat on her shoulder.

"I work for myself," Victoria says when she turns back to face him. Her tone rings true, but it holds a hint of irony he can't put his finger on.

"Who hired you to feed me this information."

"Timo." But she's dropped the damsel-in-distress act; seeing her cold smile now, he realizes just how ill-fitting it was on her. "Do you really want to ask?"

It's a warning. He needs to learn how to take a warning.

He throws open the locks on his door and holds it open for her.

"Please go," he says.

"And you'll stop asking?"

He's going to say yes, but the lie catches on his tongue.

He's waited too long.

Victoria smiles at him sadly. And searing heat blazes through his chest, followed by incredible pressure — he grasps hands around hers. They're already slick with his blood.

"I'm sorry, Timo," Victoria says. "I liked you."

And she pulls the knife out of his chest.

Everything is so sharp now — the sound of her boots on his floor, the bitter scent of the coffee he brewed after dinner, the faint drip of water from the bathroom faucet he's meant to fix for weeks. The metallic taste of blood on his tongue. Every mote of dust dancing in the lamplight, the faint scuff of chair legs from the apartment above his. The oddly sweet sound of Victoria humming to herself as she cleans up her blood, pockets his electronics, wipes all traces of herself from his apartment.

He thinks she looks back at him before she closes the door, but he can't tell, the world is already gone staticky and dark around the edges.

Timo Cho closes his eyes.

AUTHOR'S NOTE

Writing the third book of a 5-book series was a challenge. It was technically tricky, emotionally exhausting, and *incredibly* rewarding.

Knowing I had readers waiting for the next installment of the Bulari Saga really helped buoy me. Plus, I've spent a few years now with Jaantzen and his crew while working on the Bulari Saga, the prequel novellas, and various short stories. And one thing I've learned is that they don't give up very easily.

Neither do I.

They'll be back in *Heat Death*, and you can bet they'll be fighting tooth and nail to win.

Close-kept mysteries are beginning to unravel. Starla's about to kick some serious ass. Gia's going to have to make some tough choices about where her loyalties lie. And Jaantzen's battle with Leone is about to shatter out of either of their control.

Get *Heat Death* here:

WWW.JESSIEKWAK.COM/BOOK/HEAT-DEATH

If you're not on my newsletter list and want to get sneak

previews, character backstory, and side stories that fill in bits of history I don't have time to cover in the main series, head to www.JESSIEKWAK.COM.

And while you're there, please drop me a line to say hello. I love to hear reader thoughts and feedback on my stories — it keeps me going!

As always, the most powerful thing a reader can do to help an author keep writing new work is to spread the word.

Please, leave a review at your favorite retailer or review site.

And if you know someone who would love to lose themselves in the Bulari Saga, point them towards the first book (*Double Edged*), or tell them to sign up on my website to get a free copy of *noNegative Return*.

Thank you!

See you in the next book,
Jessie Kwak

Jessie Kwak has always lived in imaginary lands, from Arrakis and Ankh-Morpork to Earthsea, Tatooine, and now Portland, Oregon. As a writer, she sends readers on their own journeys to immersive worlds filled with fascinating characters, gunfights, explosions, and dinner parties.

When she's not raving about her latest favorite sci-fi series to her friends, she can be found sewing, mountain biking, or exploring new worlds both at home and abroad.

Author photo by Robert Kittilson.

Connect with me:
www.jessiekwak.com
jessie@jessiekwak.com

DID YOU LIKE THE BOOK?

As a reader, I rely on book recommendations to help me pick what to read next.

As a writer, book recommendations are the most powerful way for me to get the word out to new readers.

If you liked this book, please leave a review on the platform of your choice — or tell a friend! It's the easiest way to help authors you enjoy keep producing great work.

Cheers!

Jessie